"Seems to me friends help each other."

Neither of them broke from staring at the other.
Neither of them relented from their position.

"You got an objection to being friends with me?"
Ward asked.

Red sniffed. "Seems to me friends don't push at each
other, making impossible demands."

"Push? Impossible demands? Red, I have no idea
what you are talking about. All I've done is rescue
you and Belle from Thorton, bring you to a safe place
and make sure you're taken care of. How is that
pushing and making demands?"

She sniffed again and gave him a look dripping with
disdain. "I guess it meant nothing to you, but I recall
a kiss or two."

He gave her a look rife with disbelief. "Didn't see
you resisting."

"Maybe," she said with annoyance in every syllable,
"I was just being polite."

This was not going at all the way Ward had planned.
Red was supposed to welcome his offer of friendship,
admit that a kiss or two was appropriate, see that his
desire to help was genuinely generous. Maybe even
confess, to even a small degree, that she liked having
him around...

Linda Ford

The Cowboy's Convenient Proposal

&

Claiming the Cowboy's Heart

LOVE INSPIRED
INSPIRATIONAL ROMANCE

LOVE INSPIRED®

INSPIRATIONAL ROMANCE

ISBN-13: 978-1-335-44872-9

Recycling programs
for this product may
not exist in your area.

The Cowboy's Convenient Proposal &
Claiming the Cowboy's Heart

For questions and comments about the quality of this book,
please contact us at CustomerService@Harlequin.com.

Love Inspired
22 Adelaide St. West, 40th Floor
Toronto, Ontario M5H 4E3, Canada
www.Harlequin.com

Printed in U.S.A.

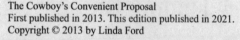

CONTENTS

Linda Ford lives on a ranch in Alberta, Canada, near enough to the Rocky Mountains that she can enjoy them on a daily basis. She and her husband raised fourteen children—four homemade, ten adopted. She currently shares her home and life with her husband, a grown son, a live-in paraplegic client and a continual (and welcome) stream of kids, kids-in-law, grandkids and assorted friends and relatives.

Books by Linda Ford

Love Inspired Historical

Big Sky Country

Montana Cowboy Daddy
Montana Cowboy Family
Montana Cowboy's Baby
Montana Bride by Christmas
Montana Groom of Convenience
Montana Lawman Rescuer

Montana Cowboys

The Cowboy's Ready-Made Family
The Cowboy's Baby Bond
The Cowboy's City Girl

Visit the Author Profile page
at Harlequin.com for more titles.

THE COWBOY'S
CONVENIENT PROPOSAL

In him we have redemption through his blood,
the forgiveness of sins, in accordance with
the riches of God's grace that he lavished on us
with all wisdom and understanding.
—*Ephesians* 1:7

Don't we all need God's grace in our lives?
This book is dedicated to those I love who are in need
of a special awareness of God's grace and love
and forgiveness. I won't name names,
but you know who you are.

Chapter One

Eden Valley, Alberta
July 1882

Ward Walker wanted nothing more than to get back to the ranch. He'd spent the better part of three days locating a man and delivering a message from his boss about purchasing a prize stallion.

With no interest in the men crowding the saloon nor what they were so concerned about, he sat back waiting to get something hot to eat before he headed back.

"I perceive you are all anxious to see Red." The man to his right lifted a bowler hat from his pomaded hair and held it out. "You willing to pay?"

Each hand dropped in a coin.

He waved the hat toward Ward.

"Ain't interested," Ward said, not bothering to keep a growl out of his voice.

The man roared with harsh laughter. "You'll change your mind soon enough."

"Doubt it. I'm just waiting for a dish of stew." In his twenty-three years he had learned to stay away from trouble as best he could.

As if summoned by Ward's words, the barkeep swung from the back room with a bowlful of steaming food. Ward turned his attention to his meal.

The man shook the coins from his hat into his palm and pocketed them. Grinning widely, he bellowed, "Red."

The silent expectation in the room held Ward's interest despite his vow that he cared only about eating.

"Aw, Thorton, she ain't coming," one disgruntled cowboy murmured. "I want my money back."

"She'll come. She knows what to expect if she don't." The way the man smacked his fist into his palm sent tension crawling up Ward's spine, the words bringing with them memories of another time, another man who said similar things and followed through with fists or boots, or anything he could lay his hands on.

"Red. Get out here. Now." The harsh voice practically stole Ward's appetite. But he had to eat to survive so he took a scoop of the succulent stew.

The gray blanket hanging crookedly in the doorway on one side of the room full of crowded tables fluttered. The men cheered and from behind the curtain stepped a woman with flaming-red hair in a mane of curls down her back. Her blue-green eyes flashed rebellion, as did the set of her mouth. She pulled a man's shirt closed across her front.

"Girl, shed that shirt."

The girl scowled fiercely.

"Need I remind you …?" The man's chair squawked back.

The girl shuddered.

Ward's fists curled as she shrugged out of the shirt to expose a red dress with a bodice that was far too revealing. Her skin flared bright pink.

"That's better. Now give us a little dance. And smile."

Red speared the man with a look so full of heat that when Ward jerked toward him, he thought he'd see scorch marks on his face. Instead, all he saw was a leer. Ward couldn't decide the man's age. Somewhere between his own and already worn out. The man had a clean-shaven face and wore a black coat that looked as if it might have belonged to a preacher, but the narrow set of his eyes and the humorless smile convinced Ward that the man was no preacher.

Red turned, revealing pale shoulders. Her dress didn't quite cover a red streak the width of a belt in the center of her back.

He didn't need such evidence to know that man named Thorton beat the woman, but seeing the bruise filled Ward with rage. He jerked to his feet, sending his chair skidding away. He'd walked away from this kind of abuse once before. He'd regretted it every day since. He would not walk away again. Not even from people he didn't know and who were none of his business.

Thorton jerked about at the noise of Ward's sudden rise. "Something bothering you, boy?"

"You beat this woman."

Thorton laughed. "Only way I can get her to do what I say. She's a bit headstrong, you might say. Ain't that right, fellas?"

The raucous laughter of the men fueled Ward's anger until it burned like an out-of-control forest fire. He was long past being reasonable and keeping his nose out of trouble. "I don't aim to stand back and allow some poor woman to be used as a punching bag."

"Is that a fact?" Thorton grinned. "Now ain't he a feisty little rooster?"

Ward caught Red's startled look, then she shook her head hard. As if telling him to leave it alone.

But he could not. Would not. "I'm telling you to let her go."

Thorton grabbed Red's arm. She cringed, then straightened and faced him squarely, defiance blaring from her eyes. But Ward knew it was only a defensive gesture. One he had grown familiar with. *You can beat me all you want but you can't control my mind.*

"She's mine," Thorton said. "I do with her as I please. Besides, I have a duty to control her. The good book says—" The man puffed up his chest as if expounding words of utmost importance "'—A man should rule his own household.' I aim to do exactly that."

Ward stepped closer. He had no plan. He didn't know if Red was the man's lawful wife or not. He only knew he would not allow the abuse to continue.

From somewhere a gun appeared in the hand of a man to Ward's left, leveled at Ward. "We paid to see her dance."

Ward hesitated, his gaze slowly shifting from the gun back to Red.

"This the way you want it, boy?" Thorton shoved Red away. She stumbled. Ward reached to stop her fall but she spun about as smooth as a fox and pushed the tipped chair of the nearest man, sending him crashing to the floor. Several men tumbled like dominos. The gun went off. Bedlam erupted.

Ward glanced down at himself. Saw no blood. He looked for Red. She was sprawled flat-out, a bright pink stain on her skirt.

"That'll bring the Mountie," a man near the door bellowed.

Men scattered, bursting through the door. Ward

figured they must have about bowled over anyone approaching the saloon. Horses pounded away. Thorton had slipped into the back room. Only Ward and the saloonkeeper remained. And Red.

"Best get her out of here," the saloonkeeper said.

Ward didn't pause to ask questions or wonder. He scooped Red off the floor and beat it out the door. He scrambled to the back of his horse, Miss Red in his arms. No one asked him what he was doing or challenged his actions. Without a backward look he headed for home.

The bloodstain on Red's dress spread but his sense of decency forbade him checking it. Unless her life seemed threatened, and it didn't. He explored her scalp with his fingers, found a knot the size of an egg and discovered her tangled curls felt all springy and satiny under his fingers.

"I'll take you home and turn you over to Linette," he said. Linette was his boss's wife and she took in strays and injured people, fixed them up and made sure they had a safe place to continue their lives. "What with Eddie—that's the boss—and the other cowboys, I don't expect you'll be bothered by Thorton again. Sure hope you're not married to that man or we'll have to deal with the law."

He urged the horse to a trot. He longed for a cool breeze, but the heat of midsummer beat down on them.

If he rode steady he could reach the ranch by the evening. At least with the long summer days there would still be some light. Not that he feared getting lost. 'Sides, if he did, the horse knew his way home.

Red moaned and clutched her head. She'd be confused when she came to, so he tightened his arms around her waist to prevent her from falling.

He knew the precise moment her senses returned. She stiffened like a rod. If he hadn't expected some sort of reaction, she'd have shimmied right out of his arms and likely landed on her head again, or under the horse's hooves.

"Relax. You're safe. Got a little gunshot wound, but I think it'll wait till we reach the ranch." He realized she hadn't heard his earlier words about Linette and Eddie, and repeated them, then gave his name.

She squirmed about to direct those green eyes at him. None of her defiance had faded. "Put me down right this minute."

"Ma'am...miss...you don't have to worry anymore. 'Less you're married to that—" Best not call him a beast just in case "—that man." He realized women married scoundrels. Usually because the man in question tricked them with words of love. Love? He snorted softly, hoping she wouldn't notice. Love made a person do foolish things. Made them regret decisions. Sort of messed up a man's or woman's thinking. He'd long ago decided it wasn't for him. Nope. He'd accept responsibility, work and do anything for people he cared about. But he would not allow his heart to rule his head.

She made an unladylike noise. "We are most certainly not married."

"Then you're safe. I'll take you to the ranch."

"I do not want to go to your ranch."

"It's not mine—"

"Put me down this instant. Or better yet, take me back."

"You're safe with me."

She exploded into a ball of flailing legs and arms. Managed to scratch his cheek before he could corral her arms. She kicked the horse, sending him into a panicked bolt.

"Whoa. Whoa." Ward had to turn his attention to getting the horse under control before they both ended up on the ground miles from home. It should have been easy, but Red made sure it wasn't. He couldn't hold both her and the horse with only one set of hands, and she slipped under his arm and jolted to the ground.

"Ooh."

No doubt she'd felt the pain of her wound, but he didn't have time to give her more than a passing thought as he fought to calm the horse. "Settle down. You're okay." Free of Red's vicious kicks, his mount settled.

Ward turned to see how Red fared. Her skin had turned pale as a sheet. Yet she flashed him continued defiance. He was beginning to understand the peculiar frustration of dealing with Red. He rode to her side and offered a hand. "Come on, get on and I'll take you—"

She slapped him away. "I'm going back." She slapped the horse on his withers.

Ward held the horse under control. "Look, lady. You'll be safe from Thorton where I'm taking you."

She took a step, wavered. He kind of figured she was a little dizzy and probably her leg hurt some.

"Leave me alone."

"Yes, ma'am." He kept pace at her side as she took another step and another, continuing to sway like a tree before a brisk north wind. Only difference being a tree had roots that anchored it to the ground. Red had no roots, no anchor. Nothing to keep her from toppling.

He figured he'd be there when she went down.

She paused, sucked in air, pressed a palm to her eyes and slowly folded to the ground.

Ward jumped down and scooped her up. "Here we go again."

She moaned. Her eyes fluttered and she sank against his chest. She'd be a whole lot less trouble this way, but for all he knew she was bleeding to death under that crimson-stained dress.

He kicked the horse into a gallop. "Let's get home as fast as we can."

Red struggled briefly and ineffectively twice more before he topped the last hill. Thankfully the little town of Cross Bar wasn't any farther away. But at least it was far enough to discourage frequent visits. Maybe far enough to keep Thorton from riding after him.

He sauntered past the empty winter pens, thudded over the bridge and passed the new house where the foreman, Roper, lived with his new wife and the four children they'd rescued and adopted. Through the kitchen window, Roper saw him pass, lifted a hand in greeting, then saw Ward had his arms full and leaned closer.

The bunkhouse lay in darkness. The men would be out with the cows or sleeping.

He glimpsed the empty table in the cookhouse as he passed. His stomach growled. He hadn't eaten more than a mouthful of that stew back at the saloon. Maybe Cookie would rustle up something for him.

He continued up the hill toward the big house. As he drew closer, he saw Linette and Eddie through the window. Eddie glanced up as he'd heard the sound of Ward's approach, and went to the window. Ward waved and motioned toward the woman in his arms.

Eddie turned away and strode from the room, Linette in his wake. By the time Ward reached the door, they had flung it open.

"What do you have there?" Eddie called.

"Woman named Red. She's been shot."

Linette sprang forward. "How bad?"

"Haven't had a look. It's her leg."

"She's unconscious?"

"Off and on."

Linette reached for Red, but Ward didn't release her until Eddie took her and strode into the house. Ward leaped from his mount and followed.

"I ought to warn you. She's a little feisty."

Eddie chuckled. "Seems pretty standard behavior around here."

Linette's look held both denial and affection. "Let's get her into a bed so I can see how badly hurt she is."

Ward followed as far as the hallway leading to several bedrooms. He plucked his hat from his head and watched Eddie duck into the doorway Linette indicated. "She's in good hands now. I'm going to see if Cookie has anything for me to eat."

Linette turned. "Wait. Who is she? Where did you find her?"

He twisted his hat. He knew nothing about her except her name and he wasn't even sure "Red" was her real name. He'd simply rescued her from a man who ruled with his fists or a belt…likely both and other things as well. "All I know is her name's Red and she was in a bad situation."

Linette studied him a moment, then nodded. "She'll get the attention she needs here."

Ward slapped his hat to his head and headed out the door. He cared for his horse, then went to the cookhouse to seek something to fill the hollows of his hungry stomach.

Only as he ate the generous plate of mashed potatoes

and gravy and thick slices of beef, raised right on the ranch, the food failed to satisfy the emptiness around his heart that he seldom acknowledged…that he'd carried since he'd walked away from his brothers and left them to deal with a situation that mirrored the one he'd found Red in. Sure he'd done it for the right reason, figuring the beatings would stop if he left.

But how could he be certain they did? Would he ever see his brothers again? Or his mother? Love had made her blind to the faults of the man she'd married a few years ago as a widow. The man who became Ward's cruel stepfather. Again he reminded himself, love made a person unable to see the facts.

He pushed the plate away and bolted from the table.

Red sat upright so fast her head spun and pain shot clear through her brain. "Oww." She pressed her palms to her head. "That hurts."

"Take it easy." Cool hands touched hers. "You're safe here."

Safe? Was it possible? "Where am I?" She glanced around the unfamiliar room. She lay on a bed with a small table across her knees. This certainly wasn't a room she'd been in before. Dark green drapes hung at the sides of a window. Brilliant sunlight spilled into the room. The bed was covered in a bright quilt full of swirls of color. She stole a glance at the woman before her. "Who are you?" The woman had plain brown hair. Oh, how Red wished her hair was brown and straight and would stay in a tidy bun. The woman smiling at her had the gentlest eyes she'd seen anywhere since Mother died. Red's throat clamped at a rush of regrets sweeping over her.

"I'm Linette Gardiner. You are safe in my home. I'm

guessing you have your memory back. Perhaps you can tell me a bit about yourself now." She removed the bed tray on which rested a half-full cup of tea. Red had no recollection of having drunk the top half but it seemed she must have.

"My memory back? How long have I been here?"

"Two days."

Two days. Her blood burned through her veins with desperate urgency. She tried to swing her feet to the floor and fell back as pain ripped through her head and leg.

Linette caught her hand. "Sit back and relax. You're injured."

"Am I alone?" She moved her head gingerly, ignoring the pain, as she checked out every corner of the room.

"You are alone and safe. I know your first name is Red, though I suspect it is a nickname. Can you tell me your full name?"

"It's—" She paused.

"Don't push it if you can't remember. I'm sure your memory will return in good time."

Her memories were intact. She was Grace Eileen Henderson, eighteen years of age. But her name no longer fit. "Red Henderson." She had a little sister, Belle, who was eight years old. Her lungs spasmed. She couldn't get her breath.

"No need to be afraid." Linette rubbed her shoulder and soothed her with a sweet voice. But the panic would not ease.

"I have to get back." Without Red's protection, what would be happening to Belle?

Linette sat back and studied her. "But why? Ward told us how that man treated you."

She couldn't tell the real reason. They wouldn't understand. No one would. Her situation would only make good people like Linette view her with even more alarm than she did now. "Where's my dress?"

"You're welcome to keep the one you're wearing."

Red rubbed the soft cotton of the muted brown dress. No doubt the color would also mute her coloring, stealing some of the red from her hair, turning her complexion muddy. More than enough reason to wish for many more dresses the same. But she could just imagine how Thorton Winch would react to her wearing an outfit that covered her from neck to wrists to ankles. A great lump of longing swelled within her. If only she could own a dozen such dresses. "I would like my own gown back, if you please."

Linette hesitated a moment, then nodded. "Very well. I shall get it." She slipped from the room.

As soon as she was gone, Red pushed carefully to her feet and waited for the dizziness to pass. Ignoring the pain in her leg, she made her way to the window. The scene spun crazily. But she squinted to focus. She was in the second story of a house that sat on a hill overlooking a large collection of other buildings. This must be the ranch that cowboy had talked about. She eyed the barn and the horses corralled outside it. A cowboy with a rolling gait moved among the horses. She studied him. Was it the man who had kidnapped her? She'd tried to escape his clutches on the way here. Would he likewise try to prevent her from leaving?

She could not allow it.

"Here it is." Linette stepped into the room. "Oh, you're up. You shouldn't be."

Red cautiously turned to face her. The red satin dress hung over her arm. "I'm fine."

"I regret I couldn't get all the stain out." She showed the dress with a faded brown stain on one side.

"Thank you." She clutched the dress to her as if it were something treasured. But it wasn't that she cared about the dress. Only about not provoking Thorton. Bile rose in her throat. Oh, how she regretted her gullibility. She'd trusted the man when he said he was a preacher and could take her and Belle to his sister. They'd be safe, he promised.

He'd lied. She'd never again trust a man.

She shuddered. Two days. What had happened to Belle? She must leave.

"I heard she was feeling better."

A man's voice pulled her attention to the doorway and her cowboy rescuer. He'd given his name as Ward Walker. He was solid-looking with a thick thatch of black hair.

"You." She managed not to spit the word out.

He grinned. "Yup. Me. Glad to see you have your memory back."

For two heartbeats she wished she didn't, but the alternative was unthinkable. "Don't expect me to thank you."

He chuckled. "Yup. I see you're back to normal. You were mellow when you didn't remember your name." He shot a triumphant look toward Linette. "I told you she was feisty."

Feisty? He had no idea how quickly she'd learned to keep her opinions and objections to herself. She had to return to Thorton. There was no alternative. She would demand transportation back this moment, but the room suddenly tipped to the right and black folded inward from the corners.

Ward rushed forward and caught her before she hit

the floor. "You're too weak to be up." He carried her to the bed and eased her down on the pillows.

For some reason her fingers refused to release him. She clutched his shoulders, finding strength and steadiness there. That was all it was, she reassured herself. Holding on to him kept the world from spinning.

"You're safe here. No one will hurt you." His intensely blue eyes drilled straight through her, invading her mind, probing her heart. If only she could accept his words, allow herself to settle back and feel safe.

But she had Belle to consider. Besides, no decent man would ever look at her without judgment or lust in his eyes. She'd performed dances that made her grateful her mother couldn't see. And men touched her, their hands soiling her soul every bit as much as Thorton's belt damaged her body.

"I can't stay," she murmured, unable to break from his promising gaze. "Please take me back."

He straightened. "Never." His eyes blazed. "I saw how that man treated you."

She lowered her gaze. "I can take it."

He perched on the edge of the bed. "I understand how you fear him, but there is no need. He can no longer harm you. No one here will let him."

Linette murmured agreement.

"So you rest and get better. Things will sort themselves out. You'll see." He patted her hand.

She nodded. Obviously she was going to get no help from him or likely anyone here. They all saw themselves as noble rescuers. But she would find her way back. She must.

Ward watched her closely. "Your coloring is coming back. That's good."

Self-consciously she brushed her hands over her hair.

For half a wooden nickel she would shave off that offensive red hair. Wouldn't Thorton find that idea just lovely? "I'd like to get up now."

Ward shook his head. "Think you better give your head a chance to get back to normal."

"For all you know, this is normal." He knew nothing about her or her circumstances and she was happy to leave it that way.

Ward's eyes crinkled with amusement. "You forget I saw how nimble you are on your feet."

He was too close, too big, practically blocking everything else from view. "I still am. Let me show you." She shoved him aside and swung her feet to the floor, feeling the blood drain from her face. Her skin grew clammy. No way could she stand up without clutching support. For sure she couldn't do anything nimble. But he didn't need to know it. She pulled in a breath, sucked strength from it and forced her legs to hold her upright. "See? I'm fine."

But by the way Ward hovered at her side and the anxious look on Linette's face, she knew she had not convinced them.

"I'll just sit a moment on that chair." She indicated the hardback chair a few feet away.

Ward jerked it closer. She didn't know if she should be annoyed that he didn't think she could walk that far or grateful that she didn't have to prove she could. Her knees waited until she reached the chair before they buckled. Still she sat straight, trying hard to convince everyone in the room she was okay. It was hard to say if either of the others thought she was fine. She knew she wasn't.

She could not make it back to the saloon without help. Help was not to be found from Ward or Linette.

Where would she find it?

"I'll let you handle her." Ward nodded toward Linette and headed for the door. He paused, turned to consider Red. "I'm glad you're on the mend and hope you'll soon feel safe here."

She scowled at him with all the strength she could summon from her uncooperative body. What right did he have to come into her life and complicate matters? He knew absolutely nothing about what was at stake.

She could not continue staring at him. It made her head hurt like fury. She settled for simply nodding—let him think what he wanted from that—then lowered her gaze and studied her fingers, noting how they twisted together until there were spots of white and red. Let them think what they wanted about that, too. Put it down to tension or pain. They would never guess how worried she was.

Ward finally left, his footsteps echoing down the hall.

Determination filled her, giving her strength to remain sitting upright. "I'm fine," she insisted.

She had to get her strength back. But with Linette hovering, she couldn't move. "I think I'd like to rest now."

Linette hurried to her side and held her elbow.

She let Linette ease her to the inviting bed, and snuggled down like she meant to have a long sleep. Linette spread an afghan over her, then tiptoed from the room. Red sighed. It was tempting to close her eyes and give in to the lethargy of her body.

But that would not get her back to Belle.

She remained tense, waiting for Linette's footsteps to fade, then she pushed herself to the side of the bed and took deep breaths to stop the dizziness. Holding carefully to the frame on the foot of the bed, she again made her way to the window and rested her forehead on the glass. Men went back and forth outside. Too many for her to slip away unnoticed. Even if she had the strength.

But she must find the strength somewhere. Somehow.

Too bad she no longer believed God would help her or she would pray for His intervention.

Chapter Two

"Boys." Eddie stepped into the cookhouse as the cowboys ate their breakfast. "Red is missing."

Ward dropped his fork and stared. Yesterday she could barely stand. Now she was gone?

Eddie continued. "Her room was empty when we got up this morning. I'm telling you, Linette is some concerned about her. Figures she's lost her memory again and is wandering about, lost and alone. Or worse, passed out somewhere." He scrubbed at his neck. "Boys, we have to find her before Linette gets it into her head to go looking. We can't have that. Especially in her condition." Linette was in the family way, and Eddie worried constantly about her.

Ward was already on his feet. "I'll check the barn." He was out the door while Eddie ordered men to various corners of the yard to search for the missing woman.

Ward raced to the barn. Had she wandered out in the dark? Fallen in the river? He shuddered as he imagined her alone. Further injured. Suffering. He'd rescued her from a harmful situation. He could only pray she hadn't fallen into a worse one. The door squawked a protest as he pushed it open and stepped into the warm, dusty interior. "Red," he yelled, wondering if she could hear his voice. Would she respond even if she did? He headed down the alley, paused at the first stall. It was empty. The horse that should be there was gone.

Gone? Had the animal let himself out? Probably not, since it was Moon that should have been in that stall and Moon liked the comforts of the barn too much to wander.

Suspicion crept into Ward's thoughts. Red kept saying she wanted to go back. He went to the tack room and counted the saddles. Sure enough. One missing.

His jaw clenched. Even though he knew it was useless to search the rest of the barn, he did so. More out of wishing she was here than thinking she was. Then he headed back to the cookhouse. Eddie paced the floor, waiting for someone to return with good news to ease his wife's worry.

"'Fraid I have bad news," Ward said. "There's a horse missing. And a saddle." Even though Eddie looked ready to chew nails, he might as well tell it all. "There were small footprints in the dust. Lady-sized."

Eddie groaned. "She stole a horse? Don't hardly call that gratitude. Do you?"

Ward didn't say one way or the other. "I'll ride after her and get the horse."

"You do that."

Ward hesitated. Did Eddie want him to turn Red over to the Mountie as a horse thief? Though Ward was beginning to think the only place Red would be safe was behind bars.

"Just get the horse back." Eddie spun about and paced to the far side of the room. He stared out the window as Ward waited. With a gut-deep sigh, Eddie turned. "And bring her back, too, or Linette will have both our hides."

"Boss, you expect me to tie her to the saddle?"

Eddie grinned. "Ward, charm her into coming back."

"Yeah, right." So far neither charm nor superior strength had convinced Red she didn't need to go back to that man Thorton. "Why in the name of all that's right would she want to return?"

"I don't know. Doesn't make sense. He must have some hold on her, though I can't imagine what it could be."

Ward turned and headed back to the barn. Whatever Red's reason, he intended to stop her. No way he could stand by and see a person subjected to the abuse he knew she received. As he saddled up, he prayed for a way to convince her. *And, Lord, keep her safe.* In her condition she could have fallen from the horse and received further injury.

Following her tracks presented no challenge and he galloped down the trail. The sun rose higher in the east, bringing with it the promise of heat.

Was Red in that silly dress she clutched in her arms yesterday? If so, she'd soon be burnt a matching color. Though anyone riding back into her situation deserved to suffer some misery. Might make her reconsider her decision.

But worry soon replaced his annoyance. And a large dose of confusion. He knew firsthand the pain and fear of living with someone who controlled with fists to the flesh and a belt across the back…or anywhere it landed. Why would she return to such a situation? Eddie said the man must have a hold on her. But Ward couldn't imagine what that could be.

He settled into a lope. An hour later he glimpsed her in the distance and urged his horse to a gallop.

As he closed the distance, she turned, saw him and kicked poor old Moon into a jarring trot. Ward knew from experience how rough a ride Moon was and almost felt sorry for her.

He easily overtook her, grabbed the bridle and pulled them to a standstill. "What do you think you're doing?" At least she'd chosen to wear the brown dress rather than the revealing red one.

"I'm going back where I belong." Her green eyes blazed with defiance.

"You know the kind of trouble you can get into for stealing a horse?"

"About the same you will be in for kidnapping me."

"Kidnapping!" She had to be joshing. "I rescued you."

"Don't recall saying I needed rescuing."

He reached out and touched her back where he'd seen the red welts and knew a fleeting sense of triumph when she flinched. "You planning to tell me you like that kind of treatment?"

"Wasn't planning to tell you anything."

"I know what it's like to have a belt used on me. I know what it does to your mind."

Her eyes darkened. She pressed her lips together. For a moment he thought she might soften. Admit the pain. Relent. But then her shoulders went back and her chin went up and he knew she wouldn't give in.

"Nothing touches my mind."

Ward shrugged. "You'll never convince me, 'cause I know better. Not only does it affect your mind, it affects your heart. Teaches you to build guards around it so no one can get in."

"Speak for yourself." She jerked away and urged the horse forward.

He grabbed the bridle again. "You ain't going anywhere."

She yanked at the reins, trying to get free. When that didn't work, she slapped his hands, tried to kick his horse.

"Stop it."

"Let me go."

They stared at each other, both breathing hard. He knew his eyes were as hard and unyielding as hers, which blared brittle, green shards. "Why would you want to go back to such a situation?"

He could feel her measuring him, trying to gauge him. He could see her throat work as if she struggled to swallow.

Finally she nodded. "He has my little sister. Belle's only eight."

The words thundered through him. A person would do anything to protect a little sister...or brother. Hank was only six when Ward left, Travers, thirteen. He did a little mental arithmetic. That was seven years ago. How had time passed so quickly, silently...sadly?

He wished he could know if leaving had made it better for Hank and Travers.

"Has he hurt her?" Each word ripped a piece of flesh from his heart.

All the starch left Red and she sank forward. "You talk about how cruel treatment touches the mind and heart. I see it in her. But so far I've protected her from worse." She scrubbed at her eyes. "I have to get back to her."

He understood that there were other kinds of torture, especially for a little girl. He nodded and together they rode onward. "We need to get her out of there. You, too." Though technically Red was out of the situation, he now understood why she would return. Why she felt compelled to.

"He will never let us go."

He heard the resignation in her voice. But he wasn't about to accept defeat. This time he would fight to make sure a man like Thorton could not continue to rule by the power of his fists. "Have you ever considered going to the Mountie?"

"Thorton never lets us out together unless he's with us. If I ever went to the Mountie on my own, I fear what would happen to Belle."

"I figured as much." He considered the situation for the next few miles. "Here's the plan. I'll go with you to the Mountie and he'll make Thorton release your sister."

Red didn't answer for a moment as she studied his suggestion. Finally she nodded.

He considered her from under the brim of his hat, wondering if she only pretended to agree. He was learning she didn't easily go along with plans others suggested. More than that, he understood why she would agree to something with her mouth while dissenting with her mind.

The sun reached its zenith as they neared town. It blared down on them without pity. One of the first buildings was the Mountie station. A horse stood patiently at the front. Hopefully it belonged to the lawman. Their whole plan rested on him being there.

Ward swung from his saddle and hustled over to help Red dismount. He guessed from the way she pursed her lips she might have protested but reconsidered and allowed it with barely a hesitation and likely only because her leg hurt. But after she gained her feet she pulled away so they marched side by side toward the door. Ward fell back to let her step in first.

The Mountie sat behind a desk, writing in some sort of ledger. He glanced up at their arrival. Ward got the feeling he saw them both in detail but his eyes lighted on Red and he slowly rose to his feet. "Thorton said you'd been kidnapped. This man the one responsible?"

Ward's neck tingled. His plan didn't include getting arrested and maybe hung.

"He didn't seem particularly worried about it, I might add. Said you'd be back soon enough." The Mountie considered Ward from head to toe, no doubt silently examining him for a weapon.

Ward could assure him he carried no hidden pistol or knife. In fact, he kind of counted on the Mountie's authority to accomplish what they needed. "I didn't kidnap her. She was injured. I took her to a friend to be doctored."

"That right, miss?"

Red dismissed his question with a wave of her hand. "I'm here to tell you the truth."

"Always interested in the truth."

"Thorton's got my little sister under lock and key. That's how he knew I'd be back."

The Mountie came to rigid attention. "That's a serious charge. One I intend to follow up on."

"We're counting on it."

He grabbed his wide-brimmed Stetson. "Let's go talk to Thorton Winch."

Ward and Red trotted after the Mountie. Red would have burst into the saloon ahead of him but he pressed her back. "I'll deal with this."

Ward could feel Red's hot impatience as they followed the Mountie inside. Mr. Winch jolted his chair to all fours when he saw the three of them. "Told you she'd be back."

"She tells me you have her little sister locked up here."

Thorton chuckled loudly. "She's addled. Don't know why I keep her." But Ward saw the evil glint in the man's eyes and knew he would beat Red unmercifully if he got his hands on her.

Ward didn't intend he should get the chance.

"Have a look, Constable." Thorton waved his arm to indicate the whole place was open to him.

"I'll show you where she is." Red stomped past Thorton, being sure to stay out of arm's reach.

Ward and the Mountie followed.

Red threw open the door to a tiny room with a narrow bed against one wall. But the place was as clean and tidy as an unused manger. "She's gone." Before either man could think, she dashed back to the grinning Thorton and tried to claw his eyes out. "What have you done with her? Tell me."

The Mountie peeled her off the man. "Sorry to bother you," he murmured to Thorton.

Red broke from the Mountie's grasp and raced outside.

Ward noted that Thorton appeared totally unconcerned. The man knew he had Red in his clutches.

Without a doubt his ace was Belle, Red's little sister. Where had he hidden her?

Red swallowed back a yard-wide wail as she stood in the center of the street. She stared the full length one way. Where was Belle?

She turned slowly and studied the other side of town. Slowly her thoughts settled. Thorton would not let Belle go if for no other reason than it forced Red to dance for the despicable creature who considered himself her owner. Belle was around here somewhere. Close enough that Thorton could mock Red's frustration. She shuddered. He delighted as much in tormenting Red as in anything else.

Where would he hide Belle? Likely any number of men would help him. Men of the same quality as he. Like Mr. Shack, who ran the feed store. Or dirty Old Mike Morton, who worked at the livery barn. Mike had a little cabin behind the barn where the owner allowed him to live.

The perfect place to lock up a little girl.

Without a backward glance or a considering thought, she steamed down the street, crossed behind the store to avoid being seen approaching the livery barn. She reached the tiny cabin. Sure enough, it was locked solid and the windows were boarded up tight as a drum. She tapped the door. "Belle?"

Did she hear a rustling? "Belle?" She dare not call loudly and alert any of Thorton's willing cohorts, but she was certain something—or likely someone—moved inside.

The padlock was solid. No way she could hope to break it.

The wood on the windows was thick and nailed to last eternity.

No willing tool stood ready for her use. She glanced toward the sky, her frustration longing to escape in a scream. But she bit back any sound.

She looked to the right and the left. Saw the woodpile behind the store. Where there was wood, there was an ax. Exactly what she needed. She clambered over the debris between the yards, found the ax with its head buried in a log, wriggled it loose and stomped back to the shack. Gritting her teeth, she swung the ax with all her might against the padlock. When it refused to give, she attacked the door. Chips flew but the door did not give way. Again and again she swung. If only she was stronger she could inflict real damage.

The racket brought Old Mike from the barn. "What-cha' think you're doin'? That's my house. Get away."

When he tried to drive her off, she swung the ax at him.

He wisely backed off.

The storekeeper and several other men joined him in a knot.

"Someone fetch Thorton. He'll put a stop to this."

"Yeah. Seems he's the only one who can make her behave herself."

Their words lent power to her arms and she swung harder. Now she could see inside. "Belle, keep back. I'm going to free you."

"Who's she talking to?"

"She's strange. Just like Thorton says."

A whole section of the door gave way. Holding the ax ready to use as a weapon, Red poked her head through the opening. Belle sat shivering on a crude bed. "Belle, honey. It's me. Come here." She held out her arms.

Belle's eyes were wide and staring.

What had these men done to her in the three days that Red had been missing? She swung about and faced them, the ax lifted like a sword. "Anyone touch either of us and I'll leave you in pieces."

The men kept back a safe distance.

She turned back to her sister. "Belle, come here. I'll look after you. Just like I always do."

Whimpering, Belle slipped from the bed.

"What's going on here?"

Red slowly turned to face the Mountie with Thorton on one side and Ward on the other.

"She's trashed my house." Mike pointed. "Arrest her, I say."

"Red, what are you doing? Give me the ax." The Mountie gingerly reached for her weapon.

Red didn't budge. Didn't offer to release it. Nor would she until Belle was safe and sound. "Have a look for yourself." She stepped aside and indicated the Mountie should look in the hole.

He watched her carefully as he edged forward. She kept her back to the shack as she watched the circle of men for any threat, but she knew the moment the Mountie saw Belle because of his indrawn breath. "Come on, child. You're safe now."

Red kept her eyes on Thorton. She saw his intention to escape and sprang forward, waving the ax.

Ward also saw his intention and grabbed an arm and twisted it behind Thorton's back.

The Mountie lifted Belle through the opening. She glanced about at all the men and pressed her back to the shack.

Red dropped the ax and held her arms out. Belle hesitated a moment, then raced to her sister.

"Thorton Winch," the Mountie said, "I'm arresting you for kidnapping and a number of other charges. Take a good look at the sky. You won't get many more chances."

As he was led away, Thorton turned to Red. "Don't think this is the end. I'll get away and I'll find you."

The Mountie jerked his arms. "You aren't going anywhere.

"Mike Morton, you are under arrest, too. Ward, would you bring him along?"

Thorton gave Ward a look fit to cure leather. "I'll find you, too, and make you regret your part in this."

The Mountie pushed him along.

The men shrank away, muttering they didn't know about a child. She expected most of them told the truth.

In a few minutes Red and Belle were alone.

"What are we going to do?" Belle whispered.

"We'll be fine."

"Who's going to take care of us?"

"We'll take care of ourselves." She spoke so reassuringly she almost believed her words. But she had no money. No clothing except the dress on her back and grateful she was for the brown one Linette had given her. But they had their freedom.

"Let's go." She took Belle's hand and headed out of town, a different direction than the one that had brought her back a few hours ago.

"Where we going?"

"To a new life." One, she vowed, where she would never again depend on a man. Or trust one.

They marched bravely onward until Belle dropped to the edge of the trail.

"We're lost. And I'm hungry." Silent tears trailed down her pale cheeks.

Red hated those tears and that silent cry, even though she felt like sitting at Belle's side and joining her in a good wail. Her leg hurt even though she'd looked at it closely when Linette changed the dressing last night and knew it was a minor injury. Her head pounded like a thousand horses kicking to be released. "We'll be okay."

Belle shook her head. Not that Red blamed her for not believing. She had no plan. No options. "Come on.

We can't sit at the side of the road feeling sorry for ourselves."

Belle didn't move.

Red dried her sister's tears on the skirt of the brown cotton dress. "Something will work out. It always does, doesn't it?" Even though she said the words, she could think of too many times when things had gone wrong to be convincing.

"Can I call you Grace now?"

Red looked past Belle to the low bushes beside the trail. "I'll never be Grace again. Continue calling me Red." She yanked on a lock of hair. Why had she been cursed with hair that drew unwanted attention?

Belle sprang to her feet. Her eyes widened as she stared down the road. "Someone's coming." She bolted for the bushes.

"Belle, wait." But Belle didn't slow until she was well out of sight.

Red shared her sense of panic. Had Thorton escaped? She squinted at the approaching rider. He led a second horse. That fact alone sent shivers up and down Red's spine. Slowly she backed away, aiming for the opposite side of the trail as Belle. That way if Red was caught, Belle might hope to escape.

To what? Starvation in the wilds?

She spun about. Her head did not like the sudden movement and dizziness made her stumble and fall to her knees.

"Red. Hold up. It's me."

She recognized the voice. Ward. Interfering again.

But her annoyance was laced liberally with relief. Surely he'd give her a ride.

To where? She had no place to go.

* * *

Ward was too far away to do anything but kick his horse to a gallop, and watch helplessly as Red fell to the ground. The woman seemed to have a knack for getting into trouble. But right now he didn't have time to analyze that observation. He had to take care of Red and her little sister. Where had Belle disappeared to?

He jumped from his horse and trotted over to Red who now sat on the ground, her legs drawn up, her face buried in her knees. He squatted at her side. "Are you okay?"

"I'm fine. Just turned too fast and fell." She eyed him with squinting disfavor. "Could happen to anyone."

He chuckled. "Yup. Happens to me all the time."

She snorted. "Sure it does."

"Well it does every time I have a blow to my head that leaves a lump the size of a turkey egg."

She stared away.

He looked in the same direction. Saw nothing of interest. Some scraggly bushes along the trail, poplars with their lacy leaves dancing in the breeze, and further off, dark green spruce and pine. In the distance, the blue-gray Rockies. "Where you going?" Seemed to be nothing much out there for her to aim for.

"To freedom."

"Yeah, sure. But where will you hang your hat?"

"No hat to hang."

He guessed she had little of anything to hang. She'd left without pausing to collect her belongings. All she took with her was her little sister. Who—if he had to guess—hid from the sight of a man. No doubt men represented danger in her young mind. Maybe in Red's not-so-young mind as well. "Even without a hat, you need a place. You can't survive out in the open. Do you have any family?"

She didn't shift her gaze. "Just Belle."

"Uh-huh. Friends? Anyone who would give you a home?"

The look she gave him dripped disbelief. "Do you think if we did, we would have fallen into the clutches of a man like Thorton?"

"Guess it was a stupid question."

"It sure was."

He sank to his backside and drew his knees up in a pose that mirrored hers. Together they stared down the trail. "I got a place. Ain't much. Just a tiny cabin. Someday it's going to be more. Got plans for a big house."

"What you want with a big house? You got a girl?"

"I got a mother and two brothers. It's for them."

"No pa?"

"He died."

"Where are they now?"

Her question unleashed a tornado of memories, infiltrated with regrets and pain. "Back in New Brunswick. Travers is three years younger than me…" When he and Travers said goodbye, Travers swore he would come and join Ward when he thought Hank could take care of himself. The Travers he remembered never went back on his word. "Hank is ten years younger," he continued. "He'd be thirteen by now. I ain't seen him since he was six."

She shifted to see his face. "How come?"

"I left."

"Who is taking care of them?"

"My stepfather." The man had vowed he loved Ma and the boys. *Love!* A word easily spoken. It meant nothing. Taking care of others was all that counted. That and kindness.

"Oh." Her voice was small, tight. "That why you left?"

Something in her tone drew him. He met her probing gaze. "He didn't care for me. Just me being there made him angry."

Understanding flickered through her gaze. "He used a belt? Fists?"

He nodded, and in that moment they formed a bond—one based on the shared experience of abuse. He looked deep into her hurting soul, found a reflection of his own. He knew then what he must do. "I'll take you to my cabin. You can stay there as long as you need."

"What about your family? Aren't you expecting them?"

He closed his eyes, shutting out her gaze, as a newer, fresher pain surfaced. "They aren't answering my letters." He'd had but three letters in the years since he left—two from Ma and one from Travers. Nothing in almost three years.

"Oh. I'm sorry." A cool hand touched the back of his, and he jerked his eyes open. She pulled her hand to her knee and looked into the distance, but she'd touched him. Offered comfort. That tiny gesture slipped into his troubled heart and mind like a warm summer breeze full of sweet scents.

"So you'll accept my offer?" He hoped she'd agree willingly. Let him help her and Belle.

She developed a keen interest in the blade of grass plucked from nearby. Her hesitation gave him plenty of time to reconsider, but rather than withdraw his offer, he silently begged her to accept it.

Slowly she turned and faced him. "What would you expect in return?"

The question sliced through him like she'd used the ax she'd threatened the circle of men with. Then the meaning of her words hit him with peculiar force. He sprang to his feet and backed away three steps. "I am not that sort of a man. I made an offer out of concern for you and Belle. I have no ulterior, despicable motives." What had Thorton demanded of her? His cheeks burned to think of the sort of things that went on in the back rooms of a saloon. Some would see Red as soiled, ruined. But all he saw was a woman who needed help to escape a bad situation. He could offer that.

She didn't lower her gaze, nor did her silent demand ease.

"If you accept my offer, it will be clearly understood that I—" he could think of no gentle way to say it "—I do not want repayment of any sort. My only concern is making sure you and Belle are safe from the kind of treatment you received at Thorton's hands and that you have a place to live."

Still she considered him, looking up from her seated position. He felt her careful examination of his words. Of him. As if she probed his thoughts, his heart. His very soul.

He met her gaze without once blinking. She would find him reliable, trustworthy, perhaps even noble so far as he was able.

Finally she spoke. "Very well. I will accept your offer until I can find something suitable that allows me my freedom and independence."

Her answer was less than satisfactory. After all, he had no intention of infringing on her freedom, though she'd had none whatsoever until he intervened. She might remember that. And how much independence did she expect? She had neither means nor opportunity to pursue such. "I'm not asking to own you, only help you." But at least she had agreed to use his cabin. "Then let's get on our way. Where's Belle?"

"Belle, come."

Nothing.

"She's afraid of you."

"Now, that hurts. If you'd said she's afraid of men, I'd understand, but you make it sound like it's only me."

"That's because you're the only man here. So at this point she's only afraid of you."

"Do you always have to win every argument?"

He might as well have accused her of some heinous crime the way she glowered at him. "I most certainly do not. Do you turn everything into a confrontation?"

"A what?"

"Yes. See, a simple comment about Belle being afraid of you becomes a—a—"

"Yeah. What?"

"A challenge. That's what."

He slapped his forehead. "I can see this is going to be a fun time."

She slowly rose to her feet, planted her hands on her hips and stuck out her chin as she faced him. "Do you mean to say you will be residing in this cabin? Because I did not understand that part. If that is so, then I change my mind. We'll find some other place."

He groaned. "I will be living at the ranch. That's where I work. But unless you have a means of getting supplies, filling the wood box, bringing in meat… Well, do you?"

She squinted without answering.

"I thought not. So I expect you'll be happy enough to let me do that. Which—if you can bear the thought— means I will occasionally come by to perform those necessary tasks." Suddenly the idea held a lot less appeal than it did just a few minutes ago.

"Just so long as we understand each other."

"Oh, I think we do."

"Fine."

"Fine."

Her gaze slid past him and her scowl vanished. "Belle?" Her voice grew soft, gentle, inviting.

Ward's first instinct was to spin around, but remembering Red's words that Belle was afraid of him—the way she'd said it still irritated—he stepped aside so he wasn't blocking Belle's view of Red and slowly, cautiously turned about.

Belle stood at the far edge of the road.

"It's okay. He won't hurt you." Red's words were as much warning to Ward as encouragement to Belle, and irritation scratched at his decision to help.

Ward let Belle assess him. Though the wariness never left her eyes, she crossed the road to take Red's outstretched hand. She carefully kept Red between herself and Ward.

"He has a cabin we can use until we sort ourselves out."

If not for Belle's presence, Ward would have pointed out how she made it sound as if accepting his offer was a last resort. She gave no account of the fact it was a generous offer made from a concerned person. After all, he was preparing a place for his mother and brothers. Having Red and Belle there would be inconvenient should they arrive. But he already knew the frustration and folly of pointing out flaws in her words. Still, he couldn't keep from murmuring, "I'm only trying to help."

"You think that will be okay, Belle?" Red asked.

"I guess so."

No one acknowledged his generosity, so Ward had to

settle for feeling like poor-quality chicken feed. "Then let's ride."

He made his way back to the horses and left them to follow. Or not. Whatever they decided. He had done his best. Not much else he could do. But he knew he would not ride away and leave them at the side of the road even if the pair got it in their minds to turn all prickly.

Shoot. They were already more prickly than he cared to deal with.

He reached the horses and turned back to them, standing exactly where they were when he left. "You coming or not?"

Their hesitation was palpable. "I get it. You don't want to come with me. But you don't have a lot of options. And I don't aim to leave you here. So let's get moving."

They sure did know how to look less than enthusiastic as they picked their way across the grass to his side. He cupped his hands to help Red mount.

Belle drew back, her fear as thick as stew.

"I have to lift you up to sit behind your sister," he said, wanting to warn her before he touched her.

She nodded but her eyes flooded with wariness.

He grabbed her about the waist, heard her indrawn breath, felt her stiffen, but before she could reconsider he had her perched behind Red.

He swung into his own saddle and led the way.

"How far?" Belle whispered, likely meaning only for Red to hear.

"It will be almost dark before we get there."

The sooner she learned that Ward meant her no harm nor posed a threat, the better for them all. How long before either of them felt comfortable with him?

Chapter Three

Belle's arms clutched about Red's waist. Feeling the fear and desperation in her little sister, she almost forgot the way her head pounded, the pain driving deeper with each thud of her mount's hooves. She shivered, though the sun beat down with enough heat to bake biscuits on the dirt trail. Where were they going? She took some comfort in the fact it was the same direction as the ranch. She could always flee there for protection should the need arise. Of course that depended on how far Ward's cabin was from the ranch. He rode a few feet ahead, leading the way. Why had he offered his cabin? Did he have an ulterior motive? Or was it born from knowing what it was like to receive the blows of fists?

She urged the horse forward until she rode at Ward's side. "Where is your cabin?"

He pointed in the general direction of the ranch. Some help that was. Would it hurt the man to give exact directions?

"It's nothing like Eden Valley Ranch. For one thing it doesn't have the backing of a rich family back in England. Nor does it have the thousands of acres of the Eden Valley land grant. But I'll be able to run enough cows and horses to make a good living." He sat easy in the saddle as only a cowboy used to long hours on the back of a horse could.

Red shifted, wishing she could be half as comfortable. But her leg hurt almost as much as her head. She was tired and admittedly, a tad cranky. She didn't need a cowboy to point it out to her.

Ward continued talking as if his cabin was the most important thing in the world. Maybe it was to him. For her, it was only a place she would go to because she had no other option. Resolve drove away a great deal of her discomfort. She would find a place as soon as possible. She allowed herself to dream a little. Wouldn't it be nice if Belle could attend school and later, they could celebrate Christmas together in their own home? She'd trim the tree with red ribbons tied in bows of various sizes. There would be gifts. Nothing extravagant. Perhaps a new dress for each of them. Warm mittens. Woolen coats. Maybe she could splurge for one extravagance. A storybook for Belle and a book of poetry for herself.

Poetry? She mocked her dreams. How foolish. That pleasure belonged to the past. As did such dreams. She couldn't afford half a penny candy let alone frivolous things. With every ounce of self-control she could muster, she jerked her attention back to Ward, who still talked about his place.

"I wanted to get a simple cabin built first in the hopes of persuading my family to join me. Once they're here, I figured there would be plenty of hands to help make it larger. Next spring, I hope to buy enough cows to start my own herd." His voice rang with hope and pride.

Red accepted that she had neither hope nor pride left. Nor was she bitter about it. Not with Belle safely behind her, Thorton locked up and a chance to make a better life for them.

"Red," Belle whispered. "When did you eat last?"

She let the horse drop back and spoke low, hoping Belle would be the only one who heard. "Been a while. But we'll manage. You and me, we're survivors, remember? Nobody and nothing can defeat us. Especially not a little bit of hunger."

"I have an awful big hunger."

No doubt Old Mike never thought to feed a little girl. Red was glad Belle couldn't see her face or she might guess at her anger. She could take all sorts of mistreatment, but it made her boil inside that people seemed to forget Belle was a child. Children should be protected, guarded, treated as gifts from God. They should never know anything but trust. "We'll be okay. You'll see."

Ward slowed until he rode beside her. "We'll rustle up some food soon." He'd overheard them.

Seems the man was determined to stick his nose into everything she did. However, she was grateful for his help. Or was she? She gave a humorless smile. Not really. She didn't want him or any man extending favors. If she never again saw another man or had to accept anything from a man's hand, it would suit her just fine.

They continued on the worn trail. Grass whispered as the wind passed over it. Birds scolded the intruders. The gentle scent of pine trees filled the air. They climbed a hill, the Rockies rising up in the distance.

Belle leaned over to get a better view. "Are we going to live in the mountains?" Awe rounded her words.

Red thought of all the places a person could hide in that rugged expanse. She'd heard men tell tales of treacherous cliffs and impassable barriers, but they'd also spoke reverently of roomy caves, rushing water and ideal camping spots. *Where a man could live forever in peace with a boundless supply of fish to eat and fresh water to drink.* It sounded ideal to Red's ears. Ward shifted in the saddle to answer Belle's question. "We'll be pretty close to the mountains. Some mornings it feels like you can reach out and touch them right outside the window. But the distances are deceiving. It would take a hard day's ride to get to the foot of one of those giants."

Despite her resistance to anything he might offer, he made the view from his cabin sound appealing. And the way his eyes flashed blue as if reflecting the sky back, Red found herself drawn into his description.

"Every time I see them out the window, I think of a portion in the Bible, one of the Psalms, 'They that trust in the Lord shall be as mount Zion which cannot be removed, but abideth for ever. As the mountains are round about Jerusalem, so the Lord is round about his people from henceforth and forever.' Reminds me that God doesn't change."

Belle sighed heavily. "Red says we don't trust God anymore, even though Mama and Papa said we always should." The accusation in her voice brought a choking argument to Red's throat, but she would not list all her reasons in front of Ward.

Ward pushed his hat back and gave Red an unblinking look. But rather than accusation or disapproval, she thought she saw sympathy. "Sometimes it's hard to trust. Awfully hard."

She couldn't jerk from his gaze and, as it deepened, something warm and gentle seemed to brush against a dark and angry spot buried deep within.

With an effort, she shifted in her saddle, keeping her attention on things close by, ignoring the mountains.

But again and again her gaze was drawn to the distance. If she could escape to the mountains. Find safety.

Resignation sighed into her soul. Ward's cabin would have to do. For now.

If they ever reached this cabin.

She'd been half slouching in the saddle, weary from too much riding, too much struggle, too much life, but now she straightened and stared ahead, though she saw neither the mountains nor the narrow trail. What if there wasn't a cabin? What if it was all a trick? Had she, in her desperation to escape Thorton's clutches, fallen into a worse situation? She began to shake and sucked in air. She could not let Belle know of her concern. Whatever came, wherever this man led her, her first and foremost thought was to protect Belle.

Perhaps she should get Belle to slip from the horse now and hide in the trees. Then when she knew what lay ahead she could come back for her, either to take her to a real cabin or to escape into hiding. But the idea of abandoning Belle for any reason did not rest easy in Red's mind. Instead, she would be attentive and prepared to take evasive action if things turned sour.

The sun ducked behind the mountains, sending rays of light upward into the sky.

"Look," Belle said. "God is sending out fiery arrows to show us the way."

Despite the knot of disbelief in her heart, Red couldn't help thinking that's exactly what it looked like. For half a second she let herself think her life could be different, that God was directing her to a place where she could forget the past.

But reality could not be wished away or fancied out of existence. She was headed into an uncertain future. Moreover she was Red. A woman who would forever be known as a saloon dancer. Many would question if dancing had been the only thing she did. It had been, though few would believe it. Seems Thorton wasn't interested in anything more than forcing her to dance for others so he could collect the money he demanded before each performance. That and controlling her, humiliating her.

He'd never allowed any other man to go beyond touching. She shuddered at the memory of those harsh fingers feeling her. Then she forced herself to sit motionless so as not to alarm Belle.

"There's the ranch." Ward pointed.

Red pulled back on the reins. The horse stopped moving and Red stared. "You said we were going to your place." It was the Eden Valley Ranch. The place she'd ridden away from before daylight. Had he tricked her?

He didn't turn toward her, which was probably for the best. He might not like the suspicion and anger tightening her face. "Have to let the boss know I got his horse and saddle back."

"What is he going to do?"

"Horse thieves aren't treated kindly around here."

"I have firsthand knowledge of not being treated kindly."

He turned to consider her. "They're usually hung."

She pressed her hand to her throat. "So you're really turning me over to a hangman? This was all just a ruse to get me to come along." Belle's hands dug into Red's ribs. She shouldn't let her anger make her forget to guard her words. "It's okay, Belle. I'm not going to hang. Now or ever." She yanked on the reins and jabbed her heels into her mount's ribs. The animal jerked so hard, Red almost came unseated, and then it took off in a bone-pounding trot. She kicked again. "Faster, you lazy animal."

But faster wasn't something this horse understood. She'd do better to try to escape into the trees, and she pulled the horse off the trail. It went reluctantly, crashing through the brush. Red ducked to avoid branches. Belle clung to her, a high-pitched sound whistling from her.

The horse jerked to a halt and stood quivering, surrounded by trees. Despite Red's urging, it refused to take another step.

"Get down, Belle. Hurry." She held out an arm to help Belle to the ground, then dropped down beside her, grabbed her hand and raced into the trees. They were making too much noise. Ward would have no trouble tracking them. She stopped. "We have to be quiet." To their right was a thicket of bushes. "There. Crawl in out of sight."

Belle clung to her. "Me?"

"I'm coming, too. Hurry up." They fought through the tangles and crouched on the ground. She wrapped her arms about Belle and held her tight. Red panted, the sound ragged and loud. She forced herself to breathe slow, deep.

The soft thud of horse hooves approached. The leather of a saddle squeaked.

Red didn't move, didn't release the air in her lungs.

No sound came from the horse or the cowboy. How long could she hold her breath? Her head felt funny.

"I know you're in there and I'm not leaving." Ward sounded so sure of himself that she wanted to jump out screaming and scare his horse so Ward would get dumped off.

She let the air whoosh out of her lungs. Stupid man probably wouldn't get thrown no matter what she did.

"I'm not about to get myself hanged."

Belle twitched and turned toward Red, her blue eyes big and full of fear.

"Nobody is hanging me," she assured her little sister.

"I doubt Eddie will want to hang you." Ward didn't need to sound so regretful.

"You might as well come right out and say you consider it foolish for him to show any leniency."

"Yeah, well, he hasn't had to fight you every mile of the ride."

"You tricked me."

He groaned. "I thought you might like a meal. There's little in way of supplies at the cabin."

"I'm awful hungry," Belle whispered.

Red considered her options. They were pretty unappealing. Either hide in the bushes while Ward waited, determined to take her to the ranch, or admit defeat. Either way, she was destined to go to the ranch.

"Let's get out of here," she whispered to Belle, and they scrambled from the bushes. She drew herself up tall and straight. She'd go to the gallows, she'd face her punishment. But no one would see a shadow of fear on her face.

"We're ready." She marched back to the trail where the horse munched on grass. Stupid animal. If it had run like a horse was supposed to, they would be far away now.

Ward swung to the ground and came to assist her back to the saddle.

She grabbed the saddle horn and pulled herself up without assistance, but as she reached for Belle, Ward swung her up. Red didn't wait for Ward, but headed straight for Eden Valley Ranch and whatever justice Mr. Gardiner would mete out.

She kept her attention on the trail as they edged downward, passed empty corrals, clattered over a wooden bridge and turned toward the big house. But with each step forward her enthusiasm and determination weakened.

Ward drew abreast of her. "He isn't going to let you hang."

"I guess not. Who would look after Belle if he did?" Did she manage to keep a defensive note in her voice?

"I expect Linette would give her a home. She's given Grady one."

Red had seen a little boy previously but assumed he was Linette and Eddie's son. "Good to know someone would show my sister some Christian charity."

Ward sighed long and loud. "Linette is a very sweet, patient woman."

He didn't need to say what he really meant. That Red wasn't. But before she could point out that it was hard to be sweet and patient under her particular circumstances, the cowboys poured from the building she knew to be the cookhouse. They didn't make a sound.

"They're staring." Belle sounded scared.

"Guess their mamas didn't teach them it was rude." She kept her attention fixed straight ahead.

The door in the house up the hill opened and Eddie stepped out, Linette on one side and a little boy on the other. They waited as Ward escorted her toward them. They stopped ten feet from the watchful trio.

Ward swung from his horse. Red would have dismounted on her own, but her skirts made it awkward at best and with Belle pressed to her back, impossible. So she allowed Ward to grasp her by the waist and assist her. It meant nothing that his hands were steady, and his shoulders where she was forced to rest her hands, solid. As soon as her feet touched the ground she sprang away, brushing her skirt clear up to her waist trying to flick away the feel of his touch.

Ward's eyes narrowed as if realizing what she did. Then he quirked one eyebrow and lifted Belle down so quickly she didn't have time to protest. But she skittered over and grabbed Red's hand, burying her face in the brown cotton of Red's borrowed dress.

"It's okay, honey. You're safe with me," Red assured her.

"With me, too," Ward said, his voice so quiet she could almost persuade herself she didn't hear. Just like she could almost believe he wasn't more than a bit offended that she tended to put him in the same category as a man like Thorton. Not that she really thought he was. But still, he was a man and she and Belle were at his mercy and that of his boss. She intended to be cautious around them.

"I see you found them," Eddie said.

"You have a child." Linette sounded every bit as sweet and patient as Ward said she was and it almost made Red want to weep.

Ward turned to his boss. "This is Belle, Red's sister. They both need a home. You have your horse and saddle back so if you're okay with that, I plan to take them to my cabin."

Linette sprang forward and grabbed his arm to shake it. "You'll do no such thing. It's isolated up there. They'll stay here with us." She reached for Red's arm, but Red backed away.

Isolated sounded about right to her. "That's very generous of you, but we've already accepted Ward's offer."

Once Linette heard where Red had spent the last few months, she'd want her as far away as possible.

"I won't hear of it." Her eyes flashed determination.

Ward neglected to say his sweet, patient boss's wife was every bit as stubborn as Red. Red allowed herself a moment of admiration for the woman before she rallied her arguments.

"Belle's been through a difficult time. I think she needs some time alone to get over it."

Linette studied Belle, who buried her face in Red's skirts. Each breath released on a shudder. "The poor child." She nodded as if she'd made up her mind. "If you think she needs time alone, then you can live in the little cabin across from the cookhouse." She pointed to the place.

In the dusky shadows, Red saw a tiny log cabin facing the roadway that ran through the midst of the ranch buildings but tucked into a cluster of trees that went on and on to the river. It was almost tempting to live where she could dream of finding friends. But once they knew the truth, no one would accept her. Better to be isolated.

Linette, guessing at Red's resistance, spoke to Ward. "I won't hear of her living alone in your cabin."

Red turned to Ward as well. "We had an agreement." She kept her voice low, but knew from the flash in his eyes that he understood she wanted to jerk every word from her mouth and spear him with them.

Linette appealed to her husband. "Eddie?"

Eddie cleared his throat and spoke to Red. "I don't know what your circumstances are, but in the future if you are in trouble and need help, I hope you will come and ask rather than steal a horse."

She'd forgotten the threat of hanging. "I apologize. But I had to rescue my sister."

"In that case…" He seemed to consider his next

words. "I won't seek justice, seeing as the horse and saddle have been returned, but I think you owe it to Linette and I to accept our offer."

Linette grinned like the decision had been made.

Red sent a silent appeal to Ward, who shrugged.

"Can't argue with the boss's wife," he said.

Red seemed to have little choice in the matter. But she vowed it would be temporary. Only until she found something else. "Thank you," she murmured, managing, she hoped, to sound grateful as no doubt they all thought she should.

"I'll show them the way," Ward offered. "And make sure they have food."

Linette thanked him, then turned back to Red. "I'll check on you in the morning and see if you need anything. In the meantime, get settled, make yourself at home and have a good night's sleep."

Red allowed Ward to take the reins of her horse and struggled down the hill with Belle still glued to her skirt. Evening had crept in and filled the hollows, so she felt as she and Belle were alone with Ward.

A cowboy stepped from the cookhouse and Ward handed him the horses. Ward signaled Red and Belle to follow him to the cabin, where he opened the door and indicated they should enter.

Red took a step forward. She paused at the doorway, unable to make out the interior in the darkness.

Belle whimpered and pulled on Red's skirt, hampering any further progress. Red extricated Belle from the material and tipped her face up. Even in the growing dusk, Red could make out Belle's eyes—so wide they practically swallowed her face.

Red's heart burned. Why should her little sister know such insecurity, such terror? Had Thorton's treatment of the past few months, and before that, the death of their parents and Red's attempts to support them, robbed this child of any childhood innocence and faith? "Belle, honey, what's wrong?"

Her hand still clutching Red's skirts, Belle lifted one finger toward the cabin. "It's dark. Like that other place." Her voice shook.

Red straightened, silently cursing herself for not taking into consideration where Belle had spent the past three days. In almost total darkness in an unfamiliar cabin. Not unlike the one they now faced.

Ward must have had the same realization as he sprang forward. "Wait there while I light a lamp." His footsteps thudded into the darkness of the cabin.

Belle shuddered. "He's disappeared."

Red knelt and pulled her little sister into her arms. "No, honey. He's only inside."

A yellow light flickered and grew stronger. It shifted, making Ward's shadow lurch like something alive. Belle squeaked in terror. Red feared Belle would shred the brown skirt as she squeezed her little fists tighter and burrowed closer.

"It's a lamp, honey, so we don't have to go into a dark room."

The light steadied, grew larger as Ward headed for the door. He stepped out, the lamp before him. The yellow light filled his nostrils and highlighted his eyebrows, giving him a wild appearance.

Red swallowed a nervous giggle. "It's okay—" She meant to reassure Belle but Belle didn't hear her as she tore from Red's side with a piercing scream and ran into the dark.

"Belle!" Red called, racing after her. "Belle, come back."

But Belle continued her headlong flight.

* * *

Ward stared past the golden lamplight, trying to see where Red and Belle had gone. But the light effectively narrowed his vision to a tiny circle. Not that he needed to see to know what happened. His ears proved more than sufficient.

Belle had run screaming into the woods, Red in her wake.

Birds exploded from the trees at the noisy disturbance.

Belle's fear of him, and Red's distrust, were starting to wear his patience a might thin. He only wanted to help them. Get them away from men like Thorton Winch and that creepy guy with the boarded-up shack. Two or three times he'd considered he might have taken on more than he anticipated. His already tense jaw tightened further, making his teeth hurt. He would not abandon this pair, no matter how difficult they proved to be. One thing he'd learned…walking away was not the answer, even if he'd done so with the best of intentions.

He lowered the lamp and hurried after Red. She stood at the back of the cabin, calling into the darkness.

"What happened?"

"You."

That was it. One word, chewed up and spit out like something dirty. "What did I do this time?" He didn't care that he sounded put out.

"You looked like a monster the way the lamp flared on your face." She gave a brief, humorless chuckle.

"Thanks." He'd about had his fill of insults.

"Well, it's true. You scared her whether you meant to or not."

"Whether?" His frustrations of the day were about to boil over. "You think I might have intended to frighten her? What kind of a man do you take me for?" He held up one hand. "Don't tell me. I don't think I want to hear."

"Good, because I don't want to say something I might regret."

He snorted. Not something he usually did around ladies. But seeing as she wasn't acting like a lady, he didn't think it counted. "Do you mean to say you sometimes regret what you say?" He expected she caught the way he emphasized *sometimes* and the way doubt dripped from his voice, but he was beyond caring what he said to this woman.

"Not often." She gave him a look of pure defiance. "Now are we going to look for Belle or not?" She stomped away without waiting for his reply.

Great. Now the pair of them was going to wander around in the dark. If he'd known how much aggravation they would turn out to be...

Who was he fooling? He would still have done the same thing. He would have rescued Red even if she accused him of kidnapping. He would have followed her back to the saloon, confronted Thorton and, yes, offered them his cabin. Having her in Eddie's cabin suited him even better. He'd be able to make sure she and Belle were safe.

He'd not done well on that front so far.

He had to find Belle. Chasing after her would serve no purpose. She'd just hide. But he recalled she'd complained of hunger. "I have an idea."

"I hope it's better than your last one."

He wondered which idea that was, because so far he thought his ideas had been good. "What idea do you mean?"

"Holding the lamp to your face and scaring a little girl half to death."

"That wasn't— I didn't— Oh, what's the use? You're determined to twist every word and action of mine into some sort of attack."

She stepped back into the circle of light to glower at him. "I most certainly do not."

"Uh-huh, you do. Now can you keep quiet long enough to hear my plan?" He paused for good measure. "Unless you've thought of one?"

Her glower deepened as she was forced to acknowledge she had not. "Go ahead. Talk."

He chuckled. "Knew you wouldn't admit you had no plan."

"You gonna tell me this wonderful plan or flap your jaws?"

He grinned at her. "Like I asked before, you ever lose an argument? No, wait. What I mean—" He leaned closer until they were almost nose to nose. "Do you ever admit it?" The lamplight reflected in her eyes, filling them with something he hadn't seen before—wasn't sure what to call it. Perhaps fear. Or loneliness? Even though it was barely a shadow, hardly a hint, he knew it was there, and knowing, all resentment left him.

He straightened. "Belle is hungry."

"So what? We've been hungry before. Expect we will be again."

He decided it wise to refrain from saying they would not go hungry while they lived in this cabin. "I'm going to build a nice fire over there." He pointed to where Eddie had dug a fire pit, lined it with rocks and placed logs around it at a safe distance to use as benches. "And start cooking up a meal. I'm guessing she'll soon come out of hiding when she smells the great food I cook."

He grinned, meaning it as teasing. After all, he was a cowboy and only cooked out of necessity, and even then it was the simplest of fare. But at the way her eyes widened and the loudness of her swallow, he guessed she was as hungry as Belle. Right then and there he vowed to make the best meal he'd ever made.

He led the way to the fire pit and soon had a roaring fire going. Red reached out her hands to the flames. For the first time he considered she wore only a brown dress. Belle had on a shapeless gray thing that had seen better days. That observation coming from a cowboy who spent weeks in the same clothes indicated a large degree of wear and tear. Good thing he could count on Linette to help him on that score.

"You stay here. Maybe she'll come back when I leave."

Red's gaze jerked from staring at the flames to look at him. "You're going?"

"Just to get supplies."

He dashed across the road to the cookhouse. "Cookie, quick, lend me a bottle of that meat you put up."

Cookie crossed her arms and looked at him like he'd suddenly sprung a second head. "What for? My cooking not good enough for you?"

He jerked to a halt and swallowed hard. He had no desire to offend Cookie. "I've got two hungry females over there." He gave a wave in the general direction of the cabin.

"Didn't the boss send you out to bring back his horse and saddle? Instead, you come back with two women?" She sniffed her disdain.

"The horse and saddle are in the barn. Red and her sister are going to stay in the cabin."

"A horse thief! Whose idea was that?"

"Linette's."

Cookie's scowl disappeared in a wreath of confusion.

"They understand why she had to do it." As quickly as he could, Ward explained how Red had to rescue her little sister. "And now she's out in the trees, hiding in fear." Before he finished, Cookie started filling a basket with jars of meat, bottles of preserved vegetables, fresh produce and some biscuits.

"You tell her to come over in the morning and I'll have freshly baked cinnamon rolls."

"I'll tell her." He grabbed the supplies and hurried back to the cabin. He dumped meat and vegetables into a cast-iron pot. As he worked, he thought of how Red looked and sounded scared when he said he was going. She'd unwittingly allowed him to see that she liked having him there, though she would deny it with every breath she had. Not that he intended to mention it. He would simply accept it as a step forward. Balancing the lamp in one hand and the makings of a meal in the other, he made his way back to the fire. No one sat beside Red or anywhere around the fire. "She hasn't come back yet?"

Red shook her head. "Belle?" she called. "Come on, honey. It's nice and warm here."

"She do this often?" Ward asked as he fashioned a spit over the fire and hung the pot. He dug a hole nearby and dropped in several hot stones, put a pan of potatoes still in their jackets on top and left them to bake.

"Do what often?" He doubted Red tried to keep the challenge out of her voice.

"Run away."

"Did you see the little room in the saloon? Well, that's where she's spent the last four months. Apart from when Thorton thought to take us out for a walk, and he made plenty sure to hold tight to her hand. So, no, she doesn't do this often."

"I'm sorry. I never realized, though I suppose I should have." He'd seen the little room, even noticed how the window was barred, allowing only slits of light to enter. "She'll have lots of chance to roam free out here."

"Hope she doesn't get lost."

Ward thought it best to not echo his worry along the same line. After a bit the stew bubbled, and he moved it down the spit to simmer while the potatoes cooked. The smell of food was enough to flood his mouth with saliva. He'd eaten a fair-sized breakfast but nothing since. He guessed Red hadn't eaten since the day before, and who could guess when Belle had last eaten. He hoped the aromas floating from the pot should soon bring her in. "How's your leg feeling?"

"It's fine."

"I suppose your head is fine, too?"

"Yup."

"Would you admit if it hurt like fury and your leg pained clear to your eyeballs?"

She laughed, a sound that startled him, expecting, as he was, another fierce argument. "I'll admit it hurts some, but seeing as there's nothing for it but to endure, doesn't seem much point in bemoaning the fact."

He'd told himself the same thing many times so couldn't argue. Somehow hearing her say it made him like her just a little. "You will keep an eye on your leg and make sure it doesn't get infected? If you see any sign of it, let me know. Linette will have ways of treating it."

"I can manage on my own."

"I was only being helpful." He felt her wariness and

recalled her earlier words. "And I don't expect any form of repayment in return."

"I would pay cash for the use of the cabin if I had any. I don't. Nor do I aim to repay favors with favors."

He sighed loud and long. "I would not take either." He tested the potatoes with a fork. They were cooked. He trotted back to the cabin for dishes, paused to fill a bucket of water at the well. Back at the fire, he handed her two plates, forks and cups.

"Thank you," she said.

He chomped down on his teeth to keep from saying it was good to see she had a measure of manners. "Call out and tell Belle the food is ready."

"Belle. There's food. It smells mighty good. Can you smell it?"

They both waited silently for a sound of the little girl. To his right, the grass rustled.

"She's coming," he whispered.

"Ward made lots of stew and there's baked potatoes. When was the last time you had a whole potato?"

The grass rustled some more, then Belle hovered at the edge of the darkness.

"Come on, honey," Red urged.

Belle darted glances at Ward as she made her way to Red's side, going the long way around the fire to avoid having to pass him.

He tried not to let it bother him and failed miserably. Instead, he had to be content with handing them a heaping plate of food. He handed Red a potato. She took it. But when he held out one toward Belle, she shrank back. Red reached for it but Ward withdrew. He wanted Belle to trust him enough to take it from him. After all, he had provided the food. Besides, he was getting tired of being treated like one of the bad guys.

Belle's fear was palpable, but so was her hunger. He offered her a towel. "It's hot. Hold it with this."

She snatched the towel, took another moment to consider the potato carefully, then, doing her best not to touch his hand, took it.

It was a start. Satisfied, he sat down with his own food. "I'll say grace."

He didn't need to look at Red to feel her resistance. But Belle met his eyes steadily a moment before she bowed her head.

He prayed, and then they ate in silence. When he saw they'd cleaned their plate, he offered them another helping, which they didn't refuse.

The evening deepened. Despite the warmth of the fire, he felt coolness moving in. "I need to do my chores." Though likely Slim or Roper had seen to them by now.

Red sprang to her feet. "You go. We'll be fine."

Ward picked up his hat from beside him and slammed it on his head. "What's your hurry?"

"I didn't mean…"

"Don't bother backpeddling. But if you don't mind, I'll see that you're settled in the cabin and the fire is dowsed before I leave." He grabbed the lamp and strode back to the cabin. He set the lamp on the tiny table.

Red slipped into the room. "Guess you can't blame me for being leery. I want to make it on my own. Owe no man anything."

"I could carve it in the log by the table so you don't forget."

"What are you talking about?"

"Lady, my stepfather made no secret that my presence set his teeth on edge. So I walked away from my family because I figured if I left they'd be better off. But

I've never known if it was so or not. Instead I wonder. And I regret leaving. My only reason for helping you is to make up for leaving my family. It's nothing to do with you. So don't think I plan to take advantage of you. You mention it again and I will carve 'I want nothing in return' in that there log." He slapped the chosen place.

"Well, fine then. Just so long as we understand each other."

"I'm pretty sure we do. There's the bedroom." He pointed toward the door. "There's the stove. I can light it now if you think it's too chilly in here, though likely you would then roast like trussed chickens. There's food in the cupboard. Not much. I'll be back with more in the morning. The place is yours."

He headed for the door, which was all of three steps away, and Red bolted out of his way. He stopped to give her a long, steady look.

She lowered her head and mumbled something that sounded vaguely like "thank you."

He nodded briskly and stepped outside. "Call your sister. I'm going to put out the fire."

At her call, Belle dashed past him to join Red.

He carried the dishes to the cabin and set them in a pot without any comment, then grabbed a shovel from the corner.

Smacking out the lingering flames and covering the embers with dirt allowed him take care of most of his frustration.

He wondered if rescuing this pair would in any way ease his guilt about having left his own family, or if he had bitten off more than he cared to chew.

Chapter Four

Red and Belle stood silent and motionless as Ward called from outside, "Goodbye. Be safe."

Red knew Belle didn't breathe any louder than she did as they listened to him stomp away from the cabin. As the sound faded she strained, but couldn't tell if she still heard his footsteps in the distance or if it was the pounding of her blood against her eardrums. So she waited, not daring to move until she was certain. It seemed he had truly left, and her breath whistled out.

"Is he gone?" Belle whispered.

"Yes." Thankfully. She was grateful for his help. Truly she was. But she didn't plan to accept more than she was forced to.

"Are you glad?" Belle asked, easing away from the dark corner as if still uncertain it was safe to do so.

"We're finally on our own. Just you and me." Apart from Linette and Eddie up the hill, a cookhouse and cowboys across the road and Ward, no doubt, flitting back and forth. She would have much preferred Ward's isolated cabin, but this would do for now.

"I'm glad, too." Belle turned to study the room. "We gonna sleep here?"

"Yup. Just the two of us. Let's have a look around."
The room held a small stove that would serve as a
kitchen range as well as a welcome source of heat on
cold nights. There was a tiny table, two chairs, a shelf
with a few supplies and a bookcase with a few odds
and ends. There was another doorway and they went
to the small bedroom.

Belle edged over to the bed and touched it. "How
long we staying here?"

Red crossed to Belle's side, perched on the bed and
caught her sister's chin. "Honey, we need some place
until I can come up with a plan. But as soon as I do,
we'll leave. We'll find a place on our own where we'll
always be safe and always together."

Belle's gaze clung to Red's. She could see her little sister wanted to believe in a future that held promise and possibility. Understood her hesitation to do so.
Her faith in good things had been shattered in the past
few months.

Red pulled Belle to her lap and held her tight. "We
got away from Thorton and Old Mike. They're both in
jail and will never hurt us again."

"They'll stay in jail forever?"

"I hope so. But long enough they won't bother us
again."

"Red, he prayed. He said we could trust God."

She heard the wistful note in her sister's voice and
understood Belle referred to Ward.

How was she to deal with this? She had no trust left.
Not for God and certainly not for any man. But how
could she admit she felt God had abandoned them and
rob Belle of any hope? On the other hand, she didn't
want her to trust anyone but themselves for their future.
She closed her eyes and tried to marshal her thoughts

together. It took too much effort, made her head ache. She'd deal with the matter later.

Belle looked intently into Red's face. "You don't like him, do you?"

The question startled Red. There was something about Ward that got under her skin like a red, itchy rash. His insistence on helping even though it was evident he didn't care a whole lot about her. The way he took objection to her comments. Yes, they might have been a little barbed, but she couldn't help it. It had become part of her armor. Yet, despite his contrary ways, he exuded strength beyond the power in his arms. It came from deep inside him. Born, perhaps, out of his own pain and experience. She had to respect that. Might even find it slightly appealing.

But she could not let herself like him. To like a man, she would have to trust him, and she could not, would not, ever again trust a man.

Belle waited patiently for her answer.

"Honey, we don't know him well enough to have much of an opinion about him."

Taking her cues from Red, Belle sighed. "Too bad he's a man. Otherwise I might like him."

Laughing at her little sister's wisdom, Red hugged her tight. "Let's check out the bed." She pulled Belle down beside her and they flopped backward on the furs. "I think we'll be very comfortable." Sharing a narrow bed with her sister was not going to be difficult. Having her so close, she could feel her breathing would comfort her.

They returned to the other room and examined the items on the shelf. Containers of flour, cornmeal and sugar. "Guess we won't starve to death."

"Can I help you cook things?"

"Of course you can. We will have so much fun. Just the two of us." She glanced at the darkened window. Would they see the mountains through that window? She touched the log where he had threatened to carve words. Her chest seemed wooden as a strange wistfulness filled her. She'd once known a secure home. So had Belle, but she wasn't sure her sister could remember happy family times.

Red didn't know what the future held nor where they would go from here, but perhaps in this little cabin she could give Belle some enjoyable times. Teach her to be happy and trusting again, though not too trusting. Look at the predicament they'd landed in because Red trusted people too much.

Belle stood in the center of the room and spun around. "I love it here." She jerked to a stop so quickly she almost tumbled over. "No one will bother us, will they?"

A storm of emotions raced through Red. Anger that Belle should know such uncertainty, hatred toward the man who'd stolen the innocence of them both, despair at how little she could offer her sister. Then determination, solid as a rock, pressed down all other feelings. She would do anything, everything, she could to protect her sister from any more hurt.

"If anyone bothers us, I'll take a shovel to the side of his head."

Belle's eyes widened. "You'd hurt him?"

Belle meant Ward. Red meant anyone who threatened them. "If he tried to bother us, I would."

Rocking back and forth, Belle considered Red silently. Then she came to a decision. "Maybe you shouldn't hurt him."

Red's head snapped back. This from a little girl who

had as much reason to hate men as anyone. "Why do you say that?"

"Well, if you hurt him he might not want to help us. It's scary and dark out there." She tilted her head toward the door and Red knew she referred to the half hour or so she'd hidden in the bushes. "Besides, I like this." She went to the table, climbed up on a chair and pressed her hand to a picture mounted on the wall.

Red hadn't paid any attention to it, but now she moved closer. A sampler done in various stitches, pretty flowers and designs around words. The words, done in black cross-stitch, *"Whither shall I flee from Thy presence? The darkness and light are both alike to Thee."* The words brushed a dark spot deep within. "It's very nice. I wonder who made it," Red said.

"I think someone's mother."

Red sat down on the bed and Belle sat beside her. "Why do you think so?"

"Because Mama made one like this for me, didn't she? Remember? She hung it over my bed and said I should never forget the words."

The memory rushed toward Red. She tried to dam it back. She could not let her thoughts hearken back to those happy, innocent days. Everything about her past filled her with crippling regret.

"I 'member her making it."

So did Red. The dam broke and she was back at her childhood home. She was warm, happy, secure in her parents' love and protection. Seems the house glowed with treasures, each representing love. Mama sat in a rocking chair that had been Grandma's and told stories of sitting on her own mother's lap ensconced in the same chair where Red remembered sitting on Mama's knees and later, where she and Mama took turns rocking Belle. What a sweet baby she'd been. "A gift from heaven for us all," Mama had said time and again. "After losing so many babies, God has granted us Belle to fill our hearts with joy." Indeed the happiness in the house had reached new heights with the safe arrival of Belle. Mama had once said she might not live to see Belle marry and asked Red to promise she'd see Belle was properly cared for. Red had readily agreed, never suspecting an accident would thrust the role upon her so unexpectedly.

"Mama hung it over my bed on my fourth birthday."

"I'm surprised you remember."

"I didn't till I saw this one. Then I 'membered."

"I remember, too." Mama had stitched a cradle with a baby in it, a window behind the cradle with light pouring in. She'd carefully selected the scripture. "I want something that will encourage Belle her entire life. No matter what may happen," their mother had said.

Oh, how disappointed her parents would be that Red hadn't protected Belle as she'd promised. She would live with that regret to her dying day and the moment she stepped into heaven, she would beg their forgiveness.

Not that she was sure God would let her into heaven after the events of the past year and her vow to never forgive Thorton.

"I remember the words, too," Belle said.

Red did, too, though she no longer believed them with childlike innocence and wondered if Belle did.

"'I will never leave thee, nor forsake thee.' Red, do you think Mama would be angry that I did forget them for a little while?"

"I don't think so."

"Red, do you still pray?"

She wished she could avoid the question. She had no

desire to rob Belle of whatever faith and trust she still had. But she couldn't lie. "Not much."

"Me, either, but when I was locked in Old Mike's cabin I remembered a prayer Mama said and I said it out loud. That's what I was doing when you came for me."

Her curiosity overcame her doubt. "What prayer was that?"

"'God, You are a very present help to me, and I am receiving Your help even now as I pray. Thank You, Father. You are my refuge and strength, and because this is true, I will not fear anything or anyone.'"

Red pressed her tongue to the top of her mouth. Her nose stung. She could not breathe for dread of unleashing so many frightening emotions she feared she would drown.

Why had God forsaken her? Where was He when they needed help?

"God heard me. He hasn't forgotten me."

Oh, if only she could have the faith of her little sister. But never again could she be innocent and trusting. Nevertheless, she was glad Belle had found comfort in her prayers. She jumped to her feet, ignoring the protest from her injured leg. "Let's make the bed."

Together they folded the fur back. It would be much too warm this time of year. They punched the mattress into better shape and smoothed the blankets. She had no way of knowing the time, but it was dark and she was tired. Enough reason to go to bed. They had no other clothes but what they wore, so preparing for bed simply meant washing their faces and removing their shoes.

They lay curled together, Red's arms around her sister.

"Red?"

"What?"

"We gonna wear these clothes day and night forever?"

Red giggled. "I don't expect they'll last forever."

"Seems I've been wearing the same thing for almost that long."

"I wish I could offer you more, but this is what we have for now." There was a time when loving parents had generously provided all they needed. They would never again know that sufficiency. Truth was, Red had no idea how she would provide even basic necessities for them. Only that she would find a way that did not require depending on a man.

Even if for now, she had accepted help from two men, if she counted Eddie. Knowing it was Linette's will that she and Belle stay in the cabin marginally eased her concern at taking charity from a man. Taking it from a woman was an easier pill to swallow.

A fresh thought entered her mind. Perhaps Ward had come in answer to Belle's prayers. God, no doubt, still heard her words.

She fell asleep, soothed by the gentle snores of her little sister.

The next morning she woke to Belle tickling her nose. "Wake up. It's morning and I'm hungry."

Red groaned. Her body hurt from so many hours on horseback and her leg reminded her of her injury. "You sure it's morning? I don't see any daylight."

"'Cause you got your eyes closed." Belle peeled one eyelid up.

Red brushed her hand aside. "It's cold in here."

"You could start a fire in the stove."

"I could, could I? Or we could wait for the sun to warm the place."

Belle crawled over Red and pushed into her shoes. "I'll help you."

Red rolled over to study her eager sister. "First thing

I'm going to teach you is how to build a fire so I can get up to a warm room."

"Okay." Belle rushed out of the room. The stove lid rattled. "Show me now," she called.

With a long-suffering sigh, Red climbed out of bed. Her hair must be a rat's nest, but they lacked comb or brush. She settled for running her hands over her hair to tame it out of her eyes.

"Hurry up." Belle waited in the doorway, her hands on her hips in a pose that reminded Red of their mother.

Pain sucked at her insides. She closed her eyes and waited for the hurting to disappear. "Let me get my shoes."

Belle tipped her head to one side and sighed as if the request was unreasonable.

Red chuckled. "I'm hurrying." She fastened her shoes, then went to the stove. "First, you need some kindling." She showed Belle how to build a fire and they watched with undue fascination as the flames took hold.

Soon the heat warmed Red and her brain began to function. For a minute she allowed herself a moment of joy that they were alone and safe. Thank God Thorton was behind bars. God had answered Belle's prayers and she was grateful for that.

"What are we going to eat?" Belle asked, eyeing the cupboard of supplies.

"What would you like?"

Belle considered her as if wondering what she could ask for.

"Ask and if it's possible with what's on hand, we'll have it."

Belle held Red's gaze in a hungry look. "You remember how Mama made teddy bear griddle cakes?"

Another memory flooded Red's thoughts. Belle was little, still in her high chair. Mama had stood at the stove, wiping her brow in a weary gesture. Mama seemed to be tired a lot and Red had done all she could to help. But Belle fussed.

"She's got a touch of tummy upset," Mama had said. "I wish I could have kept nursing her. The cow's milk doesn't agree with her."

"But we were so grateful for fresh milk."

"Yes, I still am. God provided generously. Now I'm praying Belle will adjust to it soon." She had set a place of griddle cakes before Belle.

"I'll feed her."

Mama had nodded. But Belle had refused to eat. In the end Mama had made a thin porridge and persuaded Belle to take a few spoonfuls.

Over the ensuing weeks, Belle had remained fretful, refused to eat more than a few mouthfuls at a time. She started to lose weight, grew peaked. They were all concerned. Mama had spent a lot of time on her knees beseeching God to make Belle strong.

One day Mama got up and fried pancakes in the shape of a teddy bear, round belly, round head and round ears. She had dropped raisins in for eyes. Belle was charmed. From that day forward food took on interest.

How times had changed. Since they'd fallen in with Thorton, she'd had to endure Belle begging for food on many occasions.

Red wanted to forget those worrisome months. Almost as much as she wished she could forget how Mama had prayed. How she constantly gave God praise for Belle's health.

"I don't know if there are any raisins, but we can surely make pancakes."

"Can I help?"

"Certainly. Who knows? One of these days I might

be sick and you'll be in charge." She'd been teasing, but at the sudden quivering of Belle's lips she wished she'd considered her words more carefully. She hugged her sister. "I don't plan to get sick anytime in the foreseeable future. Now you get a mixing bowl and the flour and we'll get started."

As they mixed up the batter, the room grew overly warm.

"Belle, open the door and let in some air."

Belle paused at the window next to the door. "Everyone will see us."

She understood how Belle felt. The isolated cabin would have been a better choice for them. Maybe she'd convince Ward to take them there. "We don't have to open it all the way." Seeing Belle couldn't bring herself to face what lay outside the four walls, Red crossed to her side. She planted a log on the ground, holding the door open enough to let in the air but not enough for them to see across the road.

As she straightened, sunlight smacked into the mountains. She stared. Dark folds contrasted with shadowy blue. A thousand unfettered thoughts swirled inside her head. Verses her mama had quoted often. *We will not fear though the mountains shake.* Emotions she didn't want to own bubbled to the surface. Hope, joy, longing for things she would not acknowledge.

She was Red. She had danced half-naked before men. She'd been touched in ways that made her cringe. Guilt and loathing quenched all other feelings.

"I like the mountains," Belle said with utmost conviction. "What did he say they made him think about? God is like the mountains?"

"Something like that." She would not repeat the exact

phrase: *As the mountains are round about Jerusalem, so the Lord is round about His people.*

"I thought you were hungry."

"I am."

"Then let's get the griddle cakes made."

An hour later they had washed up the dishes and cleaned the little cabin. Belle avoided the window, but sat cross-legged on the floor where she could see out the ajar door.

Red glanced out the window once, saw cowboys streaming from the cookhouse and jerked out of sight. But the open air beckoned. "Let's go out back." No one could see them behind the cabin.

Belle jerked to her feet and hurried to the table. "There's too many people out there."

Too many men, she likely meant. "I'll make sure it's safe." She edged toward the window and studied the surroundings. Not a man in sight. "Nobody out there. Let's go."

They dashed outside and around the cabin. The shovel stood against the corner and Red took it with them. She hadn't forgotten her promise to use it on any man who threatened them.

They sat on the benches around the cold fire pit, listening to the sound of birds and squirrels noisily going about their morning activities. Red lifted her face to the sun. "It's very peaceful."

Suddenly birds erupted from the trees in a great burst of noise. Sounds of horse hooves thundered through the air.

Belle bolted for the cabin. "Men coming," she wailed.

Red's initial alarm gave way to reason. "Belle, it's only the cowboys riding out to work." This was a ranch, after all. She followed on Belle's heels into the cabin. "They aren't interested in us." But she spoke to an empty room. "Belle?"

* * *

He slowed his horse and waved goodbye to Roper and the others. He'd already spoken to Eddie. "I'm asking for light duties around the ranch for a few days until they're settled."

Eddie had readily agreed.

Ward saw Red and Belle race to the cabin. What had frightened them? The door slammed behind Red. Ward studied the area around the cabin. Tipped his head and listened intently. He heard nothing to alarm him. Saw no wild animals prowling nearby. Yet something had sent them fleeing for safety.

Then it hit him. They'd heard him approach and run from him. "Horse, I'm not the enemy here." Yet over and over, he felt like it. If he had a lick of sense he would turn around and head out to the hills with the rest of the cowboys.

But he flicked the reins and continued toward the big house.

He asked Linette for some things the pair could wear.

"Goodness, what an ordeal they've endured. They must be frightened." She waved him inside and instructed him to wait while she found suitable clothing. "I have the things the Arnesons can no longer use." A couple had come to the ranch in the spring, ill and too weak to care for themselves. Linette had nursed them as they grew steadily weaker. When they passed away, Eddie had buried them in a nearby plot. They had earlier lost a child and still had her clothes. She quickly found items for both Red and Belle. And agreed to Ward's request to give Red a day or two to settle before visiting them.

He rode to the cabin, dismounted and paused. "Hello, it's me."

Silence.

"Red. Belle. It's me. Ward. I've brought some things." He stepped forward.

Red emerged from the narrow door, her fingers curled around the handle of a shovel. Her fire-bright hair sprang out in disarray. Her eyes flashed defiance.

He roared with laughter.

She glowered, indicating she didn't find it amusing.

"You gonna brain me with that?"

"If I have to."

"Guess you should have done it yesterday before you decided to come along with me."

"Being here don't mean you can come and go as you please."

His amusement ended abruptly. "Red, I promise I will not come and go without regard to the fact you and Belle reside here. No one will." Eddie had warned the others to give them plenty of space until they were ready to socialize.

"Do you mind putting that aside? I don't care to have my skull split wide open when I turn my back."

She hesitated, then propped it next to the door.

He would have felt a lot better if she'd put it against the outer wall where he'd left it. "No one will bother you here. And the woods belong to God. He won't mind if you enjoy them."

She nodded. "Only until I get on my feet."

"I brought some things for you." He untied the sacks hanging from the saddle.

She said nothing as he carried the supplies to the door.

"You're welcome." He was beginning to think she would rather chew her tongue to shreds than express gratitude to him for anything. "Where's Belle? Some of it's for her."

Belle peeked through the crack of the bedroom door. "What you bring?"

"Well, this bag—" he lifted it "—is heavy with food stuff. Cookie makes about the best cinnamon rolls ever. She has some for you at the cookhouse." He paused long enough for the idea to settle in. Then he lifted the other bag. "This is full of clothes you might be able to use. Linette sent them."

"Belle, you gonna come see?"

Belle opened the door wider but kept it between them. That was okay. He understood her caution.

He tossed the lighter bag on the table and set the heavier one beside it. "Who wants to see inside?"

Belle got as far as the edge of the door and hovered there like a dragonfly.

Red finally left her post outside the door and stepped inside. "Who is Cookie?"

"She's the cook. Big, boisterous woman. Her husband, Bertie, helps her. He's more gentle. But Cookie is a fine cook and a good woman. Every Sunday they hold church services in the cookhouse and Bertie preaches us a sermon. Only it ain't as much a sermon as a friendly talk." He had no idea if they cared about any of this, but he figured if he kept talking about ordinary things the pair might relax. "Linette and Eddie want to get a church built in Edendale—that's the little town close by. Not hardly even a town, but it's growing. I sometimes wonder if Sundays will be any better with a real church and a real preacher. I like Bertie's talks." He ran out of steam. Could think of nothing more that might interest them. Still neither of them moved.

Perhaps the food would hold more sway. He dug

into the sack and pulled out the brown-paper-wrapped
bundle, set it on the table and folded back the edges.
"Cookie thought you might be a bit shy about visiting
her this morning, so she sent fresh rolls." The aroma
from them was about more than a man could resist.
"Cookie says it's best to eat them while they're warm.
But I can tell you they're pretty good stone-cold and two
days old, too." He reached into the sack again. "Didn't
know if you liked tea or coffee so brought them both.
Cinnamon rolls with a hot drink is about as good as it
gets."

Belle rocked back and forth. He could hear her swallow from where he stood. "What can I drink?"

"Cookie thought of that, too, so she put in canned
milk. Says it's real good for making cocoa. You ever
had hot cocoa?"

Belle edged closer. "Mama used to make it. Red
knows how to make it, don't you?" She appealed to
her sister.

"Certainly."

"That's good." Ward waited, wondering if Red would
offer to make tea or coffee or hot cocoa. Or would she
stand there, guarded and ill at ease until he left?

He shifted his gaze out the window. Up until a few
days ago, he'd been content to go about his merry way,
writing letters back home, not getting a reply but planning, building and hoping for the time the others would
join him. He'd given little thought to how he lived each
day. Just did what was next. What Eddie sent him to do
or what appeared before him. Choices weren't difficult.

Now he seemed unable to make an ordinary decision
as to whether he should invite himself for tea or leave.

All because of one hotheaded, red-haired woman
who got under his skin in a way that he didn't mind.

He'd been in such a rush to get things together for Red and Belle, he hadn't even taken time to eat one of Cookie's rolls.

The least they could do was invite him to share the goodies. Ignoring the way Belle drew back when he moved, he reached for the kettle, shook it and discovered it heavy with water. He lifted the stove lid, stuck in a couple of sticks of wood, then set the kettle to boil. "We're going to have hot cocoa and cinnamon rolls, and while the kettle heats we're going to put the supplies on the shelf."

Neither female moved.

He didn't care. He pulled out a jar, held it out to Red. "Where do you want it?" Not that there was much of a decision to be made. The kitchen consisted of two narrow shelves and a larder box.

She scowled at him. Then, her lips in a tight line, she grabbed the jar and stuck it on the shelf.

He took out the items one by one and handed them to her.

Belle slipped forward, one cautious step at a time. She hovered two feet away, swaying back and forth. "Who made that?" She pointed to the picture over the table.

He stopped removing items and looked at it for a moment. His mother had sent it in a package that contained the only letter he'd received from her. Afraid the picture would get damaged kicking about the bunkhouse, he'd asked permission to hang it in the cabin after Linette and Eddie had married and moved into the big house. No one lived in the cabin then, and he thought it would be a safe place for the picture.

At Belle's question, he was awash in memories of his mother making the picture during long winter evenings with Pa at the table reading while she worked. Pa had developed a keen interest in the free land to the west. He slid his gaze to Belle. "My mother did. A very long time ago when my father was still alive."

"Did she try running away?"

"Not that I know of. Why?"

"Doesn't *flee* mean to run away?"

That was exactly what he wanted her to do. Run from that horrible man she'd married after Ward's father had died, and come West where he could look after her.

"Did you?" Belle asked.

"What?"

"Run away?"

Red touched Belle's shoulder. "Don't ask so many questions."

"It's okay. I didn't run away. I left. Like I said, I thought things would be better if I wasn't there. Sometimes to flee means to run toward something, too." He hoped that's what he'd done—run to freedom for both himself and the rest of his family.

"Are you scared of the dark?"

Strange questions, but he could see Belle had a real need for answers so he considered his reply. "No. But it is harder to know what's ahead or what to expect. So I suppose I'm more wary in the dark."

"It was scary dark in Old Mike's cabin."

Red grabbed Belle by both shoulders and leaned over to stare into her eyes. "Honey, no bad man is ever going to hurt you again. You hear?"

Belle nodded.

Red straightened and faced Ward with a fierce look, wordlessly warning him she would not allow him to hurt Belle.

Her continued distrust started to fester. "Not all men

are bad. My father wasn't. I'm guessing yours wasn't." He gave them a moment to acknowledge it. "And I'm not."

He and Red dueled silently as she considered his words.

"I'll prove it if you give me a chance." He kept his words low, inviting. Though for the life of him he couldn't explain why it mattered so much.

He only knew it did. He would somehow, he promised himself, win the trust of this pair.

As he waited for some sign of agreement or disagreement from Red, he understood winning her trust might prove a whole lot more challenging than winning that of her little sister.

Chapter Five

The kettle steamed but no one moved. Red felt Ward's relentless challenge. Let him prove they could trust him? How was she to do that without putting both herself and Belle in jeopardy? No. "A person has to earn trust before it is given."

His gaze did not falter, forcing her to shift away to avoid his intense insistence. "True. On the other hand, it's impossible to convince someone against their will. All I'm asking is you stop judging me as being like Thorton Winch."

Belle nudged Red.

Red jerked her attention to her sister. "What?"

"He's not like Thorton."

Red squatted down to Belle's eye level. "Honey, you can never be too cautious."

Belle's eyes brimmed with a combination of assurance and hope. "He prayed. And he has that." She shrugged one shoulder in the direction of the sampler.

"If you're so sure, why are you still afraid of him?"

Belle hung her head for a moment. She shuddered, then met Red's eyes again. "There's a lot of scary feelings inside me."

Red hugged her sister and looked at Ward, surprised to see a reflection of her own dismay.

"No child should live in fear." His words were solid, full of unspoken promises, as if he vowed Belle would never have a reason to be afraid of him. Their gazes melded. She understood he meant so much more than Belle's situation. Likely his own little brothers. Something inside her wrenched as she felt a sense of connection at shared pain, uncertainty and regret over the past. She recognized in his blazing look a silent vow to make up for what he'd lost, his regret over his decision to leave his family. And more. A deep conviction about what was right and wrong and determination to stand up for the right.

In that moment she allowed herself to think of him as a man who could be trusted. She retracted the thought as quickly as it came. She'd trusted too readily and too often and knew the dangers of doing so. Her willingness to believe Thorton was an honest preacher man had brought disaster.

From now on she would guard her thoughts. And heart. She yanked away from his gaze. Flung about for something to do so she could ignore him. Saw the steaming kettle and snatched it from the stove. He'd set out three heavy china mugs alongside the cocoa tin and a container of sugar. "Why don't you stay for cocoa?" Her words were not overly warm, but it was the best she could manage at this point.

"Thanks." He opened the can of evaporated milk. "Left before I could enjoy Cookie's cinnamon rolls. Intend to do so now." His tone informed Red he wasn't waiting for an invite from her.

"Well then, by all means."

Belle rocked back and forth, her face wreathed in tension.

Red immediately regretted her reluctance. For Belle's sake, she had to try to be civil when he was around. She pressed back annoyance. Wondered at the skitter of fear that tailed after it. Then smiled—it was forced and false, but it was all she could manage. "Here, I'll measure the cocoa and sugar. You pour in the hot water." She set the kettle on the table between them.

Ward looked at Belle and then back at Red. He smiled, too, though his seemed almost genuine, as if amused at the predicament his presence created for her.

She kept a smile on her lips while signaling a warning from her eyes, informing him she would do her best to ease Belle's anxiety but it didn't change anything inside her. From the way his eyebrows lifted and his smile deepened, she guessed he'd read her silent message. She did not care for the amusement flashing from his eyes.

She grabbed a spoon and dumped a measure of cocoa and sugar in each cup and gave the mixture a quick stir.

Ward moved to her side and tilted the kettle to partially fill each cup.

Belle edged closer. "That how Mama made cocoa?"

Red forced cheeriness into her voice. "That's right. We used to have it every bedtime during the winter. Do you remember?"

Belle nodded.

"Mama did it for me as long as I can remember and then for you as soon as you were old enough. Remember how we would sit close to the stove and Mama or Papa read to us?" Red's voice caught and she pretended to be preoccupied with stirring the hot mixture.

"Did Papa used to read poems?"

Ah. The ache of loss scalded her insides as if she'd

downed the kettle of boiling water. How she'd loved listening to Papa's slow, deep voice read poems, filling Red's mind with word pictures and dreams.

"I 'member something about daffodils."

Gentle, sweet memories of a different time and different place flooded Red's thoughts. "William Wordsworth. 'And then my heart with pleasure fills, and dances with the daffodils.'"

Belle clapped her hands. "I remember."

"My pa liked poetry, too." Ward's voice sounded thick.

She was reluctantly pulled into another shared regret. Thankfully he was at her side and her attention on preparing cocoa, so she could avoid looking at him. She failed, however, to avoid a tug of sadness as his loss found an echo in her heart.

She poured a dash of milk into each cup. "I guess it's ready."

Belle hesitated a moment, then slipped to one chair. Only one remained.

"I'll get a stool." Ward ducked out of the cabin so suddenly that Red and Belle looked at each other and giggled.

Belle leaned over her cup of cocoa. "Smells good. Can I start?"

"I suppose we should wait for him."

Belle looked at the door. "What if he's gone a long time?" Her voice thinned with worry.

A slow anger simmered through Red. Belle was only asking for more pain if she started thinking she could count on a man for anything. "Belle, we have each other. We'll be fine even if he doesn't come back."

Belle's eyes shadowed with doubt, but she nodded

agreement just as Ward stepped back inside, carrying a thick log squared on both ends.

Red didn't miss the way Belle visibly relaxed at his return and it served to increase her uneasiness.

He plunked the log by the table, sat on it and pointed toward the second chair. "It's yours."

Still full of caution, Red sat down and pulled a mug toward her.

Ward grabbed the other mug and grinned around the table. "I always pictured sitting around a little table like this with my mother and brothers." His smile faltered a bit. "But it's nice to share it with you." He must have seen the protest on Red's lips and corrected himself, saying, "Nice of you to share it with me." He passed the cinnamon rolls.

Belle took a bite and closed her eyes, sighing with delight. "These are so good."

Ward grinned. "That's what I said."

Red hesitated. She knew it was childish but she didn't want to agree with him, and wished Belle hadn't done so. But she couldn't deny herself a bite of the delicious-smelling treat. As soon as she tasted it, all resistance fled. Pleasantly sweet with just the right amount of cinnamon, the syrup soft and the bread as light as cake dough. It would have been criminal to refuse such delight. But now there was no way she could pretend to disagree with Ward. She would simply keep her opinion to herself, but despite her intentions she sighed with pleasure.

Ward chuckled. "I've never known anyone to voice a contrary notion about Cookie's rolls."

There was nothing for it but to enjoy the roll and take a second one. And allow a certain amount of serenity to surround the trio at the table. It was hard, she discovered, to keep up any level of resistance and annoyance when lost in the pleasures of good food.

Belle must have felt something similar, for she seemed to relax and even took another roll when Ward offered it, and didn't show a bit of fear. Red knew she should be glad, but she couldn't help but worry Belle would only end up getting hurt again.

Finally Ward drained his cup, eyed the bottom as if wanting a refill of hot cocoa. Instead he planted his hands on his thighs. "Were you comfortable last night?"

"We were fine."

"Is there anything you need?" He glanced at Red. She shook her head.

"We're fine."

He turned his gaze toward Belle. She studied him, measuring him. He let her. She ducked her head, but Red could tell there was something on her mind. Hopefully Ward would not be aware of it.

"What do you need, Belle?" he asked.

Ward's voice was soft and inviting. Far too inviting. He shouldn't be allowed to speak so alluringly.

Belle lifted her face to Ward, her eyes wide with hope and longing. It was enough to fill Red's heart with pain that her little sister should have unsatisfied needs. She'd done her best to take care of Belle but knew she'd failed miserably.

"I'm listening," Ward urged.

"A doll." The words seemed to struggle from Belle's throat, yet rang so full of childish dreams that Red closed her eyes to control a rush of hot tears. She sucked in air until she had her emotions under control.

She opened her eyes to see Ward watching her. Tried to hide any remnant of feeling. But it was impossible when his eyes reflected pain and a desire to help this child.

"Red, can I talk to you outside?" He rose and waited for her to follow, taking her compliance for granted.

Belle stiffened. "I'm sorry. I didn't mean to say that."

"Belle, honey, it's okay." Red squeezed Belle's shoulder.

Ward stopped, turned to face Belle. "You have no reason to regret asking. I only want to talk to Red about how we might get you a doll."

Red followed Ward outside into the warm autumn sun. "She didn't expect you to do anything. She was only voicing her longing. After all, she's just a little girl."

"Exactly. And she's been through more than a child should have to endure. So asking for a doll seems to me to indicate she still knows how to be a child. I think we should do all we can to encourage that."

"We?" She tried to sound as if he'd overstepped a line, but to know he felt some call to help a hurting child did something funny to her insides, as if warm, melted butter had been dripped to parched areas.

He narrowed his eyes, maybe expecting her to refuse. She wanted to, but honestly could not think of how she could without making Belle pay for her decision.

Taking her silence for agreement, he said, "I'm pretty good at carving. I think I could carve a simple little doll for her. Nothing fancy. If I ask Linette for some scraps of material, you might be able to make some clothes. What do you think?"

A man who would carve a doll for a little girl? She tried not to think what kind of person would do that— a kind, generous one who cared about the feelings of a child—but the thought burrowed past her barriers and landed behind her heart in a spot full of memories of a different life. She held her breath and forced the truth of who she was to the forefront, blocking out every other possibility.

She was Red. A woman ruined by her life in a saloon. Ruined for a decent man.

Ward watched her. No doubt thought she struggled to deal with his suggestion. Let him think so. It was a much nicer quandary than the real one.

"I won't do it if you have an objection," he said.

Oh, she had objections, but not to getting Belle a doll. In fact, she couldn't even say what they were. Only that they had a Ward-shape to them. Something about him proved a threat to her need to stand on her own. Alone against the world. Her sister's sole protector. A lonely job but a welcome one.

"Go ahead. Carve a doll and I'll make clothes for it. Belle deserves a little pleasure in life."

Ward stepped closer, forcing her to raise her eyes and challenge him or back away. She would not show weakness, and met his gaze with fierce directness.

"I think we all deserve to enjoy life."

"Yeah? I noticed how some people intend to enjoy themselves no matter what the cost to another." She knew he understood her meaning as his eyes narrowed and turned as icy as a winter river.

"I don't mean that kind of thing, and I'm almost certain you know that."

She wouldn't let so much as a flicker of her eyelids indicate he was right. "Really? So what kind of thing do you mean?"

He held her gaze for a heartbeat and another until she feared she would have to blink first. Then he smiled.

The sudden change made her dizzy. The bang on

her head still hurt. No doubt the cause of her slight loss of focus.

"I mean the kind of things God gives us freely to enjoy—the sun." He raised his face skyward and closed his eyes.

She tried not to stare at the look of bliss on his face. Concentrated on studying his rugged jawline, noting his clean-shaven cheeks, his bronzed skin from hours outdoors. But taking stock of that sort of thing proved as unsettling as the longing his words drew from her heart.

"Then there's the mountains." He pointed to the west. "Tell me you can look at that view and not feel blessed."

Thankfully he didn't seem to require a reply because she would have found it impossible to say she wasn't moved. Though perhaps as much by his freedom in expressing his feelings as in the view.

"And need I point out the wildflowers? Have you seen the abundance in the spring?"

"Didn't see much from the inside of a saloon." She hoped her hard words would make him stop. Remind him of who she was.

"You are no longer a prisoner inside a saloon. So stop thinking like one." He studied her, waiting for her reaction.

She vowed she would not give him the pleasure of seeing how his words knifed through her arguments and attacked her resistance. It was true she must now learn to live like she was free. Yet some aspects of her past must never be forgotten. And if she ever thought they could be, then she knew full well someone would remind her.

Ward nodded. "I see you understand my meaning. Are you going to tell Belle we're going to make her a doll, or do you want to keep it a secret?"

Red pulled her thoughts back to what mattered—her sister. "Belle is used to not getting what she wants. So I think knowing she's going to get a doll will give her about as much joy as getting it."

"'Spect you have a point. So let's go tell her."

Red had half a mind to tell him she could give Belle the news without his help, but realized it would be churlish. So she led the way back inside.

Belle sat hunched forward at the table, already accepting disappointment. Her posture and attitude tore at Red's heart and for the first time, she allowed herself to acknowledge the gratitude she felt toward Ward's generosity—not only in offering to carve a doll but also for his hand in rescuing them.

She knelt by Belle. "Ward has offered to carve a little wooden doll for you, and I'll make some clothes for it. Isn't that nice?"

Belle lifted her head and stared openmouthed at Red, then at Ward, who stood so close behind Red she could feel him in her pores. An unsettling feeling.

"Really? Truly?"

Red nodded. "It will take a little time, but you will get your doll."

"And I won't have to wait until Christmas or something special?"

"Nope. 'Cause you're special every day of the year and you deserve a special treat."

Belle threw herself into Red's arms, tumbling her off balance. She fell against Ward's legs. He grunted at the impact, then reached down and planted his hands on her shoulders to steady her.

A thousand sensations raced through Red. Joy at her sister's happiness. And a great longing to know protection such as Ward's hands provided day after day.

How foolish to dream of impossible things.

She knew her life would never include anything but standing firmly on her own. She eased Belle back and scrambled to her feet. Could not look at Ward for fear he would see the longing she must deny.

She could not face denial and rejection in his eyes. Nor the truth about who and what she was.

Ward struggled with a string of warring emotions. Knowing Belle feared to ask for something most children took for granted seared his thoughts. Children should not suffer at the hands of adults.

His anger was laced through and through with regret and doubt. How had Hank and Travers fared after he left? And Mother? Had his stepfather ever used his fists on her? To Ward's knowledge, he hadn't while Ward was still there. The man's anger seemed directed entirely at Ward, which is why he left. Only he could never be sure his leaving solved the problem and he wondered if it had been transferred to the others. Would he ever know?

So when Red had gone all prickly at his suggestion to carve a doll for Belle, Ward couldn't help but point out the truth to her. She was free. But when Belle squealed with joy, and bowled Red off her feet right into Ward's shins…well, he experienced a sensation he could not put words to. He wanted to do more than save them from Thorton. Wanted more than to keep them safe from despicable men. He stared at the tabletop, saw the remnants of their snack. Lifted his eyes to the wall. Beyond it lay the mountains. They represented what he wanted—only he couldn't say what it was. Just knew he'd had it when his pa was alive and they were a happy family.

Perhaps that's what he wanted—his family happy and secure again. Unable to give them what he longed for them to have, he settled on giving it to Red and Belle on a temporary basis. Seemed temporary was all that life offered—temporary happiness, temporary… His jaw tightened as words failed. Seemed love was fleeting at best and a deception at its worst. His insides hardened at the knowledge, and he shifted his attention back to Red and Belle.

Keeping them safe and making them happy would ease his conscience until such time as they found a more suitable arrangement. He vowed to redouble his efforts to contact his family and persuade them to join him.

"Have you had a look around outside?" he asked.

"Only got as far as the fire pit." Red wouldn't meet his eyes, which suited him fine. He had no wish for her to see his confusion and he already knew her green-eyed direct stare unsettled his rational thoughts. What was there about her that made him turn into an over-anxious schoolboy?

"Come along, then, and I'll show you around."

Ward saw stark terror in Belle's eyes at his suggestion, but before he could assure them he respected their caution, Red spoke.

"No need. We saw the ranch as we rode up yesterday."

"I wasn't thinking of showing you the ranch buildings. But beyond the fire pit is lots and lots of room to roam. You can be as alone as you choose."

He waited as Red and Belle studied each other and knew the moment Belle decided she might like to see the outdoors. Her eyes flared with anticipation.

No doubt Red saw it, too, and sighed.

"Red, I might get a little tired of being shut indoors all the time." Belle did her best to sound reasonable.

"We aren't locked up. We can go out back anytime we want."

"I might like to run." Belle rounded her eyes in appeal.

Ward watched Red fight an internal battle, then she faced him. "Guess we might like to see what's out there."

He chuckled at her begrudging tone. "Then come along." He stepped outside.

Red and Belle paused at the doorway and peered one way and then the other.

Knowing how cautious they were about confronting others, he assured them everyone was busy elsewhere. A quick glance up the hill showed Linette at the window, but he didn't say anything. Linette would give the pair space as long as she thought they needed.

Belle clung to Red's hand, though he suspected it was also the other way around. But they'd soon learn they were safe here.

They skirted the fire pit and he led them to an almost invisible trail through the trees to the edge of the river.

"The water level is low this time of year, but it's deep and fast in the spring." To their left were the empty wintering corrals and the noisy pigpen. "We'll go this way," he said, turning to the right and following the river. The big house stood on the hill, but they veered away from it and continued to climb. He slowed his steps, allowing Red, still clinging to Belle's hand, to fall in at his side.

At the top of the hill he stopped. "Have you ever seen a prettier scene?" The ranch buildings were hidden from view. Before them lay rippling hills that crept up the side of the mountain. The mountains filled the horizon, still wearing tiny snowcaps and shining in the sun. Dark pines filled every crevasse.

Belle broke from Red's grasp and stepped forward. "I guess you can see heaven from here. Maybe Mama and Papa can see us." Her expression rapt, she lifted her face toward the sky.

Beside him, Red jolted. He guessed she objected to Belle's observation but knew she wouldn't say anything to dispel the child's awe even if they both knew heaven wasn't in the mountains. He reached out, intending to touch Red's arm and signal her to let the child enjoy the moment, but when his fingers brushed her arm she gave a startled cry and jerked about to face him, wariness and defiance warring for supremacy in her eyes. She hastily backed away and her heel caught on a rock.

He lurched forward to catch her but it was too late. She went down with a jarring thud and her head whammed to the ground hard enough to do damage.

Chapter Six

Red lay flat on her back, struggling to get her lungs to work.

Ward knelt at her side. "Red, are you okay?"

His words were but a distraction as she fought to draw in air. He slipped an arm under her shoulders and eased her to a sitting position. "Take a breath."

She spared enough energy to send him a look full of annoyance. Did he think she purposely refused to breathe? And then a gasp shuddered in.

"Thank goodness. You had me worried there."

She leaned forward over her knees, fighting to get enough oxygen into her body.

"Are you okay? You hit your head pretty good."

"Fine," she gasped. "Help me up." She knew she crossed a dangerous line by asking for his aid, but she lacked the strength to pull her body upright unassisted.

He grasped her hand, caught her shoulder and lent his body for support as she struggled to her feet. Swaying with dizziness, she clung to him. He was solid, his touch gentle. She closed her eyes. This might be the closest she'd ever get to heaven.

Heaven. Belle had said something about it. Right.

That she wondered if she could see it beyond the mountains. Mama and Papa might be watching. *Oh, dear parents, forgive me for my failure in caring for Belle. For my failure to uphold the standards you set out so clearly for me.* She'd had few options once she'd fallen into Thorton's clutches.

She tried and failed to keep back a groan.

Ward took it for pain and held her steady. "Maybe you should sit down again."

But her pain was not physical. It came from deep inside, beyond human touch. Except, against her inner warning, she found something satisfying in leaning on Ward.

It was only her foolish weakness. She eased away and stood on her own. "I'm fine."

"So you've said a number of times."

"You don't have to sound so doubtful."

He favored her with a lopsided smile. "Are you going to expect me to believe you're fine just because you say so?"

"What a silly question. Of course it's true."

His smile grew more crooked. "See, that's just it. I don't believe it just 'cause you say so. I see the way both of you get all tense when I step into the room. That's not okay in my book. You fall and bang your head for the second time in a matter of days and can hardly breathe. That's not fine so far as I'm concerned." He shifted his gaze toward the mountains. "You are afraid and hurting. Denying it don't change it."

A thousand wishes and regrets roared into her like a storm off the towering mountains, tearing her pretense of being fine up by the roots and leaving her grasping for something to cling to. She fought panic. She frantically sought for some idea to steady her. For a moment she thought she would drown in hopelessness and despair. Then she found the only thing that mattered and her world steadied. Belle. Nothing else had any importance. Only her little sister and doing what was best for her. If not for Belle...

She let her gaze drift as far as the mountains allowed. "How deep into the mountains have you gone?" she asked Ward.

He jerked about as if her sudden change of topic confused him. She felt his steady consideration, allowed herself the briefest glimpse of his blue eyes, then quite determinedly turned back to the mountains.

Slowly he turned and looked the same direction. "I've been several days' horseback ride west. There are some beautiful valleys. But also some treacherous cliffs."

"Streams of fish? Green pastures?"

"Some." Curiosity and a degree of caution filled his voice. "It's wild country. Many a man has gotten lost or been attacked by wild animals." No doubting the warning in his words.

"Are there really caves?" She saw his expression harden, fill with suspicion. "I heard there were."

"I expect there are. Why do you ask?"

"No reason."

"Red, promise me you won't head back into the high country and hole up in some cave. You'd never survive."

It irked that he continued to think she was so helpless and needy. "You might be surprised. Besides, what makes you think I'd consider such a thing?" Did he have to look so doubtful? "After all, I have Belle to consider." She tore from Ward's fearsome glare to watch Belle running about the area, searching for treasures. No doubt she could gather up rocks and sticks to take back. A poor substitute for real toys. It was the reason she'd agreed to let Ward make a doll. She'd make hundreds of outfits for it.

Her gaze drifted to the vast landscape before them. However, if not for Belle…

"No need to go into the mountains. There's lots of beautiful spots in the foothills. My ranch isn't anything like Eden Valley Ranch. It's small. There's a natural clearing big enough for a good-sized farmyard. I thought of building the cabin on the top of the hill but figured it might be buffeted by winter winds, so I chose a spot a little ways down."

As Ward talked about how many cows his ranch could carry because of the grassy hills, Red's eyes sought the distance, drawn by some force she couldn't explain. Perhaps it was the thought of disappearing. Or finding solitude. Solace. Peace. *Whither shall I flee from your presence. I will never leave thee nor forsake thee.*

.They were scripture verses but she had learned to push thoughts of God and any memory of Bible verses from her mind. So why now all of a sudden should those words flood her mind? It was the samplers. The one over the bed made by Ward's mother and the one Belle remembered their own mother making. But where was God when they so desperately needed Him? Where was He when she'd fallen into Thorton's clutches and called out for aid? Now it was too late. Her disgrace separated her from God more effectively than the vast valleys and mighty mountains hemmed her in.

Belle was several yards away, running from one thing to another. "Come along," Red called. "We need to get back. I'm sure Ward has to return to the ranch."

He sighed. "Why is it I get the feeling you are always trying to rush me away?"

"I can't imagine why you'd think such a thing." The man would have to be dull as dirt to not hear her impatience.

He managed a halfhearted chuckle. "Only the fact that you are rather less than hospitable."

"I guess I don't need to point out that I have no right to extend or refuse hospitality." Yes, she and Belle might be safe from the likes of Thorton and his friends, but they still did not have their freedom.

"I don't mean to run roughshod over your need for privacy, as you well know. Only you're afraid to admit it."

"I'm not afraid." Of anything. Except what he could do to her and Belle if he chose. That and facing people with guilt branded on her life.

Belle joined them, making Ward keep any more of his opinions to himself. Only a lift of his eyebrows communicated how much he didn't believe her protests.

"Can we come here whenever we want?" Belle asked.

"Anytime at all," Ward answered.

"Even if you're not with us?"

Ward sent Red a questioning look as if wondering where this line of questioning was going. Red shrugged slightly, indicating she didn't know.

"You can certainly explore without me."

Belle grew motionless. "What if we get lost?"

"I'll make sure you're safe." Red looked about, fixing landmarks in her mind.

"If you always keep in mind the mountains are to the west, you can't get lost," Ward said.

Belle rocked back and forth, her worry unabated.

Ward squatted at her side and turned her toward the

Rockies. "See that big round nose of a mountain? It's a landmark. And if you can see it, you know the ranch is straight east of that point."

Red burned the information into her brain.

Not that she'd really rush into the mountains and hide forever, but it was tempting. No men. No probing stares. No whispers behind white-gloved hands of women who would never consider the circumstances that put Red in the saloon. Or if they knew them, would not accept them as adequate excuse.

A cave in the mountains sounded mighty appealing.

But Belle seemed satisfied with Ward's answer and turned her attention to the collection she'd gathered up. Just as Red expected—pretty rocks, bits of wood.

"This one looks like it has a face on it." She showed a rock to Red, then, fighting her fear, she showed it to Ward.

It was true that a child should learn not to fear everyone, but in Belle's case, a little fear and caution was wise lest people think they could take advantage of her. Red caught Belle's hand. "Let's take your things to the cabin."

The look Ward gave her left no doubt that he recognized her not too subtle attempt to keep Belle a safe distance from him.

She blithely ignored him.

They reached the cabin. Just before she ducked inside, she turned to Ward. "Goodbye and thanks for bringing the things." She would wait until he left to look at the items Linette had sent, but curiosity made her wish he'd hurry and leave.

He tipped his head back and laughed. "Red, you are something else. Your hints about me leaving are less than subtle." He held out a hand in protest when she drew herself up to demand an explanation. "Promise you won't hit me with the shovel."

Belle poked her head around Red. "She was going to when you first came."

"I was not."

Ward chuckled. "I wouldn't be surprised." He turned toward the back of the cabin.

"What are you doing?"

He grinned over his shoulder. "Going to chop some firewood."

"I can do it."

"I'm sure you can, but you won't have to." He paused and slowly turned to face her full-on. "Red, it's about time you accept that I aim to make sure you're safe and well taken care of."

"I'm not your mother or brothers, you know."

He considered her steadily, his expression going through a range of emotions. His smile flattened from amusement to sadness.

She shouldn't have mentioned his family, although he made no secret that his guilt over them was the reason he helped her and Belle. And then she detected a flash of anger and she pushed Belle behind her into the cabin and pulled the door closed. She confronted Ward, prepared to deal with whatever avenue his ire took.

But the anger disappeared as quickly as it came, replaced by strong-jawed determination.

"No matter what you say or do, I will not walk away from you and Belle." He ground about and disappeared around the corner. In a second or two she heard the sound of an ax delivering blows to logs.

A thousand regrets and wishes battered the inside of her head. If only she could be Grace again. But it would never be. No point in wishing for the stars when your feet were mired in pig slop.

Tucking away her sadness, she pasted on a smile and stepped into the cabin. At least she had Belle.

Ward swung the ax over and over, neatly splitting log after log. Sure, he laughed at Red's attempts to hurry him on his way, but his amusement was short-lived. Would she ever stop treating him like public enemy number one? After all, he'd gone to a great deal of trouble to help her. Yes, he had ulterior motives and she knew it. She understood he was doing for them what he wished he'd done for his family. Still hoped to do.

He paused and wiped his brow on his sleeve. Would he ever hear from his mother and brothers? He suspected his stepfather waylaid his correspondence, but surely one of them could get the postmaster to slip him a letter or find some way of contacting Ward. He tried to believe there was a good reason for not hearing from them, but deep inside he suspected they'd decided to put him out of their minds. Blaming him for leaving them to manage on their own.

He swung his ax. Again and again. If he could go back in time he would do things differently. Or not. How could anyone be certain of what they would do given another chance?

He had plenty of wood split and stacked most of it in a neat pile inside the shed Eddie had built against the cabin wall. Then he set to work shaving off kindling. Satisfied with the amount he'd created, he filled his arms with wood and headed for the cabin.

The closer he drew to the door, the more he grinned, imagining Red's protest. What would she say this time to encourage him to hurry up and leave?

He paused before the cabin and knocked, then listened to hurried steps cross the floor. The door rattled and Red pulled it open.

"I thought you'd be gone."

"Yeah, you hoped so." But she knew it was him or she wouldn't have opened the door quite so readily. In fact, she might have greeted a caller with the shovel still resting nearby.

She followed his gaze to her weapon of choice. "Never know when you might need a shovel." Her voice carried a shrug.

He laughed. "That's true. I brought wood."

"Who'd have guessed?"

"Woman, you do have a way with words. A person could practically cut your sarcasm with a knife." Yet it somehow tickled him to try and guess what would come out of her mouth. "Too bad it doesn't fill the stomach. Then you and Belle would never go hungry."

"Who says we ever have?"

Ward dumped the wood in the box beside the stove and turned to Belle. "You ever been hungry, child?"

She looked up from her play at the table, her eyes wide as full moons and nodded.

At the stark look in her eyes, he regretted involving her in this exchange. "Belle, I promise you that as long as I'm taking care of you you'll never go hungry."

Her glance slid toward the shelves as if mentally counting the number of meals stored there.

"The shelves will never be bare."

He turned and encountered Red's hard stare. But beneath the surface he thought he saw something else. At a loss to think what it might be and feeling very close to the edge of a precipice, he prepared to leave. "I'll be back later."

Belle glanced up from her play. "Bye."

Red sat across from Belle, studying him.

He waited for her to say not to hurry back or something similar.

Her gaze held steady, driving deep into his thoughts, searching for... He didn't know. Nor if he could provide it. He could provide meat, firewood, even a doll for Belle, but how could he give Red what she needed when he didn't know what it was? So he returned her look for look, silently promising his best.

Then she smiled, a trembling, uncertain flash that disappeared so quickly he almost wondered if he'd imagined it. But he knew he hadn't.

"Thank you for everything." She ducked her head and developed a great interest in one of Belle's rocks.

He couldn't move. He'd come to expect sharpness, sarcasm. Come to half enjoy it. But gratitude? It slipped past his reason for helping them and started a fresh journey in his thoughts. One that had nothing to do with trying to make up for leaving his family behind.

And everything to do with starting over.

He spun on his heel, too confused by this sudden shift in his thinking to know what to say.

He strode away from the cabin with no destination in mind. Then his thoughts cleared. He'd promised Belle a doll and he meant to get started on it. He veered toward the cookhouse, hoping to catch Eddie there.

Cookie greeted him at the door with a welcoming whack between his shoulders. "How'd they like the cinnamon rolls?"

He sucked in air to refill his lungs before he could answer. "They thought they'd died and gone to heaven."

"Good. Good. You think they like them enough to trot themselves over here and enjoy them with me?"

"They're both a little fearful yet." Ward glanced past Cookie. Only Bertie sat at the table, peeling potatoes.

"We'll give them time, won't we, love?" Bertie asked his wife.

Cookie snorted and returned to the stove. "Best thing for them would be to meet us and learn they needn't be afraid of us."

Ward half agreed. "The boss around?"

"Up at the house."

"I need to talk to him." Leaving Cookie muttering about how no one had any reason to be afraid around her, Ward left and jogged up the trail to the big house.

Eddie opened the door. "Come on in. Linette's waiting for a report."

As Ward crossed to the sitting room, he tried to think what he would tell them.

"Are they getting settled?" Linette asked. "I'd feel so much better if they were here where I could care for them."

Eddie took her hand. "You must allow people to deal with things in their own way."

"I know you're right, but they must be lonely and afraid. Ward, how are they? How is her wound?"

"She said her leg is fine." Though he'd noticed her favoring it a time or two. As soon as she realized she did, she stopped. "They're very wary about people. Red hesitates to accept help. I wouldn't be surprised if she suggests a way she can repay you."

Linette smiled gently. "If she mentions it to me—or to you—" she nodded toward Ward "—you say the only thing I want in exchange for what little we can share with her is for her to become secure and confident."

Red's goal was to get on her feet and become independent. "Belle seems to relax when she knows no one will suddenly show up. I took them up the far hill." He told how Belle had played but kept Red's behavior to himself. And his own. The way his heart had thudded when she tripped and fell. Then raced like a runaway horse when she'd taken his hand and accepted his help in getting to her feet. Behind that emotion lay concern about her questions about caves in the mountains. He'd be keeping a close eye on them to make sure they didn't decide to go in search of one and disappear. "Belle said she'd like a doll. I promised to make her one if you don't mind me using some scraps of lumber." He directed the latter to Eddie.

"Help yourself."

He turned back to Linette. "I wondered if you had some scraps of fabric you might give Red to make clothes for the doll."

"I'll do better than that. I'll make them myself."

Ward didn't want to argue with the boss's wife, but he had to give his opinion. "I think it might be good for her to make them."

Linette chuckled. "I expect you're right, and how keen of you to realize it. How did the clothes I sent fit?"

"I left before they looked at them. I'll ask when I see them again."

"And when will that be?" Linette watched him carefully.

"I haven't given it much thought." He kind of thought he'd spend most of the day there, but maybe that wasn't what they needed. "I'm not sure how much to leave them alone. What's best?" Surely Linette would know. She had a knack for helping others.

Linette looked out the window toward the cabin. "Do you know how they got into the situation where you found them?"

"No. Except I know it was not Red's choice."

"You said we all needed to give her time and space to learn to trust us. Perhaps your own words are the best advice for all of us. So long as she has what she needs."

Ward nodded. No doubt wise words from a wise woman, and he would heed them even though he wanted to do otherwise. At least Red was close enough she could call for help if she needed it, and he could see them flit out to the fire pit as he worked in the barn.

The next morning the sensation of starting a new journey returned. Yes, he might salve his conscience over leaving his family by helping Red and Belle, but it was far more than that.

He'd spent the previous afternoon selecting a piece of pine to carve into a doll. Linette had sent a package of fabric along with thread and needles. Thinking of how Red thought Belle might enjoy the prospect of a doll as much as getting it, Ward decided he would do as much work as possible on it where she could watch.

He hurried through the chores Eddie assigned him so he could start work on the project, but it was Red he was anxious to see. Would she be all prickly today or welcoming? Either way he looked forward to showing her the piece of wood he'd selected and handing her the material for doll clothes.

He found them sitting on the logs beside the fire pit. This time they didn't skitter away at his approach. In fact, Belle waved as he rounded the corner of the cabin. Red never left off watching him.

He greeted Belle, then returned his gaze to Red, aware something had shifted between them, uncertain how to describe it even to himself. He managed a suggestion of a smile before he revealed the length of wood, his knife and the package Linette had given him.

"What's that?" Belle eyed the wood.

"It's going to be your doll."

"It is?" Her doubt was evident.

"You wait and see." He moseyed over to sit on a log a healthy distance from the pair and held the wood for them to see. He'd rough-cut the basic shape and figured they could likely see the shape of a body and head. "This is going to be the face. I'll carve the body here. I figure to attach arms with screws so they move."

Belle edged closer as he flicked open his knife and started carving off curl after curl of wood. She hung back at a safe distance but too far to see how each cut brought out the developing outline of a head.

He held it up. "Can you see the beginning of her head?"

She nodded.

Ward spared a glance toward Red. It was meant to be fleeting but her gaze caught and held his, delving deep, as if searching for answers or something more. He had no idea what she sought or if he could provide it, but he let her look as long and hard as she wanted. She blinked, sucked in air and shifted her attention to her fingers.

His thoughts circled for a way to interpret the moment. He found none and returned to carving the doll, hoping it would tempt Red to move closer, but she seemed lost in contemplation of her hands. Perhaps if he talked about something else, something that might be of some interest to them.

"When Grady came to the ranch, he was awfully scared. Cried if anyone looked at him. Seems no one but Linette could get near him." He concentrated on his handwork for a moment but managed to sneak a glance at his audience. Belle watched every move of his fingers. Red didn't give any indication she heard him except for the way she cocked her head toward him as if anxious to catch every word.

Satisfied he had her attention but wishing for more, he continued to talk about Grady. "For Christmas last year I carved some animals for him."

"How come he's at the ranch?" Belle asked.

Ward studied his answer. Seems life should be sweeter for children. "His mama died and he had nowhere to go, so Linette brought him with her."

"His papa died, too?"

Ward wondered how much to tell her. "No, his pa is alive but he can't take care of Grady." Or didn't care for the responsibility. Eddie had told him how Linette had challenged the man to take Grady and raise him and how she continued to send letters hoping to persuade him.

"How old is he?" Belle asked.

"He's five."

"He's happy?"

"Linette and Eddie care about him very much." But he knew, as did everyone on the ranch, that Grady would have times of sadness wondering why his father didn't want him.

His answer seemed to satisfy Belle. "How long does it take to carve a doll?" she asked.

"Well, this particular doll is extra special because it's for you. So I might take a little longer in order to make it real nice."

Her eyes sparkled with joy at being made to feel special.

Ward turned toward Red, expecting appreciation in

her expression, but instead her eyes were wide and filled with fear. "Red, what's the matter?"

She blinked back her feelings and gave a smile that went no further than the corners of her mouth. "Nothing. I'm—"

"I know. You're fine." If he heard it one more time… "Only you're not and you might as well stop pretending you are. Your life has not been pleasant. Your future is uncertain. Likely your head hurts and who knows what else is not sitting well with you—"

"Now that you mention it, I am wearing borrowed clothes."

"I noticed. Nice dress." The dark blue fabric made her eyes look more blue than green.

"I got a different dress, too," Belle said.

"I noticed." A faded red dress fit well. "You look very nice, too."

Belle smiled but the tension in the air did not dissipate. It lay so thick between Red and Ward that he was tempted to cut it away with his knife.

"I have something for you, Red." He picked up the package from Linette. However, she refused to move closer so he shuffled over and held the parcel toward her.

She stared. "What is it?"

He jiggled it teasingly. "Only one way to find out."

Still she did not reach for it.

Belle stood inches away, bouncing on the balls of her feet. "Red, hurry up and open it."

Red slowly, reluctantly, took the sack from Ward's hands and opened the drawstring. She pulled out fabric, a pair of scissors, needle, pins and thread.

"For doll clothes," Ward explained.

Belle reverently touched several pieces. "All satiny.

And this one so cuddly. Maybe my dolly can have a blanket, too?" She fingered a soft piece of wool.

"You will have the best-dressed doll ever," Red said. She turned to Ward. "Let me see the size." She measured a bit of fabric against the length of the wood.

Ward held very still as she bent over the beginnings of the doll in his hands. She was so intent on her task that she seemed unmindful of how close they were. He studied her hair. She'd brushed it and tamed it into a thick braid, but already bits of curls escaped and crowned her head.

She marked a couple of places in the fabric with pins, and then sat up straight.

There were but six inches between them, but the distance seemed vast. He felt alone in a totally foreign way. In an attempt to corral the sensation, he returned to carving the doll.

They worked side by side, she often leaning over to measure this or that, he holding up his work frequently to let them see his progress. Belle sat on the ground in front of them, watching progress on both fronts and playing with her collection of rocks and twigs. At times they seemed to be animals she herded around. Other times she talked to them as if they were family members.

At first Red and Belle said little or limited their conversation to how long would the arms be? How big the head? Did Red think he should carve curls into the head? She did.

"At least they will be blond," she murmured.

Ward studied Red. Shifted his gaze to Belle. Her hair wasn't as curly as her sister's and was more brown than red, though it had mahogany glimmers. He turned back to Red. "You don't like your hair?"

She puffed out her lips in a rumble. "Hate it."

"It's kind of pretty."

The look she favored him with dripped with a load of denial. "It makes everyone stare."

"Yeah, well, only because it's eye-catching."

"I could do with plain."

He thought of her statement. "Don't most women prefer beautiful to plain? Don't they like to be noticed?"

"Can't say being noticed has been such a treat."

Aah. Now it made sense. He tried to think of a way to tell her that people would no longer view her as Thorton had. Nothing came to mind. "What's your real name?" Perhaps if she stopped using Red she might start to think of herself as someone besides that woman.

She didn't even glance up from stitching together a seam.

Belle did, though. "It's—"

"Belle." One word with a heap of warning attached. She flashed a defensive glance at Ward. "Red is the only name you need to know."

He regarded her, waiting for her to meet his look, and when she finally did he saw defiance and perhaps, if he let himself imagine it, a longing that dug deep into his heart. "Someday you will tell me your real name." It was part promise, part prayer.

"Dream on, cowboy." She jabbed the needle into the fabric so viciously he half expected to see her draw blood from her finger. But she deftly guided the sharp point away from her flesh.

Perhaps if he talked about his family it would make her realize she no longer had to be Red. She could be free of that part of her life and again become the woman she was born to be. "My ma used to say she wished she had a daughter so she could make doll clothes. She told us that when she was a little girl she'd fashioned all sorts of costumes for her doll and dreamed of doing the same for a daughter. She had a collection of paper dolls in families and hundreds of outfits she'd collected over the years. She would let us look at it only under supervision. She figured—and rightly so—that as boys we might not treat it as reverently as she wanted. If she ever had a granddaughter, she planned to pass the collection on to her." He stopped, unable to go on as a lump of despair swelled in his throat. Travers was twenty now. For all Ward knew, he was married and had provided Ma with a granddaughter. Or Ma might have had a child or two in her new marriage. Maybe Ward had another brother or sister.

He stared unseeingly into the distance. An idea—not new to him—plagued his mind. Perhaps he should forget his ranch and go back and see if he could find his ma and family. They might be in the same town, though he no longer thought so. His letters had been returned marked *No Longer Living Here. No Forwarding Address.*

However, returning was not an option at the moment. Not with Red and Belle to care for.

But would he ever see his family again?

Chapter Seven

Red watched Ward struggle with his memories and emotions. It was bad enough to lose one's family because of death, but to not know where they were or if they were okay… Well, she couldn't imagine how she'd feel if Belle disappeared.

She owed him something even if most of the time his attention was an annoyance. Perhaps she could repay him by helping him now. But how? She couldn't assure him that his family was safe. Nor could she minimize his sense of loss. To do so would be insulting.

Seemed he liked talking about his mother. Perhaps if she talked about hers, he would feel better. Though she shrank back from letting herself remember those sweet, innocent times. But Belle ought to be allowed to remember how precious and loved she was.

So she began a story. "Ma taught me to knit when I was four. I remember so clearly the moment that I finally realized the loop on one needle had to go through the loop on the other. Once I did, I was unstoppable. I knitted a long scraggly-looking scarf that Pa wore everywhere. Said it was his favorite. It finally fell apart when I was about ten." She laughed. "I don't know who

was more relieved to see it gone—Mama, Papa or me."
She let the memory glide over her regrets and guilt
and give her a moment of sweet love. "From scarves, I
graduated to doll sweaters and hats. I don't remember
using any sort of pattern. I expect Mama told me how
to make the sleeves and shape the item. I thought my
work was beautiful. It wasn't until after Belle was born
and I pulled out my doll stuff to give her that I realized
just how crude it looked. So I spent many a happy evening knitting new sweaters and bonnets and leggings
for Belle's dolls."

"Red, what happened to my dolls? And all Mama
and Papa's things?"

"An uncle inherited everything." The pleasantness of
her memory was dashed away at the cruelty of an uncle
she'd never met, didn't know existed. Apparently Papa
had borrowed heavily from him and part of the agreement required Papa naming this uncle as beneficiary
in his will. But the man had no regard for the needs
of two girls. And everything that was near and dear
to them was junk in his eyes. "He disposed of all the
earthly goods as he saw fit." Most of it went to a man
who owned a store that handled a variety of goods. Red
would never forget the way he'd gloated over some of
their treasures. *People love this kind of stuff.* He'd measured the family Bible with dollar signs in his eyes. He
did the same for the wall hangings Mama had made and
all Belle's pretty little dresses and her cradle.

Slowly, in measured tones, she continued the story,
as much to remind herself of how far she'd fallen as for
any other reason. To his credit, the uncle secured them a
place in the home of a fine family. In return for Belle's
keep, Red did housework. She didn't mind. They had

their own room and were together. But it proved temporary and they moved. Then moved again.

At that point she stopped talking. She could not bear to recall how Thorton had "taken them on," as he so generously said, promising to take them to his sister where they would "do well."

If only she had known the truth. But by the time she did, she had no option. Thorton kept Belle under lock and key in order to obtain Red's cooperation. He beat Red if she proved the least bit rebellious.

"Then what happened?" Belle's eyes were wide.

Red fought a storm of conflicting emotions—regret at the way she'd failed in her duty toward Belle, guilt at the life she'd been forced to live warred with the joyful, peaceful memories of family life as she'd known it. She tried to control the raging conflagration inside. Struggled to find an answer for Belle.

"We went from one place to another." She tried to keep the bitter note out of her voice.

Belle's expression was wreathed with fear. She shifted back until she rested against the far log bench. She ducked her head and pulled her playthings close.

Red swallowed back regret. She should have stopped talking before she stirred up Belle's memories of the past few months. She turned to Ward, her eyes burning with a warning not to ask for more details.

He smiled narrowly and resumed carving the doll.

She fought to retain her resentment. Instead she found a yearning she would never admit. What sort of man carved a doll for a little girl who wasn't his? Wasn't even related to him? Or carved little animals for a waif of a boy? Or rescued people who weren't sure they wanted to be rescued? She examined the last question. All that mattered was Belle was safe. But what did her future hold?

Ward looked up from his carving.

She turned away from him but not before he had caught her watching him. She couldn't face him, suspecting her confusion revealed itself in her expression, and she put aside the little dress she was sewing and sprang to her feet, not caring that he might wonder what drove her so urgently.

She stepped away from the logs and the cozy little scene that had drawn her into sweet memories of the past and fears of the future. Two steps in one direction and she stopped. Where was she going? Where could she go to escape both the memories and the uncertainties? Shifting direction, she made several more steps and stopped. If she didn't express some purpose, Ward would think she wandered aimlessly. Or like the daffodil poem Belle recalled… "I wandered lonely as a cloud that floats on high o'er vales and hills." Oh, if only she could float above everything as free as a cloud.

And as lonely.

Despair threatened to choke her. She must not think such thoughts. Her life was worth living for Belle's sake. Curbing her emotions, she stretched her arms overhead. "Got a little cramped sitting for so long," she murmured, hoping she sounded convincing. She picked her way back to the log bench and gathered up her sewing, aware that Ward watched her the whole while.

Even after she resumed stitching together the dress, his gaze remained on her. She could feel it. Even as she felt his nosy concern. Determinedly she kept her head bent over her task. Let him think what he wanted. Wonder at her strange behavior. He would never understand. Nor would she attempt to explain how precarious was her position in life. She would not fit in any respectable society and had no intention of returning to the other side.

He shifted closer.

She glanced out the corner of her eye, wondering if he would take the hint to keep his distance. Yet, even though there was a yard of log to her right, she did not move. For the life of her, she could not make herself even when his elbow brushed her. She caught her breath, waiting, wondering, then with a heart-wrenching jolt, recalled invasive, cruel touches. She forced herself not to reveal any of what she felt. But her arm stiffened as his brushed hers.

He didn't jerk away, only let their elbows touch. Nothing more. Her heart ticked beneath her ribs, slowly resuming a steady beat. Warmth spread from her elbow to her lungs, freeing her to take a deep breath and filling her with a sweet reminder of being touched out of love. She closed her eyes and forced her lungs to inhale and exhale in a slow rhythm. But trying as hard as she could, she was unable to pretend she didn't feel something that frightened her while at the same time, promised to fill her yearning emptiness.

He leaned closer to whisper, "You will never again have to worry about Thorton or men like him. Not while I'm here to take care of you."

She jerked about to meet his gaze, his face barely six inches from her own. So close she felt as if she might drown in the blueness of his eyes. And the sincerity of his promise.

What about when he wasn't there? What would people say about her past? It wouldn't be nice; she could guarantee that. And men who would recognize her and think—? She shuddered. Her soul was dirty.

He nudged her elbow. "You're fine. Remember?"

Only she wasn't and she couldn't fake it at the moment, knew her eyes likely revealed her failure to do so.

"Red, you're safe here."

He'd misinterpreted her worry. His dullness edged every thought with annoyance. "I might be safe but I'll never be free of my past." She knew the moment he understood her meaning.

His eyes went from sky-blue to stormy navy. He shook his head. "No one need know about your past."

"There will be those who recognize me." She resisted an urge to cover herself with her hands and protect herself. She tugged at her braid to remind him that her hair was unmistakable. "And even if they don't, I know who I am and I will never forget." Her words came in a hot rush.

She was not surprised when he jerked away to face straight ahead. His elbow lost contact with hers. She knew enough to expect that sort of reaction from decent people. Slowly, every movement a pain, she folded away the fabric, returned all the supplies to the sack and rose to her feet. "Belle, I think it's time to do something else."

Belle scrambled up. "What?"

Red had no idea what they needed to do and grabbed the first idea that surfaced. "I'll show you how to make biscuits."

She felt Ward's surprise at her sudden decision. She hesitated a heartbeat, wanting somehow to explain. But what could she say? That there was no place in her life for hopes and dreams?

Belle couldn't seem to make up her mind whether she should follow Red or stay with Ward. "Will you come with us so I can see my dolly growing?"

Red kept her groan silent. She didn't want him to follow. "Maybe he has to get back to work." Keeping her back to him ensured she wouldn't know his reaction. But she waited, wondering what he would say.

"Red? Are you trying to get rid of me?" His quiet question opened up a chasm of regret and longing. If only things could be different.

They couldn't, and there was no point in wishing otherwise.

"Red?" He said her name with gentle prodding.

Belle tugged Red's hand. "Can he taste my biscuits when they're done?"

Red stared straight ahead and considered her options. Did she really want him to leave? No. But neither did she want him to stay.

Belle shook her hand as if to remind her of the unanswered question.

Slowly she turned. "Would you like to join us for tea when the biscuits are done?"

He held her gaze in silence as if assessing how much welcome her invitation carried. It carried little. Still he nodded. "It would be my pleasure."

Red nodded and turned her steps toward the cabin. Belle jerked her back. "You gonna leave him there?"

When had her little sister grown so demanding? And so social?

Thankfully Ward answered before Red could dredge an excuse to her brain. "I'll sit out here and work on your doll for a little while longer."

She finally got Belle inside. But the change of scenery did not end Belle's demands.

"How come you don't like him? He's making me a doll."

"That's very nice of him."

Belle crossed her arms, knowing she had not convinced Red of anything. "And he wants to help us."

Red would do anything to take her little sister back to happy, safer times, but with Mama and Papa gone and the two of them at the mercy of those who tried to help, it was time to remind Belle that not all offers of help were sincere. She squatted down to eye level with Belle. If the situation wasn't so serious she might smile at the stubbornness in Belle's blue eyes. Belle was innocently beautiful—subdued, not as eye-catching as Red. Red hoped Belle would never lose her innocence but that didn't mean she could be allowed to be too trusting. "Belle, do you remember the gifts Thorton brought us? The pretty dresses?"

Belle nodded, the stubbornness still evident.

"Do you remember how he promised to take care of us?"

A shadow of doubt surfaced.

"Perhaps you never heard all he said. So I'm telling you now just to make sure you understand what happened. Thorton told Mrs. Stanley, the lady we were working for, that he had a sister back in Baltimore who wanted a young woman for companionship. He assured us all that a younger sister would be an asset and we would be generously provided for. Do you remember that?"

"Some." Belle's expression grew troubled.

"Remember how he carried a Bible under his arm and pretended he was a preacher? You know what happened next."

Belle's bottom lip quivered. "He made me stay in that little room and made you work for him."

"That's right." She tenderly wiped a tear from the corner of Belle's eyes. "I regret reminding you of all this, but you must never forget that not all promises are to be trusted." Her voice hardened until she could barely push the words past her teeth. "Never take anyone at their word."

Belle nodded, her eyes awash with misery. "Does that—" She swallowed hard. "Does it mean I can't have the dolly?"

Red pulled Belle into a tight embrace. "I think it's okay to have a doll. Just don't let it make you forget to be careful."

Belle clung to Red. "I won't."

"Now who wants to learn how to make biscuits?"

Belle pulled away and raised her hand. "Me. Me. I want to."

"Then let's do it." Red promised herself she would live her life for her little sister. Nothing else mattered.

Certainly not the loneliness edging her heart.

Nor the thought of Ward sitting patiently outside, generously carving the figure of a doll for Belle.

Yet awareness of his gentleness to her little sister allowed a tiny bit of regret to sneak past her defenses.

Ward stopped carving to listen shamelessly to the conversation drifting from the cabin. Red had left the door and windows open to let in fresh air but would no doubt shut them if she thought he could hear them.

He'd wondered how they'd fallen into Thorton's clutches. Hearing the trickery of the man made him jab his knife into the log seat beside him. He hoped Thorton suffered greatly in jail.

Of course Red was right to teach Belle to be cautious. And she had every reason to be mistrustful of promises. She had no way of knowing how sincere Ward was.

It was up to him to show her he could be trusted. But how? Every kindness triggered suspicion from her.

The conversation inside the cabin had shifted to "Measure the flour. That's the way."

"Chop until it's all mealy. Good job."

They laughed about something. He imagined the two of them working side by side and smiled. They liked doing things together.

That gave him an idea.

He would work on the doll only when they were with him as they had been this morning. And he'd invent other things to do together.

He studied the toy. The head was taking shape nicely. Soon Belle would have her doll to play with and then he'd start another project. He considered the options.

"Ward," Belle called from the doorway. "I made biscuits. Red says come and taste them."

He closed his knife and stuck it in his pocket. Blew the bits of shavings from the doll and strode toward the house.

Belle waited at the door. "Can I see her?"

He gave her the doll. "You can play with it until I come back tomorrow to work on it some more."

"I can?" Her eyes glistened. She hurried to the corner where her rocks and pieces of wood were arranged, laid her doll down and started whispering to it.

Ward shifted his gaze to Red, saw her struggle with joy for her little sister's pleasure and her ever-constant caution.

He edged closer. "It's a long way from done but she sees the possibilities."

Red's eyes flared like green flames. "A person can be waylaid by the thought of possibilities."

He considered her words. "I get the idea we aren't talking about dolls."

"You sure are astute."

He chuckled.

She scowled.

"I know you're hoping to drive me away with your sarcasm but be warned, it's failing miserably. Red, I like you when you're feisty."

She looked about ready to spontaneously ignite. "You don't know who you're messing with."

That brought a chuckle to his lips. "Or it could be I do."

She jerked her attention from him. Her gaze darted about the room as if not quite knowing how to ignore him. It settled on the plate of biscuits in the middle of the table. "Belle, do you still want to serve tea?"

Ward leaned close to whisper, "Do I hear a broad hint in your voice? Like maybe you'd be relieved if she'd changed her mind so you could suggest I be on my way?"

Her look might have scorched him if he wasn't too busy grinning.

"I haven't changed my mind." Speaking louder, he turned to Belle. "Those are delicious-looking biscuits."

Belle tucked her doll under her arm and trotted to the table. "You like them with syrup?"

"It's all we've got," Red informed them both in her most severe tone.

"I like syrup best of all." He grinned without a trace of repentance, knowing his continued enjoyment of this exchange about drove Red to distraction. He tried to imagine what it would be like if she stopped being all defensive. He got a sudden image of Red smiling and joyful as she served tea to him and Belle. The idea jolted clear through him. It was something he'd like to see in real life. But like Red said, *In your dreams, cowboy.*

He sat on the upright log stool as Belle and Red sat across from each other on the chairs.

It was Belle's tea party and she took charge. "Ward, will you pray over the food?"

Ward didn't dare look at Red, but wondered if she thought the same thing as he…. Did Belle think they might need divine intervention to eat her baking? Most likely she was only playing house. He bowed his head and folded his hands. "Lord, bless this food we are about to receive and bless the hands that prepared it. Amen."

Belle studied him with wide-eyed innocence. "That's me, right?"

He realized she meant his prayer to bless the one who'd prepared the food. "That's right. And Red, too, for helping you." He shifted his gaze to his left. Red stared at the biscuits, her throat working. If he wasn't mistaken, her eyes looked watery. "Red, is something wrong?"

She dashed away any hint of tears. "Something in my eye." Her look dared him to argue otherwise. But they both knew it wasn't true.

He couldn't help wonder what had touched her deeply enough to bring any sign of emotion to the surface. Could he get her to tell him? Smiling at his foolishness—she'd probably tell him anything but the real reason—he split open a biscuit, spooned on syrup and took a bite. "Good. Really good."

Belle beamed with pride. "I like cooking."

He finished the biscuit quickly and scooped up another. "I like eating."

He ate only two biscuits, though he could have downed a half dozen but he didn't want to deprive them of the fruit of their labors and certainly did not want to give Red a chance to accuse him of gluttony. He glanced around the room. He'd been inside a few times when Eddie lived here but having Red and Belle occupy the place gave it a whole new feel. His gaze lighted on the bookshelf. According to Belle, their father had enjoyed reading poetry. Just like his father. It gave him an idea.

"Do you like to read?" He meant the question for both of them but kept his gaze on Red. Saw a sudden, unguarded jolt of pleasure. Knew her answer before she spoke.

Her expression grew disinterested.

How did she do that? Knowing she'd learned to mask her feelings because of her situation with Thorton, he did his best to imitate her skill and hide his anger and regret. "Reading is okay for those with nothing else to do," Red answered.

He chuckled, not surprised that she refused to admit her true feelings. "How busy does this little cabin keep you? Never mind. I only had in mind to suggest a source of books." He let the words sit, waiting for Red to swallow her defensiveness and ask for more details.

Belle, likely knowing her sister would not easily give in, spoke. "I can read a little. Red taught me how."

"You ever had a real reader?"

"No. Red told me she had them when she learned to read. She used newspapers for me to learn." Her eyes sparkled. "One paper had a story in it. You know, a chapter at a time. Red made me skip parts of it." The look of accusation in her eyes brought a chuckle from Ward.

"I can imagine why."

"She said it was too grown-up for me."

"I think there might be a reader or two in the place I mean." He waited, watching Red fight an internal fight.

Finally she gave him a look rife with annoyance. "So where is this secret stash of books?"

"I'll tell you on one condition."

Her eyes narrowed, her lips tightened.

He curled his hands into fists that she still thought he might exact unwanted favors from him.

"Red, just answer one question honestly." He didn't give her a chance to get any more defensive. "Do you enjoy reading?"

Surprise flared through her eyes. She sucked in a gasp as if his question had physically landed a blow to her lungs. For a moment she didn't answer, then she blinked and nodded. "I like reading."

"Wait here." He hurried out the door and jogged across to the bunkhouse, where he snagged up a green canvas knapsack. He hadn't looked at the contents in years but it went everywhere he went. Usually it was tucked under the bed as it had been here.

He loped back to the cabin.

Red and Belle still sat at the table. Belle appeared excited. He'd say Red's expression held more doubt than anything.

Well, he was about to prove to her that her doubts were unnecessary.

"Come and see what I have." He rested the knapsack on the floor and untied the cords holding the top closed. On the top was a worn quilt. His fingers lingered on it. "Ma made me this. Said to always think of her when I saw it. Not that I needed anything to make me remember her." He pushed aside a choking homesickness and set aside the quilt before his feelings grew stronger.

Next were some family pictures. He blinked back

the sting in his eyes and instead let pleasant memories crowd his mind. He showed them to Red and Belle. "My parents on their wedding day. And this is me and Travers when we were schoolboys." His voice refused to work and he simply handed Red the picture of Hank at about two.

"Is this your little brother Hank?" Red asked, her voice curiously gentle.

He nodded but kept his attention on the stash of books. "These were my pa's. I took them when I left." Mostly to ensure his stepfather wouldn't destroy them out of spite. He lifted out the first volume. "Pa's favorite book of poetry." The pages were thumbed from much use. "Pa read from that book almost every night, especially during the winter."

To his regret, Ward had often wished Pa wouldn't insist on reading the poems aloud. "Travers and I often got the giggles as we made faces to each other. Pa said nothing but sometimes lowered the book to look at us with a pained expression. If he were alive now I would want to listen to him read each of these poems." He set the book aside and dug through the other until he found the collection of readers. "There you go, Belle."

She took them reverently. "Thank you," she whispered, and shuffled around to sit her back to the wall next to her collection of playthings. No doubt she was as fascinated with the illustrations in the books as Ward and Travers had been at that age.

He turned to Red. "Feel free to enjoy any of these books."

She lifted her face to him. If he wasn't mistaken, tears glistened in her eyes. He tried to think what they meant. Was it something he said? Or sharing memories of his pa? He wished he could retract every word that made her sad. But all he could do was brush a silvery tear from each cheek.

She jolted at his touch.

Had he overstepped the boundaries of what she would allow? But he did not immediately withdraw his hand as their looks caught and held. Hers full of so many things he couldn't name. How could he make her see he accepted her? No judgment. No expectation of favors.

He waited for her to jerk away. Nail him with a sharp comment, but she only stared at him as if overwhelmed by her feelings.

She looked so sad and lost. If only he could read her thoughts and know where he fit in them. If only he could ease her distress. Without giving himself time to think about his actions, he leaned forward and kissed her.

It could barely be described as a kiss. His lips only touched hers, and then he drew back as startled as she as a hundred surprising thoughts exploded inside his head. He liked kissing her. He would do it again if she allowed.

He knew from the look on her face that she most certainly would not.

Chapter Eight

Red sprang to her feet. How dare he? After all his promises that he expected nothing in return for his help. He wasn't any different than the rest of the men she'd seen while in Thorton's care.

How foolish that she'd allowed herself to think he might be.

All his talk about family had knocked down more than one barrier around her heart and wave after wave of longing had swept over her. She'd once known the kind of life he talked about. Once, even, had dreamed of a time when she would enjoy the same sort of life with a husband and later, with children. Now her past made that impossible. Who would marry her once they learned? Not the sort of man she cared to share the rest of her life with. Most people would assume the worst once they heard she'd worked in a saloon. The cruelty Thorton had subjected her to had never defiled her in the worst way, but it had been malicious. He'd taught her to obey his wishes to avoid his beatings. If that failed, he only had to threaten to give Belle a taste of his meanness.

Ward had stolen a kiss. She scrubbed her hand across

her mouth. It wasn't the same as the kisses she'd endured at the saloon, yet it angered her to the depth of her soul…because she'd unlocked gates and allowed him to see far too deeply. And he'd misunderstood it as invitation.

She hurried to the table and gathered up the remains of their little tea party. Even that mocked her. She'd been as guilty as Belle at pretending.

Well, no more. She would accept his help only until she found something else, and she would. She had no idea how, but she would find a way to be on her own. No expectations. No dreams.

He slowly got to his feet. "Feel free to enjoy the books."

"Thank you," she murmured, keeping her back to him.

"I best be leaving." She heard his hesitation, his confusion. His footsteps went toward the door. Stopped.

She held herself so still her muscles vibrated. She would not turn. Did not want to see the look on his face. Didn't matter if it was disgust or something else.

His footsteps resumed. They did not continue to the door but came toward the table.

She forgot how to breathe. Her heart pounded a protest against her chest wall. She stiffened as he stopped so close behind her that she could feel the heat from his body. Now he would no doubt claim what she owed him. The best she could hope for was she'd be able to send Belle outside to play.

"Red?" His voice lacked the harshness she expected. "Red, I apologize. I didn't mean to kiss you. Don't know what came over me. But when I saw you crying, I wanted nothing more than to make you feel better. Somehow I thought to kiss away your troubles. I had no right. I'm sorry. You can be sure it won't happen again."

And then he hurried to the door. She didn't move until his footsteps fade away. Then she crumpled to the log stool, buried her face in her hands and gritted her teeth to keep from crying. Of course he regretted kissing her. He was a decent man. Slowly she brought emotion after emotion back into submission, then pushed to her feet and finished cleaning the kitchen as Belle showed her doll the pictures in the books Ward had lent her. Thankfully her little sister was so engrossed in the books she remained unaware of Red's state of mind.

Red allowed herself a glance at the treasure of books. She loved reading.

Her movements fueled by anger, she grabbed the pictures, intending to stuff them and the books back into the sack.

But her fingers lingered on the wedding picture of his parents. She saw Ward's likeness to his father. Saw a happy couple with dreams of a blissful future. Agony gouged at her innards. Their happy future had been shattered by death.

Seemed even normal people couldn't hope for a pleasant life.

What chance did she have?

None. None at all.

She jammed the pictures into the sack and crammed the books on top, yanked the ties closed and shoved the whole thing into the corner by the door.

Startled, Belle stared at her. "Don't you want to read?"

Her desire to read almost overwhelmed her, but she couldn't pretend she was normal and could pursue normal activities. "Not right now. Do you want to read the story to me?"

"I might not remember."

"You will with practice."

As Belle haltingly read the book, Red pushed her wayward thoughts back into order. She knew who she was…what she was. Her dreams were dead. But she had Belle and would devote her life to raising her sister.

Her emotions settled, she spent a pleasant hour helping Belle read. But despite her best efforts, her mind wandered to events of the day. And Ward's kiss. Meant to comfort, he said. Was it possible he could kiss her and not think of her as Thorton's prize? She shuddered.

Belle looked up at her. "You cold?"

"Let's go out in the sun." They slipped out back, grateful there seemed to be no one about to observe them.

Only she couldn't escape her memories outdoors, either. Seeing the log benches reminded her of sitting beside Ward. She hoped he'd return for Belle's sake to work on the doll. Only it wasn't the doll she thought of. It was the sight of his hands as he worked, the touch of his elbow on hers…

"Belle, let's go for a walk." She didn't give Belle a chance to answer before she headed up the hill. She'd go until the trees hid her.

She didn't follow the river as Ward had shown them, but veered into the woods. The trees thickened about them. Dark shadows covered the forest floor. Birds protested at their intrusion. A raven scolded loudly. But her thoughts did not have the decency to stay behind. No amount of running would outdistance them. In fact, they grew stronger in the shadows. More fearsome until she shivered with tension.

"Let's go home and make supper." Poor Belle had not protested Red's headlong flight. Perhaps she knew something had upset Red. When they started back she took Red's hand.

"We're going to be okay." Her little sister's voice was firm.

"Yes, we are." She would not pay any heed to the frisson of fear shuddering up her spine.

The feeling would not leave her even as she and Belle prepared a simple meal and ate. Thankfully Belle was content playing with her doll and reading the books. Red tried to distract herself from her fearful thoughts by working on doll clothes. But the tingle of worry would not leave her.

She would not give it recognition by trying to decide what caused it.

Later she lay in darkness with Belle asleep beside her and the wooden doll, wrapped in a square of wool, held close.

The sensation of dread, or whatever she chose to call it, hovered on every breath.

It rose with her the next morning. Even the sight of the sun flashing on the mountains did not ease it. She paused in making breakfast to study the sampler on the wall. *Whither shall I flee from Your presence?* Seemed there were two things a person couldn't run from—God and their thoughts. About all she could do was keep so busy neither could bother her. But a little cabin didn't require a lot of work and making doll clothes gave her far too much time to think.

She studied the knapsack. Would reading bring forgetfulness?

But somehow she couldn't bring herself to take out a book. They were Ward's.

"Belle, let's go outside."

They stepped outside. A couple of men rode from

the barn and headed west. Red caught her breath and stepped back to the protection of the cabin, but the men didn't even glance her way.

Red swallowed hard. She hadn't bothered to check for the presence of others before they left the cabin. Her confused emotions made her careless. She glanced up the hill to the big house, but the windows were in the shadow of the morning sun and she couldn't tell if anyone watched. The windows of the cookhouse were mirrored by the sunshine and again, she couldn't see if anyone saw her.

Belle had skipped ahead and now returned. "What's wrong?"

"Nothing."

Belle caught her worry and shrank to her side. "Did you see Thorton?" She squeaked the words.

Red forced calm into her heart. "Honey, Thorton is in jail. He'll never bother us again. Now, what would you like to do?" She took Belle's hand and marched around the cabin as if she didn't have a fear or worry in the world.

"Can I play here?" She held her doll. "I think Sally likes this place."

"Certainly."

Red settled on a log bench and watched her sister play. If she had a book to read, she would enjoy the warm sunshine as much as Belle. There were books in the cabin. Ward's books. He'd offered them to her but would he expect anything in return if she selected one to read?

"Sally and I are going for a walk." Belle marched the wooden doll around the clearing. She paused at the corner of the cabin. "Do you think Ward will come back today?"

Red made a noncommittal sound. She wondered the same thing. After her reaction to his kiss yesterday, would he take offense? Decide to let them manage on their own? After all, from the beginning she'd insisted they could. And she meant to prove it.

Belle circled back to the log. "Maybe he'll give Sally arms and legs today."

Red said he might but not to count on it. She would not admit the weight and fear she'd carried since yesterday came from wondering if he would. Insisting that's what she wanted had become hard, heavy work.

It had been a long night for Ward, worrying as he did that Red might not forgive him for stealing a kiss. He'd apologized because he understood it went beyond what Red would accept, but he didn't regret it one bit. He'd fallen asleep with a smile on his lips as he thought of her leaning forward, unconsciously needing, wanting to be kissed.

The early morning hours had dragged. It seemed his chores took longer than usual. One horse needed something for colic. The horses required a ration of oats. One of the cowboys was feverish and Ward had to fetch Linette to check on him.

Linette questioned him as they walked down the hill to the bunkhouse. "Is Red ready for visitors yet?"

"I don't know."

"Warn her I won't be delaying much longer. Besides, Grady is anxious for a playmate."

"I'll mention it." A foolish thought tugged at his brain. He liked having Red and Belle to himself. How selfish of him. And yet it warmed a cold spot behind his heart that had been there since he'd said goodbye to his family.

"If she needs anything, just let me know."

They reached the bunkhouse and Linette examined the cowboy. "He'll be okay. Lots of rest and fluids. I'll get Bertie to tend him."

Finally Ward finished his work and strode toward the cabin. He'd seen Red and Belle sneak around to the privacy at the back.

Not wanting to frighten them, he made enough noise heading after them to give plenty of warning.

Belle ran forward and held the doll toward him. "We've been playing."

He guessed she meant her and the doll. "I hope she's been good company."

Belle giggled. "She's my best friend."

He followed Red's movements as she left the log bench and pressed into the shadows of the cabin. He couldn't see her expression to measure her feelings.

He stepped toward her.

She crossed her arms across her middle as he approached.

His feet were suddenly heavy and awkward. He almost stumbled, though nothing caught his boot. She looked scared and defensive. Had he done that to her? Lord, forgive him if he had. "Hi, Red."

"Good morning."

"Thought I'd do some more work on Belle's doll."

Belle followed behind him. "Here she is. Her name is Sally and she's wondering when she can have arms."

Red's mouth opened and closed. She swallowed loudly enough for him to hear, then stared at the mountains.

Ward took the doll. "She'll have her arms as soon as I'm done giving her a proper head and body."

"Good. She needs her arms to do her school lessons."

Belle skipped away and settled on a log bench where she picked up a reader and gave it her full attention.

Red still stared into the distance, her shoulders drawn almost to her ears. Tension seemed to hold her in a vise. "Red, what's wrong? Is it about yesterday?"

She slowly brought her wide-eyed gaze to him. "Sally was my mother's name. I don't know if Belle is aware of that. She was only five when Mama died. How much does she remember?" Her voice was a thin, sharp whisper. She breathed hard and pressed her hands to her stomach as if enduring pain.

He could no more deny her the comfort he ached to give than he could erase her past. He drew her to his chest and eased her around the corner out of Belle's sight, lest the little girl see her sister's distress and be upset.

Red stiffened, refusing comfort in his arms, yet she didn't slip from his grasp as if needing what she would not allow herself. It gave Ward encouragement.

"What happened to your parents?"

She gasped in air.

Perhaps he shouldn't have asked. But he couldn't pull the words back, so he simply held her gently, giving her time to decide if she wanted to answer or not.

"There was an accident."

"They both died at the same time?" He knew what it meant to lose one parent. But two at once? His chest felt like a great weight had been dropped to it.

"Someone from a nearby mine was trucking dynamite through town. Someone explained what happened but I don't remember. I didn't care. Still don't. I went from a happy daughter to a sixteen-year-old orphan with a little sister to care for."

The air shimmered with pain and regret.

"Poor Belle. She was so young. Does she remember any of the good or just the bad?" The agony in her voice shredded Ward's heart. He must reassure her.

"Belle is a happy child and her fears seem to be disappearing rapidly. It appears to me you've protected her from being completely aware of everything going on around her. You should be proud of yourself," he said.

She sucked in air until he thought her lungs would explode. Then let it out in a windy gust, "Proud? How can I be proud? I am ashamed of who I am." She flashed brittle green eyes at him and he knew from the rigid set of her shoulders that she had said more than she intended to.

"You can hardly blame yourself for the fact Thorton tricked you."

Her glower did not weaken. "How do you know about that?"

He smiled uncertainly, wondering how she would react to his admission. "I overheard you telling Belle." She needed to hear the truth plain-spoken. "What happened to you is not who you are."

She blinked. The only sign she gave of hearing him. Then she whispered, "Who am I?"

He silently prayed for wisdom to say the right thing. "You are a good big sister. You are a responsible adult. But above and beyond that, you are loved by God."

The hardness in her eyes grew until he could have been looking at matching emeralds. She shrugged away from the weight of his arm. "I used to believe in God's love."

"He hasn't changed."

"But I have."

"God doesn't." She had to believe it. For her own peace of mind.

"A person can be cast from His presence because of their actions."

He reached for her hand, wanting to pull her back. Not just to himself but to faith in God.

She stepped away.

"Red, remember the verse my mother stitched. 'Whither shall I flee from Your presence? The darkness and light are alike to Thee.'"

"It's easy to believe when you haven't experienced the things I have."

He lifted his hands in defeat. "It's pointless to argue." All he could do was pray for her healing. "I'm going to work on Belle's doll. Why don't you come along and make some clothing?" As he suspected, she put aside her own misery to do something for Belle and retrieved her sewing kit while he settled on the log bench.

After they'd worked in companionable silence for a while, and he reasoned she'd had time for her emotions to settle, he brought up his plan. "I have a surprise." He intentionally spoke to Belle.

Her eyes lit. "What?"

"I brought a picnic lunch. Cookie packed the basket and informed me all little girls enjoy picnics." He hoped big girls did, too.

Belle bounded to her feet and jumped up and down. "I don't think I've ever been on a picnic. Have I, Red?"

Her smile was sad. "Mama and Papa took us on frequent picnics. Do you remember a place by the river where the trees grew together at the top so it was a leafy, green room? That was one of their favorite places."

Belle stared at her sister. "Were there wild roses? With prickles?"

"Lots of them. In June it smelled so good."

Belle looked at a fingertip. "I remember getting a

prickle in my finger because I wanted a pretty flower. Papa picked it for me and kissed my finger. He said a kiss was the best medicine."

Moving slowly for fear of startling her, Ward shifted his gaze to Red. She stared at Belle but he saw emotions play across her face. Felt her sadness like someone had lassoed his heart with a tight rope and jerked him facedown in the dirt.

"He used to say that." Her words squeaked from a tight throat. She turned. Her gaze connected with Ward's. Silently daring him to pity them.

He smiled past his pain at what this pair had endured. He wanted her to know he cared how she felt. If a kiss would make it better, he would give her one, or as many as she needed, but somehow he understood—he knew not how—it would take more than a kiss, more than a thousand kisses to fix her pain.

"Then I really, really like picnics," Belle informed them. "Where are we going?"

Ward eased his gaze from Red's. "I think I know a real good spot."

Belle looked skyward. "Is it time for lunch?"

Ward studied the position of the sun. "I think I might have time to carve a leg for Miss Sally first." He could tell Belle struggled with wanting two things at the same time.

"I might be able to finish this dress," Red said, her voice almost normal.

Ward knew she would deny everything he'd just seen—her pain and, beneath it, her hope. He was content to let her take her time in dealing with her past but he prayed God would heal her heart.

They worked steadily for an hour or so but Belle grew more and more restless until finally Ward closed his knife. "I guess poor Sally will have to wait until tomorrow for her other leg." He handed the doll to Belle. "You think it's time to go on our picnic?"

She nodded, mute with excitement.

He turned to Red. "What do you think? Is it time?"

She slowly slid her considering gaze from Ward to Belle and grinned at the little girl's excitement. "I think it must be." She turned back to Ward and her smile faltered only slightly before she ducked her head and gave her full attention to gathering together her sewing materials. She tied off a knot of thread and held up a little yellow-print dress. "It's finished."

Belle squealed. "Oh, thank you, thank you. Sally is going to wear a dress to her first picnic." She hung the dress on her wooden doll. It almost looked like a real doll, though Belle's imagination made it into far more. To her it was real and alive, her best friend. "Aren't you excited, Sally?"

Ward picked up the basket he'd left at the front of the cabin. He led the way, first toward the river. He stopped several times to point out things to them—the tracks of a deer, the tree that had been cut down by a beaver, the sound of water rippling over the rocks.

Red's expression grew more peaceful with every yard they covered. He understood it was difficult to harbor anxiety in the beautiful surroundings. They followed the river around a bend and walked through rustling reeds. He could see his destination and turned aside to an almost invisible pathway. A few more steps led them to a room-sized clearing with fallen trees providing natural seating. The trunks of the trees and the overhead branches formed a secluded room.

He led them to the center. "This is where we are having our picnic. It's like our own outdoor room."

Belle sighed in pleasure. "A picnic room."

Red looked upward to the waving roof of branches, lowered her gaze to the wild roses. Slowly, she turned full circle. "It's very nice." Her husky voice revealed far more than her words. And the look she favored him with caught him by surprise. "It's a lot like the place Mama and Papa would go. Thank you."

He nodded, his throat too tight to speak. He'd wanted to please her, make her remember better times, but he hadn't expected gratitude. He put the basket down and tried to sort out his thoughts. What else would they do on a picnic? He and Travers had always played tag or hide-and-seek. Was that appropriate for girls? Only one way to find out. "Who wants to play a game?"

"Me. Me." Belle jumped up and down. "What game?"

"You have any favorites?"

She looked confused and he realized she'd been allowed few childhood games the past year or two. "Do I, Red?"

Red's smile faltered only a bit. "You used to like playing chase." The mischievous look she gave Ward tipped his heart sideways. "You would chase Papa round and round until you caught him, and then he had to chase you until he caught you."

Belle eyed Ward with a begging look. "Will you play chase with me?"

"It sounds like a lot of work. And what does Red do?"

She plunked down on a fallen tree. "I watch."

"Uh-huh." How had he gotten roped into this? But he couldn't deny Belle. Any more than he could disappoint Red. Despite her teasing indifference, he knew she ached for Belle to enjoy happy times and happy memories. "Okay. I'll play."

Belle ran away with a scream of delight. "You have to catch me."

How hard could it be for a grown man to catch an eight-year-old girl? He soon found out it was more difficult than he could have imagined. She could slip through tiny openings and duck under overhanging branches that slapped him in the forehead and tossed his hat to the ground. Red chuckled. "Better leave your hat here."

He scrambled over the undergrowth and dropped the hat beside her. She looked up, as innocent as could be except for the flashing amusement in her eyes.

"Why do I get the feeling you are enjoying this more than you should?"

She widened her eyes. "It's good to see Belle having fun."

"Uh-huh." He studied her with narrowed eyes but she kept her expression blank. He turned away. "Funny that it's me chasing through the trees scratching my face." He made a show of rubbing a spot where a branch had attacked him.

Just before he stepped out of the clearing, she giggled. "Yup. It's funny."

He grinned as he trotted after Belle. He didn't mind a bit being laughed at. In fact, it felt downright good. He finally managed to catch Belle and swing her off her feet to a good deal of squealing. Then he had to let her chase him. She seemed tireless but he soon hollered, "Uncle. I give up. Let's eat."

Belle grabbed his hand and marched back to the clearing.

Ward grinned. It felt good to have the little girl's trust. As soon as Red saw them, her mouth pinched into a frown.

Ward sighed. It was going to be a good sight harder to earn Red's trust.

He could only hope and pray that one day he would. Why did it matter so much? Well, because of his pride. He was a good man, and they ought to know it. But it went deeper. Back to his own family. If he could help this pair find what he'd failed to give his own family, somehow that would help ease his conscience.

If only Red would accept his help as it was given— freely and generously. He wanted nothing more from her. Not favors as she hinted. And not her heart.

Chapter Nine

Red understood Ward was doing his best to bring back good memories for Belle. Just as he made no secret of his desire to help her remember better times. On one hand she appreciated it. On the other, she wondered why it mattered to him. More important, how would Belle feel when they moved on?

If not for disappointing Belle, who could not remember going on a picnic, she would have gathered up her skirt and marched away. Instead, she allowed Ward to pass her a thick sandwich full of savory beef, seasoned with sharp mustard sauce. She tried valiantly to maintain a sense of annoyance but the peace of her surroundings, the enjoyment of good food and her pleasure at watching Belle play defeated her attempt.

Accepting the inevitable, she leaned back and looked up at the bright sky laced with the branches of evergreen trees. There was a time such a sight would have filled her with sweet thoughts of God's love.

She jerked her attention from the sky to the fallen trees. One of them formed a sidewalk for Belle's doll, Sally. Would she ever hear the name, or be able to say it without a thousand regrets and a world of longing catching at her heart?

Ward looked into the picnic basket. "Looks like that cake was the last of it. I hope you both got enough to eat."

Belle glanced up from her play long enough to tell him her opinion. "I did. It sure was good."

"I'll be sure to tell Cookie. She'll be pleased." He turned to Red.

"It was very good," Red allowed. "And I'm plenty full. Give my thanks to Cookie." She wondered at the way his eyes flickered as if remembering something.

"Why don't you tell her yourself?"

She didn't care that her expression likely revealed her surprise and a whole lot more. Did he expect her to walk over and tell Cookie? "You aren't bringing her to visit, are you?"

"Tomorrow is Sunday, and Cookie and Bertie have a little church service in the cookhouse. I thought you might like to go. Then you could thank her yourself."

"It's impossible." How dare he even suggest it?

Belle left her doll stranded on the fallen tree and rushed to Ward's knees. "Would Grady be there?"

Ward's probing gaze left Red just long enough for him to cup Belle's head and smile at her. "He's there every Sunday. He used to be the only child." He made it sound like Red was responsible for the child's loneliness.

She stiffened her spine, preparing to defend herself.

But before she could voice her protests, he turned to her, his gaze intense, demanding, even challenging. As if he silently dared her to face the crew at the ranch. And maybe even God.

Her own gaze hardened as she pressed her lips into

a tight line. Before she could reiterate her refusal, Belle stood before her. "Red, I never had a friend. Not since I was real young. I kind of remember the kids next door. There was a big boy who would give me a push on the swing and another boy about my age. He had a pretend farm under the tree. They had a baby, too. Sometimes I got to hold her. But that was when I was little. Maybe Grady would like to be my friend." She swayed back and forth as she talked.

Red sighed. Belle had already turned Grady into her best friend. And she knew to refuse Ward's invitation would rob her little sister of the chance to meet a child and enjoy a playmate.

From the way Ward grinned, she guessed he knew it, too.

The look she gave him should have erased all amusement, but he only grinned wider.

"Say yes. Please, Red. Pleeeeease." Belle pleaded with her eyes as much as her words.

Red studied her eager sister. She didn't want to face the residents of the ranch. They knew who and what she was. She could well imagine the speculative glances the men would give her. And the censure…

But what about Linette and Cookie? They'd shown friendship.

Their kindness only deepened her guilt and regret. She wasn't sure she could accept any of this.

She especially had no interest in attending a church service.

However, it might afford her a chance to ask Linette if she knew of any jobs a girl like Red could obtain. She clenched down on her back teeth, not wanting to think of the sort of position people might think she was qualified to fill. Finally she nodded. "Fine. We'll go."

Belle squealed and spun in a circle, then raced back to share the news with her doll.

Red would not look at Ward. She couldn't bear to see him gloat.

"I'll take you over in the morning." His voice was gentle, almost soothing. "Red, you won't regret it." He made it sound so simple.

She regretted it already, but having something to gain allowed her to overlook her misgivings. She shivered, but not from cold. "It's time to go back to the cabin."

Ward knew as well as she there was little cause for hurry.

Her promise to go to the service provided her an excuse. "If we're going to church, I need to make sure our outfits are ready. And I'll need to see to baths." She'd already planned the latter even without church attendance. "Come on, Belle."

Her sister walked her doll the length of the log and fell in step behind Ward.

Back at the cabin, he didn't immediately leave despite Red's barely contained hints.

"I'll get a tub for you." He ducked into the wood shed and emerged with a big square washtub. He carried it to the cabin and parked it in front of the stove.

Still he did not leave. Instead, he plunked two big pots on the stove. "I'll carry in some water." He filled both pots and the bucket.

"Thank you." Would he ever leave so she could wallow in her regrets?

He stood at the door, turning his hat round and round as if measuring the brim.

Seems he didn't intend to leave.

"We can manage the rest." She nodded toward the tub.

Dull red colored his cheeks. "That was unnecessary."

She didn't relent.

"Red, stop forming everyone's judgment for them. People aren't nearly as harsh as you make them out to be."

"Is this a warning about tomorrow? You telling me how to conduct myself?"

He sighed. "That is not my intention at all." He crossed the floor to plant his face inches from hers. "What I'm saying is that you should give people a chance rather than slap them alongside the head with comments like the one you just sent my way."

She tried to hold his demanding stare without blinking. But her eyes watered from the strain and she ducked her head. Was she really too defensive?

He made a noise of exasperation and headed for the door. "All I'm saying is let people decide what they want about you. Stop saying things that blatantly tell them they shouldn't like you." He strode from the door.

She waited until the sound of his footsteps faded, then sank into a chair. Did she do what he said? By her comments and attitude inform people how they should view her?

How could she help it? It was how she judged herself.

Determined to ignore her confusion, she searched through the items of clothing Linette had sent. "I need to thank Mrs. Gardiner for lending us these clothes." Besides the clothing, Linette had sent a brush and comb, hair ribbons and a bar of sweet-smelling soap.

Belle looked up from her play. "Are you going to buy us new things?"

"As soon as I can."

"When will that be?"

Red set aside the soap she'd been sniffing. "I'm going to find a job and we'll have a place of our own."

Belle glanced about. "This is a nice place. Maybe we could stay here."

"No, we can't."

Belle's face wrinkled in confusion and worry.

How could Red make her see the dangers of being so dependent on others? Never again would she allow either of them to be in their situation. Not one minute longer than absolutely necessary. "Belle, I want to take care of us."

"You're afraid everyone is like Thorton." Belle shivered. "Sometimes I think they are and then I look at Sally." She held up her doll. "Ward can't be bad like Thorton."

Red sat back. She couldn't rob Belle of her assurance. "You might be right." She returned to the stack of clothing. For herself, she selected a simple gray dress with white collar and cuffs. With a few tucks here and there, it would fit well enough. For Belle she selected a pretty blue dress. At the rate Belle was growing, these things would soon be too small.

The reality of a child's needs fueled Red's determination. She must find a position soon in order to provide for the both of them.

Later that night, she and Belle were bathed and in clean nightgowns. Belle crawled into bed to play with her doll but Red wasn't a bit tired. She'd already disposed of the water, cleaned the tiny kitchen, swept the floor and even dusted the shelves. She'd worked on outfits for the doll until her neck protested and she'd set the sewing aside. How was she to spend her time? She eyed the knapsack. A book held a lot of appeal.

She knelt before the bag and ran her fingers along the seams. She gingerly loosened the tie and inhaled the scent of mothballs and old wool.

The little quilt lay on top. She lifted it to her face and sniffed. But all she smelled was mothballs. No baby scent. Nothing remotely like the woodsy, leather scent of Ward.

What had she expected?

Her movements jerky, she started to set the quilt to one side, then changed her mind and pulled it to her chest. His mother had made this for him. Ward had experienced a painful family situation and still seemed to know how to be happy.

He'd always been able to choose. He'd been in charge.

She dropped the quilt to the floor. From now on she would be in control of her life.

She turned back to the sack. The first book that came into view was the book of poetry. Her breath stalled halfway up her throat as her mind filled with images of her father reading poetry. It was a regular nighttime habit and had been the background to her evening activities. As she sewed, did schoolwork, knitted doll clothes or played, and later as she entertained Belle, Papa's voice had spoken words of music and imagination. Keats and his "A Thing of Beauty Is a Joy Forever."

Where had the beauty and joy of her life gone?

Probably his favorite was Elizabeth Barrett Browning's poem, "How Do I Love Thee? Let Me Count the Ways." Papa didn't need the book to recite it. He knew it by heart and would say the words to Mama with such feeling she blushed.

Red sat on the floor with her back to the wall, the books forgotten as she wept silently for the parents she'd lost, the life that had been snatched from her and the bleakness of her future. She felt as if she were rudderless, homeless, hopeless. *Oh, God.* But she could not pray, ask relief from a God who'd abandoned her and who would now see her as dirty and shameful.

Her tears dried. She remained on the floor, staring at the darkness beyond the lamplight. Darkness that engulfed her soul. The lamp flickered and she shook her head. She realized that her leg ached where her wound still healed. How long had she sat there? What difference did it make? She turned the lamp down and crawled into bed, trying not to disturb Belle.

The next morning she woke aching from head to toe and regretting her agreement to attend church. With heavy limbs and a heavier heart, she made breakfast and endured Belle's excitement over the outing.

Finally Belle slowed down. "Red, why are you so sad?"

Red tried to dredge up a smile to convince her sister she wasn't. She failed miserably and her lips trembled. She swallowed hard and widened her eyes, determined she would not cry in front of her little sister.

Belle hurried around the table and threw her arms around Red. "If you don't want to go, it's okay. I don't mind staying home."

Red hugged Belle. She knew how much Belle wanted to go. And she deserved to. It was time life became more ordinary for her little sister. "No, we'll go."

Belle tipped her face upward and studied Red. "Is it because you don't like Ward?"

"I—" She faltered. She liked Ward just fine. But there was no future in it. She closed her eyes and willed in strength. "There are times I miss Mama and Papa so much I can hardly bear it."

Belle crawled into Red's lap and cuddled close. "We have each other."

Red laughed despite her tears. She'd told Belle that

was all that mattered so often yet she wondered if either of them believed it. Today it was especially hard to cling to the idea, but she must. It had to be enough. "You're right. Now let's get ready."

A few minutes later they were dressed. She'd pinned her hair back into as tight a bun as she could fashion and hoped it would stay in place. She did not have a bonnet of any sort but, unable to face the shame of appearing bareheaded at a church service, she had fashioned a bit of lace into a covering and hoped it would suffice.

Belle looked sweet and innocent in her dress with her hair curled into ringlets. Thank goodness she had been spared the bright color of Red's hair.

She peeked out the window and watched cowboys file in. Even though no one glanced in her direction, she ducked back out of sight and pressed a palm to her chest as if by doing so she could control the pounding of her heart.

Belle took her place at the window. "I see a little boy up on the hill. It must be Grady."

If not for Belle's eagerness, Red would change her mind about attending.

"Here comes Ward." Belle dashed to the door, pulled it open, and he stepped inside.

"My, don't you two look nice?"

Belle pirouetted. Then grinned at Ward. "So do you."

Indeed he did. Red couldn't help but stare. He wore a crisp white shirt, black jacket and black trousers. His hat was a new brown Stetson. It appeared he had shaved only a few minutes ago. His blue eyes shone like sky reflected in water as he smiled at Red.

If she let it happen, she could momentarily forget her guilt and pain.

She fought a mental battle. If only she could pretend

her past hadn't happened but even if she could, others would be eager to remind her.

When Ward offered his arm to guide her across the yard, she hesitated. Touching him only deepened the chasm between who she was and what she wanted. She shifted her gaze past him to the distance between the cabin and the cookhouse. Without something to keep her headed in the right direction, she'd never make it.

She rested her hand on his arm.

And gave him a ferocious warning look.

Ward had prayed long into the night for Red to forget her past and accept the future that lay before her. But from her deep scowl he knew she hadn't yet reached that place. Maybe today would bring a change. He hoped so.

They approached the cookhouse as a Roper, Cassie and their four children stepped inside.

"I don't—" Red started to protest.

Ward pressed his hand to hers, anchoring her to his side. "Settle down. You'll find a warm welcome here. In fact, I better warn you that Cookie has a big embrace."

If he hoped to drive the fear from Red's eyes, he failed. She didn't move. Seemed incapable of it as she stared straight ahead, her expression wooden. "Take a deep breath."

She continued to look toward the cookhouse.

Slim came up behind them. "Morning."

"Morning, Slim," Ward said. Although he sensed Red's anxiety, he couldn't ignore how Slim stood holding his hat and waiting. "Red." He touched her arm to bring her attention back from chasing after her fears. "This is Slim Hawkins. Slim, Red Henderson." He wished he had another name to give, but it was the only one she admitted to.

Red nodded but did not offer her hand. In fact, she shrank back as if afraid Slim might want to touch her.

"Her sister, Belle."

"Nice meeting you, ma'am and Miss Belle." Slim adjusted his hat back on his head. "I'll head inside." He continued to the cookhouse.

While Belle bounced impatiently, Red appeared frozen. Had he made a mistake urging her to attend? But he couldn't believe he had. After all, she couldn't hide forever. Sooner or later, life had to be lived. "Come along." He ushered them toward the door. Getting Belle to move required no effort, but he gently touched Red's elbow to get her attention.

She turned toward him, her eyes stark in a face grown too pale.

"Red, are you okay?"

His words and worry seemed to be just the thing she needed. She blinked. Determination replaced the fear he knew he'd seen.

"I'm fine."

"Not only don't I believe you, I am getting to hate that word. *Fine.* Every time you say it, you mean quite the opposite."

Her look was meant to scald him. "Don't ask if you don't want the answer."

His annoyance fled as quickly as it had come and he chuckled. "I might believe you're fine now because you're feisty."

She adjusted her skirt and murmured, "I am not feisty."

Not freeing her even when she tried to escape his touch, he led her to the door. He paused before he opened the door. "Remember what I said. Cookie is enthusiastic."

Then he stepped inside, Belle at one side, Red at the other. Several of the men sat at the table.

Cassie sat beside Roper, their four children on either side. She saw them and smiled, but waited for Ward to bring Red and Belle forward.

Bertie and Cookie glanced up and noticed he had visitors with him.

"You're Red." Cookie steamed toward them. Belle ducked behind Ward, and Red edged closer to his side. "And this little one must be Belle. So glad to finally meet you." She reached them and, paying no heed to Ward's presence, grabbed Red in a bear hug.

He'd wondered if Cookie would overwhelm Red, who fought so hard to remain untouchable. He would step in and rescue her if he thought she needed it.

She looked fearful and stiff in Cookie's arms, and then she closed her eyes and he could almost believe she sighed. As if finding something in Cookie's embrace she'd ached after for a long time.

And then Cookie released her. Red stepped back, keeping distance between herself, the bigger woman and Ward. Ward wanted to close the distance, grasp her elbow, but Cookie demanded his attention.

"And where is that little gal? Hiding behind you, I think." Cookie nudged him aside and grinned down at Belle. "I heard you like my cinnamon rolls. Guess what I made for afternoon tea, just for you."

"Cinnamon rolls?" Belle sounded intrigued.

"You guessed it. Now how about a hug?" To Cookie's credit, she let Belle take her time about deciding.

"You won't squeeze me to death?"

Cookie hooted. "Ain't never done so yet. Never hear any complaints, either."

Ward, Slim and Bertie all laughed derisively.

"Pay them no attention." Cookie held out her arms and Belle went into them, getting the gentlest hug Ward had ever seen Cookie give. She released Belle. "Didn't hurt a bit, did it?"

"It was kind of nice."

His nose tingled and Ward didn't dare look at Red for fear of seeing a matching emotion in her eyes that would make him reveal a weakness he didn't care to admit. Men didn't cry over little girls being hugged.

Cookie waved for Bertie to join her. "This here is Bertie, my husband and a fine man, if I do say so myself."

"So pleased to have you join us. Why don't you find a place and make yourself comfortable? As soon as everyone is here, Ward can make the introductions."

Ward headed toward the benches beside the tables. Red caught his sleeve. Surprised at her touch, he turned, saw again the fear that made her eyes too wide. He moved closer to her side and whispered, "What's wrong? And don't even bother with 'I'm fine.'"

She narrowed her gaze. "I just want to ask if we can sit at the back."

He studied her as she allowed him the faintest glimpse of truth in her. She didn't want to sit where she would be more visible than necessary. But she'd trusted him enough to ask. The knowledge dove straight to his heart and made him feel good all over. "Of course." He led them to the back corner and sat between Red and the rest of the room. Belle cuddled close to Red but perhaps as much because she sensed her sister's feelings as anything, as her gaze darted eagerly about the room and she smiled widely at Cookie. Belle appeared to be ready to enjoy the day.

The door opened and Eddie and Linette entered with Grady at their heels.

Belle sat up straight and drew in a quick breath.

Linette and Eddie hurried to them. Linette spoke first. "It's so good to see you again, Red. Are you quite recovered from your wound?"

Ward wanted to smack himself on the forehead. He'd plumb forgot her injury. And she certainly never mentioned it.

"I'm fine. Thank you."

"You're certain? No sign of infection?"

"It's almost better."

"No recurring headaches?"

Red slanted a glance to Ward as if informing him he was her only headache. He almost choked with amusement and knew his eyes brimmed with his silent laugh.

"I'm fine. I never thanked you for caring for me. Thank you. And thank you for the lend of the clothes."

Linette squeezed Red's hands. "Why, it was my pleasure and the clothes are yours to keep."

Red faced Eddie. "I apologize for borrowing your horse without permission."

Ward swallowed hard to contain a burst of laughter. Borrowed without permission, was it? Seemed like another term for stealing.

"In the future, remember you have only to ask if you need something."

"Yes, sir. I appreciate your kindness."

Ward's amusement faded. Why did she sound so sweet and grateful for them, but acted like Ward was an intrusion when all he wanted was to help?

Linette and Eddie greeted Belle, and then introduced Grady.

He hung back.

"He's a little shy but he'll soon get over it," Linette assured Belle when she saw her disappointment at Grady's lack of response.

"Did you see my dolly?" Belle held it out for Grady's inspection. "It's not finished yet. Ward is carving her another leg and some arms. Did he carve you something?"

Grady nodded.

"Can I see it?"

Linette smiled. "Grady, would you like to show her your animals after church?"

Grady nodded.

"Then it's settled. You'll join us for dinner."

Red opened her mouth. Ward saw a refusal coming and forestalled it by turning to the others. "Everyone, this is Red Henderson and her sister, Belle." He went around the gathering. "Roper, the foreman, and his wife, Cassie. Their children. Daisy, thirteen, Neil, twelve, Billy, who is six, and little Pansy."

"I'se two." The blue-eyed, golden-haired girl held up two fingers.

Roper and Cassie and the three older children all smiled at the little one.

Ward had told Red about how Cassie had come West with Linette and decided to start her own business in Edendale feeding travelers and providing the store with bread and biscuits. Laughing, he'd explained how Roper had found the four orphaned children needing a home and struck a deal with Cassie to help her establish her business in exchange for help caring for the children.

"Now they're married and the children have a permanent home."

Red tried to hide the tears that came to her eyes, but he'd seen.

"Sometimes life has a happy ending." He wanted her to believe in it.

"I've seen the children out playing. I'm glad things worked out for them."

He knew by the hard overtone in her words that she didn't expect the same for herself.

Realizing he'd been sidetracked from his intention to introduce Red to everyone, he turned back to the cowboys and introduced them. There was Slim, Blue and Cal, who were regulars at the ranch, and also a half a dozen other cowboys who would work for the season, then move on. Each one greeted Red and Belle kindly, though he saw a knowing gleam in young Stone. He'd be speaking to the man in private about respecting Red.

Bertie cleared his throat to signal they should all be seated. He waited as they sorted themselves out, then asked them to bow their heads while he prayed. Bertie was simple in his approach to God, but sincere. He'd never come right out and told about his past other than to compare himself to the prodigal son. Following his "amen," Cookie led them in some hymns, her enthusiasm making up for any lack in musical ability.

Ward was used to the plain service but wondered how Red would react.

She sat facing straight ahead, not joining in the singing. Not giving any indication she was even aware of her surroundings. Perhaps she remembered earlier times. Better times. From the things she said, Ward knew she'd been raised in a Christian family.

Which might serve to intensify her guilt over the life she'd been forced to live.

Cookie sat down and Bertie took the floor again. He welcomed Red and Belle and the others. Then he opened his well-worn Bible. It was obvious from the way he handled it that he loved God's word.

"Today, I feel led to talk about the passage in Matthew, chapter eighteen, that tells the story of a man who had a hundred sheep but one was missing. He searched high and low until he found that one sheep and brought it safely back to the fold. He was happier about that one lost sheep than the ninety and nine who were safe and sound. That's how valued each of us is to God."

They were words that reiterated Ward's thoughts. He didn't look at Red, but under the cover of the table he reached over and squeezed her hands, not surprised to discover them clenched tightly in her lap. She didn't give any indication that she was aware of his action, but he reasoned she had to be and chose to allow it. He could only hope and pray she felt the tug of God's love in the search for one lost sheep.

Bertie finished with a reminder that God saw all his little sheep with the same love.

One of the men spoke up. "I heard a song about that. I'd be pleased to sing it, if you'd like."

Bertie waved the man up. "By all means."

The man cleared his throat and began to sing. He had a wonderfully strong voice that carried Ward into the beauty of the song.

"There were ninety and nine that safely lay in the shelter of the fold. But one was out on the hills away..."

By the time the song finished, the room was still and silent except for a sniff from Cookie. Linette dabbed at her eyes with a hanky. Ward didn't dare look about for fear others would see the tears stinging his eyes. Maybe the others felt the same.

Bertie went to the man's side. "That was wonderful. Just wonderful. Thank you so much."

Cookie rose and plowed toward the man and patted his back vigorously enough to cause him to cough. "I'll never forget that song. If you're around for a bit, be sure to favor us with another solo."

The man hurried to his seat.

Finally, Ward allowed himself to look at Red expecting to see a glisten of tears. She faced him, her eyes glittering. But not with tears.

With a fearsome look of disbelief.

He opened his mouth to protest. Had she not heard the words from Bertie's mouth? The song sung by the visitor? The words of God Himself in the scripture?

How could she not believe?

At the look in her eyes he closed his mouth. Now was not the time or place to ask his questions. But he would demand answers at the first opportunity.

Chapter Ten

Only by blocking the words from her mind could Red sit through the service. Yes, the man in the story had gone looking for his one lost sheep. Because it was innocent and pure. Not likely would he have gone looking for a wolf. Or a pig. She knew by Ward's behavior he thought she should see herself as the lost sheep. If it made him feel better to see her as an innocent lamb, well, let him have his pretense.

The man singing the solo had a lovely voice. But she sighed with relief when he finished and sat down.

Now everyone could say goodbye and leave. Except she'd been railroaded into having dinner with Linette and Eddie. Perhaps she could say she had a headache and needed to rest. Linette would doubtless be sympathetic, thinking her recent injury bothered her. It wouldn't be a complete fabrication. She'd clenched her jaw so tight throughout the service that it hurt to the top of her head.

Cookie clapped her hands. "Tea and coffee will be ready in a few minutes. Everyone make yourselves at home." She winked at Belle. "There'll be cinnamon rolls and other goodies, too."

Belle jumped to her feet. "Can I go talk to Grady?"

Red pulled herself away from her thoughts. "Give him time to get used to you." But before Belle got two steps away, Linette and Eddie, with Grady between them, made their way toward Red and sat across the table from them.

Grady shyly went toward Belle and within moments they moved away to play. Leaving Red with no one to cling to. Though she realized the irony of a big sister, who was supposed to be taking care of her younger sister, seeking protection from her.

Her dread knew no bounds. Now Linette and Eddie would quiz her on her family and desire other details about who she was and from whence she'd come. How much had Ward told them? No doubt he'd said he'd rescued her from a saloon. She stiffened her spine and prepared herself for the inquisition.

However, they didn't ask a single question. Instead they talked about the little things Grady had done that pleased them. "He's learning his numbers and letters," Linette said. "I do my best to teach him, but what we really need is a teacher. And a real church." They gave Red the details of their plans for a church in Edendale.

Linette leaned forward. "Forgive us. I'm sure you're not interested in all this talk. Now that you're feeling better—"

It took Red a moment to realize Linette referred to her injured leg and head.

"You can come for tea."

Wonderful how these people were so determined to take care of her, include her, even though she didn't need it and certainly didn't welcome it.

Linette waved Cassie over. Once the other woman joined them, Linette sighed expansively. "The three of us should get together for a nice visit. The children would enjoy it."

Red watched Belle showing her doll to Daisy and Pansy. Then she turned to Grady and said something that brought a smile to the boy's mouth. Yes, Belle appeared ready to form friendships.

Red wanted only to run back to the cabin and pull the door closed.

Linette continued speaking. "Perhaps we could join forces in teaching the children."

Cassie nodded. "I'd like that."

Red rocked her head back and forth.

"You don't approve of the idea?" Linette said.

Ward had moved away to talk to Eddie. She suddenly wished he was at her side and would intervene. Though what could he say? That a saloon girl shouldn't be allowed to associate with innocent children? Where did that leave Belle? More innocent and undamaged than many people would believe. And not nearly as guarded around others as Red.

But Red was no longer an innocent child. She'd seen the seedy side of life. She'd experienced far too much. Like the day Thorton had convinced everyone he was taking Red and Belle to his sister. Instead he'd taken her to a small house, saying they had to rest for the journey. In the middle of the night, he'd jerked her from her sleep and dragged her from her bed where she'd slept next to Belle. Her concern for Belle had made her choke back her screams,though she fought like a tiger.

"You're mine," he'd said. "You little redhead."

She'd never hated her red hair more than at that moment, and she'd glowered at him, tried to scratch his face.

"Now it's time you learned to obey me." He'd taken

his belt and laid it across her back. Again and again. She tried to fight him off, but he'd grown more violent until she'd finally sunk to the ground in outward defeat, overcome by pain. Inwardly, she'd seethed and vowed she would never be his slave.

Except she was.

Over the months, he'd used the belt time and again if she exhibited any independence. And sometimes out of sheer meanness. She would have fought him tooth and nail, but all he had to do was threaten to do the same to Belle and she would dance, indecently clad, for any man. Anything to protect her little sister.

She pushed the past to the farthest corner of her brain and refused to acknowledge it. But the dirt and degradation would never go away. Even if no one else knew, she could not associate with innocent children.

Thankfully, her troubled thoughts were interrupted as Cookie and Bertie handed out mugs, poured tea and coffee and served a variety of tasty baked goods. Conversation turned to general things such as the beautiful summer weather.

She focused on enjoying tea and cake.

Belle sat beside Grady and kept up a steady one-sided conversation. Even though Grady's shyness kept him quiet, Red suspected he'd have trouble getting in a comment even if he wanted to. His eyes flashed with interest and he seemed enthralled by Belle's attention. Pansy sat on Belle's other side, equally taken with Belle's chatter. Billy tried to pretend disinterest but didn't get far from the conversation, though it would more correctly be called a monologue. Red smiled at Belle's eagerness.

Neil hung about the men, interested in what they had to say.

Daisy, she noticed, never got far from Cassie.

Red rose. "We should be going back."

"Oh, no," Linette said. "Have you forgotten you promised to come for dinner?"

Red hadn't forgotten but hoped Linette had.

Linette continued. "It will allow the children to play together longer." She turned to Cassie. "You and Roper and the children are invited, too, of course."

Cassie shook her head. "Thank you, but I think we better get Pansy home for a nap." She spoke to the other children. "If you want to play with Grady and Belle until mealtime, you may."

But the three elected to leave with Cassie and Roper.

Linette watched them depart. "I don't think the children are ready to be parted from their new parents yet. Ah, well. In time they'll grow secure." She gave her attention back to Red, which made Red want to twitch. "Bring Belle to the house so Grady can show her his things. You're welcome, too, Ward."

Trapped. Unable to say no without appearing rude and denying two children the pleasure of a playmate, Red murmured thanks and followed Linette and Eddie up the hill. Ward tagged along at her side. Her thoughts churned. This would provide an opportunity to speak to Linette. She must ask about a possible position.

A little later as the children played, the four adults sat in the room overlooking the ranch buildings with the mountains rising in the background. On the walls hung spectacular paintings.

"These are beautiful." Red rose and circled the room, admiring the pictures of the mountains, the ranch, bright flowers and serene wooded scenes.

Eddie came to her side. "Linette's handiwork." No doubting his pride at his wife's accomplishments.

Linette joined them.

Red smiled at her. "You're very talented."

Linette thanked her. "Would you like to see the rest of the house?"

"I'd love to. Especially if there is more of your artwork on display." And especially if it would get her away from Ward, hovering at her side as if he feared she couldn't manage without his help.

Linette laughed merrily. "When I look out my window and see such lovely views, it's hard to stop drawing or painting." She led the way through the house. "It is fashioned after Eddie's family estate back in England. Of course he and his father expected it would be used for fancy entertaining, but they didn't take me into account. When Eddie and I fell in love I made it clear I would use the extra rooms to help others."

"Like me?"

"You and others. Whoever the Lord brings to my door, I will welcome. No judgment, no turning my back on people regardless of race or position in society. At first, his father balked at the idea but soon realized things are different in the New World. People are judged differently…by who they are, not where they've come from."

Red didn't say anything, wondering if Linette spoke of her background and if she meant the words for Red or spoke generically.

They stepped into Grady's room. A pencil sketch of him hung over his bed. "Oh, it's sweet." She'd love to have a similar drawing of Belle but didn't dare ask.

"I sent a smaller version to Grady's father in the hopes it would melt his heart toward his son."

"What do you mean?"

Linette told of meeting Grady's mother on a ship

crossing the Atlantic and how, when she lay dying, the woman begged her to take Grady to his father in Montreal. Linette readily agreed. "But he took one look at Grady and said he had no use for a little boy. He signed over guardianship to me. But I am determined to see them reunited."

Red had heard a condensed version of the story from Ward but hearing it from Linette gave it power and emotion that seemed to thicken the blood in her veins.

Linette's expression grew fierce. "Every child needs and deserves approval and acceptance from their father."

The words churned through Red like a sudden storm. She'd once known her father's approval. She closed her eyes, not allowing herself to think how disappointed he would be with her now.

"Well, never mind. I know God will answer in His time and His way. In the meantime, Grady is loved here. In fact, I almost fear having my prayers being answered. I would miss him terribly. It's a good thing there will be another child in the New Year." She fairly glowed as she patted her stomach.

Red had guessed she was in the family way and congratulated her. They moved on to tour the kitchen. Soon they would rejoin the men.

"Linette, maybe you can help me."

"If I can, I most certainly shall."

"I need a position or job of some sort so I can provide for Belle and myself. Would you know of anything? Perhaps you have a friend that needs a maid. Or someone who needs a housekeeper."

Linette brushed her hands along Red's arm. "You're welcome to stay here."

"I need to establish a life for Belle and myself."

Linette considered Red's request a moment, then shook her head. "I wish I knew of something. I'll ask around." She lifted a finger. "But you might send an advertisement to the *Macleod Gazette* offering your services as a maid or housekeeper or whatever you've a mind to do."

"I'll do that. Do you have an address?"

"Better than that. I have some old copies of the paper. You might even find something in one that is what you desire." She gathered a handful of papers from a shelf in Eddie's office. "Here you go."

"You're sure Eddie won't mind?"

"He's done with them. We always pass them on to whoever comes by. This time it's you."

Red took them. "Thank you." She hesitated. Hated to ask for anything more, but she couldn't write a letter without paper. "Would you mind lending me paper and an envelope?" There was pen and ink at the cabin.

Linette pulled open a drawer and removed an envelope, affixed a stamp and handed it over along with several sheets of paper. "Consider it a gift. My contribution to your future. And I will certainly pray for you."

Red nodded. "Thank you." Too bad someone hadn't prayed months ago. Or offered to help. But with the possibility of finding a job filling her mind, she didn't dwell on what might have been.

Later, as Ward escorted them back to the cabin, he commented on the newspapers. "Trying to catch up on the news?"

"It's a start." Not wanting to get into an argument about whether or not he could take care of her, she did not tell him the real reason for wanting the papers.

But that night she pored over the pages, searching the advertisements. She found one that made her laugh.

Wanted: Hardworking young woman who is capable of caring for six motherless children and doing farm chores. Must be pure of heart and sweet of spirit. Willing to marry suitable candidate.

The requirements certainly eliminated her. Not that she had any desire to take over a farm home with six motherless children.

What did she want?

Or more to the point, what job was she suitable for? She doubted anyone would let her be around children or proper ladies once they discovered her past. She could try hiding it. Change her name. But her hair would give away her true identity to anyone who had ever seen her. So that left chambermaid in a hotel, a cook, or perhaps a hired girl on a ranch like Eddie's. She truly didn't care, so long as she was left alone and could care for Belle.

But there were no such ads in the paper. Discouraged, she set them aside.

The next morning, Red's determination returned, renewed and strengthened. She would find a job somehow, and silently worded an advertisement.

A knock sounded on the door.

"Come in." Ward didn't usually come until later, when he'd attended to his chores.

The door opened and Eddie stood in the opening with Grady at his side. Eddie nudged the little boy.

"Can Belle come out to play?" Grady asked.

Belle sprang up from the corner where she sat surrounded by her playthings. "Can I, Red? Please?"

Red wanted to slam the door, keep the world away from them. She knew it was only a matter of time before her past would confront them in a cruel fashion. But she couldn't deny Belle. "I don't want you wandering away."

"We'll stay close to the cabin."

"Very well."

Eddie squeezed Grady's shoulder. "Have fun. I'll return for you later or if you want to go home, you go up the hill." He shifted his attention to Red. "If he chooses to go home, could you watch and make sure he gets back safely?"

"Of course."

With a tip of his hat, Eddie strode toward the barn.

Red saw Ward in one of the pens. He seemed to be studying her. No doubt wondering how she would handle this intrusion into her privacy.

She stiffened her spine. She'd handle it just fine. Without anyone interfering, thank you very much.

Belle carried her doll in one hand and picked up as many of her other things as she could. "Did you bring your animals?" she asked.

Grady dug little carved animals from his pockets.

"Good," Belle said. "We'll start our own ranch." She led the way to a tree beside the cabin, its green leaves dancing in the gentle breeze. It stood tall and proud in full view of everyone in the cookhouse, the big house up the hill, the barn, the pens....

Red stared out the door at the pair, already organizing the play ranch. She wanted to keep an eye on them, make sure Belle remembered how to play with other children.

She picked up her sewing, pulled a chair toward the open door and sat so she remained half-hidden from view. From her perch she watched the children, happy for Belle's sake. Her attention wandered. Beyond the children, Ward held a horse by a rope lead and guided it about in a circle. Each movement was sure and gentle. She caught wisps of his voice, steady and assuring. At first the horse pranced and tossed its head, but Ward's manner soon calmed it.

She couldn't take her eyes off the man and animal. Uncertain emotions trembled through her. The horse recognized Ward's gentleness. It soothed its fears. Ward had that way about him.

He led the horse to a post, snubbed it up tight and went inside the barn.

Red sighed and shifted her gaze back to the children. With twigs they had created corrals for Grady's little animals.

Belle looked up. "Red, can we get some pieces of wood from out back?"

"Go ahead."

The pair trotted around. She listened to their murmur as they discussed what they needed.

The horse in the corral snorted. Red looked up. Ward placed a saddle blanket and saddle on the animal. Even from where she sat, she saw the way it trembled, sensed the fear. Her heart kicked against her ribs, then took off in a gallop.

"No," she whispered, seeing Ward prepare to swing to the saddle. Every fear, every worry consolidated into one thought. He would be thrown. Hurt.

She jerked to her feet, moved outside where she could see better.

He settled into the saddle and nodded. She hadn't noticed Eddie. Why didn't he stop Ward? Instead, he loosened the rope and set the horse free. It shook from head to tail, tossed its head, reared once, then bucked in a fury to get Ward off his back.

Red edged closer, unable to breathe, but not wanting

to take her eyes off Ward. If he got injured... A vise held her lungs.

The bucking stopped.

"Open the gate," Ward called, and Eddie did so. Ward rode the horse through the opening and headed down the trail away from the ranch.

What if—

She would not let her thoughts go that direction.

"He's a good horseman. He's in control."

She hadn't been aware of Eddie standing at the corner of the corrals, watching her.

"Of course he will." She returned to the cabin, grabbed up her chair and parked it in the sunshine. After all, the day was far too pleasant to spend indoors. What's more, she could see the mountains from where she sat.

Eddie moved away, apparently unconcerned with Ward's well-being.

The children played in the shade of the tree.

Red studied the distant mountains. But not until she saw Ward and the horse trotting back to the barn did she notice how the sky formed a perfect blue background to the jagged ridges of the mountains.

Ward waved.

She nodded. She'd only been apprehensive because she knew he couldn't do his job if he had a broken limb. That was all. Nothing personal about her feelings. She picked up a dress that needed mending and jabbed her needle through the fabric.

Eddie collected Grady at lunchtime.

Belle chattered so much over lunch that Red finished long ahead of her. "Eat up," she said.

"Okay." Belle ate her meal hurriedly. "Can I go out and play again?"

"Let's go out back."

"Can Grady come, too?"

Red couldn't say no to her little sister, though she feared the risks involved in getting too close to anyone. Sooner or later someone would discover the truth about them and point it out. But her argument lay flat and lifeless. Linette and Eddie must surely know where Red had been and what she'd been forced to do. Yet they welcomed her. And what had Ward said? Something about letting people get to know her and decide for themselves what they thought of her? Did he mean to suggest they would accept her?

She didn't see how that was possible. Not when her own heart condemned her.

"Can he?" Belle asked again.

"If he comes, you can play with him."

But it wasn't Grady she listened for that afternoon. When the little boy came midway through the day, Red resumed her place outside the cabin and continued the mending as the children played together. After a bit, she returned inside to start supper preparations, leaving the door open so she could keep a watch on the children. Each time she glanced out the door to where they played, her gaze drifted onward to the corrals, the barn and beyond. Previously she'd known only gratitude when no one hung about, but today the place seemed deserted. Where had Ward disappeared to? No, she corrected herself. Where was everyone?

Eddie took Grady home later. Belle came in to wash for supper. They ate fried steak, boiled potatoes and green beans that Cookie had preserved from the garden. Earlier Red had made bread, and they had thick slices of it with syrup for dessert.

Belle helped clean up and dried dishes as Red washed.

At the sound of footsteps nearby, she forced herself not to turn and see if Ward approached. A quiver in the pit of Red's stomach made her think she had forgotten to eat even though she washed the dishes that proved otherwise.

"Hello." Ward's firm, steady voice greeted them from the open doorway.

Something wrenched inside her. A syrup-sweet sensation of hope and despair.

"Hi, Ward." Belle bounced to his side. "Did you see the farm Grady and I are building?"

He cupped his hand over Belle's head, adding to the sweetness in Red's heart.

"I did. It looks to me like you and Grady had a great deal of fun playing together."

"We did. Grady says he can come every day if it's okay with Red." She flung about to confront her sister. "It's okay, isn't it?"

Red nodded, her tongue strangely wooden.

Ward flashed a smile full of summer sky, then turned to Belle. "Maybe you won't need your doll so much anymore."

"Oh, yes I do." She ran to the corner where Sally sat amidst the playthings. "She really needs all her arms and legs. Are you going to finish them?"

Ward pulled pieces of wood from his pocket. "I thought I would. Are you ladies wanting to sit outside and enjoy the evening?"

"I am." Belle dashed outside and disappeared around the corner.

"I'll be along in a minute." Red wiped the basin clean

and hung the towel to dry. She expected Ward to follow Belle, but he waited.

She adjusted the chairs around the table and delayed the moment she would have to go to his side. Her feelings were too fresh, too fragile, too foreign to feel comfortable around him.

Finally she could delay no longer and pasted a brave smile on her face. "Shall we?"

"Yes, ma'am." His grin slipped past her defenses and landed in her syrupy heart. But she wouldn't be controlled by foolish emotions, and lifted her chin, faced straight ahead and marched out the door.

How could she appear calm and collected when her insides bounced about? But she needn't have worried about it. Belle chattered nonstop as Ward carved a leg and arms for the doll.

Belle leaned over his shoulder, watching. "You're almost finished."

"Your Sally will soon be whole."

Belle giggled.

Then he would no longer need to visit every day. About time, Red told herself. But it wasn't relief she felt.

Ward attached the arms and leg and handed the doll to Belle. "There you go."

Belle pressed the doll to her chest. "Oh, thank you. Sally says thank you, too."

Ward pushed to his feet. "It's time to say good-night."

Red stood, too, and they moved to the cabin. As soon as they entered, Belle rushed to the bedroom. "I'm going to get ready for bed. Me and Sally."

Red turned. "Thank you and goodbye."

"Goodbye? I'll be back tomorrow afternoon."

Relief rushed through her. She cut it off. He didn't need to keep checking on them. Sooner or later they would have to manage on their own. Just as soon as she found something. Tonight she would write an advertisement and send it to the paper. "We'll be fine on our own." She said it as much for her sake as his.

"No doubt. But I need to get more wood."

"But—" She hadn't even considered the amount of wood they consumed. From now on, she would ration its use.

He brushed her cheek with warm fingertips. "Red, stop scheming on how not to use wood. There's lots out there for the taking. I don't mind bringing in more."

His touch did things to her insides she didn't want to admit. Filled her with such longing. Had she fallen into a pretend spell, like Belle with her doll, letting herself act as if this could be her life? It could not. Neither she nor Ward truly thought so. He liked to think he could take care of her more as a way to prove to himself he could, rather than because she mattered. What he really wanted was to take care of his mother and brothers. She was only a temporary substitute.

Ward watched her carefully. Did he see a glimpse of her confusion? "Promise me you won't try to get along without using any wood. You need to cook meals and soon you'll need to warm the cabin."

Did he mean in the fall? She wouldn't be here that long. He caught her chin and stared into her eyes. "Red, promise me."

"If we need it, I'll burn wood."

He sighed. "Why is it I don't feel like that's the promise I want?"

She shrugged. "Must be because you have a suspicious nature."

He laughed. "Something you've taught me." His gaze, warm with amusement and welcome, slipped past her defenses. Oh, she wished he wouldn't laugh so easily, smile so broadly. It made it so difficult to keep her guard up around him. Made her wish she could be something else—someone other than who she was. A draft of loneliness blew through her.

He sobered. His gaze intensified, silently laying claim to her emotions. Then slowly, as if anticipating each second, he lowered his head and kissed her.

She had plenty of time to turn away but she didn't. Somehow, despite all her arguments to the contrary, she wanted the assurance and protection his kiss signified. The touch of his lips slipped into her heart and grabbed it like a giant fist squeezing out a drop of longing, threatening to turn it into a rushing stream that would drain her. Leaving her empty and powerless. Still she could not end the kiss.

He lifted his head. His eyes were awash with yearning.

She didn't want to see it. Admit it. Knowing as she did that once the emotion died, reality would set in. And remembering who she was, what she'd done, the look in his eyes would turn to loathing. She stepped back. Crossed her arms over her middle as if she could hide the truth.

"I'll see you tomorrow." He hurried out.

She told herself she didn't notice a husky tone in his voice. She'd heard passion-thickened voices before and dared not believe it wasn't the same thing she heard in Ward's voice.

That night she waited until Belle had fallen asleep to sit at the table. Before she began her letter she had to find the address, and she spread out a paper to search for it.

That's when a headline caught her eye. She bent over the page and read the story carefully. When she was done, she sat back. This was it. Where she would go.

Chapter Eleven

Ward hummed as he strode to the bunkhouse. He'd given Red plenty of time to turn from his kiss. But she'd lifted her face in welcome. Then let the kiss continue. She was changing. Beginning to believe she was a good person. Worthy of love and respect. What happened to her was not of her doing. No one should blame her for it. She shouldn't blame herself.

Perhaps she was beginning to see that.

He realized he hummed a little tune, and stopped before he stepped into the bunkhouse.

Cal looked up and chortled. "Look at the smile on his face. I'd say he's fallen for that redhead across the way."

Ward waved away the comment but he didn't deny it. Yet he couldn't admit it even to himself, knowing Red might let him kiss her but she wasn't ready to open her heart and life to him.

Or anyone.

He climbed into his bunk and stared at the ceiling. Not that he needed to worry. She wasn't looking for love. He thought of his little cabin and the fledgling ranch. His goal had been to provide a home for his mother and sisters. Now Red fit so easily into the picture that he felt guilty. He'd abandoned his family once before and here he was mentally doing the same…putting Red in their place. His heart beat slower, each pulse heavy with determination. He could see how letting himself fall for Red could prove a substitute for missing his family.

He flipped to his side. He couldn't let that happen. His family must come first. He wasn't so foolish as to think love would satisfy the deep longings in his heart.

But just before sleep came, he smiled and thought of Red's kiss.

The next day Eddie kept Ward busy. Not until after supper did he have time to hitch a horse to the stoneboat and head over to the cabin, intending to bring in more firewood for Red.

First, he stopped to speak to her. "I would have been here sooner—" he started to explain.

"I expect Eddie thinks you should do some work once in a while. Besides, when will you learn I don't need you taking care of me?"

He ignored her gibe. "I see Grady was here again. That's nice. Everyone needs a friend. Friends make each other happy." He wanted her to accept him as a friend. To allow him to make her happy. To help her. Take care of her. Knowing she would object to the latter statements, he added, "Seems to me friends help each other."

Neither of them broke from staring at the other. Neither of them relented from their position.

"You got an objection to being friends with me?"

She sniffed. "Seems to me friends don't push at each other, making impossible demands."

"Push? Impossible demands? Red, I have no idea what you are talking about. All I've done is rescue you and Belle from Thorton, bring you to a safe place and make sure you're taken care of. How is that pushing and making demands?"

She sniffed again and gave him a look dripping with disdain. "I guess it meant nothing to you, but I recall a kiss or two."

He took off his hat and scrubbed at his hair, not caring that he likely turned it into a rat's nest. Then he gave her a look rife with disbelief. "Didn't see you resisting."

"Maybe," she said with annoyance in every syllable, "I was just being polite."

"Polite?"

"Stop sputtering. Yes, polite. Or maybe I thought you would tell Eddie to toss us out to fend for ourselves if I didn't let you."

He would not sputter but he sure felt like it. "You know that's not true. I can't make it any plainer that I'm happy enough to make sure you're safe."

"You make it equally plain that it's only because you haven't been able to contact your mother and brothers."

He slammed his hat on his head. This was not going at all the way he had planned. She was supposed to welcome his offer of friendship, admit that a kiss or two was appropriate, see that his desire to help was genuinely generous. Maybe even confess to liking, to even a small degree, having him around. "It's not just because I haven't been able to contact my family."

"So you're doing it to give you the right to steal a few kisses?"

"Woman, you don't know what you want, do you?" He turned to leave, then remembered he meant to chop wood. He confronted her. "I did not steal any kisses. You gave them. Freely, and I'm pretty sure you liked them. You don't fool me one bit."

She threw a towel at him. It fluttered ineffectively to the ground.

He laughed and continued on his way. Recognized another hole in her argument and called, "Besides, if you're so all fired set on leaving, why do you care if refusing a kiss might make me tell Eddie to throw you out?" As if Eddie would contemplate such a thing. But why should he encourage her to trust Eddie when she wouldn't trust him? "You aren't making any sense."

She slammed the door.

He headed for the woods, muttering under his breath about how difficult it was to figure out a woman like Red. But before he had placed three logs on the stoneboat, he started laughing. One thing about Red, she had a way of keeping him guessing and right now he was guessing she didn't like him pointing out she hadn't resisted his kiss. He could hardly wait to see what she would do next.

As Ward returned with wood, Red did her best to avoid him. She washed the windows and scrubbed the log walls. Both activities enabled her to keep an eye on him. To make sure he didn't sneak up unexpectedly, she told herself as she secretly watched him sweat over his labors.

"Sure putting a lot of elbow grease into this place," he commented as he passed with a load of wood. "Especially for a woman who says she doesn't care."

"Who said I don't care?" Oh, she should not have said that. It sounded as if she wanted to stay. "I'm only making sure no one will regret offering me a temporary home." Her heavy emphasis on the *temporary* was unmistakable. As was the flash of impatience in his eyes.

He gave her a long-studied look that threatened to

pry open secret places in her thoughts. She did not want them exposed. Wouldn't allow anyone access. Not even herself. There were simply things that no longer existed for Red. Like home, acceptance, love.

She puffed out her lips. She didn't need love. Didn't want it. Knew she would never receive it. Not with her past.

Ward continued to watch her and she realized she'd let her emotions play across her face. "Better get at your work," she said. She made little shooing motions with her hand.

He dropped the reins and stalked toward her, a dark, unreadable look on his face.

Alarm skittered up her nerves. Had she angered him? Would he exact payment in one of the ways Thorton had used? She glanced about. Could she hope to outrun him?

But he was already at her side and caught her by the arms, his touch surprisingly gentle. She kept her head down-turned, afraid of what she might see.

"Red, you are so prickly. Sometimes it wearies me. Yet there are other times when it catches at my heart and makes me want to hold you and kiss you until your fears subside. This is one of those times."

Before she could think what to do, he caught her chin, tipped her face upward and kissed her thoroughly. He ended the kiss and pulled her against his chest. "One day you'll admit you are safe with me. You'll realize just how nice it is." He released her and strode away, picked up the reins and drove to the woods without a backward look while she struggled to maintain her balance.

Why had he kissed her again?

And why, oh, why did she like it so much?

She rushed into the cabin. Belle played outdoors so Red sat alone at the table. She planted her face in her hands and moaned. She must get out of here as soon as possible.

She picked up the letter awaiting dispatch. Tomorrow was Sunday and she'd take it to church service and ask Linette to see it got to town. She could only hope the response would be swift and agreeable.

The next day she managed civil conversation with Ward as he escorted her across the road to the cookhouse. She'd planned to leave early and avoid his company, but he must have guessed her intent. When she opened the door, he leaned against the outer wall, all fresh and relaxed, his chin so clean-shaven she wanted to touch it. His white shirt provided a contrast to his bronzed skin that let the word *handsome* spring to her mind before she could stop it. And why did he rest one boot on its toe so he created the perfect picture of masculinity?

He grinned at her.

It was as though the sun touched her with unseasonable warmth and she jerked away. She had tried all night to forget the feel of his kiss, to forget his assertion that she might like it.

She pressed her hand to the letter in her pocket. This position would provide the perfect opportunity for Red and Belle. She couldn't have asked for more if she'd prayed for a miracle. Yet excitement did not race through her veins. Or even satisfaction or gratitude or any number of things she should be feeling. What she felt was a long ache for what she could not have.

Remembering Ward's kisses, she brushed her fingertips over her lips. Then, lest he read something into the gesture she didn't care for him to, she jerked her hand to her waist and pretended to adjust the fabric.

A woman like her could never entertain the sort of dreams that haunted her restless sleep. The warmth of his arm brushing hers tempted her to ignore the truth. Knowing she could never afford to forget the facts of her life, she pretended a great interest in something to her right and used it for an excuse to put a healthy six inches between them.

She felt his considering stare and knew he was aware of what she'd done, but she would not risk a look at him, having discovered that her resolve weakened when he smiled at her. Besides, he seemed to have developed the unwelcome ability to read her thoughts.

"I wonder how long this warm weather will last," she commented. Weather was always a safe topic to discuss.

"Not long enough." He sounded amused, as if recognizing her intent to divert him from—what? Only it wasn't him she meant to sidetrack, she wanted to stop her thoughts from admiring him, wondering if he wanted to kiss her again.

They reached the cookhouse and were greeted with the welcoming scent of cinnamon and Cookie's exuberant hug. Red successfully dismissed her wayward thoughts.

Belle waved at Grady. "Can I sit with him?"

She'd noticed the children sat with their parents throughout the service and then were free to go to the others. "I prefer you to sit with me. You can talk to him afterward."

They sat on the back bench. Ward quirked an eyebrow at her when she made certain Belle was between them.

Let him think what he wanted.

Again, Cookie led them in singing a few hymns. Not wanting to attract unwanted inquiries about not joining in, Red moved her lips silently. Then Bertie got up to speak. She closed her mind to his words, though once or twice his sincere tones drew her reluctant attention. She heard enough to know he talked about the lost being found. Maybe it was his favorite topic.

The service ended and Linette and Cassie moved over to sit across from Red.

"Grady is certainly enjoying playtime with Belle," Linette said. She turned to Cassie. "Why don't you send the children to join them?"

She took Red's agreement for granted but then it was Linette's house, her yard. Why shouldn't she?

"I might send Daisy down with the two little ones. Neil prefers to be with Roper. If you don't mind?" She addressed Red.

Red nodded. "That would be fine. I'm sure Belle would enjoy it." At this rate, her little sister would soon be a social butterfly.

Cookie again served goodies. Red guessed they were delicious, but for her they had a cardboard flavor. She excused her tension as trepidation over the response to her letter, uncertainty about the future or even reluctance to venture into the unknown. Certainly not as already missing Ward when she left. That made no sense. She would not even entertain the idea.

She hoped to have a quick private word with Linette but no opportunity presented itself.

"You'll come up to the house?" Linette asked.

Red nodded. How else was she to deliver the letter to Linette without everyone knowing?

"You, too, Ward."

The man grinned from ear to ear and fell in at her side following Eddie and Linette. The two children scampered ahead.

"Red," Ward murmured. "You're awfully quiet. Is something wrong?" His gentle, caring words scrubbed every reasonable explanation for her behavior from her mind. Ward-shaped longing and missing rushed through her like a flash flood leaving the bare rocks of truth exposed. She wished with all her heart she could dream of being more than someone for him to care for…a way to ease his concerns about his family.

She couldn't be.

Why, she'd never even seen his little ranch, though he talked of it often enough. She recognized how far that thought had veered from insisting she couldn't be more—didn't want to be.

"Only thing wrong with me is I didn't sleep well last night."

"You're not sick are you? Your leg is healing okay?"

She let out a gusty breath. "Ward, I am fine. Just fine."

He snorted. "Huh. Seems to me people who are just fine sleep peacefully."

"And who appointed you the expert on sleeplessness?"

He chuckled. "Nice to see you back in form—all feisty."

"I am not being feisty." She emphasized each syllable to make sure he understood. "I'm just pointing out that you have no way of knowing why I didn't sleep well."

He stopped directly in front of her, forcing her to halt.

She kept her attention on the tips of his boots. A little dusty now after walking along the trail, but he'd obviously polished them in honor of Sunday. Something about that fact twisted through her brain…a cruel corkscrew.

"Red Henderson, or whatever your name is, I'm guessing your sleep was disturbed with thoughts of a kiss you pretend you didn't want but enjoyed despite yourself."

"How dare you?" She shot him a look of denial. At the warmth in his eyes and the way his gaze darted to her mouth, she wished she'd continued to stare at his boots. "I do not… Did not… Am not…" Oh, she had no idea what she meant, and closed her mouth lest she say something she'd regret.

"Ah, but I think you are." He cupped her elbow and proceeded up the hill as satisfied as a well-fed cat.

"You might not be as smart as you think you are." She knew she sounded petulant. The letter that had weighed on her mind all day now promised relief and freedom. She couldn't wait to give it to Linette.

A little later when Ward and Eddie excused themselves to look at one of the horses, she got her chance. "Linette, I'd like to request another favor."

Linette nodded. "All you have to do is ask."

She extracted the letter from her deep pocket. "Will you post this for me?"

"That is too easy to be a favor."

Red's smile felt a little crooked. "There's more. When I get a reply, will you make sure to give it directly to me?"

Linette didn't answer for a moment. "You're saying you don't want me to give it to Ward to deliver? Why?"

She waggled her hands. "I don't want to argue with him about me leaving." It didn't begin to explain her reasons, which were less about what Ward might do and a whole lot more about fearing her own weakness. It wouldn't take a lot of arguing for her to agree to stay.

However, that was not possible.

Linette laughed. "You know there's only one reason he'd argue with you. He cares about you."

"I don't fancy having to defend my decisions. Promise me you won't give the letter to Ward. Please."

"Very well, if that's how you want it. But why are you running from him?"

"I believe it's for the best that I move on."

Linette considered her so long and hard that Red pretended a great deal of interest in the painting beyond Linette's shoulder.

"Red." Linette's soft voice drew Red's eyes to her. "There's no need to run and hide. You are a beautiful, competent woman any man would be honored to love."

Red ached to tell Linette exactly what she'd endured for Thorton's amusement and then ask if she still felt a man would be honored to love her. But she knew the answer and didn't need it spelled out for her. She took the letter from her pocket and handed it to Linette. "Thank you."

Now all she had to do was wait for a response.

She could only hope it would not be long in coming.

"We'll be gone ten days to two weeks," Ward said to Red. "The heavy rains to the west are threatening to flood the lower pasture. We need to move the herd to higher ground." Eddie and the other cowboys were mounted and ready to go. A chuckwagon had already departed.

"I can manage quite fine on my own."

He laughed. "Try not to miss me too much." And with a saucy salute and a flashing grin, he rode away with the others.

Now, only three days later, she stared down the trail as dusk settled into the hollows and wondered if he'd come to his senses while he was gone. Would he think about the sort of woman Red was? What would his mother think if he ever located her?

She turned back to the interior of the cabin, determined to ignore such foolish contemplations. If she received the response she hoped for from her letter, she would soon move on. And if the reply was not what she wanted, she would continue to look for something else.

Several times, Daisy had brought Pansy and Billy to play. Belle enjoyed it thoroughly.

"I like having friends to play with," Belle said, pulling Red from her musing. "Billy knows lots of games."

"You'll have to do your lessons in the morning before you can go out and play." Her little sister could read fairly well and had improved in her sums. But it would be wonderful if she could go to a real school.

As soon as dishes were done, they sat at the table. Belle played while Red read the papers, though she'd read every word twice already. If she had yarn she could knit, but she lacked the materials and would not ask Linette for any. She owed her far too much already.

The hours trudged along until Belle's bedtime. And then hollow silence filled the room. Red wandered from one side of the cabin to the other, touching objects now grown familiar—the red checked curtains at the windows, the handle of the shovel she kept close to the door, the smooth wood of the shelves, the stack of wood that reminded her of Ward's care.

She shook her head to clear her thoughts. Ward could not figure so hugely into her life.

Her eyes lighted on the picture over the table. It lay in shadows so she couldn't read the words. Not that she needed to see them to know what they said. *Whither shall I flee from Your presence?* Crossing her arms across her stomach, she stared at the picture. If only she could hide from God. The best she could hope for was to block thoughts of Him from her mind. Which was increasingly hard to do, thanks to the constant reminder of the wall hanging, the Sunday services at the ranch and in no small part, Ward's gentle words. He'd often said God forgives, doesn't see our past.

Easy for him to say. What had he ever done wrong?

Her steps long and hurried, she crossed the cabin, spun around and made a return trip. Back and forth, chased by churning thoughts, driven by a relentless restlessness.

"Enough," she murmured, and sat down on a chair. Her gaze slid to the knapsack. She drummed her fingers on the table. A book would relieve her boredom. But she did not move. She'd long ago stuck the one book she'd glanced at back in the bag, finding the poems triggered a flood of memories she didn't care to deal with. Besides, the books were Ward's. Just holding them would make her miss him.

But surely she could read one without her emotions raging wildly. She stared at the bag, her heart pressing to her ribs as she tried to convince herself she didn't want to read. She failed that argument. They were only books, she reasoned, nothing more.

She edged toward the bag. It meant nothing that she accepted his invitation to enjoy his books. He need not know. She lifted the flap, hurriedly shoved aside the quilt, not allowing thoughts of his mother to enter her mind.

She grabbed the first book her fingers touched, making certain it wasn't the poetry book.

"Thank goodness it's a novel." She returned to the table, pulled the lamp close and opened the pages. Two hours later, she reluctantly closed the book and made her way to bed.

The next day she hurried through her chores and read as Belle worked on her sums. In the afternoon, Grady, Pansy and Billy came to play with Belle. They ventured outdoors and Red sat at the open door, enjoying the story.

A cold wind came up. Daisy came to get Pansy and Billy and Eddie took Grady home. Belle and Red retreated indoors and closed the door. She was grateful for the warmth from the stove and wood to burn. Thanks to Ward.

She made soup and biscuits for supper, read to Belle and tucked her into bed.

This time, Red didn't mind when darkness descended. She sat and enjoyed reading. She felt an unreasonable gratitude toward Ward for providing her this pleasure. Not that she would tell him.

He'd been gone a week. Not since she was a child anticipating Christmas had Red counted the days and seen them pass on such reluctant feet.

It didn't help that Belle asked several times a day when he was coming back.

"He said they'd be gone up to fourteen days."

Belle's dramatic sigh echoed the emptiness in Red's heart.

How could she have allowed herself to grow so fond of the man? Did she secretly want to be hurt?

Of course she didn't. But at some time in the past weeks she'd allowed a crack in her armor without realizing it.

Belle stared out the window. "Grady's coming," she shrieked.

It had been cold and rainy for the better part of two days, preventing the children from playing outside.

Red joined her sister at the window. "Linette's bringing him." This was the first time Linette had visited the cabin and would no doubt expect to be invited in. Red hustled to fill the kettle and put it on the stove, then rushed to open the door.

"Please come in, though it feels strange to invite you into your own house."

Grady darted over to join Belle at her toys.

Linette chuckled. "My house is up on the hill."

"I know. But you spent the winter here."

Linette grew wistful. "I did and it was a lot of fun." She accepted Red's invitation to sit at the table. "Did anyone ever tell you about it?"

Red poured water over the tea leaves and put out a plate of cookies. "A bit."

Linette chuckled. "I came out expecting a marriage of convenience. My father had arranged for me to marry a much older man back in England." She grimaced. "I couldn't bear the idea and I was so sick of the restrictions of my life. I was friends with Eddie's fiancée, and she showed me the letter she wrote telling him that she'd changed her mind and couldn't marry him. It was her suggestion to tell Eddie I'd be willing to take her place. So when two tickets arrived, I thought they were meant for me. But Eddie hadn't received his fiancée's letter and meant the tickets for her." She grinned. "He wasn't pleased when I showed up instead."

Red gaped. "What did he do?"

"Because of the weather he said I could stay until spring. By then we'd fallen in love."

"That's amazing." Red tried to sound enthusiastic but the ache in her heart made it difficult. She could never hope for such a sweet happily ever after. She poured the tea and offered cookies, taking some to the children.

"Oh, I forgot the reason I came, though it is only an excuse. I've been dying to visit." Linette glanced about. "I know you think you have to run and hide. But I hope and pray you find love and happiness here as I did." She dug into her pocket. "I have a letter for you."

Red took the envelope and studied the return address. This was the letter she'd hoped for. "Thank you." It felt heavy in her palms, though it weighed no more than a sheet of paper should.

When Linette saw that Red didn't intend to open the envelope while she was there, she turned to other things. "Do you need anything? Firewood? Food?"

"I'm fine. Thanks. Ward made sure we had a good stock of supplies before he left."

Linette grinned. "I guessed as much. Ward's the sort you can always count on."

"Yes." She wouldn't let her thoughts pursue that idea. It was his family that he wanted to be taking care of, not Red and Belle. She understood it. Didn't feel any resentment.

A little later, Linette announced she had to leave.

Red escorted Linette and Grady to the door. "It was nice of you to visit."

"I'll come again, if you don't mind."

"I'd like that." It surprised her how much the idea appealed.

The pair departed.

Red stared at the letter, afraid to open it for fear it would not be what she hoped for.

"Aren't you getting cold?" Belle called from the cabin.

Realizing she stood in the open door letting out the

warm air, Red returned inside and put the letter on the table to consider it.

"We have a letter?" Belle managed to sound curious and worried at the same time.

Her words spurred Red into action and she slit the envelope open, unfolded a sheet of paper and read it through twice. Her eyes hot with tears, she finally turned toward the anxious Belle. "It's a place for us to go."

Belle's expression turned stormy. "We have a place right here. I like it. I like Grady and Cookie and Pansy and Ward. I don't want to go someplace else." Her bottom lip jutted out.

"Honey, this was never meant to be for long. This is Eddie and Linette's cabin. We can't continue to use it. It's time for us to move on and become independent."

Belle backed away, fire burning from her eyes. "You just don't want anyone to help us. You don't want people to like us."

"Belle, that is not true." Except a shiver of truth traveled through her brain. If she didn't let people like her, then she wouldn't have to endure their shock and horror when they discovered the truth. She grabbed the paper and showed Belle the picture of three women and two men standing before a square, two-story building. "Here, look at this. This is a new mission in Medicine Hat where they want to teach school, and help people who are abandoned or homeless. You know where that is. South of here, close to the American border. Just think, you could go to a real school."

Belle examined the picture, then handed the paper back. "I don't want to go. My friends are here." She silently challenged Red to dispute the fact.

She couldn't.

"Ward is my friend even if you won't let him be your friend."

Red ignored the accusing words. Friends? That's what Ward had asked for. And she'd basically refused his offer. Why? What harm would there be in friendship?

The answer ached through her. She didn't belong in decent society. At the mission she would be accepted as a needy, damaged person. "Belle, they said we were welcome and they could find work for me, so we're going and that's all there is to it."

Belle grabbed her doll and retreated to the far corner of the room, her back to Red. The words she mumbled to her doll informed Red that her sister considered her unfair and mean.

Belle would adjust to the new situation.

Red would, too. She wouldn't let regrets and longings and dreams of things that couldn't be stop her from moving forward.

Something argumentative bounced around in her brain. She kept saying people wouldn't accept her. Yet Ward knew of her past and wanted to be friends. Linette knew and had been kind and accepting. No doubt Eddie knew and he allowed her to live in his cabin. Cookie included them. Cassie and Roper allowed their children to play with Belle.

Was Ward right? Did she need to forgive herself and accept that God forgave and loved her?

She might have believed it based on how those at the ranch had welcomed her.

Except for one thing.

They didn't know the whole truth. They only knew she'd been forced to dance in a saloon to protect Belle. None of them knew how Thorton had humiliated her until she hated not only her red hair, but her entire body, both inviting men to leer and touch her without her permission. And certainly without her wanting them to. She shuddered. A mission for outcasts was the best place in the world for her. And it would suit Belle fine, too, once she got used to it.

Despite her positive considerations, a sorrow as deep as eternity filled her soul.

She turned her back to Belle and buried her hands in her face, lest her little sister see the tears flowing down her cheeks. The way Thorton had treated her had left her hating herself.

Chapter Twelve

Ward rode after a wayward cow. He always enjoyed being out in nature, riding behind the cattle. He drank in the pine scent, the air so fresh it likely came off a glacier higher in the mountains. Here and there, wildflowers of pink, yellow, orange and red dotted the alpine meadows. The sky was as blue as deep water with only a scattering of fluffy clouds.

He was anxious for the day when he'd have his own herd to move. In fact, he might buy some cows this fall and take them to his ranch. What would Red think of his little cabin? Not that it mattered. He'd written a number of letters to his mother, his brothers, every neighbor he could remember, the postmaster, the schoolteacher, the church, even addressed a letter simply to "The Lawyer" in the town where he'd last seen his family. Surely someone would know where they were and be able to get a message to them.

If only they'd come west and join him. His usual enjoyment of nature dimmed this year. A week of trailing after a herd of cattle seemed like eternity. He wanted to spend the time with Red. And Belle, of course. The little girl was a joy to play with.

Red remained a mixed joy as she continued to present him with nothing but her feisty side. Not that he hadn't seen more. So much more. He'd seen tenderness and longing in those unguarded moments, especially after he'd kissed her. She would vehemently deny it if he was foolish enough to point it out.

Mostly she seemed intent on proving she didn't need or want anyone. In the depths of his heart he understood why. She couldn't believe anyone would let her forget her past or be prepared to overlook it. No words would convince her so he quit trying. But as far as he was concerned, she wasn't responsible for what happened to her. She'd been tricked and forced to endure unspeakable things in order to protect Belle. In his eyes that made her noble and strong.

And if anyone dared to condemn her in his hearing, they would regret their words. *Lord, help her realize she doesn't need to dwell on the past.*

A cow veered away from the herd and Ward rode after it. A few more days and they'd be back at the ranch. Maybe his absence would make Red miss him. He grinned at the idea. What would it take to make her confess such a longing?

Perhaps given enough time…

If she stayed for the winter, he could make sure she had plenty of food to eat and wood to keep warm. He could help her pass the long winter afternoons. They'd talk about their hopes and dreams, play games with Belle. He might even pull out his father's poetry book and read a poem or two to her. Would she think it too romantic?

He figured time would heal her wounds and wanted to be there the day she realized she was free of her past. They could celebrate with a kiss or two.

Realizing his grin seemed permanently fixed to his lips, he glanced around to make sure none of the cowboys observed him. He'd take a razzing if they did. Thankfully they were occupied far enough away they couldn't see him.

Three days later they drove the last of the cows to the lower pastures and headed for the bunkhouse.

"I'm going to have a nice long soak," Ward announced, which brought a burst of snickers from the others.

"Got courting on yer mind?" Slim asked, his innocent voice not fooling Ward or any of the others.

"Could be," Ward allowed.

The others jeered, though he knew they would all head out for town or to the nearby ranch where a couple of single gals lived.

"Just so long as you remember I get first dibs on the tub." He kicked his horse into high gear and headed for the bunkhouse accompanied by yells from the others as they raced after him.

A few hours later, he strode across to the cabin, certain he smelled much better than when he rode into the yard. He'd donned a clean pair of denim jeans, his favorite blue shirt and polished his boots. He couldn't wait to see Red.

Belle raced from the cabin. "Ward. Ward. You're back."

It was a greeting to warm a man's heart. He waved and called a hello to her, then his gaze riveted to the doorway. Would Red come out or would she make him go in search of her?

Then she stepped into the sunshine. Her red hair glistened like a welcoming fire. Her eyes remained guarded but pink stained her cheeks. She would no doubt deny it, but he figured it meant she was happy to see him.

He was so glad to see them, his heart squeezed like an overactive fist. He jogged the last few steps, caught Belle and tossed her in the air.

She squealed in delight.

The child still in his arms, he moved to within a few inches of Red, brushed her cheek with his fingertips. "Glad to see me?"

She shook her head no, but her eyes said yes.

He put Belle down and moved closer to Red, drawn by the secrets in her gaze, hoping those secrets included feelings for him she wasn't ready to admit.

"She's gonna make us leave," Belle said.

Ward's heart spasmed like someone had stomped on it. He'd misread her expression. The secret she held was continued resistance. All joy fell out the bottom of his heart, leaving him empty and hollow.

Red hurried inside, Ward on her heels and Belle right behind.

They faced each other like wary boxers waiting to see who would make the first move.

Belle spoke before Ward could bring his thoughts into rational order. "You tell her she's wrong."

Ward pulled a small carved dog from his pocket. "Belle, take this outside and play. Stay out of the wind." Rain had been threatening all day.

With a disdainful sniff, Belle grabbed her sweater and left.

Red didn't give him a chance to say a thing. "I'm not wrong."

"You don't have to leave."

"I can't be a substitute for your family." Her eyes had developed blinkers so he couldn't gauge her feeling.

"You aren't a substitute. Stop saying it. You are safe here. Don't you like it?"

Something flickered through her eyes but disappeared before he could do more than guess she liked it but would never admit so. He changed tactics. "Belle is happy and safe," he said.

"There's a school where we're going. She can have proper instruction." She grabbed a newspaper from the table. "Here. Read it. I've already written and received a warm invitation."

He barely glanced over the news article. "You don't have to go. I don't want you to."

She rocked her head back and forth.

He took it for an internal struggle. Suddenly he understood what bothered her. She figured sooner or later someone would point out her background and the gossip would force her to leave. Probably thought it better to go now than later when Belle—and perhaps Red—got too fond of the people and the place.

All he had to do was make it permanent. "Red, marry me. I will take care of you." That didn't seem to convince her. "Just think how good it would be for Belle. For both of you."

It took Red two full minutes to catch her breath and answer. "Marry you? That's insane." She must have misunderstood him. "You can't mean it."

"It's the perfect solution."

People didn't marry because it provided a solution to where they would live. Or perhaps they did. But he didn't love her. Not that she expected him to.

"I—" She meant to say she couldn't, but failed to force the words to her mouth. Yet she could not deny the appeal of his offer. Would marriage give her what she longed for? Would she be allowed to forget her past? Or would it haunt her? Most important, would others let it go?

"Think about it."

He had no reason to sound disappointed, as if she should jump at the offer.

"Tomorrow is Sunday," he said. "Is that long enough to consider my offer?"

She laughed—a sound as much mockery as amusement, though she couldn't deny a jolt of pleasure at his eagerness. "Give me until Monday." Why was she even letting him think she'd consider it?

"Agreed."

They nodded. She wondered if he would offer to shake hands on the agreement or— She couldn't resist a glancing look at his mouth.

He chuckled as he pulled her into his arms. "Red, do you have any notion of how transparent you are at times? I only wish you would be so all the time." He stroked her head, smoothing her tangled curls. "You have the prettiest hair."

She jolted back. "It's not pretty."

Looking deep into her eyes, he spoke volumes without uttering a word. She let herself drink copiously of his assurance that he liked her hair, maybe even liked her a tiny bit.

Liking, caring…were they enough reason to marry?

He dipped his head and caught her mouth with his own—a gentle kiss.

Belle banged on the window. "Does that mean we're going to stay?"

Red sprang away from Ward.

He roared with laughter as he went to the door and threw it back. "You might as well come inside."

Belle shut the door behind her. "Well, does it?"

Ward repeated his offer of marriage.

Red sent him a cross look. "You said you'd give me until Monday."

"You better make the right choice." Belle's warning look reminded Red of their mama. It stole away her breath.

Ward noticed her quick intake of air. His eyes narrowed with concern.

She turned away. Thinking of Mama and Papa only confused her more. What would they advise? She dare not think of the looks they would give her because of the way she had lived not so many weeks ago.

Ward plunked down on the log stool he had claimed for his own. "Who wants to hear about the cattle drive?"

"Me. Me." Belle climbed to her chair and planted her elbows on the table, her expression adoring.

"I'll make tea." Red couldn't stand to watch them. Belle would be happy to become a permanent part of this place and have Red marry Ward. Was it reason enough to risk marriage?

She wished she could say it was. In the depths of her being she wanted to marry Ward and spend the rest of her life with him, but how could she? She was dirty, soiled, spoiled. He would soon come to despise her. Even as she despised herself.

If only there was some way to erase the time she'd belonged to Thorton, go back to the innocence of her early years.

However her past could not be washed away, forgotten or ignored.

Ward recounted many amusing tales of his adventures, but Red barely heard as her inner war continued. He drank tea and ate cookies, all the while talking to

Belle, yet his gaze followed Red as if waiting for some sign of what she felt. But how could she reveal anything when she didn't even know what to think?

By the time Ward returned the next morning to escort them to church service, Red had convinced herself of one thing—her brain had ceased working. She had no idea what she wanted or what was best or what she should do.

It would require little effort for her to beg off attending church service, but Ward would no doubt badger her for an explanation, so she allowed him to tuck her hand over his arm and didn't make a fuss when he pressed it close. His warm presence partially calmed her inner turmoil, though she would never confess it to herself or anyone else.

She knew what to expect at the service and prepared to close her mind to whatever Bertie had to say. Except today her brain had not only stopped functioning, it had holes in it that allowed Bertie's words to sneak in. Within seconds she was caught up in his tale of a wild youth.

"I'd been raised in a godly home. My father was a preacher of sorts. Yet I turned my back on it and did all manner of despicable things. I hated what I had become, feared what the future held. Likely prison or worse if I didn't stop. But I thought God would never forgive me for the horrible things I'd done. Nothing anyone said or did convinced me otherwise. Until the day I fell on my face in self-loathing."

Red sat straight and unmoving, her fingers twisted together in a white knot. She knew exactly how he felt.

"It was there in the dirt that I found what I needed. Forgiveness."

She sat back. That was too simple an answer.

Bertie wasn't done. "I deserved punishment and somehow I suppose I thought if I received it in my flesh it would erase what I'd done. But God reminded me of a verse my father had us children memorize at an early age. John 1:9, 'If we confess our sins, He is faithful and just to forgive us our sins, and to cleanse us from all unrighteousness.' I'd never before noticed that tiny little word *all*. That's when I realized the cleansing was all from Him. There was nothing I could do to add to God's generous forgiveness. I rose from the dirt and went forward a new man."

Red found it difficult to swallow. He made it sound so easy to start over. But how could one forget the sin of their past? Even if it were possible, would others let her forget?

She pushed her questions into a dark corner of her heart and turned her attention to the snacks Cookie handed out. Somehow she made it through the afternoon, answering Linette's questions, saying the right things at the right time. Or so she thought until she noticed Linette's curious study and forced herself to participate more. But she was grateful beyond measure when Eddie ended the afternoon early.

"I hope you all don't mind if I take Linette and Grady away. We have a lot of catching up to do."

Linette sent Red an apologetic look. "We'll get together another time."

Red nodded, relieved she wouldn't have to spend any more time under Linette's watchfulness.

Ward rose, too. "I want to get these ladies home before the rain begins in earnest." He walked them back to the cabin.

"Thank you," Red said at the door, hoping he would

take the hint and leave her alone so she could sort out her thoughts. Instead, he opened the door wider and urged her inside, then followed. Belle moved away to play and Ward pulled two chairs close to the warm stove.

"Red, I couldn't help notice Bertie's sermon upset you. Want to talk about it?"

"You're mistaken." But her voice caught, betraying her lie.

He covered her hand with his.

She jerked away.

Ward studied her silently but she kept her attention on the front of the stove.

He sighed and shifted his attention away, allowing her to draw in a strengthening breath.

"I'm not mistaken and you know I'm not. Red, I understand your past is painful, but don't you think you should stop blaming yourself for something you couldn't help?"

She shivered, "Sin is sin."

"And God is God. Like Bertie says, He forgives."

"It's too simple."

He rested his hand on her shoulder, filling her lungs with immovable steel.

"It's too simple, for sure. But still, it's God's way. He offers us complete forgiveness. What do you think we can add to what He's done?" If his voice had been impatient or argumentative she might have objected, might have found an answering argument. But his gentle, caring words erased everything but a long, heavy guilt. There was nothing she could say to explain the weight of it.

When she didn't answer he squeezed her shoulder tight. "I'll pray for you."

The wind shuddered around the cabin.

He pushed slowly to his feet as if reluctant to leave her. Listening to the wind increase in strength, she wished he didn't have to go out. If they married—

She jumped to her feet and walked him to the door.

Marry simply to keep a person from going into the weather? Now that was the stupidest reason ever. She watched his departure from the window. Almost as stupid as wishing she could be worthy of his love.

The next morning dawned still and bright. She stepped outside to a much more pleasant day and lifted her arms to the sky.

"We're staying, aren't we?" Belle demanded for the seven hundredth time since Ward left last night.

"Belle, I told you I'll let you know when I make up my mind."

Her little sister jammed her fists on her child-sized hips and looked impatient. "You're just being prideful and stubborn."

Red couldn't help but laugh at the grown-up words from Belle. "Where'd you hear that?"

"Grady says that's what Mrs. Gardiner said to Mr. Gardiner when he refused to let her go to town. He said it was too muddy. But she said he was prideful and stubborn."

Red nodded, her grin still in place. "Maybe a person has to be sometimes."

"I don't think so." She marched away without a backward look.

Chuckling as she worked, Red hauled in several buckets of water and filled the tub to heat for laundry. She should have filled the tub last night but the rain made her choose to stay inside. Today was a nice day. She could hang the clothes outside to dry.

She'd said she'd give her word today. If he hadn't changed his mind, she would agree. He could take care of them and it would make him feel better. It would give Belle all the things Red wanted her to have—home, security, acceptance, maybe even love. He would never love Red. She didn't expect him to. It wasn't necessary. She would require only one thing from him—his promise to never hate her for her past.

As she tidied the cabin and sorted the items for washing, she continually glanced out the window, wondering when Ward would appear to demand his answer. She glanced up at the sound of hoofbeats and saw Ward and Slim ride away from the ranch, Slim going south, Ward north. She pressed closer to the glass to keep them in view.

Just before Ward rode out of sight, he turned and waved his hat in her direction.

She half lifted her hand to wave back, then dropped it at her side. If he still wanted to marry her it would be a businesslike arrangement. No need for her to get all eager and adoring.

She scrubbed the clothes, rinsed them and twisted the water out of each garment. She hung the items to dry, all the while her ear tuned to the sound of a returning horse.

Hours later, the laundry had dried enough and she removed each piece carefully, folding it into the laundry basket in preparation for ironing.

The sound of hoofbeats thudded in her ears and she spun around. But only one rider returned—Slim. Red sucked in air and turned back to her chore. Ward would return later.

In the meantime she had work to do and hoped it would keep her thoughts from rushing ahead to his visit.

She carried the laundry inside, heated the sad irons and began the job of ironing each item. It consumed her minutes but not her thoughts. Perhaps he purposely stayed away because he'd changed his mind about the marriage proposition.

Thankfully Grady came to play with Belle so Red could glance out the window every few minutes without alerting her sister to her anxiety.

But after Grady left, Belle confronted her. "What did you say to Ward?"

"What do you mean?"

Belle's look was rife with accusation. "You chased him away."

"Why do you say that?"

"Today you were supposed to say you'd marry him. But he hasn't come. You said something."

"No, I didn't." Though Belle's suspicions closely echoed her own. He'd changed his mind but not because of anything Red had said. "He hasn't come because Eddie sent him to do something. Didn't you see him ride away this morning?" Was it only today? Less than twelve hours ago?

"So you're going to tell him you'll marry him?" Belle chortled, then threw her arms about Red's waist. "I knew you'd come to your senses."

Red patted Belle's back. "I haven't said anything yet. You'll have to wait until Ward comes so I can tell him my decision first."

"You like him. You'll do the right thing and marry him." Belle was so convinced that she knew what was best that Red laughed.

"We'll see."

Later, they made supper, cleaned up, then sat and stared at the door. Darkness fell. Still no sign of Ward. Had he returned and she missed it? Was he over in the bunkhouse trying to decide how to retract his marriage offer?

"It's time to get ready for bed," she told Belle.

"No."

She might have scolded her sister except for the fact her lips quivered and her eyes shone with tears. "Belle, you can't stay up all night."

"But you said he'd be back. I want to hear you tell him you'll marry him."

"Belle—" How could she tell her that Ward might not want to hear the words? But she couldn't destroy Belle's dreams until she had to. "He said he'd come so he will. But not tonight. It's too late."

Belle nodded and sadly prepared for bed. When Red went to tuck her in, Belle threw herself into Red's arms and sobbed quietly.

"Honey, don't cry. No matter what happens, we have each other and we'll be fine. We can still go to the mission in Medicine Hat."

Belle sobbed harder. "I don't want to go anywhere," she hiccuped.

"I know. But we're strong. We'll do whatever needs to be done."

Belle flung herself back on the pillow and glowered at Red. "You're talking like we're going to leave. You promised we could stay."

She only wanted to prepare Belle for bad news but what was the use? If bad news came they would deal with it. Nothing would ever be as bad as what they'd already endured, but Belle didn't need to think along those lines.

"Honey, I'm sure he'll come in the morning."

"I know. He said he'd be back." Belle seemed satisfied, and Red kissed her good-night and left the room. If only she could find the same solace.

Chapter Thirteen

Next morning Belle rushed from bed to the window. "I don't see him."

Red laughed, though it sounded tinny even to herself. "Maybe because it's not light yet."

"Almost. I see Slim and Cal going to the cookhouse." One by one she called out the names of the cowboys as they entered the house across the road. "Where's Ward?" Belle flung about and gave Red a demanding look.

Red shrugged and kept her attention on breakfast preparations. "I'm sure I don't know."

Belle stomped over and sat at the table, her elbows practically digging holes in the wooden top. "I still think you said something to him Sunday. You looked mad when he left."

Red sighed. Nothing she said would convince Belle otherwise. She served breakfast but Belle spent more of her time glowering at Red than eating.

"Are you done?" Red asked after she'd given Belle more than enough time to finish.

"Not hungry." She pushed the plate of food away.

"It's a long time until lunch."

"Who cares?"

"You might not have enough energy to play with the other children."

"Don't feel like playing."

"Fine." Red gathered up the dishes and scraped the wasted food to the slop bucket. "Good thing the pigs will enjoy your breakfast."

Belle's only reply was a long sigh.

"I'll wash and you dry."

"Don't I always?"

Red almost bit her tongue to keep from scolding Belle for her rudeness. She wouldn't normally tolerate it but this time she let it go because it reflected her own feelings. If Ward had changed his mind he could at least have the decency to tell her instead of putting her through this torture.

The dishes were almost finished when a knock sounded on the door.

"It's him. About time." Belle was at the door before Red could take a step. She paused and gave Red a squinty-eyed look. "Now, you be nice to him, hear?"

Red laughed. "Yes, boss."

Belle yanked the door open. And her shoulders sank like the air had been sucked out of her insides. "Hi, Mr. Gardiner."

Red composed her face. She would not reveal the same disappointment Belle did.

Eddie stepped into the room, twisting the brim of his hand. "I thought you might be worried about Ward."

She nodded, not about to share her silly thoughts with him.

"He should have returned last night."

The meaning of his words made their way slowly to the center of Red's brain, and then exploded. She grabbed a chair and sat down before her legs gave out. "I thought—" Her worries seemed so selfish.

Belle's eyes were far too wide. "He's gone?"

Eddie glanced from one to the other. "No need to worry."

A little late to tell them that. "But you're worried?"

"I'm sure he's fine, but I'm going out to check on him."

Belle's breath released in a moan.

Red pulled Belle to her. She meant to soothe the younger girl but clung to her, finding comfort and strength in her warm little body. She burst with questions she dare not voice. Where was Ward? Was he hurt?

Eddie jammed his hat on his head. "I best be on my way." But he didn't immediately turn. Instead, he tipped his head and signaled he wanted to speak to Red.

She stood and eased Belle to the chair. "I'm going to say goodbye to Eddie. You wait here."

Eddie held the door for her and she stepped outside. He closed it firmly behind him. Her nerves jarred with the sound.

He rubbed at his forehead. "There's more." He leaned closer, his expression filled with urgency. "Ward told us about Thorton Winch. Constable Allen rode up to the ranch with news that he's escaped. He feared the man was headed this way."

Red collapsed against the wall. Thorton! If he found her... Then a second, more dreadful thought burned through her mind. "Do you think he ran into Ward?"

"I don't know what to think. But I want you and Belle to stay up at the big house until we can be sure you're safe. Go pack up whatever you need."

She heard his words, understood what he wanted, but she couldn't move.

"Red." Eddie shook her gently. "You need to hurry."

She nodded once but couldn't think what he meant her to do.

"Red, I can't go after Ward until I know you're safely in the house with Linette."

She nodded. Over and over.

He opened the door and gave her a little shove through it.

Her legs like log posts, she stepped inside, looked around and then reality hit her. Thorton had escaped. Ward was missing. And she delayed Eddie in searching for him.

She forced her trembling limbs to pull out the sack Linette had sent items in and tossed in the clean clothes stacked in neat piles.

Belle pushed her chair back with a clatter that shrieked along Red's nerves and she rushed to Red's side. "What are you doing?"

"We have to leave here immediately."

Belle pushed Red away from her task. "We can't leave. I want to stay forever and ever. If you're going to run away from Ward, then I'm not going with you."

"Belle, we're only going to the big house. Now gather your things together as quickly as you can." She couldn't get there soon enough. The idea of being caught by a vengeful Thorton brought bile to her throat.

"I'm not going." Belle plunked down on the floor.

Ignoring her, Red continued to stuff in items, urgency making her movements jerky. She saw the book she was reading and added it. "I'm ready. Belle, come on." She tossed a sweater at her sister.

Belle crossed her arms and refused to move.

Eddie knelt before Belle. "You can't stay here. It isn't safe."

"Why not?" Her stubborn tone informed them she thought Eddie only said it in the hopes of making her move.

"It just isn't. Red isn't running away. But we need to get you to the house where you'll be safe."

"Ward said we're safe here."

Red sighed. "Belle, we aren't right now."

"You're just saying that."

Red considered her options. Belle left her little choice. "Thorton has escaped from jail. We'll only be safe with Linette and Grady."

"There's a man watching the house at all times," Eddie assured them.

Belle bolted to her feet and grabbed the sweater. Finished, she looked at Red, her eyes wide with fear and disappointment. "You said he would never bother us again."

Eddie took the sack Red had packed, gave a quick glance around the place, paused to push the wood away from the fire. Then he eased Belle toward the door.

They hurried up the hill. Every step drove shards of fear into Red's heart. Where was Ward? Was he injured? Or had Thorton captured him? She could well imagine him taking delight in torturing Ward.

Red closed her eyes in a vain attempt to stop the horrible pictures flooding her mind. She stumbled and Eddie caught her by the elbow.

"You need to stay strong," he murmured.

She nodded. She must not let Belle guess at her fears. By the time they reached the house she ached all over from tension.

Eddie turned them over to Linette, then hurried away.

"Grady," Linette said. "Why don't you show Belle

the new toys Papa gave you?" Linette had explained how Grady wanted to call Eddie "Papa."

Belle's eyes were still much too large and she grabbed Red's hand. "I'm scared."

Red managed a smile and took Belle to the windows. "See Slim out there? He'll make sure no one gets into the house."

"We're safe? Thorton can't lock us up?"

"Thorton will never lock us up again. I promise."

Satisfied, Belle went to play with Grady.

As soon as she was out of sight, Red groaned.

Linette hugged her. "I've been praying ever since we heard what happened. We must trust God to protect us."

Red tried to convince herself it was enough.

"Come. I've prepared tea." They sat before the windows overlooking the ranch where they could watch all the comings and goings. Eddie and Constable Allen left the barn, climbed the hill and stepped into the house.

Constable Allen took off his Stetson and tucked it under his arm. "Ma'am, Mrs. Gardiner. I just wanted to update you on what's going on. All the ranchers in the area have been notified about Winch's escape. They'll be on the lookout. I've organized several of the men into a posse to find Thorton and Ward. It's only a matter of time until both are located."

Linette twisted her teaspoon round and round. "Thorton isn't the only danger Ward faces. What if he's injured? Lost? Or something equally as dreadful?"

Eddie answered, "Ward is careful, cautious even. I can't imagine something like that happening to him."

"We'll find them both wherever they are, I assure you," Constable Allen said.

At the way the Mountie kept linking the two names together, the alarm Red had been struggling to keep under control scooped her insides hollow. If she hadn't been seated, she knew she would have fallen to the ground like an old rag. He was suggesting the only thing that would delay Ward would be Thorton.

"How would Thorton know we're here?"

The Mountie answered, "He persuaded a guard it was his right to know who was responsible for having him arrested. The guard foolishly gave Ward's name. Thorton wrote to the land agent asking after Ward Walker, claiming to be a long-lost brother. The agent gave him all the information he had."

"Including where his land is?"

The Mountie nodded, his eyes full of apology.

She shuddered. Thorton knew far too much. "Does he know Ward works here?"

The Mountie gave a tiny shrug. "It would be easy enough information to get."

Ward was in mortal danger. "Find Ward." She squeezed the words from a tight throat.

Constable Allen gave a tense smile. "Trust me. We'll find him. We'll find both of them. We'll keep you informed as best we can but now my job is to locate them."

Red watched him depart as a thousand fears dragged talons across her heart.

Linette rushed after Eddie. "I expect you home safe and sound."

Eddie kissed her and left.

Red and Linette watched the pair hurry toward the barn.

Roper and Cassie and the children came into sight. Roper paused to speak to Eddie, then continued toward the house. Linette went to let them in.

"I'm going to join in the search but I don't want to leave Cassie and the children unguarded."

"Of course not. They can stay here. Come in. Children, Grady and Belle are in the kitchen."

The children went to play under the watchful eye of Daisy, and then Cassie and Linette returned to the sitting room.

Cassie squeezed Red's arm. "They'll find Ward."

At least she didn't link Ward's name with Thorton's, for which Red was grateful.

A few minutes later the men rode away to the west.

Red jerked forward. "I should have told them to check his ranch. Maybe he stopped there."

Linette gripped Red's elbow. "I'm sure they'll check. Let's pray for safety for all of them." She didn't give Red a chance to either agree or argue but bowed her head and prayed fervently God would protect them all, help them find Ward and help the Mountie capture the fugitive. "Amen."

Cassie had taken her hand during the prayer. "Amen," she said, and released her grip on Red's hand.

"Amen," Red added. She could not pray, though she wished she could. What was the use though when she knew God would not hear her?

The minutes passed, heavy and cold. Finally Linette pushed to her feet. "The children will be hungry. I'll see to lunch."

Red helped with preparations, sat at the table with the others, ate the food set before her but she couldn't even say what it was.

Gloom crept into the corners as they watched out the window. As night fell, the men returned to the barn.

Eddie and Roper staggered into the house and sighed as if weary to the soles of their feet.

The women sprang forward. "Did you find him?"

"Not a sign anywhere," Eddie said. "We went to the

cabin. It was empty. There is no trail, no clues indicating either of them. Ward has no reason to hide his trail. But Thorton—" He scrubbed at the back of his neck. "The man is a magician at hiding his tracks." He looked from Linette to Red to Cassie. "We'll be out again at first light."

Red clamped her lips together. She would not let her wail escape. Excusing herself under a mumbled excuse, she hurried from the room and sank down on a chair in the kitchen. Ward was gone. All her fine talk about how she could manage on her own meant nothing as truth after truth bombarded her. He had been nothing but kind. He had the sweetest smile, the nicest eyes. His voice triggered happy feelings inside her. She clamped her hand to her mouth. Her heart squeezed tight. How could she have been so blind?

Because even if he didn't love her, she loved him with an ache the size of this house. She'd treated him unkindly. Would she get an opportunity to make it up to him?

Her insides felt sucked dry as she contemplated her situation.

She wanted to spend the rest of her life with him. Would she ever get the chance?

What had become of him?

But she had no answers by the time Linette showed her and Belle to a guest room. Cassie and the four children had returned to their house with Roper.

She prepared for bed and lay beside Belle until her sister's breathing deepened, then she rose. Unable to even pretend sleep, she circled the room, looking at each object. Some of the paintings she recognized as Linette's work. A bookshelf hung on one wall. She lifted each book and examined it. One was a hymnal. She paged through it, remembered standing between Mama and Papa as they sang the familiar words. A folded piece of paper fell from the pages. She picked it up and opened it. Someone had written a poem, perhaps meant to be set to music for a hymn. Because she didn't want to think beyond the walls of this room, she read the words.

Grace that exceeds our sin and our guilt!
Grace that is greater then all our sin. Dark is
the stain we cannot hide. What can avail to wash
it away?

It was the anguished cry of her heart. Was there forgiveness for what she'd one?

Brighter than snow you may be today.

She fell on her knees. Was it possible God could forgive so great a sin as hers?

Oh God, is Your grace meant for a sinner such as I?
I was once an innocent believer.
Can I be a tarnished, forgiven believer?
My grace is sufficient.

The words were from the Bible but filled in the spaces between each heartbeat.

Sufficient even for someone with Red's past?

Sufficiency from God's almighty, powerful, everlasting hands. From the Creator of heaven and earth. The God that parted the Red Sea and could move mountains.

How much more could she ask?

Lord, forgive my sin, wash me until I am white as

snow. Cleanse me from those awful things I was forced to do.

She pressed her face into her palms and let the words of the poem speak her heart and her pain.

Blessed, joyous release came. She laughed softly so as to not waken Belle. God did forgive sins, even those as loathsome as hers.

Free to now pray, she silently beseeched God to keep Ward safe. Then she fell into bed and slept.

Ward smiled into the empty landscape as he rode away from the ranch.

One of Eddie's prize imported bulls was missing. He and Slim had been dispatched to locate him. He planned to ride far, wide and hard, find the bull if the animal was in his circuit and get back to the ranch as fast as possible.

His insides sang with anticipation. Would Red agree to marry him? He couldn't imagine anything more pleasant than taking care of her the rest of his life. Just the thought of it oiled his insides with peace. He'd never lost the idea he'd failed his mother and brothers, but if Red gave him a chance, he would never fail her. Not so long as it depended on him. He wasn't foolish enough to think he might not make mistakes, but he would certainly pray for God to help him. He would win her back to her own faith in God. She'd once believed. She would learn that God never changed and she could trust Him as much as she'd done as a child.

Marrying to keep her safe and take care of her made perfect sense. But could he keep her safe? He'd failed to do so with his brothers and mother. Instead, he'd abandoned them. He vowed if Red agreed to marry him, he would never leave her and Belle. He would do his best to protect them. And should he fail, he would simply keep trying.

The bull wasn't in the lower pastures so Ward headed toward higher ground, his mount clattering over a rock-infested ridge. He rode through brush and searched around hills for the missing animal.

"Okay, bull, where are you? I'd like to get back as soon as possible."

His search would take him within a couple of miles of his ranch and he veered in that direction. Could be the bull might take it in his head to pay the empty place a visit.

He reached the crest of a hill that allowed him a view of his ranch. The buildings sat in a natural clearing that was big enough for a good-sized farmyard. Like he'd told Red, he'd thought of building the cabin on the top of the hill but figured it might be buffeted by winter winds, so he chose a spot a little ways down. All he had at this point in time was a small log cabin, a wood shed and some corrals. He'd build a fine barn one of these days. He turned in his saddle. To the west lay rippling hills that crept up the side of the mountain. The mountains filled the horizon, shining in the sun. Dark pines draped from every crevasse.

"It's a beautiful spot," he murmured. "Red and Belle will love it here." Only one dark spot remained in his plans. He had not heard from his mother and brothers. He longed to give them a home as well.

Ruminating would not find the bull and get Ward back to Red to hear her answer. He'd seen the acceptance in her eyes and already knew what she'd say, but he still longed to hear the word *yes*.

They climbed higher. Reached a plateau, and Ward

gave his mount a chance to relax a bit as he glanced about for any sign of the missing animal.

"Nothing," he muttered. The sun had already dipped into the west. He'd have to turn back now to reach the ranch before dark.

Something stirred the bushes across the coulee. He urged his horse toward the rim of the plateau to get a better look. The purple shadows deepened so he couldn't make out the dark shape. He needed to get closer, and searched for a way to get down the incline. Spotting a narrow ledge, he reined the horse toward the path.

The animal sidestepped and tossed his head, indicating he didn't care for the direction Ward indicated. Why had he picked this particular horse to ride? Paddy was known to be a knucklehead who shied at shadows.

"Now, look here, Paddy. The sooner we have a look, the sooner we can head back. You won't be getting any hay or oats until we're done. So best you choose carefully where you put your feet and get us off this plateau."

The horse responded to Ward's firm hand and started down the trail. It was narrowed more than Ward anticipated. In hindsight, he should have ridden several miles to the east where he knew there was a gentler trail. But it was too late to do anything but keep going.

"Steady there, old boy." He murmured encouragement to the frightened horse. "We'll be okay." But the sun had lowered enough to make it difficult to see.

He gently urged Paddy to put one foot in front of the other. "Look, I'm not enjoying this any more than you are. But the sooner we get to the bottom, the better for both of us." Every nerve tensed for the smallest clue to guide them safely.

Without warning the ground gave way beneath them. Ward's heart jolted as they dropped into nothingness. His heart bounced to the roof of his mouth and stayed. He kicked free of the stirrups and threw himself off the saddle. He might fall a hundred feet and land on rocks but he still preferred his chances on his own to being rolled on by a horse.

For an immeasurable moment he hung in the air, and then landed on one shoulder, his air leaving his body in a whoosh. He rolled several times and came to rest on something solid. Pain crisscrossed his chest.

He blinked to clear his vision but all he saw was shapes. He squinted, saw a dark shape to the side. The cliff. He shifted carefully, uncertain if he had stopped partway down or reached the bottom.

Before him spread a gray blanket. He tried to get to his feet but swayed as pain shot through his head. He sank back to the ground.

"Paddy? Come." Through the deepening darkness he saw the horse trot away and settle down to enjoy the green grass. Stupid animal. He wouldn't even go home and alert Eddie and the other cowboys of Ward's dilemma.

Ward turned and tried to make out the cliff but his eyes refused to focus. He'd never be able to navigate a climb without proper light.

He'd have to spend the night here. He shivered. If only he had the slicker tied to his saddle. "Paddy," he called again, forcing false cheerfulness to his voice. "Oats, boy. How about some oats?" But he couldn't shake a bucket and tease him closer.

With a sigh that tore at his bruised ribs, he shifted about and got as comfortable as possible. He groaned. His situation left something to be desired. Determined to ignore his discomfort, he shifted his thoughts to other things. What would Red think when he didn't show up as he'd promised? Likely that he'd changed his mind. No doubt he'd have his work cut out for him convincing her he hadn't.

The cold stole up his legs. Thoughts of Red warmed his heart.

Why hadn't she jumped at the chance to marry him? It provided the perfect solution to her problems. Safety and the protection of his good name.

He couldn't see anything but the blackness of the night but he squinted as he considered his question. Should he have offered her more? Should he have said he loved her? He rubbed at his cold chin. Love was a highly overrated commodity in his thinking, though the love he'd seen between his ma and pa had been real enough. Yet his stepfather had vowed he loved Ma and her sons. His actions proved otherwise. Ward loved his ma and his brothers. Yet what did it mean? He'd left them. Perhaps with the best of intentions. But still, he'd left and had no way of knowing if they were safe or suffered the daily beatings meant for Ward.

Nope, far as he could see actions meant a whole lot more than words of love. He figured what Red needed he could provide without letting love cloud the issue.

The air grew colder. He was high enough up the mountain that he'd have to endure a long, cold night.

Several hours later his head jerked to his chest and he bolted awake. *You must get back to Red. Take care of her. She needs you even if she won't admit it. You can give her what she needs. Safety. Protection.* It was enough. It had to be. Would she ever tell him her real name? Wouldn't she have to if they married?

Something stung his eyes. He blinked. Sunshine.

His limbs ached with polar ice. Cold sunshine. But at least he could find his way out of there. The sun was already high in the sky despite the fact it seemed to lack warmth.

He staggered to his feet, pins and needles of pain informing him of returning circulation. He had to get to Red. Had to tell her something. He shook his head. He couldn't remember what he was supposed to tell her.

He swayed as he fought for balance. "Paddy, come here. That's a good boy." His words were mumbled sounds but the horse understood his meaning. But would he trot to Ward so he could ride out of this predicament? Of course not. He tossed his head and ambled several more yards away to make sure Ward couldn't catch him.

Ward looked about him. A hundred yards to the east he made out what appeared to be a path wide enough to allow a man to the top. Stepping gingerly on tender feet, he climbed to the top and headed across the plateau in a direct line to his ranch. Every bone in his body hurt. Every breath ripped from his lungs. But he pushed aside the pain. He had to get back to the ranch and Red.

The sun shone bright enough to hurt his eyes but failed to warm him. Several times he staggered and righted himself. How long had he been walking? He squinted at the sky. The mountains were at his back. He turned and the sun hit him in the eyes. Already afternoon. He checked the pain in his leg, saw a deep gouge that oozed blood. Wondered about the pain in his arm. Nothing he could do for it. Had to keep going. Get back to Red.

He reached an open area where he'd chopped trees not long ago. He'd soon be at his cabin and he picked up his pace in anticipation.

In his haste, he fell. *Get up. Get up.* His body slowly obeyed. *Red.* He breathed her name in and out on each breath. Each breath hammered against the inside of his skull. *Red.* He focused on her name and found strength to continue.

He staggered and righted himself. Was that the cabin? He squinted. Tried to bring his vision into focus. The walls of the cabin wavered ahead of him. It was only a few yards away. He ran. More precisely, he lurched toward the cabin. Reached the door and leaned on it. The latch released and he tumbled to the floor and lay there, beyond caring.

Inch by inch he pushed his face off the floor, got to his hands and knees and looked around. The bed beckoned and he crawled to it, pulled a blanket over himself and fell asleep.

Chapter Fourteen

Something nudged Ward from his dreams. A blow to his boot. He surfaced slowly, loath to leave the dream he'd been having about Red. They were married and living in this cabin. Only it had many, many rooms. Each room seemed to evolve from the previous one until he was lost and calling for her. *Red. Red.* Her voice answered, telling him he was safe but he couldn't find her.

His first conscious thought was how strange that she was telling him he was safe. Wasn't it the other way around? Wasn't he the one who promised safety?

The blow to his boot came again. Someone was in the cabin and it wasn't Red. It was a man.

Ward was instantly alert but he calmed himself and faked being half-asleep as he studied his guest. Thorton. Holding a gun and wearing a self-satisfied smirk.

A thousand fearful thoughts clogged Ward's brain. How had this man escaped? Had he harmed Red and Belle? Best move slowly. Find out what was going on before he did something he might regret. Like choke the man with his bare hands.

"Well, lookee here. If it ain't the man who stole my

girls from me." Thorton's smile belied the evil in his eyes.

Ward edged his feet over the side of the bed to face Thorton. Sleep had helped to restore his strength. "There's laws against owning people. Or keeping them against their will."

Thorton's laugh rang with embedded evil. "Red could have left anytime she wanted."

"You know she would never leave Belle in your clutches."

"Poor Belle. You taking care of her as well as I did? How about Red?" His eyes glinted with knowing mockery.

Ward curled his fists. He must not fly at this man even though he ached to. He had to outsmart him.

"At least I don't have to force her to stay by locking up her little sister."

Thorton's amusement died. "Thought you'd have them here with you. Where are they?"

Ward allowed his eyes to give away nothing. Thorton didn't know her whereabouts? Or was he only taunting Ward? "How'd you find me?"

"Told the land agent I was your long-lost brother. He readily told me where you had this ranch." He snorted. "Looks like your ranch is only in your imagination. You figure on bringing Red here to live?"

Ward shrugged.

"Well, sonny, you ain't never gonna get the chance. Where's my girls?"

"Can't say."

Thorton's gaze was as cold as the metal gun in his hands and Ward wasn't fooled. He was just as dangerous with or without a gun. "You've got her, and I want her back."

So he didn't know where Red was.

"You're going take me to her or else."

Ward leaned back, guessing his expression was as mocking as his feelings. "And if I don't?"

"I could shoot you on the spot."

"Wouldn't help you find Red though, would it?"

Thorton considered the question for several seconds.

Ward used the time to mull over his options, but trying to figure out several things at the same time with a brain that hadn't had enough sleep and was distracted by having a gun leveled at his heart proved a challenge.

"Where are they?"

What would best serve to get Thorton distracted from searching for Red and Belle? Besides a bullet straight through his heart.

Thorton jammed the gun up Ward's nostrils. "Take me to them."

Ward sucked back caution and a goodly dose of fear that drained his heart of blood and left him as cold as the dead of winter. He tried to gauge the time of day. A slice of a glance toward the window showed the sun gleaming on the Rockies. He must have slept several hours.

"I expect they're with friends."

"And where exactly might that be?" The gun bit into his flesh. Ward knew hatred like he'd never known in his life, not even when his stepfather had beat him. Not even when the man had beaten Travers just to get a reaction from Ward. Thorton wanted Red for all the wrong reasons and Ward would not allow it. He could only pray that Eddie knew of Thorton's escape and had taken Red and Belle into his house for protection. "I might take you where they are." He would never take him to the ranch but perhaps he might get a chance to disarm the man if they rode down the trail.

"You take me there. Then I'll decide what to do with you."

"Fine. I don't have a horse."

"I found one a ways from here. Might be yours or not. Don't matter. It will serve the purpose."

"I need to give him a few oats if he's going to make the trip back to the ranch."

"Forget the oats." Thorton urged him to the door without any kindness in the way he jabbed the gun in Ward's ribs. At least it was out of his nose. He had a rifle on the saddle. Always carried one in case he met a pack of wolves or an injured animal. If he could distract Thorton long enough to get it...

The horse that Thorton had found was knuckle-headed Paddy, all right. Ward approached the horse.

"Hold up there." Thorton's voice rang with warning. "I think I'll relieve you of this." He reached around and removed the rifle from the horse. "Don't guess you're going to be needing it. I got all the firepower we need." He tied a rope around Ward's waist and pushed him to mount.

"You best keep an eye out for wolves, then. I saw a pack several times in the past week. Other cowboys have seen them, too," Ward said.

"You're just saying that to make me nervous. Hoping you might distract me."

"Don't deny that I might not like to see you take that gun off me, but I ain't making it up about the wolves. Just saying you ought to keep your eyes on more than just me, seeing as you're the only one with a gun. I ain't got no desire to be wolf bait."

Thorton laughed, a sound full of evil mockery. "I wouldn't mind seeing you devoured by a pack of wolves.

Seems fitting after you stole my girls away as sneaky as any wolf I ever saw."

"Be that as it is. I 'spect if they get me, they'll get you as well." He enjoyed the way Thorton's eyes darted from one side of the clearing to the other. He didn't mind a bit seeing the man get all nervous and swallow hard at the thought of wolves on his trail. Despite Thorton's pretense at being convinced that Ward joshed him, it was plain he didn't fancy being wolf food, either.

Ward decided to take advantage of Thorton's nerves. "You ever seen a wolf up close? Man, when one of them bares his teeth it's enough to make the bravest man cry for his mother."

"You, maybe," Thorton said. "I ain't never cried for my mama."

Ward bit back the remark burning the tip of his tongue. He doubted the man had a mama. At least one he could remember.

Ward decided he'd pushed hard enough, but he hoped he'd given the man something to fret about. A man tensed up was a dangerous man. But Ward counted on Thorton taking chances that would give him an opening.

"Get in your saddle and show me where Red and Belle are. I intend to get back what is mine."

Ward swung up and headed down the trail. Somehow Thorton's little brain hadn't noticed there was only one trail out. 'Course he might have come that way and discovered the fork in the trail.

He led the way, but Thorton kept a firm hold on the rope around Ward's waist to make sure he couldn't pull any "funny stuff," as Thorton called it.

Ward's mind clattered with all sorts of ways to distract Thorton. If he could get the gun…

But Thorton didn't give him an opening.

Ward prayed. *God, help me stop him. I don't want him to ever find Red and Belle.* In fact he would not let it happen. He would die stopping Thorton if necessary. He hoped it wouldn't be. He wanted to spend years and years with Red. Loving her. The truth caught his breath and stopped it halfway up his throat. He loved her. He didn't care if love was risky or foolish. He didn't care if Red ever loved him back. It was enough to love her and spend the rest of his life showing her. Or die protecting her. He chuckled. How ironic that he'd discovered the truth about love only to face never having the chance to live it.

Thorton jerked on the rope. "What you laughing at?"

"Thinking of Red."

Thorton yanked the rope so hard Ward had to turn the horse to keep from being pulled from the saddle.

"You keep your thoughts off her. She's mine. Why, I bet she never even told you her real name." His voice grew low. "I could tell you." He laughed a sound so harsh and bitter that it sent cold fingers up and down Ward's spine. "But then I'd have to kill you."

Ward reined his horse forward and continued down the trail. He had no mind to discover Red's real name from the poisoned mouth of Thorton. No, sir. He wanted to hear it from Red's lips. He knew the day he did it would signify that she had let her past go. *God, help her find release from her past.* He smiled at the thought of sharing his life with her. Would he fail her as he'd failed his family? *And help me be strong and make the right choices.*

A dark shadow in the trees to the side caught his attention. He stared after it. Saw another. "Thorton, don't look now but there are wolves following us."

"Yeah, like I'd fall for that trick."

Ward kept his eye on the trees. "Give me my rifle." His low, controlled voice must have said something to Thorton.

"Not going to happen." But he turned to follow the direction of Ward's gaze.

Another shadow flitted past.

Thorton let out a cuss. "Sneaky things. Why don't they come out in the open where a man could shoot 'em?"

Ward thought that was reason enough for them to hide, but knew Thorton wasn't looking for an answer. Another shadow slipped by. "That makes four. There's probably more."

Thorton shot into the trees. Aiming at shadows made for poor target practice. Ward knew he missed hitting anything but trees. He shot five more times. Ward counted the shots. When he knew the gun was empty he spurred Paddy toward the other man. Paddy leaped forward in surprise. Before Thorton could realize his danger, Ward grabbed his wrist and whacked it across the saddle horn. The gun went flying.

Ward roared in rage and grabbed Thorton by the throat. The pair tumbled to the ground. Both horses snorted and backed away. Thorton twisted and punched and cursed. No doubt he feared for his life, and well he should because Ward didn't intend he should continue to threaten Red and Belle. The man fought hard but Ward had far more at stake. Ignoring the pain in his ribs and limbs, he pummeled the man. He intended to live to tell Red he loved her. He planned to marry her and enjoy many, many years with her. She needed to know she was loved as a woman should be. Forever and always.

Riders approached. Were they friends of Thorton's? "Hello, it's Constable Allen. You can let him go now."

But Ward wasn't letting anyone go. Not until he was done with the man.

Hands pulled him off.

Constable Allen slapped cuffs on the struggling Thorton. Ward was pleased to see Thorton's nose bleeding and a lump swelling his eye.

"Good job of stopping him."

Ward shrugged away from the restraining hands. "If you hadn't come along I would have given him what he deserves."

"Don't worry. This man will get what he deserves. He killed a Mountie."

Ward's laugh was short and bitter. "See he doesn't escape again." He leaned as close to Thorton as the men would allow. "You ever show your face around here again and you're a dead man. Stay away from Red and Belle or you'll regret it. For about a minute as you draw your dying breath."

The Mountie dragged Thorton to his horse. "Get him out of here."

Constable Allen gave Ward serious study. "You're looking a little ragged around the edges. Eddie has men searching for you." He nodded toward two men. "See that he gets back to the ranch safely."

"They'll just slow me down." Ward swung into his saddle and kicked Paddy into a gallop. He had to get to Red and Belle.

Vaguely he was aware of the throbbing in his side as he rode for the ranch.

He leaped from his horse as he approached the barn and left the animal to fend for itself. He dashed for the cabin and threw the door open without pausing to knock. "Red!" he bellowed. The word echoed. "Red? Belle?" They must be out back.

He dashed around to the fire pit. Nothing. He kicked the ashes. Cold. They hadn't been there today.

He returned to the cabin and slowly began to notice details. The stove was cold. The corner where Belle played, empty.

The cold gripped his insides as the information seeped into his thoughts. No dolly. No doll clothes. Not giving any thought to intrusion, he strode over to the bedroom door. No clothing items hung on the hooks. The whole place had the air of being uninhabited.

His legs turned to cotton and he fell against the wall. Was she up the hill with Linette? But wouldn't someone have told him? Had she gone to the mission? Was this her answer?

He'd stop her. Tell her he loved her. Persuade her to change her mind. He spun about and raced from the room, not even bothering to close the door behind him. His pace increased as he headed for the barn.

Cal appeared in the doorway.

"Saddle me a horse," Ward called.

Cal jerked back. "Ward? Where did you come from?" Then he laughed. "You look downright awful. Like you've been dragged by a horse."

"Never mind. Get me a horse."

"There ain't much here in the way of mounts. Everyone is out scouring the country for you and that escaped criminal."

"Constable Allen has the man in custody. And I'm okay, as you can see. There has to be something left to ride." He headed around the barn to the pasture where they kept a string of horses. About half of them were gone. "One of those will do."

"I don't know what Eddie will say. They were rode hard all day yesterday."

"One of them is going to ride hard again today." He slipped through the gate, eyed up the horses and chose the sturdiest-looking one of the bunch. He grabbed a halter from the fence where someone had carelessly left it. Roper would have something to say to the culprit. Then he eased about and dropped the halter over the horse and led him into the barn.

Cal followed him. "You mind telling me where you going in such an all-fired hurry?"

"How come you aren't out looking for me and Thorton along with the others?"

"The boss left me and Slim to guard the big house. Make sure the jailbird didn't sneak in."

Ward tossed a saddle blanket onto the horse, then a saddle.

Cal grabbed his arm. "Man, you're bleeding. You ought to let Linette look at that."

Ward glanced at his blood-soaked sleeve. "It'll keep. I got more important things to tend to."

"So it seems. Exactly where are you headed? Just in case Eddie wonders."

Ward slowed down and sucked in air that tortured his ribs. "Guess I should let him know what I got in mind. I aim to go after Red and bring her back."

"Huh. You need a horse to do that?"

Ward shook his head. Cal could be a little thick-headed at times but this was worse than usual. "I'll follow her all the way to Medicine Hat if I have to. I'm not letting her go."

"Guess you've got the love bug, huh?" Cal grinned like a fool.

"I don't have time for your silly games."

"You got more time than you think you do."

Someday, if Ward lived long enough, he might see Cal grow up enough to make sense. "I'll be on my way. Tell Eddie I'll be back with Red and Belle."

A number of horses clattered into the yard. Cal went to the door and stared out. "Guess you can tell him yourself. He's back."

Ward gritted his teeth. Another delay. He'd never catch up to Red at this rate.

Eddie strode in. "Cal, look after the horses." He stared at Ward. "Constable Allen told me what happened. He said you'd be back here. Said you looked pretty beat-up. He didn't exaggerate. Thorton do this to you?"

"Thorton and a fall down a mountain."

"I'm guessing that's why you didn't return when you were expected?"

"Made for a bit of a delay."

Eddie eyed the freshly saddled horse. "You running out?"

"Going after Red. Figure she's halfway to Medicine Hat by now, but I'll catch up to her."

"You're after Red, huh?" Eddie grinned. "Good to hear."

"I'd like to get on my way, if you don't mind."

"I think you better come to the house before you leave."

"Boss? I'm in an awful hurry."

"Nevertheless, if you want to ride my horses until they're wasted and worn, you come to the house before you leave." He turned away, taking Ward's compliance for granted.

Ward didn't move. "I don't need any more delays."

Cal, carrying gear to the tack room, heard him. "He's the boss." Did the boy ever stop grinning?

"Yeah, guess so."

Still he hesitated. He could delay long enough for Eddie to get out of the road, then ride away. Eddie might send someone after him. Might dock his wages when he returned. Might be angry enough to fire him, but at the moment Ward only cared about finding Red.

Red finished helping with lunch dishes and the women returned to the little sitting room with Linette to watch for riders. Red prayed she'd see Ward return. Instead she watched Eddie and half a dozen men ride to the barn and dismount. Eddie ducked into the barn. Cal came out and helped the men tend to the horses.

No Ward. A chill weaved along the length of Red's spine and drove icy spears to her heart. What had happened to him? Was she destined to lose him just when she'd decided she could love him?

She clenched her fists. *Please, God. Bring him back to me. Please.*

Eddie stepped from the barn and headed up the hill.

Linette clutched Red's curled fists. "It must be good news or they wouldn't have come back."

She nodded. Didn't Linette realize Ward wasn't among them? The thought wailed through her head, sucked the blood from her heart.

Eddie stepped inside. "Good news, ladies. Thorton is under guard. He shot a Mountie while escaping so he'll hang for sure."

"Ward?" Red choked the word out.

"He helped capture Thorton. The way Allen tells it, they had to pry him off the man."

"Is he okay?" Linette asked on Red's behalf.

"He's a little worse for wear. Guess he fell down a cliff or something. I didn't get too many details."

"Where is he?" Red wailed.

"He should be here by now." He moved to the window. "I don't believe it."

Red saw Ward leave the barn, leading a horse.

She held her breath, waiting for him to head up the hill.

Instead he turned the other way.

Wasn't he coming to see her? Had he changed his mind? Was it too late for her to tell him who she was and what she wanted? "I must speak to him." She rushed past Eddie, paying no attention to his words. She trotted down the hill, almost losing her balance in her haste. "Ward," she called. "Wait."

But he didn't hear her.

She continued her flight past the cookhouse. Didn't slow until she reached the barn.

Ward argued with Slim at the corral corner. "I don't care what Eddie said. I'm taking a horse. I intend to find Red."

Slim grinned at Red over Ward's shoulder. "I don't think you'll need a horse."

"Get out of my way."

"Turn around."

Ward tried to push past Slim.

He intended to find her. But why did he need a horse? Finally able to speak, she called. "Ward?"

Ward jolted like he'd stepped on something sharp. He lifted his head and stared at Slim then slowly turned. He saw her and blinked. Shook his head. "Red? What are you doing here?"

She smiled. "Waiting for you."

"But how? Why?" He swallowed hard. "I thought you must have gone to the mission."

"And you were planning to ride there? Why?"

Slim disappeared into the barn and shut the door firmly.

Ward closed the three steps separating them and touched her cheek. "You've been here all the time?"

"Eddie said we'd be safer in the big house." She caught his hand. "Come inside, and I'll tell you what happened."

Her touch brought him from his stunned state.

They crossed to the cabin. She wondered when the door had blown open. They sat side by side and she began her story.

"When the Mountie informed Eddie that Thorton had escaped, he insisted we stay with Linette." Still clutching his hand, she turned to study each dear feature. "Where were you? I've been so worried."

He told her of his accident. His gaze grew sorrowful. "When I came here and you were gone…" He shook his head. "I imagined you'd gone to the mission." He clasped her shoulders. "You're okay? You and Belle?"

"We're both very well." She let herself float in the warmth of his look. But there were things she must tend to. "Ward, my name is Grace. Grace Amanda Henderson. And God's grace has shown me that He loves me despite what I've done."

He cupped her cheek and rubbed his thumb along her face. "You did nothing wrong. Grace? I like it. It suits you." He searched her features as if memorizing them. A skitter of fear raced through her. Was he memorizing them because he meant to say goodbye? Had she changed too late?

"Grace, I have been a fool."

She pulled away, her heart threatening to crack with sorrow. He regretted asking her to marry him.

"I wanted to take care of you. Thought it was all you need. You were right. It was my way of making up for not being able to care for my mother and brothers. But I learned something in the last couple of days." He pulled her toward him, tipped her face toward him.

She kept her eyes lowered, unable to endure any more of his regrets.

"What I wouldn't admit to myself and wouldn't share with you is that I love you."

Her gaze flew to his face. Filled with amazement and sincerity. "You love me?"

He chuckled. "I do. In a thousand ways. 'How do I love thee? Let me count the ways. I love thee to the depth and breadth and height my soul can reach.'"

As he quoted the poem her father had so often spoken to her ma, her eyes filled with tears. He brushed each away with his finger.

"Don't cry. Please don't cry."

"These are happy tears." She sucked back an uneven breath.

He kissed her damp cheeks. "And I shall quote it to you every chance I get." He jerked back. "I'm jumping to conclusions here. Grace, will you marry me?"

She saw the need in his eyes. The need for something only she could give him. "Ward Walker, I love you. I have from the time you stood up to Thorton in that saloon. I will be honored to marry you and share my life with you." She had to be certain of one thing. "My life and my little sister."

"That goes without saying." He kissed her cheeks again.

She lifted her face and offered him so much more. Her heart, her life, her future.

He claimed her mouth and gave her a kiss full of promises. Then he pulled her into his arms and told her of his experiences the past two days.

"I am so thankful you are safe and sound. I prayed God would protect you and He has."

"I had to get a chance to tell you I love you." He kissed her again to emphasize it.

Safe in his arms, she told him of the past, not minimizing her fear and loathing at how Thorton had humiliated her.

"Grace, you did nothing wrong, though I understand how you might feel. But God has washed your past away."

She clung to his reassuring gaze. "I know. It's marvelous to feel free." She rubbed her cheek against his shoulder. "And to know the love of a good man."

"I'm blessed to know your love."

Later, having opened their hearts to each other and shared their deepest longings and fears, they walked hand in hand up the hill to the big house.

Linette greeted them at the door. "I wondered how long before you two chose to join us." Her wide smile and flashing eyes informed them that she shared their joy. "Belle's been anxious to see you."

Belle rushed toward them. "Where you been? Red, did you say you'd marry him?" She left no doubt that if Grace did not do so, she would be a sore failure.

Grace and Ward both squatted down to face Belle. Linette slipped away to give them privacy.

"You can call me Grace again. And yes, Ward and I are getting married."

Ward pulled Belle into a three-cornered hug. "Belle,

I love your sister and I love you. Will you accept me as your brother?"

Belle pulled away to give him a look rife with disbelief. "I don't want a brother. I want a father."

Grace choked back a sob. If she wasn't mistaken, Ward's eyes showed the glisten of tears.

"I'd be pleased to be your father."

They hugged long and hard.

Then joined Linette in the sitting room. "I don't need to look at you twice to know you have good news."

Grace smiled. "We're going to get married and start a new life." It would truly be a new life. One blessed by God's gracious love and forgiveness.

Linette hugged her tight. "Are you going to wait until we get a church in Edendale?"

Grace looked at Ward for his opinion and laughed out loud at the shock and refusal widening his eyes.

Her eyes twinkling, she turned back to Linette. "We haven't discussed it but I don't think we want to wait that long."

Linette grinned. "I kind of suspected that would be your answer. Now let's have a look at Ward's injuries."

Grace helped cut Ward's sleeve to expose a deep gash. "It's dirty. I hope you don't get infection."

As Linette left to get water to wash his cuts, he leaned over and kissed Grace. "I won't get sick because I have far more important things to do. I want to show you my ranch. I want to get married and start life together there."

She concentrated on his injury.

"Red—Grace, what's bothering you?"

His tender question opened her heart. "What about your family? What if you find them? And they want to join you?"

He took her hands and gently rubbed each knuckle. "It would be an answer to prayer. I can't think of anything I'd sooner have than my old family and my new family on the ranch."

"You'd have room for all of us?" From what he'd said she expected a small cabin much like the one she and Belle presently shared.

Ward chuckled. "Not in the same house. But with two brothers I think we could put up another house in short order." He sobered. "I only wish it was something I needed to do."

"Me, too." Hearing Linette's footsteps, she stole one more kiss and whispered, "I love you."

His eyes shone as bright as a summer sky.

Linette laughed. "I'm happy for you both."

Chapter Fifteen

❧

Ward's injuries weren't serious. Only some cuts and bruises that healed quickly, though his ribs continued to feel like he'd been run over by a herd of stampeding cows. Eddie insisted he take it easy for a few days and he didn't argue.

"I want to take you and Belle to see my ranch," he told Grace, pleased when she seemed eager for the trip.

Early one morning, he pulled the wagon to the cabin and helped Grace and Belle to the seat. "It's going to be a beautiful day." Truth was, even if the sun wasn't shining so bright and the sky wasn't clear from horizon to horizon, even if a cold north wind buffeted them and rain peppered their skin he would think it a beautiful day with Grace pressed to his side.

The air was golden. The trees flicked their dark green leaves.

He glanced about at the spot where he'd seen the wolves. Thankfully, none appeared. Eddie assured him they had been driven from the area, but Ward wouldn't be taking any chances with his precious cargo.

A few minutes later, they turned past a thick stand of

pines and the ranch lay ahead of them. He stopped the wagon. "There it is. My ranch and our future home."

Grace sighed.

"I'm hoping that's a good sound."

"It is." She squeezed his hand. "It's a beautiful spot." Trees dressed in dark green formed a backdrop to the north.

"I hope you'll like the cabin. It's small but I plan to add on."

She laughed, the sound ringing in the rooms of his heart. "I think you'll find I'm not fussy." Turning so she could look deeply into his eyes, her smile filling her face. "I'm happy simply to have a home."

Her words pinched his brain. "And love?" he prompted.

Her smile deepened until it felt warm and rich. "And love," she whispered.

He understood she still struggled with her doubts and vowed to spend the rest of his life erasing them. "I love you, Grace Henderson. Soon to be Grace Walker." He leaned closer and caught her lips in a kiss.

She pressed her hand to his back as if she wanted to assure herself that he wouldn't withdraw…not only from the kiss, but from his promise of love.

"Hello," Belle said. "I'm here."

Grace jerked back, her cheeks pink with embarrassment.

Ward wrapped an arm about her shoulders and pulled her close. He nudged Belle. "Get used to it. I intend to show your sister how much I love her every chance I get."

"At least when I'm not stuck on a wagon I can go somewhere else."

Ward laughed. "Who wants a closer look?" Without

waiting for an answer, he flicked the reins and continued. "There's only a small enclosure now." He pointed out the corral pen. "But I'm going to start building a barn right away. Eddie agreed to sell me a few head of cattle so we can start our own place."

He stopped the wagon before the cabin. Belle jumped down before Ward made it around to lift Grace to the ground.

Belle stared at the mountains to the west. "Wow. They're so close."

Ward grinned down at Grace. "The view is the reason I built the house here. Come and see." He led her inside. "It's not much yet." Two rooms. The larger area served as living quarters, the other, a small bedroom. "I'm going to add on right away so Belle can have her own bedroom."

"How long will it take?" Belle wanted to know.

"Not long. The logs are ready and waiting."

"Do we have to wait until it's done?"

He felt the impatience and uncertainty of the pair. "What do you want to do, Grace?" They'd discussed it and she said she didn't see any reason to delay their wedding.

She shifted away, avoiding his eyes.

He caught her chin and brought her gaze back to him, saw the uncertainty in her face. "Grace, I only ask to give you a chance to say what you want." He lowered his voice. "Not because I want to delay. And I certainly am not looking for a way out." His words grew strong as he spoke.

She nodded, her uncertain gaze shifting to blinding joy. "We can live here while the new rooms are built."

"Good. Then we'll proceed with our plans. Now come and sit at the table." He'd designed the kitchen so a window provided a view of the mountains and placed the table before the window.

She sat down, turned, saw the view and gasped. "I could never get tired of seeing the mountains."

He pressed his cheek to the top of her head. "I will never get tired of sharing my life with you."

Belle groaned. "I'm going outside."

Grace and Ward laughed. Grace explored the cupboards, then looked at the wall over the armchair. "We'll hang the sampler there." She meant the one he'd hung in the cabin back at Eden Valley Ranch.

They brought in supplies from the wagon and stocked the cupboards. Grace made lunch and grinned at Belle and Ward at the table. "Our first meal together in our new home."

Ward thought his heart would burst from his chest with a joy he could hardly contain.

They returned to Eden Valley Ranch later in the afternoon. He put the wagon away, then went to the cookhouse for supper.

Cookie jostled him. "My cooking's not good enough for you? You found yourself a new cook."

"Cookie, your cooking is just fine. But there are other considerations."

The men hooted and laughed.

Cookie thumped Ward on the back. "I'm glad for both of you. You deserve to be happy."

"And I will be."

A short while later he took some things to the bunkhouse and saw a letter on his bed. "Who would be writing me?" he wondered, and then his heart broke into a gallop. His mother! He grabbed the letter and read the return address. It was from Travers. From a town miles from where they used to live. He slit the envelope open and read the letter.

He couldn't wait to share the news with Grace and jogged over to the cabin. "A letter from my brother."

She sank into a chair as if the news was too heavy for her. "What does he say?"

"He says our stepfather moved the family several times. He doesn't know how my letter found him. It had been forwarded a number of times. He says the beatings continued after I left, though they weren't as vicious. He and Hank figured out how to avoid them for the most part. Says he followed in my footsteps and left home when he was fifteen. Three years ago our stepfather had a stroke." Ward turned to the letter and read,

He was a crippled old man after that. Ma nursed him. I tried get her to leave but she said it wouldn't be Christian. She stayed with him until he died over a year ago. A few months ago, she sold the house 'cause she couldn't abide the memories. I'm going to visit her as soon as I mail this letter to you. I don't think I'll have any trouble persuading her to accept your invitation to join you. If you don't mind, I'd like to go West, too, and see if I like it better than here.

His grin threatened to split his face in two. "Isn't that good news?"

But Grace looked as if he'd told her he meant to send her back to Thorton.

"Grace, what's wrong?"

She rolled her head back and forth.

If he wasn't mistaken, unshed tears glistened in her eyes. He caught her chin and waited for her to bring her gaze to his. At the murky depths he groaned. "What is it? Tell me."

She swallowed loudly. "Now you can take care of them."

"I can give them a home. And I'm relieved they are okay and free from the tyranny of my stepfather."

She nodded. "It's what you've always wanted."

"Yes, it is."

She lowered her gaze and refused to meet his eyes even when he lifted her chin higher. "You don't need to take care of us now."

The meaning of her words hit him and he sat back. "Grace, do you still think you are only a substitute for my mother and brothers?"

She met his scalding look with quiet stubbornness.

He leaned forward until he saw nothing but her fearful green eyes. "Grace Henderson, I love you. I want to share my life, my heart with you. Taking care of you is only one way of doing that."

She didn't blink. "You're sure you won't want the cabin for your family?"

"Oh, Grace. I'm not going to change my mind about us. The cabin is our home. You and me and Belle. I'll build a new one for my mother just like I said."

Hope flooded her eyes.

He got to his feet and pulled her into his arms, tipping her head back so he could watch her expression. "I mean exactly what I say. I love you with my whole heart and soul and plan to spend the rest of my years enjoying your company. Okay?"

She brushed her fingertips over his cheek as wonder and amazement filled her eyes. "I have trouble believing that I—Red—deserve your love."

"You aren't Red anymore. You are Grace and soon to be my beloved wife."

"Ward, is it any wonder that I love you so much my heart sometimes hurts."

"Let me fix that for you." He claimed her lips in a gentle kiss. He knew exactly when she let go of her doubts, for she wrapped her arms about his neck and returned his kiss with an enthusiasm that made him chuckle.

"Only one thing."

She grew serious, guarded, and he kissed her again. "Stop being so uncertain of my love."

She brushed her hair from her cheek. "I'm learning. You have to give me time. Now what is it you want?"

"Do you mind delaying the wedding until my family arrives?"

"I think that's a wonderful idea if they aren't too long in getting here."

He laughed. "Oh, Grace. You will keep me on my toes, won't you? One minute all uncertain and the next anxious to start our marriage."

She pulled his face toward her and kissed him soundly and sweetly. "I'm learning."

Epilogue

One month later Grace waited in the upstairs of Linette and Eddie's house. She glanced at her silvery-gray dress. The silk fabric was so soft.

Linette turned from fixing Belle's hair to study Grace. It had taken a while but all of them had grown used to using her real name—even herself. She no longer thought of herself as Red.

"The cut of your gown is perfect," Linette said. "You look positively regal, especially with your curls piled on top of your head like that."

Grace had wanted to pull it into a tight bun, but when Ward heard of her plans he'd begged her to show off her curls. "You are the most beautiful woman in the whole West and I like to admire you." So she'd agreed. She turned to the mirror. It did look rather regal.

Belle's reflection joined Grace's. "Am I pretty, too?"

"You're beautiful. But remember, I'm the bride so Ward is supposed to admire me." She tickled her little sister, and they both giggled. Ward made no secret that he loved Belle as much as he would a child of his own.

Eddie came to the door. "Are you ready?"

Grace nodded. Today was the day she'd been waiting for ever since—well, truth be told, she'd waited for this kind of love all her adult life.

Belle went first, descending the stairs to the main room. Cassie and Linette followed, then Grace rested her hand on Eddie's arm. "I can't thank you enough for all you've done."

He'd sold Ward enough stock to start his ranch operations. He'd sent men to help construct a barn and add two rooms to the cabin and put up a second cabin. They'd finished the projects just in time.

Grace and Ward had spent many pleasant hours overseeing the construction and discussing plans.

"Shall we?" Eddie said, and together they went down the stairs.

Ward watched for her from the front of the room, his smile lighting a path to her heart. She saw no one else as Eddie led her to Ward's side. He tucked her hand possessively to his side, then they turned to the visiting preacher to exchange vows.

Several minutes later the preacher said, "I now pronounce you man and wife. You may kiss the bride."

And Ward kissed her for the first time as her husband. A kiss full of sweet promise.

Then they turned toward their guests. Ward's mother and two brothers were the first people she greeted. "I'm so glad you got here in time for the wedding." The trio had arrived a week ago.

Ward's mother looked weary and worn but her eyes had the same bright blueness of Ward's.

Thirteen-year-old Hank was shy and had a woundedness about him that Grace recognized. Time and love would heal those inner bruises. Eddie recognized it, too, and offered the boy a job at the ranch. Twenty-year-old Travers had been angry and standoffish to begin with, but he and Ward had spent time riding together, working together and putting finishing details on the second house. He'd accepted Ward's offer of making him a partner in the ranch. Grace knew it would take time for the hurt to heal but the process had started.

The crowd enjoyed the huge feast that Cookie had prepared.

Finally Grace and Ward could leave the party. He helped her into the wagon and they drove away from Eden Valley Ranch.

He stopped at the door of their new home and swept her off her feet to cross the threshold. "Welcome home, Mrs. Walker." He lowered her to the floor but kept her in his arms as he gave her another kiss.

"Mmm. Seems I've waited a long time for this day."

"I know what you mean. It's only been a month but all my life I've had a hole in my heart that only you can fill."

He spoke so freely of his love that her heart constantly rejoiced.

"No regrets?" He spoke the words into her hair.

She wrapped her arms about his waist and squeezed him tight. "Not for one moment."

Ward eased her back to study her face. She let all her love and joy shine from her eyes. "You don't think Belle minded that we left her with Linette and Eddie, do you?"

Grace giggled. "She doesn't mind. She sounded so grown-up when she said, 'You two need time alone right after your wedding. A honeymoon.'"

Ward chuckled. "She was very pretty in her new dress." His smile deepened. "But not half as beautiful as her big sister. It was the nicest wedding I've ever been to."

Grace only smiled. She knew he'd been to very few and one was between his mother and stepfather. Not exactly a charming memory. "Linette was disappointed that we didn't wait for the new church to be finished." The foundations had been laid, the lumber brought in.

"It was nice of her to contact a preacher friend who was willing to come and perform the ceremony."

"Now let's enjoy our new home."

Hand in hand, they walked into the new part of the cabin. Three bedrooms.

"Three?" she'd said when he told her his plans.

"One for us. One for Belle. And one for brothers for Belle."

"No sisters?"

"They can share Belle's room until we're so crowded we have to build on again." Across the yard, far enough away to provide privacy, was the cabin he'd built for his mother and brothers.

Inside, Grace glowed with joy and thought likely she glowed outside, too, she was so happy. "I am forever grateful for God's grace that sees beyond my sin and offers forgiveness."

"I have something else to show you." He wrapped his arm around her shoulders and led her to the window over the table.

"I'm so glad you put the table here under the window so we can see the mountains every day. I will always remember you saying they made you remember how God's love is round about those He loves."

"I will always remember you declaring so fiercely that you were fine. I got a little weary of you insisting you were fine."

She rubbed his cheek. "You threatened to carve the words into the log."

"Look." He drew her attention to a log by the table.

She gasped. "You didn't?"

"Read the words."

"'Because of His grace.'"

"I thought of carving in the words 'we're fine,' but I realize it is only because of God's grace that I have my Grace whole and ready to love. I don't want us to ever forget it."

She pulled his head down and kissed him soundly, then nestled against his chest.

She laughed. He did, too, his voice reverberating in his chest.

Later, they stood before the cabin and watched the sun set over the Rocky Mountains. She stood with her back to his chest with his arms wrapped about her, feeling his warm breath on her cheek.

"I will never forget this, our wedding day," she whispered, her heart too full to say more.

He nuzzled her neck. "You are my Grace, my love and my joy." He turned her so he could kiss her.

Her heart overflowed. Ward was all she'd ever dreamed of…the dream she'd given up while in Thorton's clutches. She would never stop thanking God for His abundant grace and for the love of a man like Ward. She thought of her parents and felt their approval.

Life filled with love was so good.

* * * * *

CLAIMING THE
COWBOY'S HEART

Fear not therefore: ye are of more value
than many sparrows.
—*Luke* 12:7

To my sister, Leona, and my friend Brenda,
as you struggle with so many challenges.
Remember how much God values you.

Chapter One

Eden Valley Ranch, Alberta, Canada
August 1882

"I didn't expect it to be so heavy." Jayne Gardiner held the pistol between her fingers. She couldn't bear the cold feeling of the stock against her palm. Her hand trembled and the shiny steel barrel winked in the sun like an evil tormentor. Panic clawed up her throat like threatening flood waters. She struggled to push it back. She knew firsthand the destructive power of a gun.

She stiffened her spine. Fear would not be allowed to rule her life. She would learn to defend herself and those she cared about. She'd be ready to take action if ever another life-or-death situation arose.

Behind her, her friend Mercy laughed. "It won't bite." But then, Mercy lived for adventure. That's why she'd accompanied them on this trip west. As if ready for an escapade, she wore suede riding pants that she'd purchased before they left Fort Benton on their journey to western Canada and the Eden Valley Ranch, and her mahogany hair was pulled back in a braid.

Beside her, Sybil twisted her hands in the fabric of

her fashionable pinstripe blue walking skirt. She completed the trio that recently arrived from England. More reserved like Jayne, she wanted to come on this visit to Canada to get over her parents' deaths.

Jayne had come to visit her brother, Eddie—owner and operator of the Eden Valley Ranch—and his wife, Linette, though some might think she'd come to put the past out of her mind. She tightened her lips. People who thought that would be wrong. She didn't intend to forget the lessons her past had taught her.

Sybil shuddered, causing the golden curls that had escaped the elegant roll to bounce around her shoulders. Modern wisdom said a woman with curly hair would be of gentle temperament. Sybil lived up to the expectation. "I hate guns."

Jayne sucked back an echoing shudder. Her brown hair was thick and straight, supposedly indicating a strong-willed woman. So far, she'd proven the statement false but she meant to change that starting now. "I hate what guns do but I want to learn to shoot one." She studied the target placed about fifty feet away.

The young women were in a grove of trees that sheltered them from the wind and provided slices of shade depending on the position of the sun. They were far enough from the ranch buildings to not alarm Eddie, Linette, or any of the other caring people there who saw no need for Jayne to learn to shoot a gun. Eddie had said it wouldn't serve any purpose. It wouldn't bring Oliver back. And, he'd carefully pointed out, there were plenty of cowboys around the place should it be necessary to shoot a gun. What's more, he'd said with utmost conviction, he didn't think such an occasion would likely occur.

Jayne had tipped her chin and vowed she'd learn with

or without Eddie's help. It wasn't some foolish notion of undoing the past. She would not allow herself to ever again feel as helpless as she did on that horrible day. The events had been burned permanently into her brain.

The day she had in mind had been sunny and warm after days of damp sky. Her fiancé, Oliver Spencer, had suggested spending the afternoon together instead of abandoning her to her own amusements while he pursued his as so often happened. On several occasions, she'd objected mildly to the amount of time Oliver spent in gambling establishments. The promise of some quality time together, just the two of them, had caused her to laugh at his jokes, though, as usual, she failed to understand them. He must have thought her so innocent.

They'd been walking side by side along a street lined with shops inviting their business. She had glanced in one window and noticed a beautiful display of lace gloves and thought of purchasing a pair, but she hadn't suggested a stop because she and Oliver were discussing the future. She didn't want to distract him.

"We'll live in the house with Mother and Father. There's more than enough room. No need to own another house."

Did he mean she would go from being under her parents' direct supervision to being under *his* parents'? She wanted to be a woman with her own home. Of course, it made sense to start with. "Will we get our own home when we have children?" A hot blush had flooded her body at the intimate topic.

Before Oliver could answer, a man had jumped from an alley brandishing a gun and demanded Oliver give him everything.

Jayne had shrunk back into the recessed doorway of

the building beside them and watched as Oliver emptied his pockets of quite a lot of cash.

"It's all I have," he'd said, his voice hard with anger.

The thief had jammed the money into his pocket. "You know that's not all I want." He'd waved the pistol. "Where's the key?"

Jayne had glanced about, hoping for rescue but no one turned down the street toward them. No one noticed the robbery.

"I want it back," the robber had growled.

Jayne had swallowed hard. People passed at the intersection a few yards away. She tried to call for help but her voice failed her.

Oliver had continued to say he had nothing more. He'd even turned his pockets out.

"Where is it? I can't prove it but I know you cheated. You took everything I have." The thief had lurched toward Oliver.

She'd never seen Oliver move so quickly. His arm slashed across the man's wrist. The pistol dropped to the cobblestones and he'd kicked it toward Jayne.

"Pick it up. Shoot him," Oliver had ordered as he and the thief tussled.

Jayne had stared at the gun just two feet away but she couldn't move. She'd never touched a gun, let alone shot one. She didn't even know how.

Oliver's head had hit the ground with a thud and he'd lain stunned.

The thief had grabbed the pistol. A metallic click had rung through Jayne's racing thoughts.

"Get up," the thief had ordered.

Oliver had staggered to his feet.

"I'm done playing around. You know what I want. Give it to me."

Oliver had swayed.

Someone from the nearby intersection had called out. "He's got a gun."

Then everything had happened so fast Jayne couldn't say what came first. A shot had rung out. Oliver had pitched to the pavement. The thief had raced down the alley. A crowd had surrounded them.

Jayne had hovered in the doorway, too frightened to move while blood pooled around Oliver. Someone had leaned over him. A man had looked up, seen her and waved her forward. Her legs numb, her heart beating erratically, she'd managed to make the few steps and knelt at Oliver's side. "You'll be fine. You'll be fine." She hadn't believed the words she'd uttered.

He'd caught her hand. He'd struggled to speak past the gurgling in his throat. Something about gambling and winning from the man who had shot him. Then his words ended in a gasp. Gentle hands had pried her away. Someone had taken her home.

For days she'd sat in a straight-backed chair beside the cold fireplace and replayed the scene in her mind. The skin on her face had grown taut every time she'd come to the spot where Oliver had kicked the gun toward her. Fear as deep as the English Channel had shaken her insides. Oliver was dead because she hadn't been able to act. Hadn't known what to do with the gun that lay so close to her. All over some gambling money. The world had gone crazy.

One day Bess, her quiet younger sister, had pulled a chair to Jayne's knees and taken her hands. "Jayne, I have always admired you for your determination and sensibleness. It amazes me you sit here day after day. I beg you to get up and start living again."

Jayne had looked into Bess's sweet face and made a

decision. She would not be defeated by this event. With God's help she'd use it to grow stronger. She'd pushed to her feet and hugged her sister. "Bess, you are right. Never again will I feel so helpless. So useless."

Bess's smile had widened with relief then faltered at the conviction in Jayne's voice. "What are you going to do?"

She had no firm plan at the moment. "I'll tell you what I'm not going to do. I'm not going to be a helpless woman."

That conviction had carried her away from home and across the North American continent to a new, inviting country.

Now she lifted her arm and looked at her two friends in the grove of trees. "I will learn to shoot."

Mercy steadied Jayne's hand. "Hold it like this. Brace with your other hand. Look down the barrel to the target." She guided Jayne into position then stepped back.

Jayne's arms lowered until the gun pointed at the ground. "If I hadn't been so scared of guns I might have grabbed the one Oliver kicked toward me. He might still be alive."

"Exactly," Mercy said.

"Or you might both be dead." Sybil covered her face with her hands as if she couldn't bear the thought.

Jayne wished she could as easily block the sight of Oliver's death from her mind, but it wasn't possible. Any more than it was possible to forget she was twenty-one, no longer planning a wedding, and not ever wanting to think of such things again. Oliver had taught her that life was too fragile to make dream-filled plans.

"You don't want it happening again," Mercy insisted.

Jayne cringed. "I don't have another fiancé, you know."

Mercy laughed. "Not yet, you mean."

"Not ever." Oh, she'd likely marry. Everyone did. But nothing on earth would convince her to again open her heart to such fear and pain and disappointment. Any more than she would ever again let herself become so weak and dependent on others. Though she'd only begun the journey toward living strong and free. "But you're right about needing to learn to protect myself." And people she cared about. Never again would she stand by, shaking in fear, while someone died. "I can do this."

Mercy repeated her instructions on how to hold the gun, aim it and fire it.

Sybil crossed her arms and looked like she'd sooner be anywhere but there. "How do you know all this?" she asked Mercy.

"I sweet-talked one of the cowboys in Fort Benton to teach me."

Jayne and Sybil looked at each other and shook their heads in unison. Mercy was notorious for sweet-talking men into doing favors for her.

Mercy saw their exchanged glances and simply laughed. "Jayne, pay attention. Aim, squeeze and fire."

Jayne lifted the gun, steadied it as she squinted down the barrel toward the target. She closed her eyes and squeezed. The gun jerked upward, the noise of the shot making her squeal.

Mercy gasped. "You're supposed to keep your eyes open and focused on the target."

"Hi yii." A yell came from a distant spot.

Jayne eased open one eye. Through the trees she saw a man leaning low over the neck of his horse as he raced away. Her heart clambered up her throat and stuck there like an unwelcome intruder. "Did I shoot him?" Her voice barely croaked out the words.

Sybil fell back three steps. "He might be after us. We better get back to the ranch."

Jayne shook her head. "First, we have to check and make sure I didn't injure him." Her stomach turned over and refused to settle. "All I wanted to do was be ready to defend us against bad people. But if I've hurt someone instead—" The blood drained to her feet, leaving her ready to collapse in a boneless puddle. Much like it had when Oliver was shot. So much blood. Such a dark stain.

Tremors raced up and down her spine. Cold as deep as the worst winter day gripped her insides.

Mercy wrapped an arm about her waist. "I'm sure you only frightened him and he decided to get out of range of your deadly aim." She laughed like it was no more than a silly joke.

"We need to check." Jayne lifted the hem of her black taffeta walking skirt with its stylish Edwardian hoop underskirt and forced her milky legs to take one step forward and then another. Mercy marched at her side. Sybil hung back then, realizing she would be alone, rushed after them.

They passed the untouched target, pushed through some low bushes, wended between tall poplars with their leaves fluttering noisily in the breeze. The wooded area gave way to a grassy slope with a faint trail skirting boulders. Allowing her legs no mercy, she hurried to the trail and bent over, looking for clues.

She stopped at a round rock that could serve as a seat if they'd been inclined to sit and enjoy the view. A dark, wet streak dripped down the side of the rock.

Her heart beat a frantic tattoo against her ribs. "Look. Isn't that blood?"

The others joined her. Mercy touched the spot and lifted a stained finger. "Fresh blood." She wiped her finger clean on a bit of grass.

Jayne's eyes felt as if they might fall from their sockets. "I shot someone." She straightened and stared in the direction the rider had gone. "What if—" Would she find a body down the trail?

Mercy grabbed her hand. "It was an accident."

"Explain that to the man I shot." She pulled Mercy after her and signaled Sybil to follow. "I have to see if he's on the trail."

"Dead, you mean?" Mercy said, putting Jayne's fears out in the open.

"I knew this was a bad idea." Sybil's voice was high and thin. "Let's go back and tell Eddie. He can look for the man."

That sent resolve into Jayne's insides. Her brother wouldn't always be around to rescue her. Besides, he would be angry that she had ignored his directive to forget about learning to shoot. She squared her shoulders. "I don't need Eddie to clean up after me." She marched down the trail. But her courage faded with every step. Dark spots, some rather large, dotted the dirt. Once she touched a stain and lifted a damp finger.

"More blood," Sybil moaned. "Lots of it."

Jayne tried unsuccessfully to block the memory of blood pooling around Oliver's body. So much blood. Sybil had no idea.

They passed between two table-size boulders and turned by a stand of thick pine trees whose distinctive scent filled the air. The majestic Rocky Mountains rose to her right. Such wild country. Open and free. Had she spoiled it for some poor, unsuspecting man?

She could see down the trail until it turned and disappeared. No rider. No limp body stretched out in the grass. "Guess he wasn't injured too badly." *Please, God, let it be true.*

Mercy chuckled. "If we hear of some cowboy dying mysteriously on the trail, shot by an unseen assailant, we'll know who is responsible."

"Mercy," Sybil chided. "Show a little compassion."

But Mercy only laughed. "Jayne knows I'm only teasing, don't you? It's probably only a graze. No more than a splinter to a man who lives in this country."

Jayne's tension relieved by the absence of a body, she tucked her arm through Mercy's and pulled Sybil closer. "All's well that ends well. Now let's go back to the ranch and see if Linette needs some help." Her sister-in-law was efficiency on two legs even though she expected a baby in four months.

Sybil glanced over her shoulder. "I pray that whomever you shot won't be bleeding to death somewhere."

At the teasing, Jayne faltered. "Maybe I should ask Eddie to ride out and check the trail."

Mercy urged her onward. "Like I said, it's likely only a flesh wound. If the man needs help he will seek it."

Jayne nodded. The words should reassure her but they fell short of doing so. She couldn't get the sight of a large pool of blood out of her mind. The last thing she needed was another death on her conscience.

Who was shooting at him?

Twenty-four-year-old Seth Collins bent low over his horse's neck as they pounded down the trail. One minute he was sitting on a rock, enjoying a pleasant moment as he drank from his canteen and ate a couple of dry biscuits. The next, a shot rang out and pain gouged his right leg. It took two seconds and the sight of blood soaking his trousers for him to realize what happened. Then his only thought had been escape.

He glanced over his shoulder. Saw no sign of pursuit. Why would anyone shoot him? He was just an ordinary, poor cowboy. Except for the wad of cash he carried. Had someone followed him? He'd joined the cattle drive north from Fort Benton to a ranch in western Canada for only one reason—to earn enough money to pay the special caregiver the doctor had recommended for Pa. A man with knowledge of how to manipulate paralyzed limbs. The doctor spoke highly of Crawford, saying he'd seen great success with other stroke patients. Some, he said, had even learned to walk again.

Now he had to get the money to Montana. If he didn't, what would happen to his pa? Crawford had committed to staying three months. If he couldn't help Pa in that time he wouldn't continue on because he'd found he couldn't do anything more after that. Seth had written the man saying he'd been delayed and would be there as soon as possible with the man's wages. Crawford's response had been terse. "I have others interested in my services. Please return immediately." Seth had written again. "Please stay until I get there. I'll be home in a week and I'll pay you extra." But he had no assurances Crawford wouldn't leave and Pa would suffer. Pa was all Seth had left and he meant to get home and take care of him.

He spared a glance at his leg. His buff-colored trouser leg was dark and sticky with blood, which dripped from the heel of his boot. He would need to stop soon and tend to the wound.

And hide his money so those who shot at him wouldn't discover it.

He rode on at the same frantic pace for fifteen minutes then pulled to a stop on a knoll that allowed him a good view of the back trail. After watching a little while he decided he had outrun the shooter. Or shooters. He reined into a grove of trees that provided a bit of cover yet allowed him to keep watch for anyone following him. As he swung off his horse, his leg buckled under him. What kind of damage had the shot done?

Knowing he had to stop the blood flow, he yanked the neckerchief from his neck and tied it around his thigh. He needed something to tighten it so he hobbled toward the nearest tree, biting back a groan at the pain snaking up his leg and wrapping around his entire body. He broke off a finger-thick branch then plopped, as much as sat, on the ground, stuck the length of wood between his leg and the neckerchief and twisted until the blood stopped. Resting his back against a tree trunk, he held the tourniquet tight and considered his plight.

The wad of money was his major concern. Seemed someone had discovered he carried four months' worth of wages in his pocket and decided to lighten his load. He stared at his feet, trying to decide what to do. Hard to hide anything on the horse. He had his saddlebags, but that was the first place a thief would look after searching Seth's person. No hiding a secret pocket in his ruined trousers. He continued to stare at his feet. Hadn't he once heard of a man who hollowed out the heels of his boots to hide something?

He didn't fancy trying to pry a boot off his right leg. Figured it might start bleeding again. For sure, it would increase the pain that even now hammered against the inside of his skull. Ignoring the protest from his injured leg, he used it to pry off his left boot then took his knife from his pocket and set to work. He glanced down the trail every few minutes to make sure he wasn't being pursued.

By the time he'd worked the heel off and dug a hollow in it, his head had grown wobbly. He brushed at his eyes to clear his vision. Then he rolled his money into a tight wad and wedged it into the hole he'd made.

Now to put the heel back on. He found a rock the size of his fist to use as a hammer. Getting the heel on proved harder than removing it but after ten minutes he decided it would do. Had his foot swollen? Must have because he could hardly pull the boot back on.

His head seemed full of air. He swiped his eyes again. Tired. So tired. He shouldn't have pushed so hard the past two days. Now he was paying for it. He'd rest before he moved on. Just a few minutes.

"Mister, wake up."

Seth squinted against the blare of light assaulting his eyes. Awareness of his surroundings came slowly, reluctantly. First, pain. Then thirst. Then the persistent questions of the man kneeling at his side.

How long had he been lying on the ground? Asleep? Unconscious? Either way, he'd wasted precious time. He tried to sit up but the world spun and he decided against the idea. "Who are you?" he managed to croak.

"Eddie Gardiner. Who are you?"

Gardiner? The name seemed familiar but Seth couldn't place it. "Water," he croaked.

The man held a canteen to Seth's lips and he drank greedily before he gave his name. "Seth Collins."

"Let's get you on your horse. I'll take you where you can get help for that leg."

Seth wanted to argue. Needed to. He had to get to his pa. But his leg hurt like twelve kinds of torture. A little tending wouldn't go amiss so he let Eddie Gardiner push him onto his horse and lead him away.

He clung to the saddle, which took far more effort than he would normally exert. He managed to tell Eddie about someone shooting him. "Didn't see them."

They approached a ranch. A pretty place with a big house on a hill overlooking the outbuildings. Among the structures below the house were a couple of two-story buildings, a cluster of red shacks all alike, a log cabin and a barn. All laid out nice and neat. A bridge spanned a river on one side, leading to more pens and small buildings beyond.

They approached the big house. "This is where I live," Eddie said. "You'll get help here."

Seth managed to swing himself off his horse but didn't protest when Eddie grabbed his arm and steadied him.

A young woman opened the door.

Seth's vision was clouded with pain but he was alive enough to note the brown eyes that seemed to smile even when her mouth didn't, a thick braid of rich brown hair coiled at the back of her head and a flawless complexion. Peaches and cream, his ma used to say.

"This man is injured. He needs our help."

Someone shoved a chair under him and he sat. Several women clustered around him.

Eddie answered their questions. "His name is Seth Collins. He's been shot. I found him a few miles to the south." He gave a wave in that direction. "He didn't see who did it."

One of the women addressed Seth. "You're welcome here. My name is Mrs. Gardiner. This is my sister-in-law, Jayne Gardiner." She indicated the young woman who had answered the door. Again, the Gardiner name seemed familiar but his brain couldn't find any more information.

"These are her friends, Mercy Newell and Sybil Bannerman."

He noted Mercy had reddish-brown hair and brown eyes. Sybil was a pretty thing with blue eyes and blond curls. He hadn't seen any white women in days and now he was surrounded by them. And him in such a sorry state.

"I wish the circumstances of your visit were different," Mrs. Gardiner said.

The other three women had been whispering together and now Miss Jayne Gardiner cleared her throat. "I think I might have been the one who shot you."

Seth stared at this sweet, young thing. His mind couldn't make sense of her confession. "Why would you shoot me?" How would she know about the money he carried? He pushed aside the remnants of his fatigue. Refused to acknowledge it was pain that clouded his mind. Had someone at the ranch heard he'd collected his wages and ridden south? Were they all in this together?

"It was an accident. I wanted—" she swallowed hard "—I wanted to learn how to shoot a gun so I could protect myself and the ones I care about."

Eddie jammed his fists on his hips. "I warned you about messing around with guns. I told you to leave them alone. Now do you see why?" He glowered at his sister.

Jayne tipped her chin up and faced her brother. "I must learn how to defend myself. I refuse to be a helpless female."

Eddie sputtered but before he could get out a word,

his wife intervened. "Let's get this man upstairs so I can look at his wound."

Jayne brought her attention back to Seth. "It's my fault. I'll take care of him."

Mrs. Gardiner made a protesting sound that ended abruptly. "That would be fine."

Eddie helped Seth regain his feet and steered him up the stairs that swept to the second story. At the top, he turned them right and into the first bedroom. Seth settled himself on the edge of the bed.

For the first time he gave his leg a good, hard study. It throbbed clear to the top of his head. His trousers were blood-and dirt-caked. He didn't anticipate the skin beneath looked any prettier.

Mrs. Gardiner and Jayne had followed into the room.

"Eddie, he'll need to remove those trousers so we can get at the wound," Mrs. Gardiner said.

"Not my pants." Seth's protest sounded weak and he clamped his teeth together. Weakness was not something he cared to reveal.

"We'll wait outside until you're decent," Mrs. Gardiner said as the ladies left the room. He heard them murmur in the hallway, Mrs. Gardiner asking Miss Jayne about the shooting.

Eddie knelt at Seth's feet. "I'll help you with your boots and pants." He tugged at a boot.

Seth would have protested but had to bite back a groan. Cold sweat beaded his forehead.

"Can't you simply roll up my pant leg?" Seth asked through his clenched teeth.

"Seems to me you'd welcome a clean outfit. Do you have another pair in your saddlebags?"

He grunted in the affirmative.

"I'll get them later. First, let's get you cleaned up."

Eddie helped remove the second boot and the soiled trousers then eased Seth to the bed and covered him with a sheet, but not before Seth saw the dirty, bloody wound.

"I'll send the ladies in to tend that." Eddie piled Seth's boots and pants beside the door. Good. So long as the boots were where he could see them.

Jayne and Mrs. Gardiner again entered the room, Jayne carrying a basin of water.

He closed his eyes knowing he must endure having the wound cleansed. Ironic that it was at the hands of the same woman who had inflicted it.

Mrs. Gardiner eased back the sheet to expose his leg. "This doesn't look good."

Seth nodded. "I saw it."

"It's very dirty." She shifted her gaze to Jayne. "When did you shoot him?"

She swallowed hard. "It was yesterday."

Yesterday? He hadn't realized he'd slept through the night. The urgency of his task struck him. He could not afford this delay. He half sat then fell back. Wouldn't hurt none to have the wound cleaned up before he moved on.

Jayne pressed to Mrs. Gardiner's side. She gasped as she saw the wound. She looked at Seth, her eyes wide as she met his gaze. Whether he saw distress, regret or something else entirely, he couldn't hazard a guess.

"It was unintentional." She sounded so defensive that in spite of his pain and the awkwardness of being flat on his back with two women in the room, he grinned.

"Seems you should have tended it a little sooner," Mrs. Gardiner offered.

"Got someplace to be." Again urgency gripped his innards. The last letter from the caregiver, that one Seth picked up a few days ago at the ranch headquarters, had been dated three weeks ago and gave little information to ease Seth's concern about Pa's well-being. *Expecting you soon with necessary wages. Job here done.*

How could a man give so little assurance in his few words? Seth needed to get to Pa before Crawford left. Might be he was already gone. He'd signed up for three months and no more. If he wasn't there, who would be looking after Pa? The uncertainty burned the inside of Seth's stomach.

Mrs. Gardiner tsked.

"Is he going to be okay?" Jayne asked. Her eyes filled with concern. And well they might. She'd shot him.

"We'll fix you as well as we can," Mrs. Gardiner said. "But you're going to have to be careful you don't get an infection." She turned to Jayne. "You can clean it up." She gave instructions.

He closed his eyes to endure the pain that would surely come from having the wound tended.

At first her touch was tentative then it grew firm, more assured. She was gutsy. He'd give her that.

"Why is it so important for you to learn to shoot?" His voice sounded hoarse. He hoped they'd put it down to some strong virtue, not the pain that seemed to clutch every part of his body.

"I need to be able to defend myself and others if the need ever again arises."

He lifted his eyelids. "Again?" He ignored the pain as he eased up on his elbows to watch her.

"You best lie still." She pressed firm, damp hands to his shoulders. "Moving makes you bleed more." Her face was so close to his he could see the porcelain purity of her skin, the dark streaks of brown in her irises and something more—the determination in her gaze. He was beginning to think she was a headstrong woman who gave little heed to the results of her actions. Just the sort of woman he normally gave a wide berth to. For now, though, he must submit to her ministrations.

He sank back on the pillow. "You've been involved in gunplay before?"

"Only as a spectator. I saw someone shot to death." Her jaw muscles tightened. "And I did nothing to prevent it because I didn't know what to do. Didn't even know how to shoot a gun." Her gaze had shifted to a distant place beyond the walls of this room. "That's when I decided I would never again be a helpless, pampered woman." She gave a decisive nod. "I will learn to shoot a gun and be ready and able to defend myself and those I care about." Her voice rang with determination. "Nothing will stop me."

Seth watched her warily. He knew the folly of insisting on doing foolish acts. Good thing he would be leaving here in a matter of hours. He wouldn't be around to see the result of her decision. But pity poor Eddie Gardiner trying to keep a rein on his sister.

He hoped for both their sakes that the job wasn't too much for the man.

If he had time to spare he might offer to help with the task simply to prevent a worse disaster than having her shoot some innocent passerby in the leg. But thankfully he didn't have time. Because for a man like him who took his responsibilities seriously, this was the sort of woman who spelled a heap of trouble.

Chapter Two

The ragged edges of the wound were covered with dirt and blood. As she cleaned it, fresh blood oozed out and thickened into globs. Jayne swallowed hard, holding back nausea. She'd never taken care of an injured person. Never even entered a sick room. But she would take care of this injured man. It was her responsibility, no matter how tight her lungs grew or how hard her pulse banged behind her eyes.

"Take the wet cloth and sponge away more of the dirt," Linette said.

She dabbed at the dirt and allowed herself a moment of satisfaction. Another step on her journey to move beyond a pampered young lady who couldn't take care of herself or help others.

"You need to scrub a little harder to get the dried stuff," Linette said.

She rinsed the cloth clean and tackled the job again. When she'd finished the area around the wound, she turned to Linette. "What about the blood?"

"Clean right to the edges." Linette leaned past Jayne's shoulder to inspect the job. "Good. You've got it nice and clean. Now we need to use antiseptic on it." Linette handed her a small container marked carbolic acid.

"Won't it hurt?" she whispered to Linette.

"For a moment or two. But it's necessary."

Jayne turned to Seth. Knowing whatever pain he endured was her fault tore at her innards. "I'm going to use antiseptic. Linette says it might sting."

Gritting her teeth at what she must do, she splashed the carbolic in the wound.

His knuckles whitened as he gripped the edge of the bed. His eyes caught and held hers. The dark, pain-filled look brushed a tender spot inside her.

"I'm sorry." Her hands trembled as she set aside the bottle.

Sweat covered his brow.

She grabbed a towel from the stack nearby and dabbed at his forehead, which provided her plenty of opportunity to study him. He was big. She'd noticed that as he'd hobbled up the stairs at Eddie's side. He had a thatch of dark—almost black—hair in need of a good combing. His hazel eyes, although clouded with pain, held her gaze in a steady grip.

She turned from her musing as Linette handed her dressing material. As she placed a pad over his wound and wrapped strips to secure it, she was aware of him watching her and longed for words to assure him she had nothing but his well-being in mind.

"I truly regret that you must suffer for my ineptness."

"You're doing fine." The hoarse words grated on her heart.

She'd meant shooting him, but he'd taken it to mean her ministrations. "I'm doing my best."

"I'll get you a clean shirt," Linette said. "Yours could do with a good scrubbing." She slipped from the room.

Jayne turned to meet Seth's gaze. "I very much regret that I am responsible for your pain."

He studied her for a moment. "Who did you see shot to death?"

His question jolted through her, bringing all the memories of that day forward in a flash. "My fiancé, Oliver." She twisted the towel she held, knotting her fingers into the material.

"I'm sorry for your loss." He lifted his hand and caught her fingers. His hand was large, work-hardened and steadying.

She tore her gaze from their linked hands and stared into his eyes. Her imagination read a dozen things into his gaze—comfort, concern, perhaps even the offer of protection.

She jerked her eyes away and stepped back from the bed to hang the towel over the back of the chair. The last thing she wanted was to be taken care of by anyone. "I'll be fine on my own." Her words were firm, almost as if daring him to think otherwise.

"No doubt you shall." He sounded dismissive. And why not? He had no reason to concern himself with her and she didn't want it.

Linette returned with a clean shirt and helped Seth slip out of his dirty one. "It's a spare. Eddie has gone to tend your horse and get your things," Linette said. "In the meantime rest and allow the bleeding to stop. We'll be back in a bit to see if it has."

Jayne followed Linette down the stairs and into the kitchen. She glanced about and let out a relieved sigh when she saw Sybil and not Eddie. She did not want to face her brother and once more insist she meant to do certain things that he might not consider appropriate for a proper, genteel young lady fresh from England. His concern about her behavior was at such odds with the free rein he gave Linette. He didn't protest her doing all sorts of things Father would have objected to. Perhaps that was the difference. He didn't have to answer to Father for Linette's actions.

She dumped out the red-tinted water. No doubt Father would be shocked that she'd dirtied her hands in such a fashion. But with or without the approval of the men in her family, she meant to be more than a pretty fixture in some fancy house. She'd prove she was capable, though she wondered if anyone would ever believe it. Eddie didn't think she needed to learn to protect herself because someone else would do it. Not many years past, her father didn't think there was any reason for her to continue her studies because once she was married, Oliver would expect her to run his home and provide him with children. Other than that, she'd sit around the house doing needlework and looking content, eager for nothing more than for her husband to return and favor her with a smile.

As for Oliver, well, she'd proven she was of no use to him.

But she'd sailed across the Atlantic Ocean, crossed the hills and rivers and mosquito-ridden land of most of North America for the chance to start over. And to be a person who could take care of herself.

"Is he going to live?" Sybil asked.

Before she could reply, Linette spoke up. "He'll be fine so long as he doesn't get an infection in his wound." She turned to Jayne, squeezing her arm. "This might be the perfect thing for you." Her smile was gentle. "You couldn't help Oliver but you can help this man. You'll need to check his dressing in a couple of hours. If the wound stops bleeding he'll doubtlessly be wanting to leave. But until it does, he needs to keep still."

Jayne nodded. Linette was right. This was her chance to atone not only for what she'd done to Seth but what she'd failed to do for Oliver.

She'd grabbed his soiled trousers and shirt as they left the room. "I'll wash these and mend them." At least she had a certain amount of skill with needle and thread.

"There's a tub and washboard hanging on the side of the house," Linette said. "Scrub out the blood in cold water. I'll heat water so you can give them a good wash."

She went out to the back step, filled the tub with water and plunged the trousers and shirt into it. Though she'd never used a scrub board, she'd seen maids using one. Mimicking their actions, she rubbed the soiled shirt and pants up and down the ridges.

Mercy came around the corner of the house as she worked. "Do you remember the young cowboy named Cal?"

"I met him the first day when Eddie took us around and introduced us." Good. With repeated rubbing across the scrub board, the blood came out, staining the water a muddy brown.

"He says he'll teach me how to ride."

"You already know how to ride."

Mercy made a dismissive noise. "Side saddle. I'm going to learn to ride astride."

Jayne straightened to give Mercy her full attention. "Mercy Newell, have you taken leave of your senses? Your parents will be shocked."

Mercy's merry laugh said enough but she spoke her mind, as well. "Who is going to tell them? Besides, I intend to enjoy every opportunity for adventure this trip offers."

Jayne sighed. It was useless to try and dissuade Mercy. Besides, who was she to say what was safe and proper for anyone? If she were to listen to the voices around her, she would continue to be who she'd always been and she had already decided against that. She returned to scrubbing the clothing.

Mercy studied her for a long, quiet moment. "Why are you washing his clothes? Can't he take them with him and tend to them himself? I understand he'll only be here a few hours." She tipped her head from one side to the other as she studied Jayne. "Does this have something to do with Oliver?"

Jayne didn't bother trying to hide her shudder. "I shot some poor passing cowboy." As she talked, something became clear. "But no, this isn't about Oliver. It's about me."

Mercy wrapped an arm about Jayne's shoulders and drew her close. "You can do it."

Linette brought out hot water and helped Jayne fill the tub. "Here's the soap." At least her sister-in-law understood Jayne's need to exert more control in her life. From what she'd heard, Linette had much the same desire when she came west. She said her first hurdle had been convincing Eddie she could be a pioneer wife. Her second had been making him understand he needed such.

A few minutes later Jayne had the shirt and pants pegged to the clothesline. They would dry quickly in the warm sunshine with a breeze to aid the process.

Seth jerked awake as Jayne entered the room. He hadn't meant to fall asleep. Only to rest for a few minutes. He'd glanced at his dressing earlier. It had grown pink, which meant he was still bleeding. How much blood had he lost? Enough to make him feel weak. Not a state he liked.

Jayne moved to the side of the bed and folded back the sheet covering his leg. Her eyes softened with concern. "I'll have to change the dressing. It's blood soaked."

He nodded. "Fix it up as best you can. I can't afford to lie about."

"What's your big rush? I thought cowboys came and went and did pretty much as they pleased." She folded back the dressing as she talked. Her cool fingers on his skin made it possible to ignore the pain as she uncovered his wound.

He sat up on his elbows to study it. "Is there an exit hole?"

"Yes. Linette checked for it earlier."

He fell back on the pillow. "Well, that's good news. And the bullet missed the bone."

"This would never have happened if Eddie would have given me shooting lessons."

"Why doesn't he? Seems it would be the wisest thing to do."

A quick smile curved her lips. "He doesn't see it that way. Seems he still sees me as his little sister whom he was taught to protect." She shook her head. "I keep telling him I don't want to be protected anymore." Despite the determined tones of her words, her voice remained calm, the English accent soft and soothing. Like the song of a dove.

"How long have you been here?" Then lest she think he meant this room he added, "At the ranch."

"My friends and I arrived a few days ago. Mercy, Sybil and myself."

Three unmarried young women in the Northwest Territories. They would draw men from every direction within a hundred-mile radius, if not more. Especially Miss Jayne. The light from the window next to the bed settled in her hair like a net. Brown was such a flat word for the richest color of hair he'd ever seen.

"We left England for various reasons," she was saying. "Sybil's parents are both dead and she longed to get away from her memories. Mercy lives for excitement. The whole trip has been one big adventure for her." She eased his leg up so she could wrap strips of cloth about it. "That ought to take care of it for now." She stepped back.

Pain pulsed in the wound. He wanted to ask her to press her fingers to the spot. Her touch would ease the hurt. He turned to her, then thought better of his foolishness. "And you came to forget about Oliver."

Her expression hardened. "I will never forget. Nor do I want to." She fluttered a hand. "Not that I wouldn't gladly erase the images from my mind. But I don't want to forget the helpless feeling I had as I stood back not knowing what to do." She curled her hands in a gesture that suggested resolve.

Resolve was good but not when it was combined with stubbornness and refusal to listen to wise counsel. And he had already learned enough about Jayne to know in her case, it was. Despite her brother's warnings she'd gone ahead and shot a gun. Shouldn't the accidental shooting have persuaded her to abandon her idea of learning to shoot without a proper teacher?

She was a dangerous woman to know or be around. The kind that left others to bear the consequences of her choices. In this instance, he was the unfortunate one to pay for her recklessness. His jaw tightened as he thought of the burden her stubbornness placed on others.

He stared up at the ceiling. "What time is it?"

"Almost supper time."

He sighed heavily. "I really need to get on the trail."

"Where are you going in such a hurry?"

"I got a pa who needs me. He's all I have."

Her smile softened her expression and made her eyes dance. "He's expecting you?"

He tried to think how to answer her question. Yes, Pa was expecting him, though not likely with the generous welcome she appeared to imagine.

Taking his silence for denial of her question, her eyebrows rose. "You're planning a surprise? How nice. How long since you've seen each other?"

"Not exactly a surprise, though he isn't likely expecting me. I joined a cattle drive four months ago and haven't seen him since."

Sympathy darkened her eyes. "Well, then of course you're anxious to see him, but will a day or two make any difference? Especially if your leg needs the rest?"

"It's not just my pa." Shoot, he might as well tell the whole story. "My pa had a stroke five months ago. It left him crippled on one side and barely able to speak." As he talked the memory of the situation tightened his throat. "I will never forget finding him alone and helpless."

She patted his shoulder. "I think he wasn't the only one who felt helpless. I think you did, too."

He nodded. Held her gaze. Maybe she understood because of her own helpless feeling of watching her fiancé die. "The doctor said there were new treatments. Some patients had been having good success with manipulation of the paralyzed limbs. I would do anything to help my pa so I arranged to hire one of these people who do that. A man by the name of Crawford would care for my pa for a price, and put him through the exercises. In order to pay for his services, I joined a cattle drive. I paid him what I could up front and promised to deliver the rest at the end of the drive."

"Surely a day or two won't change that."

"I don't know. Our agreement was for three months but our drive ran into trouble crossing the Oldman River. Crawford drove a hard bargain. I sent a letter a few days ago saying I'd be there in a week. I don't expect he'll give me much leeway in my arrival time." He sat up on his elbows and checked for his boots. They were there but his pants and shirt were missing. Never mind them. Eddie would find his clothes in the saddlebags. "I need to get there. I don't want to put my pa's health at risk. But more than that, I want to see for myself how Pa is."

"You said he was all you have left. Your ma is dead?"

He nodded. "She passed away a few years ago." She'd been ill a few days before he'd gone away on a job but she assured him she was fine. "Go on and do what you need to do," she'd said. "I'll be here when you get back." She'd been there sure enough. In a pine box. He shouldn't have left her knowing she'd been ill. Pa said he didn't realize she was so sick. Seth knew even if he had, Pa wouldn't have sought medical help. He didn't think doctors had anything to offer. If Seth had been there he would have taken her to a doctor. She might still be alive.

"I'm sorry about your mother and I respect your anxiety about your father but it seems to me you better let your leg stop bleeding so you can get on your way without fear of dying on the trail." She shuddered. "This is all my fault."

No getting around that fact and yet he wanted to reassure her. But what could he say? "It was an accident." His words offered little comfort to her and certainly didn't provide an excuse in his mind. Accidents were usually the result of foolhardy choices and as such could, with a little common sense, be prevented.

"If I could ride I would deliver your money myself. I'd make sure your pa was cared for in the best possible way. I'd do it myself."

Seth held back a protest. But he wasn't sure she was the kind of person he'd send to care for his pa.

Fire filled her eyes. "See, that's what's wrong with being helpless. I need to learn to ride like a Western woman."

He chuckled. "It's a long ride for anyone not used to the saddle." She'd be off the horse and leading it before she'd gone twenty miles. The idea tickled him clear to his toes.

She smoothed the sheet over him then poured a cup of water and offered it. Her cool fingers brushed his. Such fine, soft fingers. Evidence that she'd led a privileged life. Hardly the sort of woman to shoot a gun, or ride a horse, or do many of the things required of women in the west. Yet she seemed determined. And some things she needed to know, like starting a fire in the stove, or practical things like that, but where was her common sense? Even if she thought she needed to know how to shoot a gun, there was a reasonable way to do it and a bullheaded way. His leg was evidence that she'd chosen the latter, unwilling to bide her time for proper instruction.

He knew the risks of people who didn't listen to common sense. He lived daily with the consequence. He scrubbed at his chin, vaguely aware he needed a shave.

"Linette said if your wound was still bleeding you should continue to rest. You have lost a lot of blood already. I don't know how much a person has to lose." She shuddered. "Seems like a lot."

He wondered if she meant Oliver. Had she watched him bleed to death?

She sucked in air and appeared to dismiss whatever thoughts shivered up and down her spine. "She says she'll provide you a tray so you can eat in bed."

"Eat in bed? No way. Only invalids and weak women take their meals in bed." He was neither.

"That's just your pride speaking. If it means your leg would stop bleeding, shouldn't you be willing to do it so you can resume your journey?" She sounded so reasonable that he felt like a small child having a pout.

"Very well. I'll take supper in bed." He held up his hand to make sure she understood. "But only this once so my leg will stop bleeding."

She patted his shoulder. "One meal in bed won't make you a permanent invalid."

How could he protest when she sounded so reasonable? Pride was a foolish emotion that he had never struggled with before, and now it had reared its ugly head. He didn't like it.

"I'll be back later. Try and rest." She slipped from the room.

He stared at the ceiling. He curled and uncurled his fingers and lay as still as possible, willing the bleeding to stop. Only common sense kept him in this bed. Like Jayne said, he didn't want to die at the side of the trail. That would not help Pa. But being sensible had never before been so hard.

Please make the bleeding stop. Help me get there in time. He didn't know if God had a mind to listen to a prayer from a cowboy with little faith. God sure hadn't listened to any prayer from him in the past, but Ma had often counseled him to "cast all your cares on God." He'd done little of it in the past but he was powerless at the moment to do anything else. Guess he had nothing to lose by casting.

Maybe he should ask for a hedge around Jayne while he was at it. Seems she'd need divine protection, as would everyone around her if she meant to blindly pursue her own plans despite the risks.

Seemed to him people should consider the dangers involved before they blindly followed their own path.

Chapter Three

Jayne paused outside the door to Seth's room to adjust the tray on which she'd placed soup, buttered bread, pudding and tea. It was heavier than she expected and hard to balance as she turned the knob. Never before had she realized how skilled the serving maids were to carry on one hand trays piled high with dishes. How did they do it?

"I brought you tea. Supper," she corrected herself as she then stepped inside the room. She positioned the tray over his legs. She plucked another pillow from the shelf and reached around to tuck it at his back. Their faces were inches apart. His eyes flashed pine green and held her gaze so she couldn't jerk away. Her heartbeat fluttered in her throat like she'd swallowed a tiny butterfly and it was trying to get free. Her cheeks grew warm. Why was she staring into the eyes of a stranger? And why did it cause such an odd reaction?

From somewhere deep inside, her upbringing exerted itself. She finished adjusting the pillows so he could sit up enough to eat and stepped back, her hands folded at her waist.

"Linette is going to check on your wound after you've

eaten. She has something that will stop the bleeding. She got it from an Indian woman in the area." She rattled on, not allowing herself a chance to consider her silly behavior.

He tasted the soup. "This is very good. Sure beats the beans and biscuits I've lived on for the last few days."

"I'll tell Linette you like it. I'm learning to cook, too. Linette says it's not difficult. She came out west last fall and had to learn the hard way."

"The hard way?"

"By trial and error." She chuckled as she thought of Linette's stories. At Seth's questioning look, she said, "She didn't know how to bake bread and tried to bury the lump of failed dough in a snowbank but Eddie found her doing it." Baking bread was another thing to add to her list. "And she didn't know how to cook beans and served them hard. I don't know any of those things, either, but I will learn."

"Far more practical than shooting guns."

"Did your ma know how to shoot?"

He considered her. "Well, now I suppose she did though I don't recall her ever doing so. Why would she when there was Pa and I and—"

She waited for him to finish but he suddenly concentrated on his food. "And?" she prompted.

He shrugged. "And other people. How did you get to the ranch?"

His question, so out of context, caught her by surprise and she answered without thinking. "We crossed the ocean on a ship then took a train, a steamboat and then the stagecoach."

"You and your two companions?"

"An older couple escorted us as far as Fort Benton. Why do you ask?"

"Because you talk like you are helpless yet I think it took a great deal of guts and ability to navigate that trip."

She stared at him. No one—not even she—had acknowledged that it had been a challenge. "I learned a lot."

"And maybe discovered you could do more than you thought you could."

"Maybe." She handed him his tea. His words echoed in her head. Could she do more than she thought she could? She intended to find out on this visit to the ranch. Funny that it had taken a stranger, a victim of her ineptitude, to point out something she'd overlooked.

"Thank you." She ducked her head at the surprised look he shot her way.

"For what?"

"For making me see that I'm not a helpless, pampered woman."

He grinned. "I don't know about pampered. I suspect you are a woman of many privileges but no one has to be helpless unless they choose to be."

"And I choose otherwise. In the past I have been far too compliant."

He put his spoon down and considered her solemnly. She considered him right back. "Miss Gardiner—"

"Please, call me Jayne."

"Jayne, then. There is a vast difference between not being helpless and being foolhardy."

Her breath stalled halfway up her lungs. She forced her words past the catch in her throat. "Are you saying I'm the latter?" Her words were spoken softly but surely he heard the note of warning.

"What do you think?" But he didn't give her a chance to say. "Shooting a gun willy-nilly without regard for passersby, without knowing proper safety technique sounds just a little foolish to me. Doesn't it to you?"

"It sounds to me," she replied, her tight jaw grinding the words, "like a woman ready and willing to do whatever is required to learn how to take care of herself." She headed for the door. Then she retraced her steps to face him. "I came here intending to do my best to make your evening pleasant. I meant to bring my friends to visit you."

He quirked an eyebrow. "Too big a job for you to do alone?"

"I think I can handle one lame cowboy."

"Just like you can handle a gun."

She pressed her hand to her lips. The man had a way of saying all the wrong things and igniting an irritation that burned away reason. "You know I even thought of reading a book to you so you could rest." She let out a blast of overheated breath. "But now I believe I will leave you to your own devices. After all, you wouldn't want the company of a foolish, useless—" Heaven help her, she couldn't stop her voice from quivering and stopped to get control of her emotions. "Silly woman." She hurried toward the door.

He was just like her father and her brother and, come to think of it, Oliver. None of them saw her as having any useful purpose other than to grace their table, encourage them whether or not she agreed with them and do nothing to upset the status quo.

Well, they could all look for that kind of woman somewhere else. She would no longer be such a person.

She didn't need any of them to help her achieve her goals.

Seth's voice reached her before she made it down

three steps. "Miss Gardiner, Jayne, please come back. I didn't mean to upset you."

Ignoring his call, she returned to the kitchen where the others had cleaned up the dishes from the meal.

"How is he?" Linette asked.

"Anxious to be on his way."

"Is his wound still bleeding?"

"I didn't check. I said you would do it."

"Of course." Linette went to the pantry and returned with a small leather pouch. "I'll take this along in case I need it." She headed for the stairs. "Aren't you coming?"

Jayne shook her head. "I don't think he needs two females fussing about him." Especially one he considered foolish. His words continued to sting.

Mercy draped an arm about her shoulders. "What happened?"

Jayne gave a tight smile. "What makes you think anything did?"

"Because I know that look. Right, Sybil?"

Sybil moved to Jayne's other side. "Was he rude to you? Inappropriate? I knew you shouldn't have gone up there alone."

"He wasn't rude or inappropriate."

"Then what?" Mercy demanded.

"He said I was foolish to want to learn to shoot. Said there were lots of people around to take care of me." He hadn't exactly said that but it was implied. "He seems to think I'm a threat to everyone's safety because of my desire to know how to handle a firearm."

Mercy choked back a chuckle. "I suppose he might have cause to think so."

"I'll be more careful in the future."

Sybil sighed. "I do wish you'd give up this idea but you are far too stubborn to do so."

"I'm not stubborn. I'm—I'm resolved." She liked that word much better. "I am resolved to never again feel helpless in the face of danger. To never again feel useless when something needs doing. Why, I might even learn to ride astride like Mercy plans. Just think of the things I could do." She could offer to ride to Seth's pa with the money. Of course she would never do such a thing. Despite Seth's very harsh opinion of her she understood some things simply weren't safe for a woman, like riding alone across the prairie.

Linette descended the stairs, carrying the tray. "I think that will stop the bleeding so the poor man can get on his way. Jayne, he asked that you keep him company for a few hours. I would do it myself but Grady needs to get ready for bed." Grady was the five-year-old-boy Linette had become guardian of after his mother died on the ship to Canada. Originally she meant to leave him with his father in Montreal but the man said he couldn't take care of a small boy. Jayne's heart went out to Grady. Imagine having your father turn away from you. Why, it had to be every bit as bad as watching a fiancé die from a gunshot wound. At least Grady had Linette and Eddie who loved him and had adopted him.

Jayne's resentment at Seth's comments vanished as she thought of how harsh life could be. Besides, she was responsible for his injury.

"Why don't you two come with me?" she asked her two friends. "I'm sure he'd enjoy your scintillating company." She didn't want to be alone with him, provide him with another opportunity to share his opinion of her.

"Sounds like fun." Mercy steered them down the hall without giving Sybil a chance to voice her opinion.

* * *

Seth stared at the blank white ceiling. Not even a crack so he could make childish pictures in his mind. There were days in his past when he'd thought how pleasant it would be to have nothing to do but lay about. He'd changed his mind in the last few hours. Every ten minutes he decided he'd had enough rest and his leg was well enough for him to move on. After all, it wasn't like he didn't have things to do. Important things. But he wasn't foolish enough to risk his life or limb. Mrs. Gardiner had packed the wound with some kind of powder and said she hoped that would stop the bleeding.

She'd given him a smile. "You could do your part, too, by staying still."

He meant to do his best to comply.

He grinned at the ceiling. Jayne had taken exception to his suggestion she might be foolish in pursuing her desire to shoot a gun. He'd been careful to add without someone to teach her.

Jayne's voice came from the stairs and he turned to the door. Another voice answered her. And then a third. He couldn't hear what was said.

Perhaps she wasn't coming to see him.

He lifted his head, watching the door. As the footsteps neared, paused, he held his breath.

The door opened. Jayne stepped in, her two friends behind her.

"We've come to keep you company," Mercy said.

Jayne had said Mercy wanted adventure. The way her eyes danced as if she had a secret she couldn't wait to divulge, he guessed she managed to find her share of excitement wherever she went.

"It's partly my fault Jayne shot you," Mercy said. "You see, I was attempting to teach her to shoot the pistol but she closed her eyes. Completely missed the target."

Sybil shivered. "I tried to warn them it wasn't a good idea."

Seth shifted his gaze to her. Jayne had said Sybil wanted to get away from sad memories. There was a darkness in her eyes that spoke of hard times. He recognized it from seeing it in the mirror if he looked hard enough.

Then he brought his gaze to Jayne who hadn't said anything yet. He wanted to tell her he didn't mean to hurt her. But he didn't know how without retracting his words, and he meant them. Foolish choices caused unbearable consequences. He didn't want her to learn that the hard way.

She shifted her attention to something past his shoulder.

Mercy eased closer. "Tell us about yourself."

"Not much to tell. I'm just a cowboy who's finished a cattle drive. But I expect you all have your stories." Maybe he could get them talking about themselves.

"Tons of them." Mercy appeared to be the spokeswoman. Sybil looked ill at ease and Jayne looked stubborn. Must be a mule somewhere in her heritage.

Compliant, she said? Not a hope.

"I'm going to learn to ride," Mercy said.

"Like a man," Sybil murmured, her voice conveying shock.

"Men are allowed to do all sorts of things that women aren't. It's not fair." Mercy gave another little pout. Then she brightened and gave Seth her attention. "We were talking about you, though."

He shrugged. "I'm sure you're far more interesting than I am." He'd told Jayne about his pa and even his ma. But he didn't intend to reveal any more. There were some things best left buried in the past. "Tell me about your families. I know Eddie is Jayne's brother but nothing more."

"I'm an only child," Sybil said with a heavy tone.

"It sounds like you regret it."

She nodded. "I suppose I do. With my parents dead I am all alone except for an elderly cousin."

Jayne and Mercy pressed close to her on either side. "You have us."

Sybil smiled and gave a little chuckle. "So I do. One of you set on turning the world upside down." She nudged Mercy. "And the other bound and determined to shoot her way to forgetfulness." She patted Jayne's arm as if to say she meant no harm.

Mercy laughed. "She's got a way with words, doesn't she?"

Jayne shifted her gaze about the room until it came hesitantly, and likely reluctantly, to Seth. The way she squinted dared him to point out he had said something similar to Sybil's words. "It's not like that at all. I only want to be strong and prepared."

Sybil patted her arm again. "Of course. We understand."

Mercy continued to grin at her friend.

Seth jerked his chin slightly hoping she'd understand he had no desire to continue their disagreement.

The look she gave him had the power to start a fire. He tore his gaze from her scowl. "What about your family, Mercy?"

She sobered and got a faraway look in her eyes. "I'm the only living child. I had a brother who died when he was eight."

"How old were you?"

"Six."

A lot younger than he had been. Was it any easier at a young age? He couldn't imagine it was.

"He got sick," she added, then shook herself and turned to Jayne. "Jayne here is the one with an abundance of family. Tell him."

"He already knows about Eddie. I also have two younger sisters."

He nodded encouragement and she continued.

"Bess is almost eighteen and Anne is fifteen."

"Do you miss them?"

A smile curved her lips. "More than I thought I would. The things with brothers and sisters is you get used to having them around and don't think about it much then you find yourself turning to speak to them and with a start, you realize they aren't there."

She'd so concisely identified how the loss of a sibling felt. He fixed his attention on the ceiling as a distant pain surfaced. Not as strong as it had once been but still pulsing with life. He'd reconciled that it would never die.

Mercy, the bold spokeswoman, broke the silence. "So where are you headed?"

"Corncrib, Montana."

"Got someone there waiting for you?" She waggled her eyebrows teasingly. "A wife, a girlfriend?"

"Just my pa."

"Oh." She sounded disappointed.

"What? You think I look like a man who has a wife?"

Jayne didn't give Mercy a chance to answer. "His pa is sick."

Sybil edged closer. "I'm sorry. I suppose you're anxious to get there and see him."

He heard her unspoken conclusion that his pa was on the verge of death and set out to correct it. "Pa had a stroke. He's in the care of a very capable man. But it's been four months since I've seen him. I'm anxious to see how he's doing. I'm hoping he's greatly improved."

Jayne patted his shoulder and for the first time since she'd fled his room upset by his comments, the tension in his neck eased. "I'm sure everything will work out. Doesn't God promise us that 'all things work together for good to them that love God'?'"

Her gaze delved deep into his, searching, challenging.

"I know God's in control of the universe and nature." He spoke slowly, bringing his thoughts into words. "But I think He expects us to take care of the details ourselves." He watched Jayne's expression change as she considered his answer. It went from surprise to denial to confusion.

"I think we have to trust Him even when we don't understand or we don't possess enough faith," she said.

Mercy spoke. "I kind of think Seth is right. I mean, why would God bother with little stuff?"

"Oh, no. It's not like that," Sybil protested. "He cares about everyone. We have to believe that."

"I do believe." Jayne shook her head. "But sometimes it's a struggle to feel it, especially when awful things happen."

"That's when we need to trust even harder."

Silence filled the room for a moment after Sybil's comment. Seth lacked the energy to argue against it.

"We should leave you in peace," Jayne said and the three of them walked toward the door.

The loneliness of the room lay on his chest like a weight, and fleeting memories clawed at his throat. He didn't fancy being alone any more than he had to be. "Wait a minute."

Jayne hung back.

"Do I recall you offering to read to me?" he asked her.

"That was before."

"Before what?" He knew what she meant but pretended otherwise.

She shrugged. "Before now."

The other two hovered at the doorway. Mercy nudged Sybil. "Are they talking about the fact he called her foolish?"

Sybil studied Jayne and then Seth. "I suspect so." Her gaze bored into Seth's. "Be warned, if you hurt one of us you deal with all of us."

He held her look steadily for a moment, pretending to be contemplating her warning. But he couldn't maintain a serious expression as he imagined being pummeled by their girlish punches. He grinned widely. "I'll keep it in mind."

"Good." Sybil took the girls each by an arm. "We'll help Jayne pick out some books," she said as they disappeared out the door.

He settled back, wondering if Jayne would return. He didn't regret being honest with her but hoped she would get over feeling offended.

She returned in a few minutes with four books. "Which would you like me to read?" She gave the titles.

"*The Arabian Nights.*"

"You're familiar with the stories?"

"My father used to read it aloud." He hadn't thought of that for years. At one time, Pa would read aloud every night during the winter. Stories of adventure in a different time and place. When had it stopped?

The answer came readily. After Frank's death.

All day he'd been fighting the memory but could no longer push it aside. He was fourteen, Frank sixteen.

Seth's long-time friend, Sarah, had caught Frank's attention and the two of them had been acting silly all afternoon. But when Frank teased Sarah to slide on the thin
ice of the river, Seth had begged them to be sensible.

"Life is too short to waste on rules and cautions, little brother," Frank had called as he ran onto the ice and
skidded a good distance. "This is fun."

"Sarah, don't go. The ice is too thin," Seth had said,
wanting to yank Frank back to safety.

"It's holding Frank okay." Ignoring his warning,
she'd raced after Frank.

Seth had hovered on the bank, longing to join them
but knowing the dangers.

He'd heard the crackling of the fragile ice and called
out a warning but Frank and Sarah only laughed and
continued their merriment. Then suddenly Frank had
broken through the ice. Sarah, chasing after him, had
fallen in, too.

A shudder raced through him as the horror of that
day returned to his memories. Oh, how he'd tried to
erase it from his mind. He'd succeeded in burying it
so deep he thought it would never surface. But today
proved how futile his hope for forgetfulness was.

Frank and Sarah had screamed Seth's name. Their
panicked voices echoed through his head and he closed
his eyes, which did nothing to stop the pictures playing in his head.

He'd grabbed a branch that lay at his feet and raced
to where they'd broken through. His feet had moved
like lead. His legs had refused to make the speed he
wanted. Every yard had seemed an eternity. Sarah had
clung to the edge of the ice. He couldn't see Frank and
then he'd bobbed up.

"I'll get you. Hang on." He'd flung himself on his

belly and wriggled forward, holding out the branch before him. As soon as Sarah could reach it, he'd called out to her to grab it. "Lay as flat as you can. I'll pull you out." The ice dipped toward the hole and water crawled toward him. Would they all drown in the murky water? He'd toed himself more firmly in place.

Inch by inch he'd pulled her to shore and threw his coat over her before he went back for Frank.

But Frank had disappeared. Seth called his name over and over. He'd jabbed at the hole. In desperation he'd yanked off his boots and dove into the cold water. The shock had numbed him clear through. He'd opened his eyes underwater, tried to find his brother but saw nothing. The current tugged at him. He'd surfaced before it sucked him away. So cold he could barely function he'd somehow managed to pull himself out of the hole. He didn't recall getting himself and Sarah to the house. Only the emptiness of returning without Frank. And the shocked look on his parents' faces.

Frank's body was found three days later, caught on a log downstream. The same day that Sarah had died of pneumonia.

The emptiness had stayed, a permanent, unwelcome guest that consumed their home. Consumed Ma and Pa, too, and took residence in Seth's heart.

Never would he forget how he'd failed. He had done all he could but had been unsuccessful in taking care of those he loved.

He realized Jayne was speaking and jerked his thoughts back to the present.

"Eddie read them to me, too, when I was much younger." She adjusted his pillows, straightened his covers. "Are you comfortable?"

He almost caught her arm as it passed over his chest.

If he had something to hang on to he might be able to escape the awfulness of his memories. Instead, he pushed them back, deep inside, and slammed a door to keep them at bay. But like wisps of black fog, the remnants of horror lingered. Sooner or later, he knew, they would dissipate. He steadied his voice. "Reasonably so."

"Very well." She drew the chair close and began to read the story of "Ali Baba and the Forty Thieves."

Her voice soothed him, filling him with happy memories of life before Frank had died. He drifted pleasantly on her words. When she finished he couldn't lift his eyelids, even when he heard her whisper, "Good night," before she slipped away.

What a crazy couple of days it had been. Shot. Rescued. Cared for by the hands that shot him. No one would ever believe that. It was as if God had played a role in orchestrating it.

God! He couldn't imagine that God cared one way or the other what happened to Seth or most of the people he met. The Almighty sure hadn't cared about saving Frank or Sarah from drowning. Or how his death had affected their ma and pa. And even Seth.

But Jayne had suffered a painful loss, too. And she continued to trust God. A smile tugged at his lips. She also fought back, mostly by taking control of life in every possible way—even to shooting a gun, despite the fact no one seemed to care to give her instructions. Except Mercy, and he wondered how valuable her lessons would be. He rubbed at his leg. It didn't seem she was a very good teacher.

For the safety of everyone within shooting distance, someone should give Jayne lessons.

Chapter Four

Seth wakened as someone stepped into the room. He sat up and stifled a moan at the pain that reminded him why he was in a strange bed in a strange room with a strange man standing at his side. Then his mind cleared and he recognized Eddie.

"Good morning," Eddie said.

"Morning." The word croaked from his dry throat and he reached for the cup of water Jayne had left on the table beside him.

"I brought you your things. I was here last night but you were already asleep. Linette wants to check your leg one last time."

"Thanks."

Linette joined her husband and changed the dressing. "It's not bleeding but I believe a couple more days rest would be in your best interest."

"Thanks. But I have to get going."

"We'll leave you to get dressed, then." Eddie handed him his saddlebags. "I believe your other things are waiting for you downstairs."

"Please join us for breakfast," Linette added. "Turn

right at the bottom of the stairs and the kitchen is at the end of the hall."

"Thanks." He waited until they left the room before he threw back the covers and sat on the edge of the bed. A stark-white dressing covered his wound and would keep it clean until he reached Corncrib. He pulled on his dark gray trousers, and his black-and-white-striped shirt. Putting weight on his leg caused his wound to protest but it wasn't anything he couldn't ignore. He tugged on his boots, pulled a comb from his supplies and ran it through his hair then stood tall. There. He felt like a man again. He slung his saddlebags over his shoulder and left the room.

The stairs were wide and led down to a big door that stood open, allowing a cool breeze to blow through the screen. This was the door he had stumbled through with Eddie's help yesterday. So much had happened since then that it seemed more like a week ago.

He paused at the bottom of the stairs to stare at the view. The house overlooked the neat ranch buildings he'd noticed yesterday. Several cowboys crossed toward the nearest two-story house. He gave it all a quick study then lifted his gaze. The view of the mountains caught at his breath. They were gleaming with the morning sun. So big and majestic. So powerful. The words of one of Ma's oft-repeated verses entered his mind. "God is our refuge and strength, a very present help in trouble. Therefore will not we fear, though the earth be removed, and though the mountains be carried into the midst of the sea." Ma had been devastated by Frank's death but in spite of it, Seth suddenly realized, she'd remained serene. He hadn't been able to understand. Was it because of her faith?

A faith he shared but to a lesser degree. He wasn't

sure God would lend a hand if Seth needed it. He'd called God's name several times when trying to rescue Frank. Where was God then? Or was he blaming God for an individual's own choice? Was not the individual responsible for the outcome? These were oft-repeated questions to which he could never find a satisfactory answer.

He turned to his right and strode down the hall. As he passed a room, he glanced inside at the bookshelves filled with books, a large mahogany desk and an over-size black armchair, plus some very nice paintings. One seemed to be a perfect replica of the mountain scene he'd admired seconds ago.

To his left, he glimpsed a formal-looking dining room that had an empty, unused look. Then he reached the kitchen.

"Good morning," Jayne said, smiling cheerfully as he entered. She was probably eager to see him gone. After all, he was a constant reminder that her shooting had been a failure.

She should be happy he was only slightly injured because of her foolish activity. She might have left a body on the trail. His body. Then who would take care of Pa? Maybe God had been protecting all of them— Jayne, Seth and Pa. He'd study the thought more closely when he had the time.

The room was large, dominated by a big table. To one side were cupboards and a stove, and on the east side, the rising sun shone through the generous windows.

The others greeted him. Linette held a small boy before her. "This is Grady. Grady, say hello to Mr. Collins." The boy held a half-grown gray kitten.

Seth squatted down to the boy's level, ignoring the pain in his leg. "Pleased to meet you, Grady. And what's this fine fellow's name?" He scratched behind the cat's ears earning him a loud purr.

"This is Smokey. He's a good cat. He never fights with the other cats. Not like Snowball. Snowball is always fighting. He's got a torn ear 'cause he fights too much."

"Why, it sounds like Smokey is a very smart cat." The animal pushed against Seth's hand, begging for more attention.

"He is. He can climb a tree faster than anybody and he eats slow, like a gentleman."

"A fine cat, indeed. I expect he's good company for you." He straightened to ease the pain in his leg.

"Yup. But my best friend is Billy. He lives down the hill with Daisy and Pansy and Neil and his new ma and pa, Cassie and Roper. Mr. and Mrs. Jones," he corrected as Linette opened her mouth. No doubt she meant to tell him he shouldn't call adults by their first names.

Seth's eyebrows peaked. "Wow. That sounds like a real good story."

Linette gave her son a gentle shove toward the door. "Put Smokey outside and wash up for breakfast. Seth, have a chair." She indicated one next to Jayne.

He sat. Feeling Mercy and Sybil's gazes on him, he lifted his head to give them each an inquisitive look. "Did you want something?" he asked.

Sybil shook her head.

Mercy leaned forward. "We were wondering how you would explain your—" she tipped her head toward his leg beneath the table "—gunshot wound. Jayne doesn't think you'll admit to your friends that a woman shot you."

He turned toward Jayne.

Her brown eyes flashed a teasing challenge. "They might wonder why you let a woman outshoot you," she said.

He practically choked. "Outshoot? I don't think I'd explain it like that. What I'll say if anyone asks is that I got hit by a stray bullet."

Eddie cleared his throat. "There'll be no more stray bullets. Jayne, I forbid you to continue this foolish endeavor."

She bristled like a cat stroked the wrong way. She ducked her head and stared at her plate but her lips pressed together in protest.

Eddie was right about it being foolish but hearing it from the other man's lips made Seth want to protest. Why didn't he teach his sister what she needed to know? It would surely make it safer for everyone on the ranch. He guessed from Jayne's expression that she had no intention of abandoning her plan, despite her brother's direct order.

"Would you ask the blessing, dear?" Linette said, ending the tension between brother and sister.

Eddie prayed and then food was passed around. Fried pork and eggs, fried potatoes, fresh biscuits and syrup and plenty of milk.

Seth helped himself. "I heard you were a good cook, Mrs. Gardiner. This certainly proves it."

"Thank you. The girls are learning to cook, too. If you were around longer, you would get a chance to evaluate their progress."

He pretended a great deal of shock. "I hope their cooking lessons aren't as deadly as their shooting lessons."

Beside him Jayne choked. He had the pleasure of patting her on the back. At first, he got a bit of satisfaction out of her discomfort but after the second pat, he had an urge to pull her into his arms, rub her back and assure her she would be safe because he would personally see to it. Instead, he dropped his hands to his lap. He didn't need one more person in his life to be responsible for.

After she stopped coughing and wiped her eyes, she turned and gave him a look fit to cure leather. "I could have choked to death."

He felt suddenly remorseful. "I'm sorry. It was a careless remark."

She nodded. "Then consider us even. I didn't mean to hurt you even as you didn't mean to hurt me."

He wondered if she referred to the choking incident or the words he'd spoken the previous day. But it didn't matter which. He was leaving today and would prefer to go with no ill feelings left behind. He nodded. "Agreed."

Conversation around the table turned to more general things—plans for the day, who was going where, what needed to be done.

His nerves tensed when Eddie asked Jayne what her plans were.

"I wanted to explore a bit more."

Seth relaxed. It sounded like a safe activity. He'd be in no mortal danger as he rode away. And may God have mercy on any strangers riding nearby if Jayne meant to continue with her plans.

Again he wondered why Eddie didn't simply give her a few lessons. Surely that would soon satisfy her.

When the meal ended, Eddie pushed from the table. Seth pushed back, too.

"Thank you for your hospitality. I'll be on my way now."

Linette favored him with a sweet smile. "We understand but you're always welcome at Eden Valley Ranch."

That's when he recognized the name Gardiner. Eddie Gardiner and his wife were well spoken of in the western ranches. "I've heard of this place."

"You have?" Linette asked. "I hope it's been good things."

Eddie wrapped his arm about his wife's shoulders. "What else would he hear?"

"It's been good," Seth assured them. "You're known to offer hospitality to all, regardless of race or social status. People say Mrs. Gardiner nurses the sick, helps the poor and Eddie here is considered a man of honor and integrity."

"That's lovely," Sybil said.

"We're honored," Eddie added.

Seth leaned back on his heels and grinned. "I heard a tale about feeding a starving Indian family and outrunning wolves. Is it true?"

Linette and Eddie grinned at each other.

Jayne answered his question. "It's true. My brother refused to hang an Indian who tried to steal a cow to feed his starving family. Instead, he took him meat. On the way back, wolves attacked them and Linette helped beat them off." She jammed her fists on her hips. "I intend to become just as brave and proficient."

Linette reached out and squeezed Jayne's hand. "And you shall."

Eddie opened his mouth but Linette jabbed her elbow into his ribs and he closed it without speaking. Had he been about to reissue his orders to Jayne?

Instead, he said to Seth, "I'll take you to the barn. Your horse is there."

"I'll go with you," Jayne said and no one argued otherwise. Certainly not Seth who looked forward to a private goodbye. "Wait a moment." Jayne turned aside and brought him his shirt and pants, neatly folded as if they'd come from the best Chinese laundry.

"You washed them?"

Mercy didn't wait for Jayne to answer. "She washed them, mended them and ironed them. Your clothes could not be in better hands." Her dark eyes challenged him as if informing him that Jayne had many admirable qualities.

He wasn't about to argue. No doubt she did, but shooting wasn't one of them any more than was being bullheaded about it.

"Thank you. I didn't expect this."

She tipped her head to one side and lifted one shoulder. "I doubt you expected to be shot by a woman, either."

He choked on a startled laugh.

Mercy and Sybil chuckled.

"Jayne, there's to be no more shooting." Eddie sounded like he was used to giving orders and having them obeyed.

As the three of them traipsed down the hill, he heard Jayne whisper beside him, "You can't order me around." No doubt she hadn't meant for anyone to hear her. Seth worried that things might get a little tense between her and her brother if they kept up the way they were.

Grady shouted from the doorway. "Papa, I'm coming, too."

Eddie turned to wait for him. "You two go ahead."

Jayne and Seth continued onward. He shoved the barn door open, and a cowboy nodded a greeting as he saddled a horse.

Seth found his horse in a nearby stall and grabbed his saddle and bridle that hung in the tack room. He noticed they'd been cleaned until they shone. He hadn't expected that kind of service.

The animal, too, had been groomed until his coat shone. Someone certainly knew how to look after things.

As he lifted the saddle into place, his leg spasmed painfully. It was only a gunshot wound, he reminded himself. Not much more than a flesh wound. Nothing to slow him down.

He led the horse through the door, Jayne at his side.

"I hope you arrive in good time, that the man is still tending your pa and that he is much improved."

He smiled down at her. "Thanks. I can't say it's been fun but it's been unusual meeting you."

She chuckled. "I dare say it's the most unusual meeting either of us has had."

He nodded, suddenly reluctant to leave. Like that made any sense. But something about Jayne pulled at his thoughts. Of course she did. The woman needed someone to keep an eye on her and make sure she didn't get herself into more trouble.

He chomped down on his molars. It would have to be someone other than himself because he'd had more than his share of trying to take care of people who didn't bother to take care of themselves.

"You stay out of trouble, hear?" He swung up into the saddle. "Don't go shooting any more cowboys."

A stubborn look crossed her face and then she smiled. "One has proven to be enough trouble. I won't go for two."

He laughed and touched the brim of his hat.

She stepped back and gasped. "Seth, look at your leg."

He did. His pant leg was blood-soaked.

Eddie had reached them and saw the same thing. "You can't leave like that. It would be foolish."

Seth stared at his leg then shifted his gaze to Jayne's eyes, saw her look go from shock to compassion. "Seth, you have to rest it."

He nodded. He knew he had no choice. "The money..."

"Tell Eddie about it."

Knowing the reputation of the Gardiners, he knew he could entrust his money to Eddie. "It's in the heel of my boot. Can you see it goes to Murdo Collins in Corncrib, Montana? I need it to get there as soon as possible."

He swung from the saddle and began to pry his boot off.

Eddie clamped a hand on his shoulder. "Let's go to the house and take care of that. Linette can tend your wound. Looks like you'll be here a few more days." He called to a cowboy barely old enough to call himself a man. "Buster, take care of this man's horse."

"Yes, boss." Buster's chin had likely never met a razor yet. His hair was shaggy as if it had not seen a pair of scissors in a long time. And his too-short trousers were held in place with a braid of rope.

"Kid looks like he's lost," Seth said as they climbed back up the hill.

"He showed up a couple of weeks back asking for a job. Seems he's all alone in the world. But he doesn't take kindly to help. Linette offered to give him a pair of trousers from her supply closet but he refused. Said when he earned them, he'd buy them."

"Guess you can't fault him for that."

"You have to allow a man, however young, to have a certain amount of pride. He's proving to be a good man. He took care of your saddle and groomed your horse."

He was struck by an errant thought. Maybe Jayne

also needed to keep her pride intact by being able to use a gun.

Eddie went through to the kitchen with Seth and Jayne behind him. Seth sank to a chair and removed his boot and pried off the heel. He handed the wad of money to Eddie. "Can I write a note to accompany it?"

Jayne disappeared down the hall and ducked into the room with the desk and books. She returned with paper and pencil, handing it to him with a sad smile.

He wrote a note to Pa saying he had been delayed but would be home as soon as possible. To Crawford he wrote, "There is more here than what I owe you. Please keep it in return for staying with Pa until I get home." He folded both pieces of paper and handed them to Eddie.

"I'll see this gets to Edendale right away. We should be able to catch the stage. Petey, the driver, can be trusted to make sure it gets to your pa." He left the house to tend to the task.

Seth tried to relax. The money would make its way to Corncrib as fast as he could take it himself. But what about Pa? Would Crawford stay? Or would his pa be alone, unable to care for himself?

Linette retrieved her little leather pouch of herbs. "I think it's best if you return upstairs." She went down the hall.

Seth rose, preparing to follow.

Jayne reached out and squeezed his arm. "I'm sorry."

He made up his mind. "The money is on its way. That should keep Crawford there for a few more days." No point in worrying about things he couldn't change, especially when this gave him a chance to change one important thing. "My leg will heal fine if I rest it. While I am here you will get shooting lessons from me. That way I can leave with a clear conscience knowing you won't kill someone accidentally and end up in jail." He went down the hall and up the stairs to have Linette pack the wound with the herbs.

"They'll do their work if you give them a chance," Linette said. "I suggest you don't move around much for a day or two."

"I'd sure like to sit in the sun."

She nodded. "That should be okay so long as you don't put any weight on that leg. I'll put a chair by the door." He hopped down the stairs after her and sat beside the big doors. Being idle weighed heavily but at least he could watch people coming and going.

Jayne and her friends passed the barn toward the bridge. They had said they were going exploring.

He hoped the exploring didn't involve a pistol. Surely she would wait for the lessons he'd promised… Unless she was too bullheaded to listen to reason.

Jayne pressed her lips together as she joined Mercy and Sybil. Seth was just like Eddie, barking out commands and expecting her to jump. Yes, she wanted to learn to shoot. But she would have liked it better if he'd offered rather than ordered. Like she'd kill anyone! Her eyes narrowed. Was he any different than her father, or Eddie or Oliver? Did he see her as simply a foolish young woman who needed him to protect her?

She snorted. "I don't need him protecting me." She spoke the words aloud without regard to her friends.

They stopped and waited for her to fall in between them.

"Who?" Mercy demanded.

"Why, Seth, of course," Sybil said. "Jayne, accept it.

There is something about you that brings out the chivalry in men."

"I don't want chivalry."

Sybil made a protesting noise. "Who doesn't want a man who is courteous and considerate, honorable and loyal?"

"Put that way, I have to agree but he thinks he can order me around. He acts like he has to take care of me or I'll cause a disaster." She shuddered, remembering how her lack of action had caused a terrible death. "I don't need a man taking care of me, thank you very much."

"What did he say?"

"He said he would give me shooting lessons."

Mercy and Sybil ground to a halt. "Isn't that what you want?"

"Yes. But I'd like to be asked not told." She wondered if her words sounded as petty to her friends as they did to her.

"Either way, seems to me you're getting a gift," Mercy said. "The lessons you want from a man whose eyes darken when he looks at you." She sighed dreamily.

"They do not," Jayne protested. At least Mercy hadn't said Jayne's eyes got all starry when she looked at him. As if they would. Seth was proving to be rather annoying and overbearing. "I don't need that kind of man in my life."

"Oh?" Sybil's voice was sweet. "What kind of man do you need?"

"Right now? None. My heart is locked up tightly. I won't open it again. It's like asking to be hurt."

"You'll change your mind about that one day," Mercy said.

"Nope. Not me. Now let's go follow the river and see where it goes."

Sybil laughed. "It goes to the ocean. Are you planning to go that far?"

She laughed at Sybil's nonsense. "So maybe I'll see where it comes from."

Sybil pointed toward the mountains. "From the snow up there."

"But it's August. Surely the snow is all melted. So where does the water come from that keeps flowing past the ranch?"

Mercy flung her arms wide. "Who cares? It's a lovely day. Let's enjoy it."

Jayne sighed her agreement. The sun glistened off the rugged mountains and dappled the deciduous trees. A gentle zephyr tickled her skin and danced along the grass. Birds rejoiced from every direction. She breathed deep. "It smells so good. Like the air is full of a thousand wild flowers."

They followed the river past the pens and along a grassy slope. A few steps farther and they entered a grove of trees.

"We should have brought a gun," Mercy said. "You could practice your shooting."

"You don't think there are enough injured cowboys already?" Sybil asked.

"We could go for one each."

Jayne knew Mercy was teasing but Sybil gave them both a this-isn't-amusing look.

Mercy pushed past some prickly bushes and led them into an opening. "Look at the little waterfall."

It hardly qualified as such. It was only the river flowing over some big rocks and making a cheery noise.

Sybil perched on a fallen tree. "It's so peaceful."

Mercy and Jayne exchanged looks and silently agreed to let Sybil enjoy a quiet moment. They sat on the grass behind her and waited for Sybil to be ready to move on. Finally, with a sigh that came from deep inside, she pushed to her feet. "It's very restful to watch the water gurgle past."

They continued onward and spent a pleasant couple of hours wandering along the river.

Jayne glanced at the sky. "We should get back."

As they retraced their steps, the sun shone hotter. They stopped and splashed cool water on their faces before they reached the ranch.

When they stepped into the open and headed for the bridge, Jayne looked toward the house. Seth still sat in the chair beside the door. He must be bored. The joy of the morning faded slightly. She should have offered to keep him company. Perhaps read to him again. How selfish of her.

As quickly as the thought came, she dismissed it. He surely wouldn't want her company. After all, she was but a silly woman who needed him to guide her. Or so he thought.

She sighed. She certainly was acting foolish. She didn't care about his opinion one way or the other and was grateful he'd offered to give her shooting lessons. Never mind how the offer came.

Mercy saw him, too. "Let's ask Seth about where the river comes from."

As they drew closer, Jayne saw Smokey curled into a ball on Seth's lap. The cat opened one eye as the ladies approached then closed it again and ignored them.

At least Seth had the cat to keep him company.

"To what do I owe this honor?" He glanced about the circle of friends but directed his question to Jayne.

She answered before Mercy could. "We want to

know where the water from the river comes from if the snow is all melted."

He blinked then widened his eyes. "That's a strange question."

"Do you have an answer?"

His eyes dipped into a smile. "I could say the water comes from lakes."

Mercy snapped her fingers. "Lakes! I should have thought of that."

"That isn't the whole answer, is it?" Jayne asked, caught by the darkness in his hazel eyes.

"There are glaciers up there and melted water comes off them throughout the summer. I've seen them. Even walked on some of them." He closed his eyes as if thinking of a time when he had done so. "Imagine cold ice on a hot summer day. And it's really cold."

Jayne sighed. "I wish I could see it."

"Before I leave I will take you to the mountains. Maybe not to a glacier but to one of the beautiful lakes. There isn't anything quite like the views." He again closed his eyes and sighed.

"I'd like that," Sybil said.

"Me, too," Mercy added.

Seth opened his eyes and looked directly at Jayne. He lifted one eyebrow. "How do you feel about it?"

She widened her eyes. Did he really care what she thought?

His gaze held hers. His eyes darkened, tinted now like the forest trees. She could almost hear the birds singing.

She blinked, as if to sever the spell they'd cast on her. "I enjoy seeing the country. It's beautiful." Her words came out in a breezy rush. She grabbed the girls and pulled them toward the door. "Let's help Linette."

"Bye," Seth called.

Jayne added her goodbye to that of the others.

"I thought he was anxious to leave the ranch," Mercy murmured as they headed down the hall. "Don't see any evidence of it. You sure you haven't batted your eyes at him a little too much and made him forget everything but your charming company?"

Jayne blew her breath out in a protest. "I've done no such thing." She hoped Seth hadn't overheard Mercy's comment. A hot blush raced up her neck and she prayed the others wouldn't notice and ask about its cause. She'd never admit that a moment ago she'd gone on a flight of imagination all because the color of his eyes reminded her of the forest.

If either of them noticed and commented on it, Jayne would pretend it hadn't happened. He was only a cowboy she'd accidently shot and who high-handedly informed her he meant to teach her to shoot so no other cowboys would be harmed.

He might prevent another injured cowboy but she wasn't so certain that the shooter would be unharmed. Something about the man threatened her firm resolve. No, she informed her brain. There would be no veering from her goals. No opening her heart. No inviting pain and trouble.

Chapter Five

When Linette called out for him to come for dinner, Seth hobbled down the hall, careful not to use his leg. The herbs she'd put on the wound could only do so much. He had to be responsible enough to rest the leg until it stopped bleeding.

Eddie came in the back door as Seth entered the kitchen from the other side. "Say, I think you need a crutch."

"Sounds like a good idea."

Grady burst through the door behind Eddie. "Billy and me are going to catch bugs after we eat. Daisy said girls don't like bugs." He faced Linette. "Is that right? Do you hate bugs?"

She smiled. "It depends on the kind of bug. Some I like just fine." She lifted generous portions of fried ham from a skillet.

Grady shifted his attention to Mercy who dished a mound of potatoes into a bowl. "You like bugs?"

"Can't say as I do."

Grady moved on to Sybil as she dumped cooked carrots into a bowl. "You like 'em?"

She shuddered. "No. They give me the creeps."

He continued on to Jayne who sliced a large loaf of richly browned bread.

Seth swallowed back a rush of saliva. Been a long time since he'd enjoyed a meal such as this. Oh sure, he got fed fine on the cattle drive but hunkering around a campfire with a bunch of cussing, spitting cowboys was hardly the same as sitting at a table in the company of a family and some pretty ladies while eating home-cooked food.

"You like bugs, Auntie Jayne?"

Jayne pretended to give the question a lot of thought. Then she answered. "I don't mind bugs…" She crossed to Eddie, who scrubbed up at the washstand. "Unless a brother is threatening to stick one down my back." She leaned over him. "Like you used to do."

Eddie slowly straightened, saw the knife in her hand and backed away, his arms up as if to protect himself. "Me? I don't recall doing such a thing."

She stalked him. "Funny how clearly I recall it. You were such a tease." The two of them glowered at each other then broke into laughter. She lowered the knife and he draped an arm over her shoulder.

"I was only trying to teach you not to be a sissy."

"Hmm. And yet you continue to treat me like one."

He leaned away to look into her face. "How do I do that?"

"By overprotecting me. By refusing to teach me to shoot." She tossed her head, sending waves of light through her rich brown hair. "But never mind. Seth has decided to give me lessons."

Eddie stared at Seth. "You did?"

Seth shrugged. Would Eddie feel Seth had encouraged Jayne to defy him? "If you have no objections. I figure it will be safer for everyone if she shoots under proper supervision."

Mercy huffed. "It wasn't my fault she shut her eyes."

Eddie rolled his head back and forth. "Are you sure about this? It might be a bigger task than you know."

"Yeah," Mercy said, her tone aggrieved. "How are you going to keep her from closing her eyes?"

"I'm sure she'll do just fine," Linette soothed.

"I don't know why she wants to learn." Sybil sounded truly puzzled.

Jayne waved her hands. "I'm here, you know. Stop talking about me."

But they all continued to talk, each defending their previous statements and adding to them.

Jayne jammed her fists on her hips and glowered at the lot but they paid her no heed.

Seth watched her frustration mount and he started to grin.

She met his gaze and squinted at him. "What's so funny?"

He tipped his head toward the others. Then he put his fingers between his teeth and gave a whistle that brought every pair of eyes toward him. "Jayne seems to be annoyed that we're all talking about her. She's feeling invisible."

Eddie patted her shoulder as if to soothe her which, as far as Seth could tell, had quite the opposite effect.

He wondered how long it would be before she blew her top.

Linette no doubt wondered the same thing, as she moved to defuse the situation. "Our food is getting cold. Why don't we sit down and eat?"

Eddie waited until everyone was settled then bowed

his head and said the blessing. After the food had been passed, he asked, "Where did you girls go this morning?"

All three spoke at once then by silent consent they let Jayne answer. "We followed the river for a ways. Wondered where the water came from. Lakes, of course, but Seth says there are also glaciers up there."

Eddie nodded. "Indeed, there are. Way up in the mountains."

Seth took note of the fact that Jayne had said nothing about his promise to take them to one of the mountain lakes. Did it mean nothing to her? For some reason her failure to mention it annoyed him. He'd offered her an outing. At great personal sacrifice. It would mean delaying his return yet another day. Of course, her friends were included. But it was Jayne he'd invited.

Come to think of it, she hadn't seemed any more overjoyed at his offer to teach her to shoot.

Was she reluctant to spend time with him or was it simply her independence kicking in? Perhaps she thought she and her friends could go to a glacier on their own and she resented his intrusion.

Seems the young lady would take some watching if she thought she could handle every situation on her own. Not that he meant to volunteer for the job. He couldn't even explain why he'd offered to take her to the mountains let alone give her shooting lessons other than the one big reason.

It hurt to get shot. He'd do his best to see it didn't happen to another unsuspecting person.

After dinner, Jayne and her friends told Linette they'd clean up so she could rest. Grady went to join Billy in their bug hunt. Eddie rode out of the yard with two other cowboys. The crutch seemed to have been forgotten. Seth wondered what to do with himself but seeing as he was mostly immobile, sitting in the sun again seemed the only alternative, though he'd discovered it a lonely occupation.

He parked himself on a chair out in the grass and stared at the ranch buildings. There must be something he could do to pass the time. Maybe he'd ask Eddie for a job that would last a day or two.

After a bit the girls drifted outside and sat down on the grass beside him. Sybil brought a knitting project and Mercy had an atlas. How far did she expect to go adventuring? Jayne had brought a sock and darning material.

He watched as she wove the yarn in and out.

She glanced up, saw he watched her and lowered the needle. "What?"

"I didn't say anything."

"You didn't have to. You *looked* something."

"Really? How do I *look* something?"

"Like this." She knit her forehead in a fierce look. "Or this." She waggled her eyebrows like mischief waiting to happen. "Or this." She widened her eyes and very clearly communicated surprise.

Her friends giggled.

"Fine. I get your point. But what look was I giving?"

"I'm sure you know." She returned to her work.

"I'm equally sure I don't. Why, I was simply watching you darn a sock, watching you weave the yarn in and out in perfect little—" He flicked his wrist to indicate what he meant.

"I suppose you're surprised to see me doing something useful."

He glanced at the others but they kept their heads down. Fine. He could deal with this on his own. Though for the life of him, he didn't know what she expected him to say. Why should he be surprised that she could darn a sock? Then he recalled what she'd said about needing to feel useful. Or something like that. He honestly couldn't recall her exact words. His mind had been numbed by the pain in his leg and concerned about how it delayed his trip home.

"I think nothing of the sort." He leaned closer and lowered his voice. "If you want the truth, I admire your quickness with the needle and yarn."

She jerked back and stared open-mouthed at him.

"Shut your mouth," Sybil whispered. "Or you'll catch bugs."

Mercy didn't bother to hide her giggle.

Red crept up Jayne's neck and painted round apples on her cheeks.

Seth sat back and resisted an urge to pound his palm on his forehead. He'd only meant to…to what? Encourage her? Make her see that she was more than she saw herself as? Instead, he had come across as a flirt. Him? Seth Collins? A flirt? He opened his mouth intending to explain he never flirted but instead clicked his teeth together without saying a thing. Least said, soonest mended, Ma used to say.

"Look," Mercy said. "There are the boys."

Billy and Grady ran around in the tall grass beside one of the buildings, each carrying a Mason jar.

"I wonder how many bugs they've found." Jayne's voice seemed a little gravelly.

"If they come here with jars of bugs, I'm leaving," Sybil said, already pushing to her feet.

Smokey jumped out of the grass and Sybil screamed. "Silly cat. You frightened me." She headed indoors.

Mercy closed her book, stretched and bolted to her

feet. "I'm going to explore. Can you take my book in for me?" She handed it to Jayne.

Smokey arched his back and rubbed against Jayne then leaped into Seth's lap.

"Well, make yourself at home." He stroked the cat and earned a very loud purr.

"The cat likes you," Jayne said.

"You needn't sound so surprised."

She shook her head. "I'm not surprised at all."

"Really? So you think I'm a likeable fellow?" He ducked his head and paid Smokey a great deal of attention. What kind of question was that? When had he ever been tempted to beg for attention before? It must be the result of sitting around all day staring at the world creeping by on leaden feet.

She made a humming sound. "Can't really say, can I? I hardly know you."

"Fair enough. But after I've taught you to shoot a gun well enough to trust you with one, you'll know me well enough to give me your opinion."

She squinted at him. "How long do you think these lessons are going to take?"

He lifted a hand. "I guess that depends on how fast you learn."

"I learn fast."

"Good to know."

"Then you can be on your way." As an afterthought, she added, "To your pa."

That reminder brought him up sharply. He had to get to his pa as soon as possible. He would not fail in his responsibility.

His attention was diverted as Grady and his friend climbed the hill.

Jayne introduced Billy, a boy of about six with blue

eyes and blond hair. The boys' coloring was so similar, he could have easily passed for Grady's older brother. Seth recalled hearing that Billy and his brother and sisters had a new ma and pa and wondered what had happened.

Billy pointed down the hill. "I live in that house." He indicated a two-story house beyond the other buildings. It looked recently constructed. "Heard you got shot. It hurt much?"

"Only when I breathe," Seth said.

The children giggled.

"Wanna see what I got?" Billy held his jar toward Seth.

Seth took it and examined the bug collection. "Wow. You've been hard at work catching bugs." There were a dozen or so bugs including several furry caterpillars. He offered the jar to Jayne. "You want to see them?"

She held up a hand and wrinkled her nose. "I see them fine from here."

He chuckled at her expression then turned back to admire Grady's collection of bugs. After a bit the boys set their jars aside and chased after each other.

"It's nice they have one another to play with," Jayne said.

He didn't say anything.

"It must be lonely being an only child."

He heard the question in her voice. Knew she was asking how it had been for him. But he hadn't been an only child. He'd had an older brother he adored. The hollowness in his heart cried out. He moaned then realizing he'd done so, rubbed his leg as if it hurt. It did, a little, but not nearly as much as the spot in his heart where he stored Frank's memories.

He quietly, firmly closed the door on that pain.

There'd been a resurgence of his memories in the last few hours but he intended for them to stay safely buried in the past.

Thankfully Linette joined them at that moment and saved him from Jayne's curious study.

Jayne wondered at his sudden withdrawal. One moment he teased her and the next his expression had closed off like he'd remembered something he'd left undone. She didn't think it was because he'd delayed his trip to see his pa. Seems he should be able to relax and trust that this Crawford fellow would not abandon his pa. But she had no idea what else could explain it. Not that it mattered. He wasn't part of her plans for her life.

She resumed repairing the sock but couldn't dismiss his statement that he enjoyed watching her, and stole a glance his direction.

His attention was on the boys chasing each other.

That was fine because part of her plans included being free of emotional entanglements and something about Seth threatened those boundaries.

She folded up her mending project and rose. "I'll help with supper preparations," she said and retreated indoors.

The next morning, Seth appeared for breakfast hobbling on a crutch.

Jayne watched his progress. He appeared a little awkward but it would enable him to get around without using his leg.

Linette had checked the wound this morning and said it looked good.

"I see Eddie found you one." She nodded at his crutch and smiled. Her smile made its way to her eyes, warming them in a surprising way.

"Yup. Now I can get around more and not worry about bleeding." He grinned at her.

Mornings would be a cheerful matter if she saw such a happy grin every day. She resisted an urge to thump the heel of her hand on her forehead. The last thing she needed or wanted was to be dependent on a man's facial expressions to set the tone for her day. She turned to Linette. "Is his leg okay?" She already knew the answer but had to bring her thoughts back to sensible. She hoped Seth wouldn't take her words to indicate anything more than concern that he not do further damage to his leg. She didn't want that on her conscience. No reason he should think it anything more.

"So long as he doesn't overdo it."

Seth made a protesting noise. "You could have asked me. I'm right here." He put his fingers between his teeth as if to whistle, a reminder of how he'd silenced the others yesterday. He grinned at her.

She couldn't help but smile back, and despite her resolve, her heart tumbled over itself like the waterfall they'd visited.

After breakfast, he lingered in the kitchen. When she glanced at him, he tipped his head to signal he wished to speak to her.

She followed him down the hall.

"I'm ready to give you a shooting lesson. Let's go."

Her tumbling heart jerked to a halt as she crossed her arms. "I can be ready anytime I want. Just as soon as I'm asked."

"I just asked."

"No, you told me. Just like you told me I would take instructions from you." She planted her hands on her hips as her insides twisted. "You're just like everyone else. I have the right to make a choice. So ask."

He blinked and opened his mouth. No sound came out. He closed it again and turned to stare out the front door. His shoulders rose and fell as he took a deep breath.

Was it so difficult to give her the right to make her choices? If so, he demanded far too much control. More than she would give up.

Slowly he came round to face her. "I don't know why this is so important to you but fine. I can ask. Jayne Gardiner, would you like me to give you shooting lessons?"

She struggled to put an end to her annoyance, her anger and a whole host of emotions that had nothing to do with him. With blinding insight, she realized that her cauldron of emotions had been building for a long time. They were the culmination of having so many decisions taken out of her hands because she wasn't considered worthy of making them. Added to that was how she bore the consequences of the choices others made for her. Father, Oliver and even Eddie chose as they saw best but their decisions weren't always what she cared to live with.

He shifted, and she brought her attention back to the present situation. He'd asked even though he didn't understand. That raised him considerably in her estimation.

"I would like for you to give me lessons." She waited.

He looked confused then understanding flooded his face and he chuckled. "Would today suit you?"

She nodded. "Today suits me just fine."

"When would you like to go?"

"Give me two minutes."

His chuckles followed her across the kitchen and into her bedroom where she scooped up a Western-style hat she deemed necessary for shooting and the red brocade bag containing her pistol. She'd purchased the gun at the Fort. She guessed even before she reached the ranch that Eddie wouldn't be willing to teach her to handle a firearm. There were times he was so much like their father. But she'd bought it, anyway.

She skipped back to the kitchen. Linette, Sybil and Mercy waited for her.

"Are you sure this is what you want to do?" Linette asked.

"Very sure."

Her sister-in-law smiled. "Then I'm behind you all the way. I firmly believe in women learning as much independence as they can."

"Me, too," Mercy said, giving her a little hug.

Sybil sighed. "Just don't go shooting anyone."

She laughed, then assured them she'd be extra careful and went to join Seth who waited outside.

"Where to?" he asked.

She pointed to the back of the house. "That will get us away from the ranch." As they walked, she gave him a studying look.

He had a gun stuck in his belt.

"I have my own gun," she said.

"Figured you did."

The way he said it, full of resignation and despair, brought a burst of laughter to her lips. "So why did you bring a gun?"

"A man should be prepared at all times." He grinned. "Don't you agree?" He stopped, leaning on his crutch to look at her. Their gazes caught and held. A dozen thoughts fluttered through her brain like butterflies. Did he refer to her shooting him and meant to suggest he should have been armed and ready?

The idea so amused her that she tilted her head back and laughed.

"Care to share the joke?"

She tried to stop her laughter but at the bewildered look on his face, she shook her head and waved her hands to indicate she couldn't speak.

He looked heavenward as if seeking divine help in dealing with her—an idea that tickled her so deep inside she couldn't stop laughing despite his pained look.

Finally, she wiped her eyes and took a deep breath. "I wondered if you wished you'd been armed and ready the day I shot you." She pressed her lips together to keep from bursting into laughter again. "Or if you planned to be armed and ready for today." She managed to contain her mirth but her eyes brimmed with the effort.

He shook his head and his mouth drew down at the corners. "If you can't be serious about such a grave matter..." He let the sentence trail off as if her failure defied words.

She pulled her mouth into a frown that reflected his expression. "I can be serious. See?"

He lifted his hands in a sign of defeat. "I give up. But how am I to teach you something as grave and deadly as shooting a gun if you only see it as a—" he shook his head "—a mockery."

"You sure you're not mocking me?" She giggled.

"Me? Not a chance."

In a flash of clarity, she realized that he spoke the truth. Likely he took each task with due seriousness. And she didn't find the idea of his seriousness objectionable. It made a man dependable. Not that it mattered to her. She didn't mean to depend on a man in the future.

Chapter Six

They reached a grove of trees. Tall pine, frothy willows and sighing poplar. As they stepped into a clearing, Seth looked around. The area was wide enough to give them room to shoot, and there were no rocks nearby to pose a risk of ricochet. If his bearings were correct, he had been a hundred yards farther on, sitting on a boulder when she shot him.

A stump on the far side of the clearing held a paper target. "Where did you get that?" He wondered why Eddie would have one. He didn't seem the type to be spending time in target practice.

"I got it at the Fort when I got my gun. When I explained to the store owner what I intended to do, he said I'd need a few of these."

Seth stared at her. "You've been planning this a long time."

Her eyes bored into his, full of conviction and challenge—as if she expected him to oppose her idea. But she wouldn't listen if he did, which was why he intended to give her lessons.

He broke from the intensity of her look and shifted his gaze to the target. "I see it's unmarked."

She laughed. "I haven't come within a mile of it." Her expression sobered. "But I've left a mark on you. You will never know how much I regret that."

Again her gaze found his and held it in a look that burned away every argument he might have imagined to her plan. In fact, if he let it, her look might have broken down walls he'd built around his heart to protect it from the pain of losing Frank and Sarah. That couldn't happen and he jerked his gaze away so sharply it put him momentarily off balance. Only his firm grasp on the crutch kept him on his feet.

He was here for one purpose only—to teach her how to handle a firearm so no one else would be injured. She might have shot herself. He shuddered at the thought.

"First thing is to move the target closer so you have some hope of hitting it." He hopped over and brought it to a stump much closer. "Let's see what sort of gun you have."

She dug in her brocade bag and brought out a .45 Colt Single Action Army revolver. A decent enough gun. She held it gingerly.

"First thing is always consider it loaded. Hold it like it's serious business. That way you aren't in for any surprises."

"Okay." The gun still dangled like a spider.

He gingerly removed it from her hand and walked her through the process of loading, unloading, cocking the hammer, ejecting the spent shell. "Have you got all that?"

She nodded.

"Then let's see you do it."

He walked her through it several times until each move was certain.

"Now for the stance. Your first instinct is to stand

with your legs slightly apart facing your target. However, that allows you to sway sideways. Instead— Are you right-handed?"

She nodded again.

"Then you want to put your left foot forward and hold the gun with both hands. Like so." He let the crutch fall to the ground so he could illustrate. "Try it."

She followed his instructions. She clenched her jaw so tightly he wondered if her teeth would survive her first lesson.

"Now take the gun and hold it."

She did so, extending it at shoulder height, her shoulders hunched practically to her ears. It looked most uncomfortable. If she found the task so offensive, why did she persist with it?

He knew what her answer would be if he asked. Because of her helplessness in the face of Oliver's death. He could tell her that feeling would never leave but didn't see the point. It wouldn't make her change her mind.

Not for the first time, he suspected she was part mule.

"Rock back and forth a bit. Do you feel solid?"

They went through the stance several times then he addressed her grip.

She listened and practiced the steps he gave. "You sure pack a lot more into a lesson than Mercy did."

"Hopefully with better results." He touched his leg.

Her hands wavered. He edged closer. Hesitated. But there was only one way to show her how to hold her arms. He closed the distance between them. "Like this." He reached around her, steadying each arm with his own.

He felt her arms twitch.

An answering jolt raced up his limbs and landed in his heart with the force of lightning. Thunder echoed through his insides. Here was a woman who needed taking care of.

What was he thinking? He had a father he was responsible for and he took his responsibilities seriously. He would go home, hopefully find Pa much improved and take over his care. He would devote the rest of his life, or however long Pa lived, to that job.

He didn't need any complications. Especially from a headstrong woman whose only concern was becoming independent at any cost. However foolish her choices were.

He knew where that led. He was the one who paid the price for Frank and Sarah's foolishness. He certainly wasn't about to venture in that direction again.

It was impossible to say who moved away first. Though he figured it was mutual. He knew she didn't want someone taking care of her any more than he wanted the obligation.

"My arms are getting tired," she said, shaking one then transferring the gun to shake the other.

"Let's take a break." He sat on a nearby log and she sat on another. She couldn't get much more distance between them and remain in the same clearing. The air fractured with unspoken cautions, goals that took them in different directions.

After several tense, silent moments, Jayne sighed. "You're putting a lot into this." She sliced her gaze toward him. "Why?"

Perhaps explaining his reason would ease her tension. "I'm just concerned that if you intend to shoot, you are prepared to use a gun appropriately."

"But why does it matter to you? You'll soon be gone and our paths will likely never cross again."

"I suppose that's so." She didn't have to act so relieved about it, he thought. "But I would still feel responsible. The way I see it, if you see someone doing something foolish, you do your best to stop them. If you can convince them to make better choices, you might save them from disaster." His voice caught but he hoped she wouldn't notice.

She cocked her head. "Are you speaking from firsthand experience?"

"Yes, I am. I lost two people very close to me because they wouldn't heed a warning."

"How close?"

He shrugged. "Does it matter? The point is, I will always do what I can to keep people from making disastrous choices."

She turned away and seemed greatly interested in something at the far side of the clearing. "How disastrous?"

"They died." The words tore out of his chest and scratched the length of his throat and they vibrated in the air.

"Oh, Seth. I'm sorry. An accident?"

He nodded, trying to push every remembrance of that day from his thoughts.

"Did you—" She hesitated.

He looked at her. She scrubbed her lips together and seemed to struggle with her emotions. No doubt she was remembering watching her fiancé die.

He hobbled over to her side and sat down. "I should have never started this conversation. It reminds you of a painful event."

She shuddered and his instincts to protect her took

over. He slipped his arm across her shoulders and offered his strength. "I'm sorry."

Another shudder raced through her then she turned to look into his face. Her eyes were wide and so dark he thought the pain must be searing them. Ah. How could he have been so thoughtless?

"Did you see them die?" Her words were barely a whisper.

He nodded. "I wish I hadn't."

She squeezed his hand. "Me, too."

He understood her to mean her fiancé. "The pictures fade with time."

"Do they?" She shook her head. "How do you ever forget watching someone die?"

"You don't. But you learn how to live with it and how to keep it in the past."

She clung to his gaze, probing his soul for truth.

He couldn't hide it from her. He let her glimpse the pain, the despair, the guilt—and hopefully the determination that carried him through every day until it became second nature.

"Seth, who died?"

Her question jerked him to his feet. It was one thing to talk in anonymous terms. It was quite another to talk about Frank and Sarah. "Let's run through the whole thing again. If we're both comfortable that you're ready, I'll let you shoot a real bullet."

She rose slowly. "Seth, there are some things you can't control. Like death, as you've already learned. And people. Guess you didn't learn that quite so well because you're trying to control me and I won't give you that right." She stalked to where she had practiced her stance. "I will never give anyone that right again." She shifted her left leg forward, gripped the gun in her right hand and steadied it with her left, just as he'd shown her. She held the stance firmly for several seconds than flung him a hot look. "I think I'm ready for a bullet."

It took every ounce of Jayne's strength to hold the gun steady before she turned to Seth. He'd lost friends. Knowing the pain and shock and despair of watching someone you cared for die, she sympathized with that. She even understood his need to be in control. It was how she'd reacted.

But she only meant to be in control of her life, her choices and her boundaries.

While he, foolish man, thought he could be in control of everything and everyone. It surely must put him in opposition with numerous people.

"I'm ready," she repeated.

He picked up his crutch and hobbled to her side. "One more thing. You must practice squeezing the trigger." He cupped his hand over hers. "Hold the gun like you don't want to lose it." He tightened his fingers to illustrate, crushing her flesh into the cold steel. "This way you always have control."

Earlier, he'd wrapped his arms about her to steady her arm. She'd felt safe in his solid grasp. So safe, it sent alarm skidding along her nerves. She didn't need anyone holding her or keeping her safe. She meant to be independent.

Now the way his fingers closed on hers, she felt again his strength. It raced up her arm and into her heart like a promise of protection. She gritted her teeth. If she gave the slightest encouragement she suspected he would gladly play that role. He'd become her protector, her defender, her knight in shining armor for as long as he chose to stay around. And then he'd leave and she would be the weaker, the more uncertain for having allowed him that role.

She would not do it. She would not give him control.

She nodded. "I've got it. Let me show you."

He dropped his hand from hers and stepped back. "Show me."

She held the stance he'd taught her, gripped the gun in her hand, held it steady and she crushed her fingers around the gun.

"Squeeze the trigger slowly, keeping your grasp tight all the while. That way your other fingers can't spasm when you squeeze and you won't get the same amount of recoil."

She obeyed his every instruction. In this matter, at least, she welcomed his lessons so she allowed him the right to tell her what to do. He showed her how to line up the sights on the target and made her practice until she could steady the gun on the bull's-eye.

"Good," he said when he was finally confident she had the whole procedure down. "Now for a bullet."

"Finally. I was beginning to think I might have to do this for hours, even days, before it led to the real thing."

The look he gave her said plenty but that didn't keep him from saying what he thought, as well. "Need I remind you that I am living—thankfully—evidence of you shooting live ammunition when you didn't know proper technique?"

"I haven't forgotten." She spoke meekly.

He put one bullet in the chamber, stepped behind her then lifted the gun in front of her. "Forget there is a bullet in it. Simply do everything I've taught you." Slowly, quietly, he repeated the steps as she followed them.

A frisson of fear raced through her as she cocked

the hammer. Last time she'd pulled the trigger she'd shot someone.

She knew the damage a bullet could do. Thank God that in Seth's situation, it hadn't been worse. She tried to swallow but her throat was constricted. What if she had been forced to live with two deaths on her conscience?

He brought his arm around her and steadied her hand. Her fears subsided, settled back to the dark spot behind her heart.

"Good grip. Now squeeze."

She did. The explosion of the bullet battered her eardrums.

She opened her eyes and squinted at the target. "There's a hole right through the center."

He dropped her arm and backed away.

She turned to face him, laughing.

"No thanks to you. You closed your eyes."

"I did?" Her shoulders fell as did her sense of victory. "I did."

"Guess I missed one very important step in your lesson." He leaned closer and narrowed his eyes. "Keep your eyes on the target." His eyes flashed shades of green. "Keep them open so you aim true."

"You're angry."

His breath whooshed out, and his expression softened. "Not angry."

"Do you expect me to believe that?" She put more distance between them.

He leaned back on his heels, struggling with his emotions. Suddenly he barked out a laugh. "Like Mercy said, how am I going to persuade you to keep your eyes open?"

"They're open now." In fact, they felt too large for her face as she stared at the man who had gone from anger to roaring with laughter. He sure knew how to laugh with abandon. The sound rumbled up and down her chest and tickled behind her ribs. She began to laugh, as well, though she had no idea what they were laughing at. Only that it was pure enjoyment to do so.

He shook his head and pointed at her. "Maybe I should use matchsticks."

She understood he meant to hold her eyes open. The idea tickled her and she laughed harder. Her knees weakened and she sat on the nearby log.

Seth joined her and they both sobered as they sat side by side. She stretched out her legs as did he. His went on several inches beyond hers. He was a big man, as she'd already noted. A solid man. A steady man.

Good thing he was leaving soon because she was finding it harder and harder to remember why she didn't need the care and protection of such a man.

One glance at the gun she still held brought her reason back. She drew her legs in. "I'd like to try again."

He sighed. "I don't have any matchsticks with me."

"You won't need them." She marched over to the spot where she faced the target. She could do this. All she had to do was focus on the target and keep her eyes open.

He chambered another bullet and edged in behind her. She could feel the warmth of his body, the shelter it provided from the slight breeze…the shelter from life's storms. His breath caressed her cheek as he lined up the sights over her shoulder.

Confusing emotions raced through her. Determination that she found hard to cling to when his arms were about her, dismay at what her ineptitude had cost Oliver…and herself. Fear of firearms and an emptiness that she wouldn't allow herself to investigate. Her arms quivered ever so slightly but enough that he noticed. Again he brought his hand up to steady her. "Line it up. Keep your eyes open and squeeze."

She curled her trigger finger, held her breath as she anticipated the explosion. It was so loud.

"You closed your eyes again." He held his head in his hands as if it hurt him to even think about it.

"I can't help it. It's so loud." She refused to look at him.

"Jayne, it's a gun. Guns are loud and heavy and cold and dangerous."

"I know that." He didn't have to treat her like an idiot.

"Why are you shooting one if you're so all-fired scared of it?"

She flung him a defensive glance. "Because I refuse to let fear control me."

He lowered his hands and studied her, his eyes wide as if he couldn't believe what he'd heard.

"Yes, I am afraid of guns. I admit it. But my fear held me immobile when Oliver was shot. I won't allow it to make me useless ever again."

"What happened?" His gentle voice melted her resolve. That, and knowing he had a similar experience.

She moved to the log and sat down, folded her hands in her lap. Seth sat beside her and she told him the story. "I met Oliver when I was fifteen and he eighteen. His family is old friends of my family but they'd been abroad and had only just returned." She tried to think what had attracted her to him. Strangely she couldn't remember anything specific. He didn't tease her, didn't make her laugh...at least not on purpose. He didn't give her looks that made her want to laugh and cry at the same time. Nor had his arms about her ever made her feel like she'd found a secure shelter.

She shifted to meet Seth's hazel eyes, saw the gold showing in his irises. She clung to his gaze wanting him to understand how she could have been attracted to Oliver, even though she wasn't sure she understood it herself. "He seemed so wise. So sure of himself." At first, she'd liked that but soon discovered it meant he didn't need her. Not like she needed him and wanted to be needed. "I thought him so grown-up. He did things and took me places I'd never been." Places her father would have forbidden. "Oliver liked to gamble. Claimed he was good at it. If the amount of money he spent indicated anything then he must have been. But money didn't impress me. My father is rich and could provide my every want. After a while, when he either didn't invite me on his exploits or I refused to go because I didn't care for the type of company I met, I found myself more and more alone. Gambling was his mistress and I couldn't compete." She hadn't meant to say the words aloud. Hadn't meant to spill all the detail but Seth didn't indicate shock or disinterest. He cupped his hand over hers on the log.

It gave her the courage to continue. "One day he offered to take me shopping. I didn't need anything but I was thrilled he wanted to spend time with me." She groaned. "That makes me sound needy and immature. Perhaps I was. But not anymore." She drew in a refreshing breath and continued. "Someone came out of the alley demanding money and a key. Oliver gave him all his money but had no key." She gave the rest of the details. How a gun had been within her grasp but she couldn't bring herself to touch it. How Oliver had been shot. "There was so much blood." She shuddered.

He squeezed her shoulder. "What a horrible, sense-less crime. You should never have witnessed it."

No words came to her mind. Her head was filled with regrets and wishes. "I will learn to shoot. I will overcome my fear of guns."

"Of course you will. Just as soon as you keep your eyes open and on the target."

She nodded.

"Did they catch the killer?"

"No. He escaped."

"He's still on the loose?" He grabbed his crutch and hurried to his feet. He limped to the far side of the clearing and stared out into the trees. He turned and faced her.

"Then I think it's very important that you learn to shoot a gun and shoot it well."

Tension skidded up her spine and grabbed the base of her head at the harsh tone of his voice. "You think he's after me?"

"You are a witness to him murdering Oliver, aren't you?"

She wrapped her arms about her. "Thanks for scar-ing me." She rose and took a deep breath. "But he'd never follow me to Canada. Even if he did, how would he ever find me? Canada is a very big place."

He scrubbed at his eyes. "Yes, of course. I'm sorry. I was being foolish. Forgive me?"

She nodded absently. Was it possible Oliver's mur-derer would try and track her down? "It's not like I'm in London and can identify him. It's to his advantage that I've left the country. I'd say he should feel like he got away with murder. Literally."

He gave a mirthless laugh. "You are right."

His assurances did not alleviate the tension in her

muscles. "I think I'm done with shooting lessons for today." She secured the gun back in her bag.

She waited for him to fall in at her side, and they slowly began their way back to the ranch. "I said far too much. I'm sorry." She should never have opened the floodgates on her experience.

"It is I who should apologize for expressing concerns that have no basis. I guess I'm turning into a worrier. Always seeing and expecting something bad to happen."

Sympathy and understanding erased her tension. "You witnessed the death of two close friends. That's reason enough for your caution."

"It's generous of you to give me that excuse."

She drew up and faced him. "For goodness' sake. Are we going to apologize and wallow for the rest of the day or can we be done with this?"

He burst out laughing. "Oh, Jayne, how refreshing you are. Yes, I'm ready to be done." He laughed again.

"Good. Now can we plan another shooting lesson tomorrow?"

He rolled his eyes. "The one thing you need to learn I can't teach you."

She planted her hand over his on the crutch. "I'll keep my eyes open. I promise."

He leaned closer as if examining her eyes.

She forced herself to meet his look without blinking.

He stared at her so long her eyes began to water. Still she would not blink first. She concentrated on the way the clouds reflected in his eyes, how his irises darkened to forest green, how the shards of gold were revealed when the clouds moved aside and allowed sunlight to hit his face.

Finally he nodded and straightened. "Good. Let's see you do that tomorrow."

She sucked in air to relieve the sudden dizziness. The man had the most intriguing eyes with the power to make her forget every rational thought—which was not a good thing. Being weak and vulnerable was not part of her plan.

He moved onward and she hurried along. The weight of the gun in her bag reminded her of what really mattered. Learning to take care of herself. Being prepared to take action, especially with a gun. Still, she prayed she would never have call to do so.

Chapter Seven

Seth had accepted Eddie's invitation to continue using the bed in the upstairs room though he could have likely found a bunk with the cowboys in the bunkhouse. Somehow, especially after Jayne's story, he felt the need to be close at hand.

She was right. Her fiancé's killer would likely stay in England where he could move about scot-free. Seth pressed the heel of his hand to his forehead as if he could force wisdom inside. What had he been thinking to voice his fears about the murderer? He regretted it the moment he saw his worries reflected in her eyes. He'd wanted to yank the words back. Wanted to pull her close and promise to protect her.

How could he even hope to promise such a thing? He didn't have the right and didn't want it.

But still there was a concern. The killer had wanted something from Oliver that he didn't get. Would he come after Jayne for it? *God, I'm not much of a one to ask anything of You but this isn't for me. It's for Jayne. Keep her safe.* He wished he could feel some assurance that God would hear and answer his request. He had never understood how Ma continued to believe after Frank and Sarah's deaths.

For the moment he didn't regret his injured leg. It forced him to stay at the ranch for a few days. As long as he was there he could guard her. But he couldn't stay. Besides, Eddie would take care of his sister.

But making sure she could protect herself, should the need arise, took on a greater importance. She must learn how to shoot a gun and hit her intended target.

If only he could figure out a way to make her keep her eyes open.

The next morning he rose with fresh determination. He planned to start lessons again as soon as breakfast ended. As usual, the food was excellent and the talk about the table friendly.

Grady eased forward, anxious to share some news.

"What is it, son?" Eddie asked, giving the child permission to speak.

"Billy's mama and papa are dead. Right?"

"Yes." Eddie sent a questioning look in Linette's direction. She shook her head to indicate she had no idea where the question was going.

"So Cassie and Roper adopted them."

"That's right."

"Because they had no mama and papa?"

"Yes. Why do you ask?"

The boy practically bounced off his chair. "If I find a puppy who has no mama or papa can I adopt him?"

Eddie stared at his son.

Seth ducked his head to hide a grin. The little guy certainly knew how to present an infallible argument.

Jayne nudged his elbow and they secretly grinned at each other.

Eddie and Linette silently consulted each other.

Eddie nodded and turned back to Grady. "I couldn't say without meeting such a puppy. Why do you ask?"

"Billy's new pa said someone left a puppy at the store in Edendale. I guess he needs a good home, wouldn't you say?"

"I expect there are lots of people wanting a dog. What makes you think he'll still be there?"

Grady slouched forward. "I was only hoping. That's all."

"Well, son, I can't say if this puppy still needs a home but I'll check, and I'll leave word at the store that we might be in the market for a new dog. How about that?"

Grady bounced again. "That's good."

Seth stole a look at Jayne and saw a reflection of his own pleasure. Eddie was a good pa.

The meal ended and Seth turned to Jayne but she didn't give him a chance to suggest another shooting lesson.

"You need to meet Cookie. She knows you're here and has likely seen you outside. She likes to meet everyone. Besides, she makes the best cinnamon rolls." She headed for the door and signaled he should follow her. "She always has coffee and some kind of goodies ready."

At first he didn't make any move to join her.

She grabbed his crutch and handed it to him. "Are you coming?"

"Would it do any good to say I'm not?"

"Not a bit." She grinned. "Believe me, you won't regret it."

He gave an exaggerated sigh. "I guess I don't have a choice." He gave slight emphasis to the last word.

Her eyes narrowed and he knew she remembered how she insisted she deserved to be given a choice. She smiled. "You're right, of course. Seth, would you care to meet Cookie? I'm sure she's anxious to meet you."

His grin widened. "It seems like a fine idea." He tromped down the hall. "Shall we?"

As they descended, she told him about the ranch. "Eddie came out two years ago with instructions to build a replica of the Gardiner estate back in England. However, he found the circumstances were so different that he had to adjust the plans Father had given him. At first, Father opposed him but I'm proud to say Eddie stuck to his convictions and Father came around."

She waved at Eddie who mounted up in front of the barn.

"Father especially objected to his marriage to Linette. He said her family wasn't suitable. And Linette's notions of helping people regardless of race or social position especially upset him."

"Seems to me Eddie and Linette make a fine couple."

Jayne slowed her steps. "I agree. And Father has come round."

"So this stubborn, independent streak runs in the family?" He kept his tone light and teasing because, although it was true, he had almost convinced himself it didn't matter to him. He would leave. Continue on with his plans. What Jayne did was not his responsibility. His conscience would be clear if he did his best to teach her to shoot.

"I prefer to think of us as people with principles and resolve."

The airy, dismissive way she said it made him chuckle.

She didn't give him a chance to say anything more on the subject as she went back to her discussion about the Eden Valley Ranch. "The ranch is like a small town.

Over there are supply buildings. Eddie lined one with tin to keep the rodents out." She beamed with pride in her brother.

Seth turned away. He'd had the same pride in Frank. Had thought his older brother could do nothing wrong. Then he'd gotten all goofy about Sarah and did something so stupid it cost him his life.

Jayne drew his attention back to the present as she pointed to the new house where Billy had said he lived. "Roper and Cassie live in a new house, which is large enough to accommodate them and the four children they'd adopted. You met Billy. Besides him, there's Daisy. She's thirteen and very pretty. She obviously adores her younger siblings as well as her new parents. Neil is a year younger than Daisy and imitates Roper right down to the rolling swagger. There's Billy who's six then little Pansy who's two. As the baby of the ranch she gets lots of attention."

"Four children is a lot to take on."

Jayne nodded. "Cassie and Roper handle it like old hands. I suppose it isn't hard when you all love each other."

"Still, it's got to be challenging." Love was not enough sometimes. It didn't conquer pain or make people responsible.

"See that little cabin?" Jayne indicated a log cabin next to the trail. "That's where Linette and Eddie lived the first year she was out here." She chuckled. "I don't suppose you heard their story." She drew closer to the cabin and slowed her steps. "Linette came out expecting a marriage of convenience but Eddie was still working on the big house and expected his former fiancée. He said Linette's arrival was a mistake and he'd send her back come spring." She grinned at Seth. "By spring he was head over heels in love with her."

Love again. As if it would fix everything. He knew it wasn't enough. He'd loved Frank. He'd loved Sarah in a boyish way. He'd loved Ma. It hadn't fixed or prevented anything.

Jayne turned toward the other two-story building. "That's the cookhouse. Cookie and Bertie—her husband—run it." She drew in a deep breath. "I better warn you about Cookie."

He gave her a hard look. "Warn me? Why?"

She shrugged. "It's nothing, really." But her eyes sparkled like she had a secret joke.

"Jayne Gardiner, what are you not telling me?"

She did not manage to control the twitch of a smile. "I wouldn't say anything except I'd hate to see your leg hurt."

He stiffened. "What do you think she'll do? Beat me with a broom? Fly at me with a skillet?"

She laughed hard enough for tears to fill her eyes. "Can't say as I've ever heard tell of her doing so." She sobered with a great deal of effort. "But she does like to hug her guests."

"Hug?" He stared at the cookhouse. "I need to think about this." Hopefully she thought he was teasing. When was the last time he'd been hugged? Ma had been affectionate before Frank died. After that she had grown cautious and sparse with her hugs, though she used to pat his arm or touch the back of his neck.

He realized his hand had gone to that spot of its own accord.

Jayne studied him, her face wrinkled in curiosity. "Do you have something against hugging?" Her voice was low, as if she tried to keep from revealing any opinion.

"'Course not." How else could he answer?

She patted his hand. "You'll like it. I know you will."

The smile gleaming from her eyes made him want to be hugged just to please her. He curled his fingers into his palms. When had he ever been so addlebrained?

"I just want you to be prepared so she doesn't catch you off balance."

"Okay. Fine."

She climbed the steps and opened the door. He swung up after her, keeping a firm grip on his crutch.

A mountain of a woman steamed toward them.

"About time. I thought Jayne meant to keep you to herself." The big woman bore down on him with the speed of a freight train.

He braced himself.

She engulfed him in a hug that threatened to shatter bones but filled his nostrils with cinnamon and yeast and a thousand pleasant memories.

She clapped his back twice and released him.

Jayne nudged him. "Was it so bad?"

He shook his head, unwilling to meet her eyes as something hungry and lonesome tugged at his heart and it wasn't hunger for food.

"Come. Sit. Tell me everything about yourself." Cookie herded them toward the table and put forth steaming cups of coffee and a plate of the rolls Jayne claimed were famous.

Cookie waited until he'd savored a bite of one.

"Mmm. Jayne was right. These are the best I've ever tasted."

She beamed at him. "Pshaw, they're nothing. I make them by the dozens every day."

"And the cowboys eat them by the dozens," Jayne said, earning her a beaming smile from Cookie.

"They certainly do." Seeing he'd finished the first roll, Cookie offered him another.

"Thanks. Don't mind if I do."

She let him enjoy the roll then leaned forward. "You from these parts?"

"My pa lives in Corncrib, Montana."

"I do believe someone mentioned that. Didn't Eddie arrange to have something delivered there?"

"I guess he did." Her reminder put his thoughts back on track. He had responsibilities. He must teach Jayne how to shoot so he could get to his pa. He gulped the rest of his food. "Thank you for the coffee and delicious rolls. 'Preciate them. Now, if you'll excuse me, I need to teach Jayne how to shoot a gun."

"My goodness. You've taken on quite a job from what Mercy says." Cookie turned to Jayne. "No offense but she says you're not the best shot she's ever seen."

Jayne made a protesting noise. "I'm learning."

Seth hobbled to the door. The warmth of Cookie's welcome and the homey atmosphere reminded him of a time when he belonged in a happy family. A time that had come crashing to an end all because Frank cared more about a little fun with Sarah than he did about his own safety. Or Sarah's. It had left Seth with regrets and guilt that chewed at his insides at the most inopportune times. It had also left him with the task of keeping Ma and Pa safe. He'd failed on Ma's behalf but he wouldn't fail his pa. He must get back to Corncrib and make sure Pa was safe.

Jayne jumped to her feet to follow Seth. He seemed in an awful hurry. Guess he was anxious to see her learn to shoot so he could leave. "Thank you, Cookie."

"Come again. Anytime."

Outside, she saw Seth at the corral fence beside the barn. Grady talked to him and waved his arms in animated conversation.

Seth nodded and Grady turned toward the barn. He called, "Kitty, kitty."

Within seconds, four cats raced out and tangled around Seth's legs.

Grady picked up one of Smokey's littermates and said something to Seth.

Seth nodded, backed up to the fence, rested his crutch at his side and took the kitten Grady offered. When he glanced up and saw her standing there, he smiled.

She caught up her skirts and trotted across the yard to his side. When she reached out a hand to stroke the purring cat he held, their hands brushed and warmth jolted up her arms, zapped through her heart. What was there about this man that made her forget her hard-learned lessons? Made her aware of emotions she'd never before experienced?

His hand grew still. Distractedly, she realized hers had, too.

Grady offered her a cat. "This is Smokey's sister, Sandy."

She gratefully took the cat, glad of something to divert her foolish thoughts. "Sandy? But she's gray."

"She likes to dig in the dirt. Billy said we couldn't call her Dirt so we decided on Sandy."

"I see." She glanced at Seth, saw a reflection of shared humor. As her heart clattered against her ribs, she ducked her head. Something about his strong hands softly cradling a half-grown cat threatened the barriers in her heart.

Grady patted the cat in Seth's arms. "Her name is Mouse."

"Mouse?" Jayne laughed. "Odd name for a cat, don't you think?"

Seth chuckled. "I expect they had a good reason for their choice."

"When she gets a mouse she won't let anyone near her," Grady said.

Billy came toward them. "You coming to play, Grady?"

Grady called a hasty "Goodbye" and ran to join his friend.

As Jayne and Seth studied each other her heart ticked an uncertain beat. He had strong hands. A gentle heart. He was a man worthy of trust.

He lowered the cat to the ground and slowly brought his gaze to her. But after a second it shifted past her. He scrubbed at the back of his neck, tilting his hat so it concealed his eyes.

Had he done it on purpose? Had the moment burgeoned with possibility for him as well as her? What was she thinking? There was no place for possibilities between them. She clung to the cat in her arms. Thankfully, it didn't appear to mind her tight grasp.

"Are you ready for another lesson?" he asked.

It took two seconds to realize he meant shooting lessons. If she needed anything to pull her back to rational thinking, this was it. His only interest in her was teaching her to shoot correctly so he could leave. After all, he had a father that needed and deserved his attention.

"I need to get my gun."

"I'll go with you." Side by side they climbed the hill.

She purposely slowed her steps so he didn't have to hurry on his crutch. Back at the house, she rushed to her room and got the bag containing her gun and joined him outdoors. They returned to the clearing where they'd been the day before.

"I think you need to practice shooting without bullets until you can keep your eyes open." He sat on a nearby log as she assumed her stance. "Walk me through each step so I know you remember."

She did. He obviously didn't plan to steady her arm or offer any assistance today. Fine. She needed to do this on her own.

"Now aim and fire."

She did, determined to keep her eyes open. It shouldn't be difficult. After all, there was no bullet in the gun.

She squeezed the trigger. It clicked into place.

And even though there was no explosion, she blinked.

He sighed. "You need to keep your eyes open."

"I know." And not just to shoot a gun. She needed to keep them open to the dangers of a man like Seth. A strong, protective man who tempted her to abandon her quest for independence. A gentle man who made her long for the kind of protection he would provide.

Yes, she had to keep her eyes wide open in that regard. She did not want or need protection. Besides, he had no intention of staying around to provide it.

Determination firmly in place, she lifted the gun and repeated the procedure.

She would keep her eyes open.

Widening her eyes in preparation, she pulled the trigger. *Click.* "Did I do it?"

He sighed. "Almost."

Chapter Eight

Jayne glanced at the position of the sun. It was growing late and they'd need to return to the ranch.

She'd practiced shooting a number of times but failed to keep her eyes open a single time. Oh, she'd tried. She'd widened her eyes until they felt like they might pop from her head. When that didn't work, she'd narrowed them to slits. She'd even tried closing one and then the other.

"I give up." Jayne let out a long sigh, letting her arm fall to her side, the gun still clamped in her hand.

"Really?" Did he have to sound so relieved? Though it surely wasn't his intention, his tone merely served to renew her resolve.

"No. I won't give up."

"Kind of figured that." His resignation scratched along her nerves.

"You don't have to feel obligated to teach me." No doubt, he was getting annoyed at her failure.

"I never accept defeat."

She snorted. "I guess there is always a first time." She stowed her gun away. "It's dinnertime. We should get back to the house."

He picked up his crutch and stood. But he didn't move.

She grew aware of his waiting and glanced in his direction.

He smiled. The lift of the corners of his mouth had the power to lift her heart. "Jayne, you can do it. I believe it's important for you to do this. So I will continue to help you until we're both satisfied."

She lowered her gaze in order to keep her thoughts clear. "Why does it matter to you, anyway?" Against her will, she stole a look at him to see his reaction.

He shrugged. "Maybe because I don't like to see people fail."

No longer concerned about her silly reaction, she wondered at the meaning behind his words and looked straight into his face. She studied him a full thirty seconds. Watched a chain of emotions flash through his eyes. Determination, kindness, concern and something so deep and heart-filled it made her lose her breath.

He brushed his knuckles across her jaw. "This is a wild, untamed land. You should know how to defend yourself should the occasion arise." Then, as if realizing what he'd done, he shifted away and started toward the ranch.

His touch had sucked the air from her lungs. Left her struggling to think straight.

She realized he'd moved on and hurried to catch up. As they returned to the ranch, Jayne had little to say.

She said little all throughout the meal, as well, content to listen to the others. Her thoughts went round and round. She had only one thing in mind in her dealings with Seth—learn to use a gun. And yet...

And yet. Those two words encapsulated her problem. Despite her resolve, despite understanding Seth only cared because of his sense of responsibility, despite everything, there was something about him that left her confused and dizzy.

She joined the others in cleaning the kitchen after the meal. Whatever she said to add to the flow of conversation must have made sense because no one commented.

"I'll show you how to do that pattern," Sybil said to Linette when the dishes were done. She was showing Linette how to knit a sweater for the expected baby.

"What can Mercy and I do to help?" Jayne needed something to keep her hands and her mind busy.

"Yes, what can we do?" Mercy gave her a look ripe with curiosity.

It wasn't like they didn't help out around the place. But Mercy must have wondered at Jayne's haste to get a job.

Linette suggested they could wash the windows and Jayne hastened to start the task, though there wasn't any need for her sense of urgency.

Not until Seth hobbled down the hall and out the front door did her actions slow to normal. Hopefully he would find Eddie or Roper or one of the other cowboys and amuse himself the rest of the afternoon. Jayne did not want another shooting lesson today.

As soon as the last window was done and the rags they'd used were hung to dry, Jayne grabbed Mercy's arm and hustled her out the door.

"Where are we going?" Mercy asked.

"Walking. Exploring." She didn't care where they went or what they did so long as it wasn't with Seth. All morning she had struggled to remember she didn't need or want anyone to take care of her.

"Okay." Mercy trotted along at her side. "Any place in particular?"

"Just out." She tucked her arm through Mercy's. "What have you been doing with yourself?"

"Would you believe Cookie has been teaching me how to make cinnamon rolls?"

"Really? Maybe I should come along and learn, too. Are they difficult?"

"Not with Cookie supervising. But aren't you pretty busy with Seth?"

"He'll be on his way soon." The reminder brought her thoughts back to their proper place. They both had plans and goals that did not include each other.

He'd leave to take care of his pa and she'd be in a position to take care of herself. Shouldn't the idea make her feel better?

"How are your shooting lessons coming?" Mercy asked as they walked.

Jayne admitted she struggled to keep her eyes open and Mercy laughed.

The two of them spent a pleasant two hours wandering along the road that led to Edendale then returned in time to help Linette with the evening meal.

And Jayne succeeded in paying no more attention to Seth than she would to any visiting cowboy.

The next day was Sunday. Sybil came to Jayne's room as she prepared for church, and sat down on the edge of the bed.

Sybil had already put on her golden dress and brushed her hair into a tidy roll about her head.

Jayne eyed her up and down. "You look ready to walk into the finest church in London."

"I'm ready to go to church here." Without hesitation she added, "You're spending a lot of time with Seth, aren't you?"

"He thinks he needs to teach me to shoot properly so I don't hurt another unsuspecting cowboy."

"It's more than that, I think." Sybil took the hairbrush from Jayne and indicated she should sit on the stool.

Sybil began to brush Jayne's hair.

"That feels good." Jayne welcomed a chance to change the direction of conversation Sybil had started.

"We did this for each other every day on the boat trip. I miss it."

Jayne closed her eyes and let the brushing soothe her. "I miss it, too."

"I don't want to see you hurt."

"Is it that badly tangled?" She knew that wasn't what Sybil meant. Had she seen how Jayne reacted to Seth even when she vowed she wouldn't notice his presence? But Sybil didn't need to worry. Jayne understood the boundaries of her time with Seth. He would teach her to shoot then move on. And she would stand tall, strong and confident in her ability to take care of herself.

Why just this morning at breakfast, hadn't she sat at his side, cool and detached, her determination to remember that Seth was only a temporary visitor firmly in place? But when their arms brushed as they reached for something, she had almost jumped off her chair.

Maybe the church service would arm her with strength.

Sybil stopped brushing and scooted around to look straight into Jayne's eyes. "He's just a cowboy. He isn't the sort of man you need." She pressed her palms to Jayne's shoulders to stop her protest. "He won't give you what you want."

"How do you know what I want?"

"You're a city girl. You couldn't fit into a cowboy's

way of life." Sybil resumed brushing Jayne's hair as if the matter was settled.

Sybil was right. She'd never be the strong adventurous type who welcomed the challenge of ranch life. Or whatever a cowboy like Seth did. The connection she imagined between them was simply that—imagination. And, she realized with blinding clarity, the hungry cry of a needy heart. She would not be needy any longer. Strength and resolve returned. Jayne Gardiner meant to be independent, self-sufficient, armed and ready to face any and every challenge life tossed in her path.

Seth had done his best to stay as far away from Jayne as possible yesterday. He'd sat and watched her struggle to handle the gun when every instinct told him to give her a hand.

But he'd found giving her a hand brought out a whole bunch of feelings he wasn't prepared to deal with. Besides, she didn't need or want his protection.

He must remember that in a few more days he would be on his way to his pa. Jayne would then be on her own—exactly what she wanted. Surely he would be able to avoid her easily enough today, it being Sunday.

Eddie had informed him they held church services in the cookhouse and invited him to attend. It would be rude to refuse. Not that he didn't want to go. But he suspected it would be hard to ignore Jayne for the entire service.

Seth waited until the others left to descend the stairs and follow. Unfortunately it gave him plenty of opportunity to study those ahead of him.

Linette clung to Eddie's arm as Grady raced ahead. Jayne, Mercy and Sybil walked arm in arm. The trio was such good friends.

Mercy's hair had been tamed to a coil at the back of her neck and further subdued by her bonnet. She wore a muted green dress. Sybil, her hair tidy, wore a gray bonnet. She was like a flash of evening sun in her dark gold dress. They walked on either side of Jayne.

Jayne. He could no longer keep his gaze off her.

Like the others, she'd pulled her hair into a demure coil at the back of her head and wore a navy bonnet. A faint rustling sound reached him as her navy skirt swung with every step. A blue-striped shirtwaist completed her outfit.

Her full-throated laugh rang out as Mercy said something.

He slowed his steps and leaned heavily on his crutch. He'd considered not using it anymore but Linette had checked his wound and suggested one more day. Just to be on the safe side.

The others reached the cookhouse and stepped inside except for Jayne. She dropped her friends' arms and waited for Seth.

So much for keeping his distance from her but he couldn't find a hint of disappointment in his thoughts.

"You'll want to meet the others," she said as he reached her side.

He told himself that was a good enough reason to accompany her despite his decision to confine their time together to the shooting lessons. They stepped in.

The benches had been arranged to face the table. Cookie sat behind it with a smaller man at her side. "Come in, come in," she called.

Seth and Jayne moved toward Cookie.

"Seth, this is Bertie, Cookie's husband."

Bertie held out a hand and they shook. Seth liked the friendly welcome in the man's face.

Jayne led him toward a young couple. "This is Ward and Grace Walker and little Belle." The woman had flaming-red hair. The little girl bounced on the bench with what he could only interpret as a zest for life. Ward beamed as if so proud of his wife and child he could hardly restrain himself from pointing out their virtues.

He must love them a lot.

Seth envied the man, though he didn't want the responsibility of love for himself.

Next he met Cassie and Roper and the other children. Then three cowboys. Eddie had said there were a dozen cowboys about but most of them were with the cattle. He met Cal, who kept glancing at Mercy, and Slim, a tall, quiet man. He'd already met Buster.

Introductions over, Jayne and Seth sat down side by side, in the only available place. Their elbows brushed, flooding his brain with sweetness. He told himself he had enough responsibilities and didn't want any more. Even if he somehow convinced himself he'd like to add Jayne to that list, could he even succeed? Or would he fail to protect her? He couldn't live with failure of that magnitude.

Thankfully, Cookie stood before his thoughts rambled further astray. She led them in singing three hymns. It was a rowdy choir but full of enthusiasm. Beside him, Jayne's voice was clear and sweet. He mumbled the words of the song in a sort of daze as the spot where her arm touched his grew warmer.

Then Bertie stood up to speak. "I want to warn the ladies from England that I ain't a preacher. No siree. But I know my God. I've known Him for more years than I care to tell. And there's one thing I'm certain of. He is as good as His word and you couldn't ask for more. He says in Matthew six, verse twenty six, that

He watches the fowls of the air and not one of them falls to the ground without His notice. Imagine, He watches the little sparrows. I guess one of us is worth a whole lot more than a sparrow. Why they ain't even good for a pie."

Everyone chuckled.

"But His eye is on the sparrow so I know it's on me for my good. It's on every one of you, too, for your good."

When the short service ended, Seth didn't immediately move. Bertie's words filled his heart. God watched over sparrows? So why did some fall to the ground and die? He couldn't believe as simply as Bertie did.

People shifted about and Cookie served tea, coffee and cinnamon rolls. And the whole crew sat around and visited.

Cal edged closer to Seth. "Heard you got shot." His gaze slid toward Jayne and he grinned.

Seth kept his expression bland but bristled inside. "It was an accident." His soft words gave away nothing. The man would never know that Seth resented the way the cowboy wanted to make an issue of it.

"Sure glad I wasn't in the line of fire." Cal laughed.

Beside Seth, Jayne stiffened. Then she relaxed and chuckled. "I'm glad you weren't, too. Wouldn't it be awful if I injured two cowboys? But just think of all the attention you would garner." She grinned at him.

Cal's gaze went to Mercy and lingered. When he looked at them again, he looked thoughtful. "Might be worth it. When are you going shooting again?"

Jayne laughed. "I won't be shooting anyone accidentally again. Seth is making sure that doesn't happen." She turned to him, favoring him with a smile full of gratitude that slipped into his heart like a silent intruder...though not an unwelcome one, he realized. His resolve seemed to have no lasting effect on his thoughts. Or his heart. And at the moment it didn't matter.

He smiled into Jayne's eyes, letting his heart speak for him, telling her he was glad to be able to help her. Glad to spend a few days with her.

Apparently Sundays included going up the hill for Sunday dinner for, at Linette's invitation, Cassie, Roper and their children, Ward, Grace and Belle joined the guests of the house in climbing the hill toward the big house.

Eddie took the men into the front room while the women and children went to the kitchen to prepare the meal.

Seth sat back in one of the easy chairs, content to listen to the conversation among the other men and the laughter and chatting from the kitchen. But it was not to be. The men wanted to know where he'd been, what he'd seen and any news he could pass on.

The hour or two as the women worked in the kitchen passed pleasantly enough as he told about the cattle drive, the number of animals that had successfully arrived at the ranch northwest of the Eden Valley Ranch. He described the owners and every other specific he could recall until Linette announced the meal was ready.

Extra chairs crowded the table that had been extended to its full length. Seth tried to position himself for a place away from Jayne but Linette waved him to her side.

And to be honest, he truly didn't mind. He held bowls and platters for her as she served portions for herself. He snagged a dish of butter for her when she looked about for it. He asked her advice when Linette asked him to choose between raisin or pumpkin pie.

"I recommend the raisin," she said. Her smile was both sweet and teasing, filling him with sweetness.

He chose the raisin and wasn't disappointed.

After the meal ended, men, women and children helped clean up the dishes and put away the extra chairs then they again retired to the front room.

Linette settled in the green armchair before the window. Her gaze went outside and she sighed then faced the others. "Eddie says the lumber for the new church should arrive any day. I can hardly wait, though I will miss the coziness of meeting in the cookhouse."

Seth studied the gathering as the conversation circled about him. Across from him, Jayne held out her arms to little Pansy and lifted her to her lap. The child pressed her head to Jayne's shoulder and closed her eyes.

Jayne's gaze crashed into Seth's and he saw the longing and a hefty dose of hopelessness. No doubt she had dreamed of babies with Oliver. His heart twisted at her pain and loss. If they had been alone, he might have ignored his intention of not getting involved and taken her in his arms and comforted her.

Her look went on and on, delving deep into his soul, seeking something he couldn't offer her. Assurances he couldn't give. Promises he couldn't keep. Not that he wasn't tempted to give it a try.

Pansy shifted and drew Jayne's attention away.

Seth glanced at the other children playing quietly with Grady's toys. His eyes lit on Cassie. Four children was a lot of responsibility. They could get hurt, sick, have an accident, so many things. That had to be a heavy weight for Roper, too.

As if the cowboy read his mind, he took a seat next to Seth and began to talk.

"I could never have guessed how much joy the children would bring to our lives. Bertie's talk about God watching over the sparrows really encouraged me, reminding me, as it did, that these children aren't solely my responsibility. They are, above all, God's children. He saw fit to bring them into my life and Cassie's. Then He saw fit to enable us to keep them. For sure, I can trust God with the rest. Their future, their health, their happiness." The man let out a satisfied sigh.

His words startled Seth. Was it possible to accept responsibilities and expect God to take care of them?

Chapter Nine

The next morning, Jayne and Seth left the house in the direction of the clearing for another lesson. The sun was warm in a cloudless sky. A breeze promised modest relief from the heat that would build throughout the day.

Seth walked without a crutch, limping slightly.

"How is your leg?" she asked.

"It's okay. No lasting damage."

"I'm relieved to know it." She watched him from the corner of her eye. Yesterday he had seemed a little distant, as if he regretted his offer to stay long enough to teach her to shoot well. If that was the case, she needed to make sure the lessons were satisfactorily concluded as soon as possible.

"I am determined to keep my eyes open today."

He chuckled. "Weren't you determined the other days?"

"Yes, but this time I am really determined." They reached the clearing and she took out her pistol, got into position and spoke his instructions aloud so he would know she remembered and followed them. She set her sights on the target, gritted her teeth—*eyes open, eyes open*—and squeezed the trigger. *Click.* The gun wasn't loaded so there was no explosion to startle her.

She stared at the target. She'd seen it the whole time.

Lowering the gun, she turned to Seth. "I did it. I did it." She jumped up and down and ran to his side to grab his arm and shake it. "I kept my eyes open."

He covered her hand with his, anchoring her to the spot. What was there about him that reached out to her, making her want to stay connected to him?

She withdrew her hand and backed away. "Isn't it time for a real bullet?"

"I don't think you should rush. Let's see if you can keep your eyes open more than once."

She tipped her head and studied him. "I thought you would be anxious to be on your way now that your leg is ready."

His gaze watchful, guarded even, his mouth flat, he revealed nothing. He nodded. "Not so anxious to leave before you can shoot a gun with reasonable accuracy and with your eyes open." His eyes narrowed. "I do not want to live wondering if I'm in any way responsible for someone being injured or dead."

She hurried back to the place where she must stand. So it was for his conscience. For unknown people. Didn't he care at all to stay for her sake, because he was concerned about her, or even because he might be enjoying her company a tiny bit?

She jerked the gun into position, and eyed the sights. She gripped it tight and focused and then—

Something brushed her skirts. Her heart crashed against her ribs and she screamed and bolted to the side.

"Smokey." The cat plopped down where Jayne had been standing and started to groom herself.

Seth scooped the cat into his arms. "What are you doing here?"

Jayne pressed a hand to her chest and willed her heartbeat back to a normal pace. "She about scared me to death."

Seth chuckled. "You did jump rather high."

Her breath whooshed out. "Good thing I didn't have the gun loaded or I might have shot her." Seeing the shock on Seth's face, she hurriedly added, "Not on purpose."

"How many accidents are you planning?" The way he cocked his head and studied her without revealing his thoughts left her floundering, especially as he petted the cat and received grateful purrs.

"I hardly think you plan accidents." Her fright continued to make her edgy.

He looked out into the distance as if considering her words. "A lot of accidents could be avoided if people planned not to have them."

The sorrow in his words made her think he wasn't talking about her. "You're referring to the death of your friends." He'd said so little about something that had such an obvious impact on him. She wanted to learn more. "Were they shot?" She shuddered.

"No." His answer was abrupt.

She waited, giving him plenty of opportunity to say more. When he didn't, she pretended she wasn't disappointed and returned to her place before the target.

One by one, deliberate enough to satisfy the most critical teacher, she went through the steps and—*click*—kept her eyes open.

But when she turned for his approval he still stared into the distance, his hand mindlessly stroking the cat.

Smokey was satisfied with his distracted attention.

Jayne wasn't. Yet she couldn't demand more. She didn't have the right. But her heart went out to him. He looked lost.

Smokey jumped down, jerking Seth back from wherever he had gone. He sighed and when he turned toward her, he blinked as he saw she was watching him.

Had he forgotten her presence? Was she that unimportant? She squared her shoulders. Perhaps she needed this reminder that she must depend on no one.

"Let's see if you can keep your eyes open again." His smile, likely meant to be encouraging, seemed rather forced.

But she turned and went through the steps again, keeping her eyes open at the click.

"Good."

She told herself she wasn't disappointed at his lack of enthusiasm. Why would she be? But she failed to convince herself. And it made her angry. She was doing this so she could be independent and unafraid. She had no intention of substituting one weakness and dependency for another.

"I'll do it again." And again and again, until she was the best, most confident shot in the whole of western Canada. She lined up the sights and squeezed the trigger. This time she didn't even flinch at the sound.

Without waiting for him to tell her to do it again, she did it over and over, six more times then faced him.

The grin he wore erased all her annoyance. "I think you're ready."

"I'm more than ready." She let him load the shell and as she lifted the gun, she almost did it without giving in to a little quiver of fear.

He stepped close behind her. "This time counts. I'll

make sure the bullet doesn't go astray." He cupped his hand over hers on the gun and steadied it.

Heavens but it was tempting to lean back and feel the strength of his chest, the comfort of his arms.

Instead she stiffened and squinted down the sights. *Eyes open. Eyes open.* She widened her eyes and squeezed.

Crack!

She shuddered at the sound but she kept her eyes open.

He patted her shoulder. "You did it."

Her hands shook clear to her shoulders. Her breath came in sharp gasps. "I need to sit down."

He'd left Smokey sunning by a log and she collapsed near the cat and stroked it, finding comfort in the motion and in the gentle rumble in the cat's chest. "I hate guns," she muttered.

"Is it really necessary to learn to shoot?"

"We've had this discussion already and yes, it is. My fear will not control me. I don't know if I'll ever hear a gunshot up close and not have my mind fill with pictures of Oliver's death." She shuddered again. "Death is not pretty."

"No, it's not."

She realized she clung to his hand or did he cling to hers? It didn't matter who had reached first. Nor did it matter that she meant to be strong. At the moment she was a quivering mass of nerves.

"Jayne." His voice was soft. "You might learn to shoot just fine but that doesn't mean you'd ever be able to use the gun against a living soul."

Misery wrapped about her like a wet blanket. "I know it won't be easy." She sat up straight and gave him a look full of despair and determination. "But I will if I have to. It's got to be easier than standing idly by while someone you care about is gunned down."

Her misery was reflected in his eyes. "I hope you never have to face such a situation."

"Me, too." She thought about the sermon Bertie had given. "The Bible says God watches the sparrows. If God watches us for our good why do bad things happen? I don't understand."

"What's to understand? It isn't like God said he prevents the sparrow from falling. Only that He takes note."

"That makes it sound like God stands back and observes without any concern for what happens. I can't believe that."

"Why not? Like you said, bad things happen."

"But—" She struggled to think of an argument. "He has promised to never leave us or forsake us. I don't think I could survive without the sure knowledge that God will help me."

He studied her. "You have firsthand experience with this aspect of God?"

"After I watched Oliver die I thought I didn't deserve to live. I was nothing but a useless, foolish woman." She raised her eyebrows. "Just as you said."

"I wasn't referring to something like that. I only meant if you were insistent on doing something without being properly prepared you put yourself and others at risk and that would be foolish."

She drew in a deep, sustaining breath and released it slowly, willing tension to leave with it.

He dropped a hand to her shoulder. "Jayne, I think you are very brave to learn to shoot a gun when it brings back such dreadful memories. It doesn't hurt to be prepared."

She nodded, clinging to him with her gaze.

He didn't shift away, didn't blink. He simply met her look for look.

The moments ticked by as she floundered in fear and uncertainty.

He continued to offer silent support and encouragement.

She swam in the depths of his gaze until she found solid ground. Out of sheer gratitude and relief, she touched his cheek. "Thank you." His skin was warm, rough with the day's whiskers.

He smiled beneath her hand. "You're welcome."

She should move away but she liked the feel of his cheek...how it crinkled with his smile.

He reached up and caught her hand, held it to his face for a heartbeat then drew it down and curled his fingers around hers. "Jayne." His voice was a hoarse whisper. "I will never forget you."

She lost herself in his eyes, so full of power and strength and purpose.

Purpose. The word seemed to ground her, to bring her back to reality. Her purpose was to be independent. His was to teach her to shoot and then move on.

She touched his injured leg. "I expect you'll remember me every time you look at the scar your leg will have."

He blinked. His eyes went from forest green to hazel, all full of golden flecks, and he burst out laughing. "I'll always have that, won't I?"

They grinned at each other. The tension-filled moment had ended and they had settled back into a relaxed friendliness.

"Do you want to try another bullet today?"

"Not really, but I will."

He again came along to steady her arm. "I don't want to take any chances that you'll close your eyes and have the shot go amiss."

She gave an exaggerated shudder. "Nor do I." Nor could she object to his steadying arm about her.

Because it was only temporary and she could allow herself a few hours, or even days, of something that would soon be gone.

Seth had been up and down a wide range of emotions. Her question about how Frank and Sarah died punched him in the middle of his chest with the force of a hammer blow. He never talked about them. His folks had never talked about them. No friends had ever asked about them. Yet he felt he could tell Jayne and she would understand the pain, the shock, the helplessness, the anger and finally the determination to make sure something like that never happened again. She'd been through a similar experience. He almost opened the door to his memories and told her how they had died.

But once open, would he ever be able to close the doors again? And if he couldn't, would the memories and regrets and pain consume him?

It wasn't worth the risk.

Then she'd wondered if God cared about sparrows. What she really asked was did God care about people even when bad things happen? It wasn't a question he could answer.

He had reluctantly released her to shoot again at the target when he would have preferred to hold her close and tell her to forget about the gun. Guns were dangerous.

She fired one more shot. She kept her eyes open but the bullet splintered a stump to the right. Her shoulders sank. "That's enough for today. Who knew learning to shoot could be so exhausting."

Likely it was the memories and emotions that the sound of a gunshot brought to mind that left her shaking.

He took the gun from her hand and wiped it clean then dropped it into her bag. He draped an arm about her shoulders, felt her quivering and pulled her close. For a heartbeat, he considered pulling her into his arms and crushing her to his heart. He'd hold her fears at bay. But she didn't want that. She wanted to prove she didn't need anyone.

And he had other plans, as well. A pa to take care of. A heart to guard against risk.

They returned to the house and joined the others for dinner.

As they ate, Linette announced, "There are peas ready to pick."

"I'll help," Jayne said. Mercy and Sybil echoed her offer.

"Thank you. I warn you, it will take all afternoon."

"That's fine." The three girls nodded. "We don't mind."

No one suggested Seth should help. He got the feeling the garden was the women's domain so he didn't offer. Which left him the entire afternoon to amuse himself. He would check on his horse. Maybe exercise him.

As the meal ended and people dispersed, he headed down the hill to the barn. His saddle was in the tack room and he went to inspect it. Buster had done a good job of cleaning it.

A bunch of leather hung on the wall ready to be used to repair harnesses and saddles. Pa had been a leather worker, a tanner, saddle maker and repairer so Seth examined the leather with a knowledgeable eye. And he had an idea. If Eddie approved, he would make Buster a real belt.

As he selected the leather he would choose for the project, the voices of children reached him.

"Billy, that knife is sharp. Put it down."

Seth guessed Billy's older brother, Neil, was the speaker.

"I'm just looking."

"You're also touching and that's not safe."

"Aww, I won't hurt myself."

"Billy, put it back." Neil's voice was firm.

"I'm being careful."

Seth's scalp prickled. Seems Billy was set on getting into trouble. Trouble with a sharp knife could be disastrous. Seth headed for the tack room door, ready to intervene and prevent an accident.

"No, Billy. You could get hurt. Put it back."

Seth heard something thunk and he paused before he reentered the barn, out of sight.

Neil spoke again. "That's better."

"Why's it matter to you, anyways?" Billy groused.

"Because you're my brother. Remember how our mama made us promise to be responsible for each other?"

"Before she died?" The resentment level in Billy's voice lowered.

"Yes."

"That was when we come looking for Pa, right?"

"That's right."

"He was already dead, too, huh?" Billy sounded confused about the events.

"'Fraid so. Good thing our new pa found us."

"Neil, what does 'sponsible mean?"

The boys scuffed along the barn floor as they moved about.

"It means we watch out for each other. I make sure you're safe. You watch out for me and make sure I'm safe. We do the same for Pansy and Daisy."

"'Specially Pansy 'cause she's still little."

"That's right. Now let's take water to the chickens like Ma said."

They trotted from the barn. Buckets banged the side of the water trough and water sloshed. Then their voices faded into the distance.

Seth stepped into the barn and picked up the knife Billy had wanted to examine. He stuck it in the slot of wood where it belonged and where it would be safe from little fingers.

He and Frank had watched out for each other. Many a time, Frank had pulled him back from falling through the hole in the loft of the barn, or helped him get down from a tree that he'd climbed too high. And although younger, he'd helped Frank, too. One time he'd helped him hold a colt Frank had roped and found too much to hold. Then there was the time Frank got into a fist fight with several town boys. He was outnumbered but when Seth stepped in, they'd been able to defend themselves and chase away the tormentors. He could think of many other times he and Frank had helped each other.

But you couldn't take care of someone set on doing something foolhardy.

He walked the length of the barn, glanced out the back door then wheeled around and returned to the front. He stared at the busy ranch scene. A cowboy he didn't recognize rode past the far pens. Women's voices reached him from the garden.

He had to find something to do or he would drown in memories.

Eddie stepped into view toward Roper's house and Seth trotted in that direction.

"I find myself at loose ends this afternoon and idleness bores me. Could you give me a job?"

Eddie stopped and rubbed his chin. "You good with hammer and nails?"

"Good enough, I think."

"Fine. A bull damaged the wall of the oat bin." He indicated a building near the barn. "You'll find supplies in the barn if you care to fix it."

"I sure would." He trotted back to the barn, limping on his sore leg. He fetched hammer and nails then went to the bin. Someone had placed new pieces of wood nearby so he was set.

Pounding nails to fix the damaged wall did little to make him forget how foolhardy Frank had been. Reckless. Irresponsible. *Bang, bang, bang.* Every hammer blow echoed in his head.

He fixed one side and moved around the corner. His position gave him a view of the garden and the women bent over plucking peas from the vines. The sun shone hot and furious, something he hadn't noticed until he saw Jayne and her friends out in the open with nothing but broad-brimmed hats for protection. The blue sky held only one frothy cloud in the distance. A reluctant breeze barely stirred the grass. They must be sweltering in the sun.

Shouldn't he warn them not to get overheated?

Jayne's laughter drifted to him. Seems she wasn't bothered by the heat. Or did she think she was impervious? Perhaps she gave no thought to consequences.

Was she foolhardy? Or strong and brave? Could she be both?

He grabbed a nail and drove it in with one vicious blow.

It didn't matter who or what Jayne was, only that he did what he could to prevent any more accidents. Then he would be on his way.

Chapter Ten

❦

"Are you ready for another shooting lesson?" Seth asked Jayne the next morning.

She resisted an urge to rub the pain in her neck and swallowed back a moan. Who knew picking peas was backbreaking work? Or that the sun could be so demanding? "Linette needs help shelling peas. We're all going down to the cookhouse to help."

"Well, have fun."

Did he sound disappointed? Because she would be busy all morning or because it delayed him leaving? "I might be free later." She had no idea how long the job would take.

"I'll maybe see you then." With a touch to the brim of his hat, he left the house and went down the hill. What did he plan to do for the day?

"Are you ready?" Linette asked her, laden with several large bowls.

Jayne, along with Mercy and Sybil, joined her in the trek down the hill. They gathered in the shade of the cookhouse where Cassie already awaited, along with Grace, who had come to the ranch with Ward and their daughter. As they approached, Cookie came outside, bringing with her the scent of cinnamon and yeast.

They set out blankets, but since Cookie claimed she'd never get up if she sat on the ground, Cassie brought out a chair.

Daisy supervised the children playing. Their laughter filled the air like music.

Linette showed the English girls how to snap the pea pod open, scrape the tender green peas into a bowl then toss the pod into a bucket. Jayne settled into a routine at the mindless task and listened as Cassie asked Grace how she liked living in the west. It was pleasant to sit here and forget everything. Except one thought intruded. What lay ahead for her?

She didn't know but wasn't about to let the thought mar a perfect morning.

"Will your cowboy be leaving soon?" Cookie asked Jayne.

Jayne pretended she had to think who Cookie meant. "Seth? I expect so."

Mercy snorted. "Could have fooled me." She batted her eyes and tipped her head, doing her best to look coy.

Jayne waved a hand in a way she hoped said Mercy's opinion was of no matter. "Don't pay attention to her. She's prone to be dramatic." She'd never let any of them know there was something about Seth that tugged at her heart and occupied her thoughts in a way that confused her.

Mercy grinned. "I'm not making it up."

"Leave her be," Sybil said gently. "She only wants to learn to shoot a gun." She shivered. "Though I still think it's a bad idea."

Grace studied her fingers curled in her lap. "There

was a time I wished I had a gun. A big gun. And had the nerve to use it."

Jayne had heard how Ward had rescued Grace from a man who made her dance in a saloon by holding little Belle captive.

Cassie squeezed Grace's hands. "Thankfully, God sent Ward along to help you."

"If God watches us for our good why do bad things happen?" The words came from Jayne's mouth before she could think to stop them. At the way each of the other women grew serious, Jayne almost wished she hadn't asked the question but she ached to know, to understand.

Cookie planted her feet more firmly on the ground and shifted so she faced Jayne. "Maybe we only see the dark side. The pain, the sorrow, the loss. But we would never see a rainbow without the rain."

Sybil's hands twisted into a knot as she considered Cookie's words. "Is the rainbow worth it?"

"I would go through what I did again if it was what brought me and Ward together." Grace's face flooded with joy and serenity.

Jayne stared at her. Would she ever look back at what happened to Oliver and say something so wonderful had happened because of it that she thought it was worthwhile?

Grace spoke again. "But I would avoid it altogether if I could and still meet Ward."

The women murmured agreement. All of them had endured their share of loss and pain except perhaps Mercy. She never confessed to anything but joy and excitement.

"Maybe," Mercy said, "it takes something tragic to

push some people off their comfortable log into the adventure that lies ahead of them."

Sybil chuckled. "Like Jayne learning to shoot. What an adventure she started. Poor Seth, though. He didn't ask to be part of your adventure."

The others laughed. Several of them commented that the challenges of their lives had indeed led them to go places, or to try things they wouldn't have without the impetus.

"Look at you," Mercy said to Jayne. "Not only are you learning to shoot a gun but you would have never left cozy old England if you'd married Oliver." She squeezed both Jayne's and Sybil's hands. "And we all get to share your adventure. I, for one, am grateful for the opportunity."

Jayne couldn't argue with Mercy's rationale. Oliver's death had pushed her to explore new horizons. She'd never be grateful for it but she had to move forward and this was a good place to do it. She looked about the ranch but didn't see Seth. She would forever be thankful that he played a part in helping her achieve her goals.

She meant the thought to be reassuring. It wasn't. Instead, it quivered restlessly in the pit of her stomach. She popped some fresh green peas into her mouth to still the sensation. "Mmm, good."

The others also ate a few and nodded agreement.

The conversation shifted to other things until Cookie lumbered to her feet. "Time to cook up some grub for hungry cowboys."

"You'll eat with us," Cassie said to Grace and they scrambled up to prepare food for their hungry men and children.

Linette checked around the circle. "The peas are done. Thank you all. Many hands make light work."

Jayne and her friends climbed the hill with Linette and helped her prepare a quick dinner for everyone who ate at the house.

When it was time to eat, Grady entered at Eddie's side.

But where was Seth?

She caught her breath and waited.

He entered the back door and her breath eased out. She couldn't take her eyes from him.

He'd rolled his sleeves up to his elbows, exposing strong forearms. He took his hat off and hung it on one of the many hooks.

He turned, and their eyes met. She felt a strange tightening in her throat as he smiled.

Slowly, his gaze lingering, he shifted, and turned to wash.

She jerked back to helping Linette.

Mercy nudged her. "I see you don't even have to bat your eyes."

Jayne made a protesting sound and took the bowl of fresh peas to the table.

Throughout the meal, she forced herself to think about the food. The peas and potatoes tasted better than anything she'd ever had before.

But all the while, her nerves vibrated at Seth's nearness and the hope of him asking her to go to the clearing.

"Are you helping Linette this afternoon?" he asked, sending a frisson of excitement through her.

"I don't need everyone," Linette said. "Sybil wants to help me. That's all I need."

"Then I guess I'm free for more shooting lessons." Jayne emphasized *shooting* just enough to inform

Mercy it was the reason for the two of them spending the afternoon together.

A little later, Seth and Jayne returned to the clearing.

She prepared her gun. "I believe I'm ready for real ammunition today."

"Try it once without and convince me you haven't forgotten anything." He grinned, teasing lights flashing from his eyes. "Like keeping your eyes open."

She wrinkled her nose at him.

He stood with his hands on his hips and his legs wide as if preparing for a long afternoon of fun.

Her cheeks grew warm. He only wanted to see her succeed in this so he could leave, she reminded herself. She had pinned her own silly desires on the poor unsuspecting man. She jerked her attention back to the reason for being there, lined up the target through her sights and squeezed the trigger. *Click.* Her eyes had remained open. She turned and curled her fingers to indicate he should give her a bullet.

He handed her one, supervised as she slipped it into the chamber then stood very close as she took the stance he'd taught her. He steadied her hand then eased back.

She swallowed hard. She was on her own. She squeezed the trigger, squinting to keep from closing her eyes at the explosion.

She lowered the gun and studied the target. "Did I hit it?"

"Almost. You have to keep your hand steady all the while you squeeze the trigger. Grip the gun so your fingers can't move."

He dug another bullet out of his pocket but before he could hand it to her, Smokey appeared and meowed around his feet. "Go away, cat. It's not safe for you to be here."

Smokey took a step away then stopped and meowed over her shoulder.

"Go home, silly cat."

Smokey meowed louder. She returned to Seth and meowed up at him then took two steps. Again she meowed.

Jayne stared at the cat. "Is she trying to get you to follow her?"

"Nah. She's just a cat."

But Smokey continued to call at them.

"Maybe we should see what she wants." Jayne put the gun on the log and stepped toward the cat. "Where do you want us to go?"

Seth scooped up her gun, tucked it into his belt and followed them.

Smokey headed for the trees to the right, turning often to make sure they followed.

Then Jayne saw what the cat wanted and drew to a halt. She pressed her hand to her throat. "Seth," she whispered. "Look."

He was at her side. "I see it."

Under the trees lay a fawn, curled up, its wide eyes watching them.

Smokey licked the animal's face.

"Seems Smokey has made a friend."

Jayne tiptoed closer.

The fawn bleated and tried to get to its feet.

Seth grabbed her arm to stop her. "Stay back. It's frightened."

Jayne saw blood on its back leg. "It's hurt." A dreadful thought grabbed her throat. "Did I shoot it?" Her legs buckled and she would have folded to the ground except Seth held her up.

"I don't think it's a gunshot wound."

Her legs got their strength back and she straightened. "Are you sure? How can you tell?"

"It looks more like a tear." He pulled them back to let the frightened animal relax. Smokey rubbed against the fawn and purred loudly.

Seth eyed the trees around them. "I wonder where the doe is. Let's have a look." He took her by the hand and led her into the trees. They moved as quietly as possible.

They passed through into the open. It was the same place she'd found evidence of Seth's blood and she groaned.

"There." He pointed into the shadows.

All she saw was a brown rock. Then it moved. "That's the mother deer?"

"Looks like it's injured. Wait here while I see."

But she grabbed his hand and followed. They crossed the grassy clearing. The doe didn't lift its head but its sides heaved with frightened breaths.

Bright red blood covered the animal's front quarters. More oozed from a hole high in the chest.

Horror as dark as the blackest pit choked Jayne. How could she think she could shoot a gun and not hurt someone? "Is it a gunshot wound?"

He knelt over the animal. "No. This is the work of a wolf or maybe a mountain lion." He straightened, his expression hard. "Go back to the clearing where your stuff is."

"Aren't you coming?"

"I'll be along straightaway."

She rocked her head back and forth. Why would he order her to leave? "I'll wait for you. I don't fancy meeting a wild animal that will claw me to bits."

"I'm sure the gunshots you fired will have scared them away. Now go. I'll be right behind you."

She stared at him, wanting to argue but something in his eyes, the brittleness of them, the darkness behind them made her obey. She lifted her skirt and headed back. She'd barely entered the trees that circled the practice area when a bang came from where she'd left Seth.

She could think of only one reason for him to shoot. The doe. He'd killed her.

Her heart pounding, she raced to the log that served as a seat and sank down. She pressed her elbows to her stomach and her chin to her fists. Puffs of air raced in and out of her lungs without providing any relief. Her head grew dizzy.

Seth stepped into the clearing and crossed to her side. He sat close and rubbed her back.

"I had to do it. She was suffering."

"You shot her."

"I'm sorry."

The pressure of his hand on her back, the little circles that he made, eased her lungs. She sucked in air.

"Was there—" She swallowed hard. "Was there a lot of blood?"

He didn't answer.

She didn't want him to. She wished she could erase all memory of blood from her mind but the pictures were as vivid as the day they came. A sob threatened to strangle her.

Seth pulled her into his arms. She grabbed his shirt-front and buried her face against his shoulder. Only one sob escaped. When his arms tightened about her, the horror faded and she felt safe.

She stayed there until her heartbeat calmed.

"The fawn!" She sat up. "We have to help it." She jumped up and raced toward where they'd left the little animal.

Seth caught up to her and grabbed her hand. "It's wild and afraid."

She pulled away. "Nevertheless, it needs help." She continued onward, tiptoeing now so as to not frighten the fawn.

Seth followed though his expression informed her he did so reluctantly.

She paused before the fawn, far enough away so it didn't lurch to its feet. "I mean you no harm. I just want to help you." She slowly narrowed the distance and squatted down.

The fawn's eyes widened and it tried to escape.

Smokey meowed a protest and rubbed against the fawn's legs.

Jayne pressed her hand to the wild animal's shoulder and held it down. "You need someone to take care of you." She needed help and sent Seth a pleading look.

"Jayne, what do you think you can do?"

"It seems pretty obvious. We'll take it back to the farm. Fix the wound and feed it."

"We? I haven't agreed." He scrubbed at the back of his neck, tipping his hat forward over his eyes.

"Why ever not? I don't understand. I thought you'd feel a responsibility to take care of this helpless little thing."

He squatted beside her. "You take on a job like this, you better think about the consequences."

"Like what?"

"He'll be frightened of the horses, the cows and the curious children. Chances are the poor thing will pine for its freedom, refuse to eat and die before your eyes."

"Nice picture you've drawn but we have to at least try."

His expression remained stubborn.

Anger exploded in her, boiling over into her words. "You're afraid of risks. Afraid you might fail. Well, I would sooner fail trying than fail to try."

"What are you going to feed it? How are you going to keep it safe from predators? You'll end up regretting this when you have to watch him die."

She gave him a look that ought to make his insides burn with shame. "I am not so foolish as to think I can guarantee he'll live but I intend to give him a chance. Are you going to help me or not?"

He studied her then sighed. His expression full of regret, he wrapped his arms under the fawn and lifted it to his chest, murmuring calming sounds when the creature struggled.

She didn't care if he helped willingly or not. She meant to help the little creature.

Smokey trotted at their heels as they retraced their steps. Jayne scooped up her bag as they passed through the clearing and walked at Seth's side.

Seth held the fawn's legs so it couldn't kick. They rushed past the house and down the hill to the barn.

"Whatcha' got?" Billy called as he saw them.

At the sound of a voice, the fawn struggled.

"I told ya," Seth mumbled to her. "Curious children."

Jayne turned aside and went to Billy. "We have an injured fawn that is very frightened. Would you make sure none of the children come to the barn until we have it settled down?"

The boy's chest expanded. "I sure can." Then he grew curious again. "Then we can see him?"

"If the fawn is feeling well enough," she replied. Seth went into the barn and she hurried after him.

He was in the far pen. He'd put the fawn in a bed of sweet hay. Smokey curled up beside the animal.

Seth knelt at the fawn's side. "Eddie has dressings in a box in the tack room. Can you bring it here?"

Tack room? She wasn't sure what he meant but she raced down the alley. A little room held saddles, harnesses and an assortment of horse items. She opened a cupboard on the wall and saw a box of bandages and a tin of something. Likely an ointment Eddie used on his horses. She scooped up the box and raced back to Seth's side.

"Hold his front legs while I look at this cut."

She folded the fawn's leg back as Seth showed her and watched his big hands gently examine the fawn's back leg.

"It doesn't look too bad." He cleaned it, applied smelly ointment from the tin then wrapped a dressing around it.

"Let him go."

She did and the fawn struggled to its feet. It ran into the corner and tried to hide but all it could do was press its nose into the boards.

Smokey followed and purred around the tiny legs. The fawn seemed to forget Seth and Jayne were there and turned its attention to the cat.

Seth leaned close to whisper in Jayne's ear. "Smokey has found a new best friend."

She nodded. Tears were too close to the surface for her to speak. They couldn't save the doe. She understood that. But somehow, being able to help the fawn made her feel as if life sometimes made sense.

"What are you going to feed it?" Seth asked.

She faced him. "Why, I have no idea. What do you suggest?"

His expression was soft as if he, too, had found some healing in helping the fawn. "I suppose we could try bottle feeding it. Or maybe it's big enough for grass and oats." He eased to his feet, slowly backed from the pen so as not to frighten the fawn. "I'll go get some and see."

She followed him and helped pull grass. He trotted to the oat bin and scooped out a handful of oats. He paused to fill a bucket with water. They returned to the pen and put the feed down. The fawn wouldn't move with them there so they backed out, closed the gate and tiptoed away then turned to watch. The fawn nosed at the grass. Ate a few mouthfuls. Ducked his nose into the water.

"Maybe he's not hungry," Jayne said.

"I think you'll have to bottle feed him."

"But—"

"It's not that hard. Though I'm not sure who would have a baby bottle."

"I'll ask Linette." She trotted up the hill and explained her need to Linette.

"I think there is a bottle in the things the Arnesons left." She'd heard the story of the family who sought shelter with Linette and Eddie as they fought a fever. They died under Linette's care. Her admiration for her sister-in-law grew as she realized how difficult it would be to watch people die.

Linette took her to a room upstairs and found a bottle complete with a nipple. She gave Jayne milk from the supply in the house and warmed it for her. Along with a warning that wild things often didn't take to being helped.

"Seth said the same but like I told him, I have to try." Calling out her thanks, she hurried back to the barn where Seth watched the fawn and cat in the stall. Smokey licked the fawn, which seemed to calm it.

"I've got an idea," she said as they entered the stall

and the fawn bolted to its feet. She handed the bottle to Seth and scooped up Smokey then sat against the wall. She crossed her legs and put Smokey in her lap. "Bring the fawn."

He picked up the fawn and knelt in front of Jayne. He positioned the fawn so it sat with its head almost touching Smokey then offered the bottle.

At the first taste of milk, the fawn jerked back and fought. Seth let it struggle a moment then again stuck the nipple in its mouth. This time it swallowed a mouthful.

Smokey stretched up and rubbed her head against the fawn's head. She smelled the milk and licked the fawn's muzzle to capture the drips. The fawn calmed. After a few false starts the little thing managed to figure out how to take milk from the bottle.

Jayne beamed at Seth. "We might be able to save this little one."

His eyes were soft green and full of hope. "Maybe."

Maybe the fawn would be a source of healing for both of them. She could save something instead of standing helplessly by without taking any action. He could accept that some risks were worth taking.

Was this what the women meant when they said bad things had a place in life, bringing blessings in their wake?

"This morning I asked the women how they explained God's love when bad things happen. They all said good often came from bad. Or at least they can be used for our good."

He considered her words. "We can use bad things for our good. I like that. But is it something we do, or God does?"

Jayne contemplated his question. She liked how he

pushed her to think about serious things. "I'd have to say I think it's both. God can use it but we have to co-operate."

"I like that, too." He smiled. "Like getting shot. That's a bad thing. But it's allowed me to meet you and a very smart cat." Smokey meowed.

His eyes darkened to deep green as he smiled at her.

She couldn't tear herself from his gaze. Couldn't think of a rational thing to say as her heart leapt within her chest. Something shifted inside her. A thought sang through her head, echoing what Grace had said. *I'd go through it again if it brought us together.* She realized how foolish were her thoughts. How far from reality... even possibility.

She jerked her eyes free and stared down at the fawn, who had stopped struggling, and drew in a deep, steadying breath. Seth was only the cowboy she'd shot. He was here only because he felt a responsibility to make sure she didn't shoot someone else. He couldn't wait to leave.

And yet he'd said he was glad to have met her. Maybe he only meant because it gave him a chance to give her shooting lessons. Seems his biggest concern was to avoid another accident.

She stared at his hands cradling a tiny fawn and feeding it milk from a bottle. No, he hadn't exactly said he was glad. Simply that his being shot had allowed him to meet her.

So what did he mean?

She stole a glimpse from under the protection of her eyelashes. His expression gave no clue. She sighed. She was simply a responsibility to him.

The fawn tossed its head. Seth released it to run to the corner and Smokey meandered over to join it.

Jayne scrambled to her feet.

She didn't want to be a responsibility. She wanted—

She didn't know what she wanted. Fresh air and sunshine would do at the moment and she rushed out of the barn and stared into the cornflower-blue sky.

Would anyone ever view her as capable? A person to be valued?

And protected? asked a little voice.

Was it possible to have both?

She didn't know and her inner turmoil left her restless.

Chapter Eleven

Seth tidied the little pen where he'd put the fawn. He hadn't had a chance to ask Eddie if he minded. If he objected, Seth would find another place for him. Now that he'd started caring for the fawn, he meant to do his best to see the animal survived.

He put away the vet supplies Jayne had brought him. Why had he said that meeting her was a good thing? The words had come to his mouth without forethought. But now that they were spoken, he had to consider them.

Was meeting her a good thing?

He tried to think how it wasn't and smiled when he couldn't come up with one reason.

Except the one he'd started with. His responsibility was to care for his pa. No doubt most people would think he could do that and pursue a friendship—or more—with Jayne.

Not that he didn't consider the possibility. If she would let him, he would offer her protection. But she didn't want that.

Jayne was headstrong. Determined. Seeking independence.

Seth had had his share of dealing with headstrong people who left him to carry on in their wake.

He had nothing to offer her but some shooting lessons.

He left the barn and returned to the oat bin. He'd finished repairing the wall but now circled it, putting in a nail here and there, tightening the hinges on the door, looking for things to fix.

He was a fixer. A protector. He took his responsibilities more seriously than most. A long time ago he had promised himself he would not take on more unless they helped him with his current responsibilities.

He saw no reason to change that decision. Jayne was right. He was reluctant to take risks. Best he could do was make sure Jayne could handle a gun well enough to not be a threat to others and also be able to take care of herself should the need arise.

He would have avoided her the rest of the day but she assumed he would help her care for the fawn, so after supper he accompanied her back to the barn. Eddie had assured them he had no objection to the fawn in the barn.

"I asked around," Jayne said. "The consensus is he needs a good bottle feeding twice a day."

He'd pulled a carrot from the garden and broke it into pieces. "Let's see if he can eat some of this." He dropped a bite into the fawn's mouth and it chewed it. "That's good."

They fed the fawn another bottle.

Jayne practically glowed. "I believe he's going to make it. What are we going to call him?"

Seth's insides tightened. Naming the fawn only made it more painful should anything happen to it. But he couldn't quelch Jayne's joy. "How about Deer?"

When she laughed, the skin around her eyes crinkling like rays of sunshine, his insides turned to warm honey.

"You're too funny. No, we need something strong and bold."

"You mean like Thor, the god of thunder." He meant to be amusing but saw a flash in her eyes and guessed she liked the idea.

"Thor. Suits him, don't you think?"

He pretended to give the tiny critter closer study then shook his head. "I really can't picture him throwing bolts of lightning across the sky. Nope. Doesn't look like a Thor to me."

"It's only figurative." She gave him a playful punch on the shoulder. "Gives him something to live up to."

He grabbed his shoulder and groaned. "First, you shoot me and now you beat me."

She giggled. "As if that hurt."

No, it wasn't pain he felt but the feeling that gripped his heart had the same kind of power to drive all other thoughts from his mind.

A few moments later he realized the fawn had finished eating and Jayne had scrambled to her feet.

His thoughts righted and he landed back in his sensible place.

They left the barn.

Seth wasn't eager to put an end to the evening nor did she appear to be in a hurry to return to the house. By mutual consent they wandered along the roadway between the buildings.

"It's such a lovely evening," she murmured, plucking a blade of grass. "This country is so different from England."

"How so?" He'd never been anywhere but the west.

"It's big. So sunny and bright. And the mountains. Have you seen anything like them?"

"I've seen them all my life but have to say I never tire of them."

She stared to the west where the sun leaned toward the mountain peaks, filling the valleys with sharp shadows. "Linette says she could never get tired of them, either. Have you noticed her paintings?"

"Can't say I have."

"The paintings in the living room are hers."

He had seen the stunning pictures. "I didn't realize she'd done them."

"Linette has painted many pictures but my favorite is in the library. It hangs over Eddie's mahogany desk. A winter scene with snow-covered mountains and snow-draped evergreens." Her voice had grown dreamy as if she had slipped away to another place.

He'd noticed the painting and thought it beautiful.

"It's full of strength. When I look at it I think of a Bible verse I learned as a child. 'Seek the Lord and his strength.'" She shifted her gaze from the mountains to Seth.

"If God made the mountains and holds the world in place by His power, He can surely carry me through the trials of my life even when I don't understand what's going on." She shook her head. "And I so often struggle to understand life."

Her eyes widened and she pressed her fingers to her chin. "Why, of course. It's like the mountains. Even when storm clouds obscure them they are still there. Still solid."

The peace flooding her face made Seth wish he could as easily find the assurance she had. But a rock of disbelief had settled into his heart after Frank's death and over the years had grown more solid. More fixed. He figured it would take four teams of strong oxen to budge it now.

Jayne curled her hand around his elbow. "Let's walk. It's too pleasant an evening to waste."

They crossed the bridge, went past the pens, paused to watch the pigs for a moment then climbed the hill beyond and stopped under a tree that provided a view to the west.

Jayne sighed and leaned toward him. Or did he only imagine it as a queer mingling of hope and yearning filled him? But a dark shadow hovered, an accumulation of fear and caution. His arms ached to pull her close and hold her next to his heart and let his skin absorb her calm assurance. But his head told him he could never give her what she needed—protection, security, safety. He feared failure.

"The sky is alive with fire," she murmured.

The sun dipped behind the mountain peaks, fracturing light into a hundred bright ribbons of color.

"It makes me wish I could paint like Linette."

If she hadn't been leaning close he would not have noticed her stiffen.

"I wish I could do anything useful and practical." She tipped her chin up in a gesture of determination. "And I will learn how."

He longed to be able to say something that would encourage her, make her see her strengths and abilities. Slowly, the words coming haltingly, he spoke. "Jayne, don't sell yourself short. What counts is what's inside you, not what your hands can do. That, you can learn. After all, no one was born knowing how to rope or ride or bake bread."

She turned her face up to him. The deep hunger in her eyes squeezed his heart.

"What if what's inside is fear and cowardice?"

He touched her chin and smiled into her eyes, lost in their chocolate depths. "No coward would cross the North American continent nor pick up a gun and learn to shoot it after seeing the death and destruction it can cause." He trailed his finger along her jawline, marveling at the softness of her porcelain skin. "Fear is a good thing. It protects us from danger. Assessing fear and confronting it takes courage. You, Jayne Gardiner, have shown that kind of courage over and over."

She cupped his hand, stilling his fingers against her cheek. Her eyes filled with warmth and appreciation and drew him into her thoughts.

He swallowed hard. Tried to assess what was happening. Where would this go? But he couldn't think past the feel of flesh on flesh, his hand on her cheek. He couldn't reason beyond the look in her eyes.

"Seth Collins, you are a very kind and generous man. No one has ever said anything like that to me. It makes me feel…" She gave a tiny shrug with one shoulder. "It makes me feel strong and…" She swallowed hard and her eyes grew wide. "Never mind."

She didn't move but he felt her withdrawal as thoroughly as if she'd shouted it in his ear.

He slipped his hand to his side.

She put the space of a foot-long ruler between them.

Yet neither made any motion toward returning to the ranch. Instead, they continued to watch nature painting the sky in bright colors.

Distant sounds reminded him of a world beyond this place. A horse neighed. In the trees behind them, birds cooed. A noisy crow cawed as it flapped by. If he really listened, he could even hear the rippling of the river.

A breeze caught a strand of Jayne's hair and blew it across her cheek. He lifted his hand, thinking to tuck it into place, but she caught it herself.

She didn't need him. She had Eddie and back in England, her father. Moreover, she meant to become independent.

And he did not welcome more responsibilities. It should have been all the reason he needed to end this time with her. Yet he didn't move. Didn't say anything. He wasn't ready to return to the narrow life he'd built for himself and so he remained motionless and silent, drinking in the view as his eyes swept the ranch.

Beside him, Jayne seemed almost worshipful as she observed the sunset.

Then she let out a breath that seemed to come from the very soles of her feet. She turned and smiled at him. "Wasn't that wonderful? I feel renewed, refreshed." Her eyes blessed him and he knew a soul-satisfying sense that he'd had a part in making the evening special.

They turned and made their way back to the ranch, though she didn't seem in any more of a rush to end the evening than he.

They reached the bridge and she stopped to lean her arms on the side rails.

He hesitated, having no fondness for rivers. But he couldn't resist Jayne's company and joined her, elbow to elbow.

Evening shadows filled the water. Dark. Murky. Unlocking his forbidden memories. Giving them life.

"I had a brother. Frank. He was two years older than me. We were very close. Always watching out for each other." His voice caught and he couldn't go on.

She pressed her hand to his arm. "What happened to Frank?"

"We had a friend, Sarah. She lived across the road and spent a lot of time with our family." Memories came in a flood. "We almost grew up together. Mostly she was my friend and Frank put up with her. Then one day—"

She slipped her hand down his arm and tucked it into his curled fingers. He held on to the lifeline she offered.

"It was early winter. The ice had started to form on the river. The sun was so bright it hurt the eyes. One of those days when a person can hardly contain their enthusiasm and you begin to think there's nothing you can't do."

She squeezed his hand.

"Frank seemed to notice Sarah for the first time and it made him silly. Foolhardy. He dared us to slide on the ice. He knew as well as I that it wasn't thick enough but Sarah laughed and he couldn't be stopped. He went first. Sarah followed. I refused to go. I wanted them to come back. Stay away from danger." He sucked in air that didn't reach his lungs. Instead, it went to his head and made him dizzy.

Jayne gave an almost inaudible gasp. "No." The word came on breathless air.

He nodded. "They broke through the ice. I grabbed a branch and wriggled out to pull them from the icy water. I managed to get Sarah to shore and went back for Frank but I couldn't find him." His voice scraped from his throat. "They found his body three days later. Sarah died the same day he was found. I did everything I could." His jaw ached. "But it wasn't enough."

"Oh, Seth." She shifted, wrapped her arms about his waist and held him tight.

He enclosed her in his arms and pressed his cheek to her hair, breathing in the scent of sunshine and hay.

"Seth, I'm so sorry. I know how much it hurts. How helpless you must feel. But you said it yourself. You did everything you could. You have to stop blaming yourself for their choices."

He knew her words were right. In his head. His heart said otherwise. His heart blamed him. Said he should have stopped them. Should have saved them. *You were taught to look out for each other.* Pa's words reverberated through his head.

"Why did they insist on acting so foolishly?" he said.

"We all make mistakes. I guess it simply proves they were human. Like us all."

"Where was God?" He choked the words out. "Why didn't He stop them from dying?"

Her arms tightened around him and she shuddered.

"Oh, Jayne. Here I am bemoaning something that happened years ago while you deal with something a lot fresher. Forgive me for being so selfish."

"No. Don't apologize. Your pain is as real as my pain. I think—" She tipped her head back to look into his face. "It makes me feel like you can understand how I feel and why I do the things I do. It makes me feel close to you."

They looked at each other in the lengthening shadows. At that moment something healing and eternal occurred. He knew he would never be the same. Not, he silently warned himself, that his circumstances had changed.

His heart swelled with gratitude for her understanding and he lowered his head and caught her lips in a gentle kiss.

Her hands splayed across his back. She appeared to welcome the kiss and return it with answering pressure.

His heart swelled to near bursting with joy. It beat hard with exuberance three times before his lifelong habit of caution took over and he reasoned his way out of accepting what this situation offered—though he couldn't say exactly what it was, maybe a new beginning.

He broke away from her embrace. "I shouldn't have done that. I had no right."

She gave a deep-throated chuckle. "I don't think you noticed me protesting in any way."

When she would have tucked her hand about his elbow, he pretended to stop and listen for something, putting enough distance between them that she dropped her arm.

It wasn't that he didn't welcome her touch, even yearn for it. But nothing had changed. He was still Seth Collins who lived a life of caution. Who saw responsibilities as all consuming. Who didn't know how to trust God. Who had a pa who needed him and in order to prove he wasn't a failure in the responsibility department, he meant to prove he could look after Pa.

Jayne did not deserve the affections of a flawed man like him.

Jayne felt him pull back. Part of her understood it was his fear kicking in. Now that he'd shared the story about his brother and their friend, she understood why he wanted to control things so much, why he thought people shouldn't take risks and why he kept his heart locked up. But she'd also seen his tenderness and vulnerability.

He'd given her such encouragement by saying she

wasn't a coward. She wanted to give him something in return. She recalled his words. *Where was God? Why didn't He stop them from dying?*

She stopped walking and turned to face him.

He looked beyond her, avoiding eye contact.

It pinched her heart to see his withdrawal. "Seth, God was there. Why He didn't stop the accident, I can't say. I don't presume to understand His ways. But more and more each day I understand that His love is unchanging. His arms are outstretched to comfort us. I think life is meant to press us closer to Him. But so often we—and I mean me—let circumstances come between us and then wonder where God is. He doesn't move. He doesn't change." As she spoke, her convictions grew stronger. "I flounder from time to time but joy comes when I return to His side."

His gaze darted to her for a heartbeat then away again. "I'm glad you have found solace in His presence." His words were distant as if pulled from the mountain tops.

"I would wish the same for you, my friend."

He jerked his full attention to her. "Friend?"

"We are, aren't we?"

The seconds ticked by as he stared into her eyes. "Friends?" The word rounded with surprise.

She nodded, hoping he would allow it to be so.

A slow smile curled his lips. "I like that."

"Me, too."

They turned back to the trail.

After a moment he stopped. "You know, I haven't had a friend since…" His voice trailed off.

"Since Sarah?"

"I was going to say since Frank."

She reached for his arm, gratified when he didn't pull

away. "Then I'm doubly honored to be your friend." A sense of wholeness, such as she couldn't recall ever before experiencing, warmed her insides.

The next morning she dressed hurriedly and rushed to the kitchen to get milk for Thor. She glanced around, hoping Seth would be there and offer to help. Yes, caring for the fawn had been her idea but she'd never done anything of the sort before. Seth seemed to know what to do.

But he wasn't about. Her heart squeezed out a disappointed beat. She longed to see him again, bask in his smile, revel in their friendship.

Never mind, she could feed the fawn herself.

She gathered together her supplies and trotted to the barn where she went to the enclosure where Thor rested. The pen was empty. An overwhelming sense of fear and dread took hold of her. Had the fawn died and one of the cowboys removed his body? Her knees weakened. "Thor," she cried. "Thor."

Footsteps thudded. She'd ask where they'd taken him and see he got a proper farewell. She turned, tears welling up in her eyes. "Seth." He'd understand why it mattered so much. "Thor is gone."

"He's okay. Come and see." He held the gate open.

His words barely registered in her brain. She had to force a deep breath into her lungs as she followed him.

He stepped back and pointed to a wire pen with a little wooden shelter. There Thor and Smokey chased each other around the perimeter.

She laughed shakily. "He's okay."

Seth jerked his attention to her. "You thought something had happened to him?"

She nodded, unable to push a word past the conflagration of emotions.

He moved closer and touched her cheek. "I'm sorry. I didn't mean to frighten you."

She nodded, clinging to his gentle look.

He dropped his hand, turned back to watch the pair in the pen.

Her world righted. Came back to sanity and reality. "You built this?"

"He needs space to run and play. He can play here during the day but for his safety, he'll need to be shut in the barn at night."

"I brought a bottle." She clutched it still.

Together they entered the pen. Thor backed into the far corner but after a short struggle to get him started, he took the bottle readily enough.

Once Thor was sucking well, Seth backed away, leaving Jayne to feed the fawn on her own.

She appreciated his vote of confidence but felt he'd put distance between them for another reason. He was cautious about their friendship.

"Are you ready for another lesson today?" he asked.

Relieved that he didn't mean to abandon the lessons, she gave him a teasing grin. "A shooting lesson?" She hoped to remind him of the evening before when, for a moment, she had felt so close to him. Maybe he'd realize she wasn't opposed to courting lessons.

"'Fraid I can't teach you how to preserve peas," he said. Her eyes twinkled and she understood he only pretended not to know what she meant.

Thor finished and trotted away, jerking her attention back to the animal.

"After breakfast?" he asked.

"Sounds good." She looked forward to it more than

usual. Last night had made her realize how much she had grown to enjoy his company.

They left Thor in his pen and stood outside watching him play with Smokey for a few minutes then they returned to the house.

After breakfast she would have stayed to help clean up but Linette shoved her toward the door. "Don't keep Seth waiting."

Jayne did not need any more urging and went to join Seth. They went to the clearing.

"I think you're ready to go on your own," he said.

A thrill of both victory and fear coursed through her veins. "You're sure?"

He tipped his head and studied her, his eyes soft, his expression gentle. "Don't you think you are?"

She considered the question. His instruction had been thorough. She knew each step. It was time to put aside her fear and move on boldly. "I'm ready."

"Then let's see you do it." He stood at her side, observing as she loaded and aimed. "Good."

He didn't move to her back to steady her hand but remained close by. He really meant to leave her to do this herself. She considered letting her hand waver so he would put his arm around her and hold her hand. But no. She would learn how to shoot. She would do this.

She squinted down the sights and squeezed the trigger. A shudder raced through her at the explosion but she had not flinched.

Seth squinted toward the target. He said nothing.

"I missed, didn't I?"

"Try again."

She shot again. Missed again. But on the third try she hit the target. Only the outer edge but she cheered.

He gave a nod of approval. "You're doing just fine.

From now on you have to practice keeping your eye on the target. As you get better, move the target farther away."

He talked like this was the end. She didn't want it to be. Yes, she wanted to be strong and independent. But something deep inside her cried out for more. More than she'd had as a child protected by her father. More than she'd had as Oliver's fiancée, never sure of his devotion. More than she had here as a woman allowed to do things she'd never have been allowed in England.

The trouble was, she simply didn't understand what the *more* was.

She put the gun on a nearby stump and sat on the adjacent log. If only she could find the words to explain what she felt. But how could she when she didn't know them herself?

"You look disappointed." He stood a few feet away, his arms crossed, one foot tipped over the other.

She rolled her head back and forth. "Not disappointed, exactly." He waited for an explanation. "I don't know. It's like now I can shoot. So what? How is that going to change anything? It won't make me feel less like I failed to help Oliver when I could have. It won't..." Her voice grew hoarse. "It won't make me any more sure that he loved me. Or that I loved him." The words had come uncensored to her mouth and she clamped a hand to her lips. "I didn't mean to say that." Her eyes felt way too wide.

He sat beside her. "Jayne, you can't change the past. But didn't you say you can use it?"

She tried to recall when she had said that. "I said life is meant to press us closer to God. Is that what you're referring to?"

He nodded.

"Have I let my experience with Oliver press me closer?" She thought for a moment. "It's certainly changed me. Made me want to be strong. Able to take care of myself and protect others. It's also made me see that what Oliver and I had wasn't what I want now. It was enough back then but now I want to be more than a convenient addition to a man's life. I want to be more than a worthy match." She grew firmer, more impassioned as she spoke. "I want—" She clamped back the words. *I want a love that is not only ready to die for me, but to live life to the fullest with me.*

Seth waited and she scrambled for words to finish her sentence.

"I want to be fearless." It was but a fraction of the truth.

He chuckled. "Jayne, I think you are closer to that every day."

His words had the power to ease her worries and she smiled. "I guess I am. Thanks to your help."

He choked back his amusement. "I don't think I can take credit for doing anything but walking beside you."

Walking beside her. What a wonderful thought. That's exactly what she wanted. A man who would walk beside her. Honor her strengths and gently help her through her weaknesses. Why had she picked a man like Oliver who offered neither? And now she'd met one who offered both but for a limited time. She would ask him when he meant to leave but didn't want him to think she thought it was time.

"I told Linette I would get back to help pick beans." They retraced their steps toward the ranch. "I never realized how much work was involved in growing and gathering food and preparing enough for the winter."

The sun was warm overhead. A gopher stood on tiptoe beside a mound of dirt and whistled before it ducked down his hole in the ground.

Jayne chuckled. "Cheeky little thing." She breathed deeply. "Do I smell roses?"

"Over there." He pointed toward a bush with late-season wild roses.

She'd seen them before and loved them. Single petaled in varying colors of pink from palest skin tones to fullest red. She bent over the bush and inhaled the scent. She would pick one and take it home but had learned how fragile the blossoms were. The petals would fall even as she picked the flower.

A flash of blue in the grass caught her eye and she scurried to the spot. Little bluebells hung their clustered heads. Such rare beauty.

Seth waited nearby as she enjoyed the flowers.

She sat back on her heels and let her gaze sweep the blanket of blossoms. Her eyes were drawn to something on the horizon.

A man sat on a horse watching them.

She rose slowly and backed to Seth's side. An English gentleman. Nothing unusual about that. He would have fit in back in London but looked out of place here with his bowler hat and buttoned-up suit. Would she ever see a man thusly dressed and not be reminded of Oliver's killer?

As the man shifted in his saddle, Jayne caught a glimpse of his face. She gasped and grabbed Seth's arm, dragging him behind a bunch of poplar trees.

Seth stared at her. "What is wrong?" He ducked his head to look into her eyes. "You look like you've seen a ghost."

Jayne struggled to suck in air. "It's him." Her voice shook.

Seth looked about. "Who is him?"

"That man." Jayne pointed a trembling finger. "It's him. He's the man who shot Oliver."

Seth moved to where he could see where she pointed. "Are you sure?"

"I…" She tried to collect her thoughts, sort out the flashes of memory from that day. "I don't know. Maybe it's only because he's dressed like that man was."

"He's leaving. I wonder what he wanted."

Jayne bent over her knees, forcing air in and out of her wooden lungs. "What if it's really him?" She straightened and stared to where the man had been. "What if he followed me? What if he wants to get rid of the only witness?" She shuddered.

Seth pulled her into his arms and patted her back. "I regret ever suggesting such a thing."

Bile burned the back of her throat, but she focused her entire being on the comforting movement of his hand on her back, and the murmur of his words, though she didn't listen to their meaning. Slowly, her nerves calmed and she relaxed into his embrace, feeling safe and sheltered.

It was a luxury she couldn't allow herself. She must depend on no one to keep her safe. No one but herself and her skills. Thankfully she could now use a gun if she must, though she might not be any threat unless she could actually hit a target.

But she enjoyed several more moments of resting in his care then, exerting every bit of inner strength she possessed, she straightened and escaped his arms.

"If that's him, he is here for only one reason." She squared her shoulders. She would not cower in the corner if he threatened anyone again.

Chapter Twelve

Seth let her step away, although everything in him wanted to keep her right there in his arms where he could protect her. If he hadn't been so busy watching her enjoy the flowers, he would have seen the man before he turned away. He would have memorized his face and then gone hunting him.

He couldn't leave Jayne now. Not even for Pa's sake. He hadn't been able to protect Sarah and Frank from the cold waters, but he would keep Jayne safe at any cost.

"Let's get back to the ranch." He wouldn't frighten her any more than she already was. Back at the ranch there was hope of keeping her under constant surveillance. He pulled her to his side, kept her tucked safely under his arm as they rushed back to the house.

Jayne hurried into the kitchen and collapsed on a chair.

Linette rushed to her side. "What's wrong?"

She shuddered then said in a deadly calm voice, "I think I saw Oliver's murderer." She explained about seeing the rider.

Linette lifted her gaze to Seth. He saw the same horrible knowledge in her eyes. The Englishman would be in the same vicinity as Jayne for only one reason.

"Where's Eddie?" he asked.

She nodded, relief filling her eyes as if assured her husband would know what to do. "He went to the supply sheds to check on what we need."

"I'll get him."

Linette followed him to the far door.

"Keep Jayne here," he said.

"I will."

Seth found Eddie at the first supply shed. Roper was with him as they discussed a trip to town for supplies.

He told them both about the Englishman.

Eddie's jaw tightened. "Could she have been mistaken?"

"I don't know. Best you talk to her."

Eddie handed his list to Roper. "Tell the boys to keep a lookout for a fancy-dressed Englishman and to bring him in if they see him."

Back at the house they went to the kitchen where Jayne held a cup of tea. Linette sat across from her with a cup held tightly between her palms.

Eddie sat beside Linette. "Tell me everything."

Seth sat at Jayne's side, resisting a protective urge to put his arm about her.

Jayne nodded. "There was something about him. And as soon as he turned to give me a view of his face, I knew it was him."

"You're certain."

"I suppose I could be mistaken but I don't think so. I don't think I will ever forget the look on that man's face when he demanded Oliver turn out his pockets."

It was more than enough for Seth. If Eddie didn't do

something, he would. He'd find the tracks on the hillside and follow the man to the ends of the earth.

"I'll send for the Mountie," Eddie said. "Until he gets here I think you better stay in the house."

"I have to take care of Thor."

At the blank look on Eddie's face, Seth added, "The fawn."

"Fine, but stay close to the buildings."

Seth figured it indicated how frightened she was that she didn't object to her brother ordering her about.

Mercy and Sybil clattered into the room.

"We heard. Did you really see the murderer?"

Eddie left the house as the pair hovered about Jayne. Mercy pushed Seth aside to sit next to her. He glanced after Eddie then decided he would stay right there until they knew for sure if the man was a threat or not. Until the man could be confronted face-to-face.

Jayne explained yet again what she'd seen while Mercy and Sybil made appropriate comforting sounds.

Linette offered them all tea and cookies.

Seth took both gratefully, but he couldn't remain at the table. He carried his cup and cookie to the window and looked out. A rider kicked up dust as he rode off the ranch. Probably the man Eddie sent to find the Mountie.

He stayed at the window long after the dust disappeared.

Grady ran past his line of vision and crashed through the door. Billy came in on his heels.

"You got a baby deer?" His voice was filled with awe. "Billy says we can't see it without permission. Can we see it now? Please?"

Seth turned back to Jayne, saw the stress creasing her forehead. It might do her good to leave the house and forget the Englishman but forgetting the danger lurking out there would be foolish.

She sent him a desperate look.

He made up his mind and left his post and headed to her side feeling Mercy's measuring watchfulness. "I'll take the boys to see the fawn, if you like."

She bolted to her feet. "I'll go with you. I need to check on him, anyway."

"We'll come, too," Sybil said and she and Mercy fell in at their heels and the lot of them went down the hill.

The boys were soon joined by Daisy, carrying Pansy.

They went round the barn to the small pen.

"His name is Thor," Jayne said as they crowded up to the fence. The fawn curled up on the ground, Smokey between his paws.

Although Thor's eyes grew wide, he didn't move.

Jayne chuckled. "It looks like he doesn't want to disturb Smokey."

"Thor!" Sybil laughed softly. "Strange name for a little fawn."

Seth checked their surroundings, seeing nothing, then he turned to the ladies. "I said he didn't look much like a Thor but she didn't believe me."

"What does it mean?" Daisy asked.

"In mythology, Thor is a god of thunder and lightning. He carries a big hammer and smashes things. His job is to protect humans." Sybil gave the details.

Jayne grinned at her friends. "In this case, the humans are protecting Thor." Her gaze captured Seth's. He returned it with silent promise that he would protect her as well as Thor.

"Can we touch him?" Grady asked.

"Seth, what do you think?" Jayne asked. "Is it too

soon?" She turned to explain to the children. "He's a wild creature and people frighten him."

"Look," Seth whispered and they all turned toward little Pansy. She had edged around the fence to where she could reach her fingers through the wire. Thor licked her fingers then bounced to his feet and pressed his nose close to hers.

"There's one human he isn't afraid of." Seth spoke so softly he wondered if the others heard but they all stayed where they were and watched the two little ones acknowledge each other.

Daisy edged closer to make sure her little sister wasn't in any danger.

Thor skipped away then turned and tiptoed back to Pansy. She giggled as his nose touched her fingers.

"Can we touch him, too?" Grady asked.

"Why don't you let him make friends with you?" Seth said. "Stand at the fence and wait for him to come to you."

Mercy and Sybil sat with their backs to the barn to watch. After a moment, Jayne joined them.

Seth couldn't relax, not that he worried about the fawn. His concern was Jayne and the threat of a fancy-dressed Englishman. He guided the children but all the while he watched the trails leading to the ranch and kept a lookout at the trees nearby where a man could hide in the shadows.

How long would it take for the Mountie to receive Eddie's message and get here?

The boys stayed until the fawn finally came up to explore their fingers. A little after that they trotted off in search of bigger adventures. Daisy gathered up her little sister and headed back. "I'm going to help Ma pick beans."

Jayne bolted to her feet. "I plumb forgot. Come on, girls. We need to help Linette." They raced away to the garden where Linette and Cassie were already at work.

"Jayne," Seth called. But she didn't hear him.

He rubbed at his neck. Shouldn't she return to the house and stay out of sight? He followed slowly, not headed for the garden but for a spot behind the cookhouse that allowed him a nice view of the entire yard and most of the surrounding area. He hunkered down, alert to the tiniest movement.

He scanned the landscape constantly but his gaze continued to return to the garden where Jayne worked alongside the others, filling tubs with green beans. He repeatedly assured himself no one would ride into the ranch and attack her. Eddie had posted a watch at either end of the trail leading to the ranch.

A shifting shadow beyond the garden drew his attention. Every nerve in his body fired into action. He strained to make out any shape, could see nothing. But he knew something or someone had moved there. He edged his way toward the barn, saddled his horse and left as if making his way to town. Once down the road and around the corner, he cut to his left in a direction that would bring him into line with anyone leaving the spot he'd been watching. He rode as fast as he figured was safe, hoping he wouldn't draw attention to himself, but there was no way to muffle his horse's thudding steps.

He reached the area without encountering anyone. He left his horse at the edge of the trees and went to examine the place where he'd seen something. The first thing he noted was the good view of the garden it provided. He stood there a moment, watching Jayne. He heard his breath whoosh in and out. A man with a good rifle could get rid of her before anyone could do a thing about it. And he could disappear before a man on horseback could overtake him.

His heart hammered a protest against his rib. She was a sitting target. She should be indoors.

Before he told her so, he examined the ground. Footprints. And not those of a cowboy boot. A sliver of wood caught his attention and he picked it up gingerly. One of those fancy new toothpicks. Definitely a city man. No cowboy in his right mind would use such a silly thing. A sharpened piece of wood served the purpose just fine. Or a length of oat straw. Even a stem of grass.

A city man who killed without remorse and tracked witnesses across the world.

Not a man to be trifled with.

He returned to his horse and rode down the hill in a straight line to the ranch. He rode directly to the garden.

Every woman turned to him, knowing his visit had a purpose.

"Jayne, I don't think it's safe for you out here."

She blinked. "Why not? Eddie put two cowboys on the trails and another to watch the place." She pointed toward Slim who leaned in the barn doorway. "And Eddie is within calling distance." He was across the river tending to some chores. "No one is coming in here without being met by a gun-toting man." She sat back on her heels as unconcerned as the cat grooming itself in the sunny patch of grass.

"Yes, ma'am. That's so. But—" He hesitated to speak his fears aloud. He turned to Linette. "Ma'am, I saw something up the hill." He pointed to the place and five women rose and shielded their eyes with their hands to look in the direction he indicated. "Someone was there but I didn't catch him. But I regret to say that from there Jayne is an easy target for anyone with a rifle."

The women turned to confront Jayne.

"Jayne, you aren't safe out here," Sybil said.

Mercy grabbed the beans still in Jayne's hands. "You shouldn't be here."

Linette nodded. "I can't bear to think of you being a target."

"That's a terribly frightening thought," Cassie added.

Jayne looked confused, frightened and then stubbornness hardened her expression. "You think I should run and hide?" Her flashing eyes informed Seth the question was meant for him.

All the women said, "Yes."

"But the beans." Jayne indicated the rows left to pick.

"We'll take the full tub to the house," Linette said, "and you can begin stringing them."

As soon as he saw Jayne meant to follow her sister-in-law, Seth hurried to the barn to unsaddle his horse. The chore seemed to take longer than usual. As soon as he finished, he trotted up the hill, ignoring the sharp reminder in his leg of his recent injury.

Linette and Jayne worked in the kitchen.

"I can manage this on my own," Jayne said.

"Very well. And thank you. I appreciate it." As she left the house, Linette murmured to Seth, "Keep an eye on her."

"I mean to."

He circled the room, glancing out the windows. It was hot enough to require the door to stand open, which allowed him a view through the screen. Still, he felt as if a man could sneak up on him without warning.

"Do you really think he'd venture close to the ranch when it is swarming with people?" Jayne asked him.

"There's no way he'd get in and out again without getting stopped."

"Likely that is true." It was the time between getting in and out again that worried him. "Now would be a good time for you to ask God to take care of you."

"Why me? Or rather, why just me? You could ask, as well."

"I'm not sure I believe He would answer."

Her hands grew still. "You won't know if you don't ask."

"I'll let you do the asking."

"Fine. I will." She bowed her head a moment. Then lifted it again and gave him a direct look that burned through his caution straight to an unguarded corner of his heart. He needed to get away from this place soon or he'd forget the promise he'd made to himself to never take on more responsibility and never put anyone ahead of his pa.

"I said a prayer for you, too," she said, her voice both sweet and daring.

"Save your breath."

"I asked God to show you that He hears and answers your prayers."

He let out a gusty laugh. "You believe that quite firmly."

"That's right." She went back to stringing beans as confident as if it were already done.

He circled the room again, checking out each window and staring out the door a long time. "He's out there. I practically saw him."

"I did see him."

He didn't need the reminder. It was time to stop dwelling on it. He was here to protect her. He'd keep her safe.

He continued pacing the room, stopping at a painting of mountains in full summer array. The grass shone emerald, and the deciduous trees made a light green contrast to the pine and spruce. Flowers dotted the field in the foreground, where off to the right sat a mounted cowboy. He leaned closer. "Looks like Eddie."

"It is. That's one of Linette's paintings. It's good, isn't it?"

"I'm no judge of artwork but I like this. I can almost smell the fresh air and the flowers."

"Exactly. It feels alive."

He studied it a few more minutes than circled the room again, checking out the windows and doors.

"Seth, will you sit down. You're making me nervous."

"You *should* be nervous."

"Fine. I am nervous enough without you pacing around like a caged animal."

Even as he sat, his muscles twitched. He couldn't shake the feeling that someone was watching...that the murdering Englishman was very close.

He shifted his chair so his back was to a wall and he faced the door. "Hand me some of those beans. I might as well keep busy."

She moved her chair next to his and placed the tub of beans close by. He'd never pictured himself sitting in a kitchen preparing beans to be bottled, but it wasn't half-bad. Jayne sat beside him where he could protect her. She hummed under her breath as she worked. The scent of flowers and garden soil came to him from her direction. Flies buzzed against the window glass but apart from that sound they might have been alone in their own little world.

If only it could be so. Instead, danger hovered on their doorstep.

* * *

Jayne couldn't get a thought straight. She simply continued to pull strings from beans and cut them the size Linette wanted. The mindless task failed to divert her thoughts.

Seth had seen the murderer watching again.

She shivered. When she felt Seth's glance touch her, she raised her eyes, knowing they begged for reassurance. She didn't care.

He smiled but his eyes reflected her concern.

She touched his arm. "At least you're here to protect me." She wanted to say she would be fine without protection but her brave talk about being independent and looking after herself meant nothing in the face of real danger.

He nodded, his eyes forest green and bottomless.

She let herself sink into his gaze, let herself find strength and safety. She drew in a trembling breath as she found what she sought. He would take care of her. With God's help.

Oh, Lord, I press close to You. Protect us all.

She jerked her attention back to the beans and continued to prepare them as the clock on the wall ticked off the minutes.

Every tick echoed like the click of a gun. Oh, why had she allowed that word into her mind?

Her breath escaped in a groan.

Seth took her hand and squeezed. "Don't be afraid. There are plenty of people here to protect you."

She nodded, again clinging to the promise in his eyes. "I know." A teasing imp prompted her to add, "Besides, I asked God to protect us all."

His smile didn't reach his eyes. "There now. What more do you need?"

"Nothing except for that man to be arrested and sent back to England to hang."

He nodded.

That evening, after supper, she gathered up supplies to feed Thor.

Seth stopped her. "I'll do it." He reached for the bottle of milk.

She hesitated, fighting an inner battle. Part of her wanted to hide in a closet somewhere. But she'd had enough of running. "I will not give in to my fear."

He took her arm and pulled her around to face him. "Listening to fear is not a bad thing. It can prevent people from taking foolish risks."

She studied him. Saw the concern and the pain in his eyes. She pressed her palm to his cheek. "Seth, I am not going to be foolish. I am not skating on thin ice."

The darkness in his eyes informed her he understood her reference.

"We'll take Thor into the barn to feed him. How's that?"

He considered her suggestion for a moment then nodded. "If you stay in the barn while I get him."

"I will. I don't have a death wish, you know."

Their gazes clung for another second.

"And stay close to me on the way to the barn."

She had no objection to being tucked under his arm, pressed to his side as they marched down the hill. From there she felt as if no harm could ever come to her.

The words were contrary to the goals she had set for herself but provided comfort at the moment.

After this crisis ended she would return to learning to be strong and independent.

Chapter Thirteen

The next day Seth again insisted on being her human shield as they went to feed the fawn. Thor, shut in the barn for the night, raced toward them as soon as he saw the bottle.

She laughed. "Look at that. He knows where the food comes from."

They didn't have to urge him to take the nipple. He grabbed it and pulled eagerly.

She held the bottle, discovering satisfaction and peace in feeding the little animal and in seeing how it had lost its fear of her. Fear. The word covered so many things. She wanted to put her thoughts into words if she could. "I know that fear is a good thing in that it keeps us from danger. But fear can harm, too."

He quirked an eyebrow questioningly.

"Like Thor's fear of us. If he didn't get over it he might have starved to death."

Seth's gaze went slowly to Thor as if he needed to consider her statement.

"I think our experience with fear has been at opposite ends of the spectrum," she said.

He again brought his gaze to her, full of dark intensity that brushed a tender spot within. She ached to be able to help him leave his fears behind.

She went on to answer his unspoken question. "You lost Frank and Sarah because they didn't heed the fear of thin ice. But I stood by helpless and useless because my fear crippled me."

He nodded. "That's true. But I hope we are together, united with fear about this Englishman who has followed you."

She couldn't look away from his gaze. Couldn't escape his silent demand. *United.* The word pulled at her heart strings, threatening to undo her resolve. She must not allow his concern and her fear to drive her back to the person she'd been when Oliver was shot.

She nodded. "I will never again let fear control me, though."

He narrowed his eyes. "I was hoping for more cooperation than that."

She gave a little shrug. "I will only promise not to ignore danger signs."

"I guess that will have to be good enough."

She didn't bother to ask what else he wanted. She didn't object to him being her self-appointed bodyguard but she would not become a whimpering, simpering female afraid to stand up and protect herself should the need arise.

Grady raced into the barn. "Did he eat already?"

"He just finished." Jayne showed him the empty bottle. "He's a greedy little thing."

"Aww. I hoped you'd let me help feed him."

Seth ruffled his hair. "Maybe next time. Thor seems to be comfortable enough with people now."

As if to prove it, Thor bumped his head into Grady's hand then watched, his legs splayed awkwardly. When

Grady reached out to pat his head the fawn bounced away a few feet and paused to wait for Grady.

Grady trotted after him but Thor bounced away.

"I think he wants to play tag," Seth said.

The pair chased up and down the alleyway. Grady paused at the door. "Can we go outside and play?"

Jayne waited, wondering what Seth would say.

"I don't think you should right now. Let's make sure Thor knows where home is first. We wouldn't want him to get lost."

Grady nodded. "Sure wouldn't." He continued playing with the fawn as Seth and Jayne watched.

Jayne liked Seth's answer. It was wise and thoughtful. And not based on fear.

They returned to the house for breakfast. Afterward, Linette turned to Jayne. "Would you be able to help me preserve the beans today?"

Jayne recognized it as Linette's way of making sure she stayed indoors and hid a smile at the way Seth sighed.

"Sure, I'd love to assist you."

Two hours later she realized how much work was involved. They packed beans into jars, added salt and water and put them in a boiler.

"Now they boil for three hours," Linette said. "Which gives us time to get another lot ready to go."

"How did you learn all this?" It was Linette's first summer on the ranch.

"Cookie taught me. When I came west it was with the idea of being a pioneer wife. I was determined to do all the practical things I thought a woman should do. Eddie would pay a housekeeper if I wanted one but I don't."

The heat from the stove, combined with the growing heat from the August sun made the kitchen like an oven. Jayne wiped her forehead with a corner of the big apron Linette had lent her. How could Linette work so hard despite the heat and her growing belly?

Jayne glanced out the window. Seth sat on horseback, on a hill overlooking the house.

Linette joined her. "He's concerned about that Englishman." She gave Jayne a sideways hug. "And you."

Jayne didn't answer. She could hardly deny it when Seth made it obvious but she wasn't sure what it meant. In a secret place behind her heart she wished it meant he cared about her, and not just because he had an overwhelming sense of responsibility to prevent bad things from happening.

Burying a sigh, she returned to the large tub of beans. "This will take all day." Sweat dripped down her back.

Linette chuckled. "I expect it will but we'll really appreciate it when winter comes. Let's be grateful that Cookie is doing half of them."

Jayne stole another glance out the window. Seth had moved. Her heart slammed against her ribs. Where was he? Who watched to make sure the Englishman didn't come near the ranch?

She crossed the kitchen and stepped out the door to scan the surrounding area. There he was. Seth and horse stood in the shadow of the trees near where he and Jayne had spent many hours on shooting lessons. Her breath eased out smooth and warm. She should have known he wouldn't forget about her.

Why did the knowledge feel so good and right when it was not what either of them wanted?

Did he watch her? It was impossible to tell at this distance but somehow she knew he would have seen her step outside. She ducked back into the kitchen before he could ride down and order her to stay indoors.

She hummed a little as she turned back to preparing beans. The Englishman posed no threat so long as Seth stood guard.

Not until dinnertime did she see Seth except at a distance. He came in at Eddie's side, pausing at the door to take a look across the yard.

The men protested the heat in the kitchen.

Mercy entered and gasped. "How can you bear this?" She fanned herself.

Sybil did likewise.

"Would you like to take your food outside to the shade?" Linette said.

One glance at Linette's flushed, damp face and Jayne thought it would be wise. The heat bothered her though she'd never once complained.

"I'd like to," she replied.

Seth pulled her back when she started for the door. "It's not safe."

"Linette is about to perish in this heat. She needs a break." She kept her voice low.

"Let her go outside. But you need to stay here."

The others took their plates outside.

Jayne looked into Seth's eyes, saw stubbornness and caution. Or was it fear? He'd deny it and likely be offended if she suggested so. Was his fear good or not? Was it making him too cautious? How should she respond?

"How likely is it that he'd try and harm me with half a dozen people around?" The question was rhetorical.

"You can never be too safe."

"But you can worry too much." She filled her plate.

"Come on. I'm sure I can sit somewhere that is safe enough."

He grabbed a plate, flung food on it and tromped after her. He waited until she sat with her back to the wall then sat facing her, his bent knees almost touching hers.

She pursed her lips. Did he have to be so obvious that he thought her in danger? Certainly made it difficult to relax and enjoy her meal. Every time she bent her head over her plate she felt exposed and spent most of the meal scanning the trees and hills around the house, hoping and praying she wouldn't see that man.

Seth bolted to his feet and stared down the road. "Rider coming."

Eddie had also risen.

Jayne's heart clattered up her throat and clung to her teeth.

Seth pulled her to her feet and unceremoniously rushed her inside.

She would have protested except his breathing was harsh, his concern obviously genuine. A fact that caused her heart to hammer even more rapidly until her head spun.

The others entered more slowly.

"Whoever it may be, he is riding directly to the house." Eddie moved through to the front door. "Doesn't look like an Englishman to me."

Seth practically glued himself to Jayne's side. She clung to his arm. When he draped his arm across her shoulder and pulled her close she relaxed marginally. She couldn't be much safer.

"It's Constable Allen," Eddie called and he went through to the front door.

Everyone in the room let out a gust of air. None louder than Jayne, unless it was Seth.

"Come on in." Eddie led the man to the kitchen. Beside him stood a Mountie with a yellow stripe on his midnight-blue breeches. Rather than the red serge jacket she'd seen the Mounties at Fort Macleod wearing, he wore a brown canvas tunic. He pulled off his broadbrimmed felt hat and tucked it under his arm.

Eddie made introductions. "You've come about the murderer we saw?"

"Suspected murderer. And yes, I have. Who is the witness?"

"My sister, Jayne."

She had eased away from Seth's side at the announcement of the Mountie's arrival and now stepped forward. "Me."

"I need to ask you some questions. Can we…" He looked about at the crowd.

At least Grady had run to play so he didn't see and hear this.

"You're welcome to use the front room," Linette offered, pointing down the hall.

"That would be fine. Thank you."

Eddie led the way. Jayne followed, the Mountie on her heels. Not until she reached the other room did she see with relief that Seth had also followed.

The Mountie waited for Jayne to be seated then pulled out a little notebook. "Now tell me exactly what happened."

She swallowed hard, gripped her hands together and wished Seth sat at her side instead of across the room beside Eddie.

"I don't know how much you know…"

"Pretend I know nothing. Start at the beginning."

Where was the beginning? When Oliver had gambled so often? When he'd found his gambling more interesting than her company? She gave herself a mental shake. The Mountie meant the shooting.

"I was with my fiancé, Oliver Spencer, walking down a street in London, when this man came from an alley." She went on to describe the scene, leaving nothing out, not even her own fear and shame, nor the horrendous amount of blood.

"What can you tell me about the man who shot your fiancé?"

"He was just an ordinary businessman. Suit, bowler hat, white shirt."

"His hair color?"

She shook her head. "I can't remember."

"Think of the scene. Search every detail. Did his hair show under his hat or not?"

She closed her eyes. "It showed. Kind of dirty blond."

"Good. Eye color? Take your time."

She closed her eyes and brought up the scene she had tried so hard to erase from her memory. "Hard. Beady. Blue, I think."

"How tall? Picture him with your fiancé. Was he taller, shorter?"

"Shorter, and Oliver wasn't a tall man."

"Build?"

They went through a number of details.

"Now can you think of anything odd, unusual? A scar. A limp. A birthmark, say on his face or hands. A ring."

"He had a ring. On his right hand."

"What did it look like?"

"A lion's head with emerald eyes."

"Very good. I think I have enough to find this man

and send him back to England to face his crime." The Mountie closed his notebook and stuffed it back in the breast pocket of his vest and stood. "I'll check back in a few days with news."

Jayne's eyes widened in surprise. The man certainly seemed to think he'd capture the murderer in no time. He didn't appear to entertain a shadow of doubt.

Eddie showed the Mountie to the door.

"I suppose he means he'll be back with good news." Her voice felt weak as if she'd spent all her energy and she certainly felt that way. "He sounds mighty sure of himself."

"The Mounties always get their man," Seth said with assurance.

A burst of nervous energy jolted her to her feet. "I have to get out of here." Avoiding Seth's outstretched arm, she raced for her room, grabbed the brocade bag where she carried her gun and headed for the door.

Seth blocked her path. "What are you doing?"

"I can't stand being cooped up. I'm going to practice shooting."

He crossed his arms and refused to let her pass. "It's not safe."

"I've got a gun."

"That doesn't insure safety."

"And isn't the Mountie out there looking for the man?"

He shook his head. "It's a big country."

Linette drew to her side. "I think you should listen to him."

She felt the others watching her and tossed her hands in a gesture of defeat. "You all expect me to stay inside forever?"

"Yes," they chorused.

Except Seth. "Only until the Mountie gets his man." He gave a slow, lazy grin that melted right through her annoyance and restlessness.

She sighed and gave in. "Very well. But I warn you. I expect to be entertained." She glanced around at the group. Mercy looked away. Sybil was suddenly very interested in washing a pot. Linette indicated the shrinking mound of beans.

"There's always canning to do."

Jayne brought her gaze back to Seth's. He looked amused as he leaned against the door frame.

"You," she said as she leaned close. "You will keep me company seeing as you insisted I stay indoors."

He shrugged but his eyes smiled, full of promise. "I can handle it."

Mercy chortled but when Jayne scowled at her, she only gave an unrepentant grin.

Jayne tried to remain upset but she couldn't and laughed. "I want you all to realize that you are so controlling."

"Yes," Seth said, taking her elbow and leading her to the table. "But it's for your own good." He sat across from her and helped finish the beans.

The last batch of jars went in the boiler midafternoon. Linette splashed cold water over her face and neck. "Do you mind watching the boiler while I have a little nap?"

"Of course not," Jayne said. "Take as long as you like."

"There's really nothing to do. It's three hours before it's done."

"Go." She gave her sister-in-law a little shove toward the stairs.

Mercy and Sybil had left an hour ago. Only Seth and Jayne remained. She gave him a long, considering look.

"What?" He seemed oblivious.

"This is where you're supposed to ask me what I'd like to do."

"Nope. I don't think so. You'll probably suggest things you shouldn't do."

"Like what?" She was curious what he thought she'd suggest.

"Like maybe going shooting. Or walking up the hill."

Her cheeks warmed as she remembered their previous walk up the hill. How she'd kissed him eagerly, only to have him apologize. Nope, she didn't care to repeat that. Though perhaps if they changed the ending...

"Shucks. You might even suggest a trip to town."

She tapped her finger on her chin. "All very good ideas. I suggest you keep them in mind. But I already agreed I would stay indoors until the Mountie catches the man—supposing he does."

His eyes followed the movement of her finger. She purposely drew it along her jawline and back to her chin to watch his eyes move along with her finger.

What was wrong with her? Her life was in mortal danger and she played silly games.

She jerked her hand to her waist and cleared her throat. "Actually, what I had in mind was a game of checkers."

"Sure." Did he sound relieved? Had he been entertaining thoughts similar to hers?

Not likely. She put her unusual response down to nervousness at the threat of the Englishman. Her thoughts settled. She pulled the checkers game from the cupboard and put the board on a side table in the front room. The spot allowed them both a view from the window. She knew he wouldn't be happy unless he could see out.

He scanned the scene beyond the glass as she set up the game pieces.

"Ladies first."

She moved. "Eddie and I played checkers and chess by the hour when we were younger." She sat back and mused. "So much has happened that it seems like a long time ago."

Her entire life had been slashed into two segments—life before Oliver's murder and life after.

Although there were enjoyable parts to the first half—like games with Eddie, tea parties with sisters Bess and Anne and certainly, the lessons under a good tutor—she would never return to who she was at that time.

Aware that Seth waited for her to take her turn at the game, she pulled her attention back to the here and now.

There might be present dangers that frightened her but she would never let them control her as she had when Oliver was shot.

Seth tapped the back of her hand. "What are you thinking?"

"About the past."

"All of it?" He sounded amazed.

"And the present," she added, bringing her gaze to him, silent and challenging. Did she want him to have a place in her present?

Only if he acknowledged her growing strength. Not that she minded him providing an extra pair of eyes while Oliver's murderer lurked about, but he had to understand that she wanted to prove she could take care of herself.

Chapter Fourteen

For two days Seth rode the perimeter of the ranch looking for evidence of the Englishman, dividing his time between that and keeping Jayne company, mostly doing his best to make sure she didn't leave the house.

The only exception was when she fed Thor, and he stuck to her side like a burr. Thor had quickly become a pet. He raced to the fence when they approached with a bottle. He welcomed the children to play with him. So far, they had restricted the fawn to the barn or his pen but soon he would need more space.

Letting him run about the ranch posed many risks, mostly predators. "You'll have to be responsible to see that he's shut up at night," he warned Jayne that afternoon as they discussed the fawn.

"Me?"

He hadn't meant to make it so plain that he wouldn't be here. But she already knew that.

A curtain fell behind her eyes. "I'll take care of him."

The same way he would take care of her.

The next day was Sunday and there'd be so many people coming and going. Eddie and Linette invited everyone in the county to visit and attend church. But the

Englishman would not be welcome nor would he likely show his face. Instead, he would lurk in the shadows, hoping for a careless moment.

Seth rubbed at the tightness in his neck.

Jayne didn't mean to be careless about exposing herself to someone who might have her in his sights several yards away, but she was so determined not to let fear rule her that she often stood in clear view from any number of spots around the ranch.

He knew she would never consent to remaining in the house for the day so the next morning he put on his best shirt—a buff-colored cotton with pearly buttons— and a clean pair of trousers. He glanced down his leg. He'd worn this pair of trousers when he was shot and he'd figured they would go in the trash, but Jayne had scrubbed them clean and mended them so neatly he could hardly tell they'd been ripped. She certainly knew how to use a needle and thread. But despite her fine job, his trousers were about worn out.

He badly needed to buy some new duds. His boots were in particularly bad shape since he'd pried off the heel. It had taken two hours the night before to get them polished up as good as he could. He studied them. They still looked like they belonged on the range, not at a church gathering. Good thing this was a ranch church where the men were cowboys.

The others left as he waited at the bottom of the stairs for Jayne.

She came down the hall. "I'm ready." She patted her head.

His eyes followed her hand. She'd scooped her shiny brown hair into some kind of curly thing at the back of her neck. Her skin glowed with summer color. A gray bonnet dangled from her hands. She wore a shiny dress in black and white stripes with a pretty collar that framed her face.

His mouth dried. She was a beautiful woman with a brave heart.

She smoothed the skirt of her dress. The fabric rustled with the touch. A very beautiful woman used to fine dresses, luxuries and servants. Used to being sheltered and protected.

The reminder burned through his thoughts.

Could he ever take care of her the way she deserved?

He knew the answer. Had known it from the beginning. No. He had a record of failure in protecting those close to him.

She should meet one of the rich land owners from the nearby ranches. Or a colonel from Fort Macleod. She deserved the very best in life.

He kept her close as they went to the cookhouse and once inside, sat between her and the windows.

She gave him a long, steady look, then shook her head as if to suggest he worried too much.

If they'd been alone, he would have said it wasn't possible, considering the danger out there. Instead, he gave a smile that didn't touch anything but his mouth and turned to the others.

Besides those who lived at the ranch, Ward, Grace and little Belle were in attendance. And two cowboys from the OK Ranch, Buck and Matt.

Bertie's talk was simple and straightforward.

"God loves us and listens to our prayers. He will never fail to fulfill His promises." Bertie went on to tell of times when God had shown His faithfulness.

Seth believed God loved him in a distant sort of way. After all, if God made him, He must feel some sort of responsibility for him. He just wasn't sure God cared enough to answer his pleas. His doubts had started at Frank's death and simply become a habit. He never gave them much thought. And didn't intend to start doing so now.

As was the custom, after the service the guests enjoyed coffee and cinnamon buns served by Cookie.

Eddie questioned Matt and Buck. "Have you seen any strangers around? Like an Englishman." He described the man.

Matt shook his head. "Ain't seen much but the back end of cows for three weeks."

"Me, too," Buck added. Then he snapped his fingers. "We did see a campfire over toward Dead Man's Coulee. Didn't think much of it. You know how people ride through and stop only to spend the night? Figured it was only that. You think it might have been this here man you're asking about?"

Eddie shrugged. "No way of telling but if you see this man, either apprehend him or come tell me or Constable Allen."

They agreed they would.

Linette rose. "You're welcome to join us for dinner," she said to the pair.

Buck ducked his head. Matt cleared his throat. "Thanks but we thought of riding into town."

Seth grinned.

Beside him, Cal chortled. "Someone new in town? Someone I should know about?"

Matt scowled so hard it should have been enough to dry Cal's mouth to a prune. But Cal only grinned wider.

"There are two young ladies who have come with their parents. But I warn you, they're already spoken for. Right, Buck?"

"That's right." The pair scrambled to their feet, murmured their thanks and beat a hasty retreat to the door with Cal's mocking laughter following them.

Buster looked as if he couldn't decide to be shocked or annoyed. He swallowed twice then got slowly to his feet. "Seem like real nice guys, they did. Those girls are fortunate to have the interest of such fine fellas."

Seth choked back a laugh at how the young man had said what all of them likely thought and done it in such an innocent way.

Buster seemed a fine fella, too.

Seth would see to getting that belt made soon.

As everyone made their way to Eddie's house, Matt and Buck waited on their horses and called to Seth.

He went to them.

"I almost forgot. Petey said I was to see you got this." Matt handed him a letter.

He stuffed it in his pocket and hurried after the others. Yes, Eddie watched out for Jayne but Seth had given himself the responsibility of assuring her safety, and he couldn't do that if he lollygagged behind.

The women went to the kitchen to finish the meal preparations.

Seth hovered close to the door, alert to any unusual sounds. From where he stood he could see part of the trail that led from town. He watched Matt and Buck ride out of sight. The dust they kicked up would provide a perfect cover for someone to ride close. He waited until their dust died down, his gaze alert to any sign of an intruder. When he saw nothing to alarm him, he leaned in the doorway and pulled out the letter.

The envelope was wrinkled, Seth's name and address blurred. The return address was Corncrib. From Crawford. The pages had gotten wet at some point and many of the words were too blurred to make out.

"Received the money. Just in time as I was preparing to leave. I've done all I can. Your father—" he couldn't read the next bit. He could decipher only a few more words "—plans to travel…"

He folded the smudged paper and put it in his pocket. Seems Crawford meant to leave whether or not Seth returned. He strode toward the open door and looked out. Was he already gone? Seems he must be. How long had Pa been alone? If Seth left immediately, would he get back in time or would Pa die alone and untended? His insides twisted and knotted. Words Pa had said after Frank's body was discovered burned through his brain. *You didn't take care of your brother. Suppose you mean to neglect your parents, as well.*

He'd tried burying the words, vowing to never let them rise again, and yet here they were, mocking him.

A cowboy crossed the yard and Seth jerked to attention. He meant to watch for anyone who meant to harm Jayne.

How could he leave her and go to his pa?

Yet how could he neglect his pa? Pa would be all alone. At least Jayne had Eddie, the ranch hands and all her friends. Not to mention the Mountie.

He turned to the stairs. He took three at a time but halfway up he stopped. Surely Crawford would have arranged for someone to check on Pa. Made sure he had food and water. He sighed. That made him sound like a pet.

But would a day or two make any difference to Pa except in Seth's mind? Was he letting cruel, thoughtless words spoken by his pa at a time of stress drive his decisions?

He stood on the stairs. What should he do? Be a responsible son or a caring friend who made sure Jayne was safe before he left?

Slowly he descended the stairs, his decision growing firmer with each step. He would never have any peace until he knew the murdering Englishman had been captured and Jayne was safe.

Then he'd ride hard and fast to Corncrib and take care of his pa.

He joined the others and listened to their chatter. He sat at the dinner table and enjoyed the feast, then afterward he joined in the visiting. He rose often and circled the room, looking out the window for any sign of danger. Eddie often checked the windows, too.

There were so many places the man could hide then slip closer without being seen. The yard was exposed from every side to any decent marksman.

Seth had forgotten how to pray. But he was beginning to think he might need to get back into practice, because only God could see everywhere at once.

Jayne did her best to appear unconcerned about the lurking Englishman but it was impossible to relax and forget it, even for a moment, with both Eddie and Seth prowling from window to window. Bedtime finally arrived, promising relief from the constant reminder until she realized Seth meant to sleep outside her door.

"I'm sure there's no need," she protested.

"How can you be sure? You can't. So Eddie and I have agreed you will be guarded day and night until that man is under lock and key."

She looked past Seth's shoulder to Eddie.

Eddie nodded. "It seems the safest."

She sighed, went into her room and closed the door. She and Mercy and Sybil had chosen to sleep in the small rooms down a short hallway off the kitchen rather than upstairs. Perhaps the latter would have been a better choice.

She lay in bed, acutely aware that Seth was on the other side of the door. She expected to stay awake, eyes wide, listening for any sound, but she fell asleep almost instantly.

She wakened the next morning with a smile on her lips. Remembering Seth guarded her door, her smile widened.

Not wanting to disturb him if he still slept, she tiptoed about getting dressed then cracked open the door.

"Good morning." He sat on a tipped-back chair facing her door. "Did you have a good sleep?"

"I did." She studied him closely. His cheeks were dark with a day's worth of whiskers and his eyes were red rimmed. "Were you awake all night?"

"Off and on."

"Aren't you being overly concerned?"

"Don't think so."

It was on the tip of her tongue to say she wasn't Frank or Sarah and wasn't about to do something foolish like run out into the open, waving her arms, but he yawned and she only wanted to tell him to relax and get some sleep.

"I'm going to feed Thor then help Linette with breakfast." It didn't surprise her when he followed her down the hall. Nor did she object when he pressed her to his side as they went to the barn. There were advantages to his concern.

Breakfast was over when the Mountie rode in.

"Good news," he said to the adults who waited for him in the kitchen. "I believe we have your man." He dug in his pocket and pulled out a ring that he showed to Jayne. "Do you recognize this?"

"Yes. It's the ring Oliver's murderer was wearing."

"You're absolutely certain?"

Jayne nodded. "Completely."

"Good. He'll go to Fort Macleod where the colonel will question him and arrange to have him sent back to England. Miss Gardiner, you may have to go there and give evidence, though the colonel might decide to accept your statement plus the evidence I'll provide."

"What do you have?" Eddie asked.

"In the man's belongings were the stub of his steamship ticket and the copy of a newspaper article concerning Oliver Spencer's death. Pretty conclusive evidence in my opinion, plus he fits Miss Gardiner's description."

Eddie clapped the Mountie on the back. "It's good to know he is no longer a threat to my sister."

Seth didn't add his thanks or gratitude. He simply shook the Mountie's hand. Jayne would now be safe. He could leave with a peaceful heart and go to Corncrib to fulfill his duty to his pa.

As soon as the Mountie departed, Jayne bounced to her feet. "I feel like I've been set free. Now I can go outside without an armed guard."

At least she didn't look at Seth when she uttered those words so he tried not to take them personally.

Jayne rushed toward the door. "I'm going to enjoy the sunshine. Who's coming with me?"

Mercy and Sybil hurried after her. Seth followed more slowly. He really should be on his way. He could get a good start on the journey. But first he had to make sure Thor could handle being out of his pen, as they'd agreed to do for the first time today.

Jayne headed straight for the fawn's enclosure and opened the gate. "I think it's time for this little guy to enjoy some freedom, too. Come on, Thor."

The fawn trotted over to her and followed her past the barn to the open area between the buildings. Billy and Grady raced over. Neil left the chores he'd been doing and came to watch.

Cassie opened the door of their house so she could see. Cookie came out and stood on the cookhouse steps.

As soon as Thor saw the younger boys he started to romp. Soon everyone took turns playing with the fawn. Seth stood back watching but Jayne would have none of it. She had the fawn follow her to Seth's side and darted back and forth behind him while Thor pranced about. Seth couldn't resist and swatted playfully at Thor who danced away and kicked up his heels.

Jayne laughed. "I had no idea a deer would be so playful." She eyed him up and down.

What did she want? What did she think? He didn't have to wait long to find out.

She tagged him. "You're it." She raced away. "Can't catch me." She lifted her skirts and ran for the cover of the trees by the river.

At first he didn't move, overcome with surprise at this playfulness. Then he growled and ran after her. The others had moved down the road, still playing with Thor, and didn't notice the game Jayne had started.

She darted from tree to tree, making it impossible to catch her.

He changed tactics and rather than chase her, started to stalk her. He hid behind some bushes.

She stopped to listen.

He could hear her breathing and silently moved toward the sound.

"Seth?" She moved into the open to look for him.

He crouched low and used the underbrush for cover as he narrowed the distance between them.

"Are you hiding?" she called.

He waited, holding his breath.

She darted to another tree, bringing her so close he could reach out and touch her. But he waited, biding his time.

As she turned her back to look for him, he took the step that put him right behind her. "Hi, Jayne."

She screamed and spun about.

He caught her arms to keep her from losing her balance.

"Where did you come from?"

"I haven't forgotten how to play." She didn't need to know it had been years.

"So it seems." Her eyes flooded with joy. "Isn't it good to know that man is captured?"

"Relieves my mind greatly." He moved his hands up her arms to her shoulders.

"Mine, too." She scrubbed her lips together. "I owe you thanks for guarding me."

He slipped his hands to her back and pulled her closer. Either she didn't notice or didn't mind because she came readily enough. "Seems you might have resented it a time or two."

She lowered her eyes. "I realized it was necessary but that doesn't mean I had to like it."

She lifted her head and met his gaze. Time waited as they looked deeply into each other's eyes. Behind him the river gurgled by, the sound erasing doubts and cautions and even fears from his mind. All that counted was this moment and the warmth in her eyes.

"I'm glad no harm came to you." Was that husky voice his?

She nodded. Her gaze dropped to his mouth and slowly returned to his eyes.

Slowly, savoring every bit of anticipation, he lowered his head and captured her lips. Sweet as honey. Welcoming as home.

Her hands pressed on his back, holding him, accepting his kiss.

His heart swelled to near bursting.

Pa's voice echoed through his head. He didn't hear the words. Didn't need to. Didn't want to. Only knew he must answer the call of duty.

He ended the kiss but did not release her from his arms. She fit perfectly as if she had been made for him.

The thought scattered through his brain. Made for him? God made her. Did He mean for Seth to enjoy her presence?

Again Pa's voice called, harsh, demanding.

Seth still did not let her go. The river murmured softly and he remembered a promise to take Jayne and her friends up the mountains. "Do you and the others still want to see a mountain lake?" He didn't even know if there was one nearby but Eddie would.

"I'd love to."

"Then let's plan an outing tomorrow."

After that he would obey his pa's call. But he wouldn't tell her he meant to leave until they enjoyed tomorrow.

They returned to the yard.

Mercy saw them and gave Jayne a startled look.

He glanced in Jayne's direction. No wonder Mercy

looked surprised. Jayne had the look of a woman who had been kissed and enjoyed it.

Telling her he meant to leave was not going to be easy.

Chapter Fifteen

The next morning, Jayne jumped from bed and pulled on her clothes. She decided to wear the same outfit she'd worn the day she shot Seth. It amused her to think her accident had brought him into her life. She brushed her hair, braided it and left the braid hanging down her back. She studied her reflection in the looking glass. Satisfied, she hugged herself. Laughter bubbled up unbidden. She spun around her room, thankful neither Mercy nor Sybil had come in.

Seth had kissed her and held her. Then invited them to accompany him to a mountain lake. A special outing for a special reason? She would make certain she and Seth had time together alone. Perhaps she should warn her friends of her plan.

But when she entered the kitchen they had already gone down the hill to join Seth, who was hitching the wagon.

She joined them.

Sybil and Mercy sat on blankets in the back of the wagon and Jayne perched beside Seth on the seat. "I'll keep you company."

The sun shone in a clear blue sky. It would grow hot

before the day was over but the ladies all wore bonnets so they wouldn't get burned. Besides, not heat, nor cold, nor rain or sleet or snow could mar the beauty of this day. But sunshine was the best.

God, please give us a good day full of laughter and love. Her heart flowed with sweetness. Today would be special.

"Eddie suggested we see a waterfall," Seth said as they left the ranch buildings behind them. "He said it was worth the drive."

"Sounds good to me," she said. The trail led across a grass-covered hill. She leaned forward. "It's beautiful country. I love the way the hills roll away in waves of green. And the mountains fold back in blue layers."

"It's fine country."

"I told you this before but I never see the mountains without thinking of how great God is. Powerful, strong, caring. 'In the beginning God created the heavens and the earth.' I've never been more aware of it than I am here."

He nodded. "Seems He is pretty powerful all right."

She slowly brought her head around to study him, her eyes wide with surprise. "You sound different."

"Do I?"

She looked toward the pair behind them. So did he. The girls strained forward to hear what he and Jayne said. This was not the time to speak of personal things.

He pointed to a tall pine tree. "A bald eagle's nest. Do you see the male bird?" A white-headed eagle circled slowly then descended to the nest. "He's brought food for the eaglets."

Mercy and Sybil pressed forward and they all strained to see the eagle.

He stopped the wagon so they could have a better

look but Jayne felt his gaze on her. She turned, not caring about bald eagles, and let her eyes say what her heart felt, let him see that she would welcome anything he said.

"I wish we could get closer," Mercy said.

"We don't want to disturb them," Sybil replied.

"It's impossible to get close in a wagon," Seth told them. "They are magnificent up close, though. So big. So strong."

"Everywhere I look I see evidence of God's majesty and power." Jayne gave him a warm smile. Was he ready to acknowledge God was not only powerful but cared about each of them in a personal way? Ready to acknowledge a faith they could share?

He didn't say anything. Simply smiled.

The smile melted a path to her heart. She could barely keep from hugging herself, hugging him, hugging the world.

He turned his attention to the trail as it climbed a steep hill.

Mercy and Sybil remained kneeling behind them making impossible anything but general conversation.

Jayne didn't mind. This day overflowed with promise and possibility. She meant to enjoy every minute of it.

"The air is sweeter here," Sybil said.

Seth sniffed. "It's the pine trees and mountain air."

Mercy sighed. "It's adventure beckoning. I keep saying we need to go on a camping trip."

Seth jerked about to look at Mercy. "On your own? That would be dangerous. Three young ladies on their own in the woods? Three citified ladies? There are wolves, bears, mountain lions…hundreds of different threats you aren't experienced enough to deal with."

All three of them laughed.

Jayne sobered to explain their amusement. "Mercy figures it would take two cowboys each to keep us safe and—" She sought for a word.

"Entertained." Sybil's word carried a good dose of resignation.

Seth laughed. "That's a lot of cowboys. You think Eddie would spare them?"

"No," Mercy said. "I'm just teasing, anyway."

Jayne settled back with a bubble of happiness in her heart. She'd never seen a finer day.

The trail grew more rugged, required more of Seth's attention. They climbed, went past huge rocks, and sheer cliffs rose to their right and fell away to their left. The path eventually narrowed to the width of the wagon and everyone grew silent. Jayne wondered if they all held their breath like she did. Would it merely end ahead? How would they turn around?

They rounded a corner and Jayne gasped as they entered a verdant clearing. Before them water rushed downward in a horsetail of white spray where it gurgled into the river below.

"This is as far as we go," Seth announced and climbed to the ground. Mercy and Sybil scrambled down before he could offer any of them help but Jayne waited for him to reach up and assist her.

She liked the firmness of his hand on hers, the warmth of his fingers at her waist.

Mercy and Sybil skipped away toward the waterfall but Jayne remained at Seth's side as they walked at a slower pace. The roar of the water made conversation impossible.

Mist sprayed from the falls and Jayne pushed her bonnet off, lifted her face to the moisture and laughed.

She turned to Seth, saw the wonder on his face and hugged the thought to her.

They poked about the water's edge for a bit, examining the rocks and admiring the tiny flowers. One rock was dark and shiny and somewhat heart shaped. Surely a sign that Seth meant to offer her his heart. She tucked the rock into her pocket.

After a bit they sat on a damp boulder and simply took pleasure in the surroundings.

Mercy and Sybil clambered over the rocks to rejoin them.

"We're hungry," Mercy yelled. "Let's eat." She grabbed Jayne's arm and dragged her and Sybil toward the wagon.

Jayne glanced over her shoulder and called at Seth to hurry, even though she knew he couldn't hear her.

They spread out the quilts, put out the food they'd brought from the ranch and sat down. Seth sat beside Jayne, his legs crossed so his knees jutted out, touching hers.

She turned to him. "Would you ask the blessing?" As soon as she spoke, she wondered if he would feel awkward.

But he gave a casual shrug. "Sure." He bowed his head. "Heavenly Father, thank You for the beautiful scenery, which reminds us of Your power. Thank You for friends to share the day with and for the food. Amen."

Jayne squeezed his hand. "That was lovely. Thank you." She broke off the touch before her friends could comment.

The conversation as they ate was lively and full of laughter.

They barely swallowed the last bite before Mercy

jumped to her feet. "I want to explore more." She stuffed the remains of their lunch into the box. "Let's go."

Sybil rose with a long-suffering sigh but Jayne remained seated at Seth's side. "I'll stay here if you don't mind." She hoped Seth would recognize the opportunity for them to be alone.

Mercy opened her mouth to speak but Sybil jabbed her in the ribs, cutting her off.

"Come on, Mercy. Let's go."

The pair sauntered away.

"Don't go too far," Seth called. "I wouldn't want you to get lost. And watch for bears."

Sybil's steps slowed at his warning but Mercy dragged her on.

Jayne folded the quilts and stowed them in the wagon box.

Seth followed, and leaned his back against the wagon. "You sure you don't want to join them?. We could catch up still."

"No, I'm enjoying the view from here." And she didn't mean just the waterfall, though it was magnificent. Seth was a handsome man with his dark hair and hazel eyes. He had a good jawline and eyes that seemed made for smiling.

He met her gaze. His eyes flashed as he looked deep into hers, probing secret places. He bent his head.

She lowered her eyelids, silently inviting the kiss she knew he offered.

His lips touched hers. Firm, cool, tentative.

She tipped her face upward, wanting more…more of his kiss, more of him. Her arms stole around his waist. Her hands pressed to his back. Her fingers curled into the fabric of his shirt as a thousand butterflies seemed to take flight inside her and fill her heart, her mind, her every thought.

She'd been kissed before. After all, she'd been engaged to what's-his-name. But his kisses had never caused this soul-searing sensation. As if joy had become a verb and danced in her being.

He broke off the kiss and leaned back to study her. "I'm sorry. I shouldn't have done that."

Sorry? That he'd kissed her? Did it mean nothing to him, while her world spun with happiness? She shifted back, tipping her head and seeking his face for an explanation.

"I have to check on my pa. Make sure he has everything he needs."

Did his eyes say he wasn't anxious to do so? Perhaps because he wanted to spend more time with her?

"Of course. I understand your concern."

"I'll be leaving tomorrow."

Her heart dropped to the bottom of her stomach. Surely he meant to tell her he'd be back, ask her to wait.

She held her breath until her head thundered. But he didn't say the words she hoped for.

"I've delayed far too long. My pa might be in serious condition by now." He patted his breast pocket. "I had a letter from Crawford saying he left. He didn't say if he'd arranged for someone else to care for Pa. I hope he did but Pa is my responsibility and—" He gave her a look so full of resolve that she fell back a step. "I will never shirk my responsibilities."

He moved aside, putting more distance between them.

Not one word of hope. No suggestion that he meant to come back. Or that he wanted her to wait for him. His silence said it all. This was goodbye. He didn't intend to return. "You brought me here to tell me this? Why? You could have told me at the ranch." Where she would have the option to run to her room and bury her head in her pillow.

"No, I brought you here because I promised you and your friends I would take you to a mountain lake. I wanted to do it before I left."

If she'd had a sliver of hope left that he didn't mean this to be forever, he killed it. He did not intend to return.

"Jayne." He reached for her but she moved away. "I didn't mean to hurt you. I thought you understood that I wasn't staying."

"Of course I did." She forced false cheer into her voice. "You stayed longer than you intended simply to teach me to shoot. I'm grateful. I pray you will find your father well." She lifted her skirts and hurried to the path Sybil and Mercy had taken.

How could she have misjudged him so badly? Did he feel nothing when they kissed?

She met up with Sybil and Mercy returning down the path.

Sybil took one look at her and asked, "What's happened? You look like you've had terrible news."

She tried to smile but tears were too close to the surface. "Seth is leaving tomorrow."

"He'll be back." Mercy was quite certain.

"No. He's going to take care of his invalid father. I understand his concern and his sense of responsibility." She hoped her tone conveyed that it mattered not to her that he didn't intend to return.

But the way both her friends hugged her, she knew they weren't convinced. Her leaden feet followed them down the hill.

They jumped into the back of the wagon. She climbed up and sat between them, keeping her back to Seth.

If she looked at him she might forget her pride and demand to know how he could kiss her like that and walk away as if it hadn't happened. She'd gladly fall on her knees and beg him to stay if she thought it would change his mind.

But nothing would shift Seth from his guilt-driven responsibility.

Chapter Sixteen

The next morning, she prepared a bottle for Thor.

Seth stepped into the kitchen behind her. "I'll help."

She kept her back to him. "I told Grady he could feed Thor. It doesn't require both of us to help him." From now on she'd do it without his help. Might as well start now.

He thankfully accepted her excuse and let her go.

Despite the searing pain in her heart, she laughed at the way Thor bounced with excitement at seeing Grady. It took the fawn a moment to realize his playmate meant to feed him.

Grady laughed. "I think Thor is better than having a dog. Don't you?"

"He's sweet." She'd never see the fawn without being reminded of many precious hours spent in Seth's company. Her hand pressed to her chest as she tried in vain to stop the pain that threatened to burst her heart.

"Can I take him outside to play with?" Grady asked.

"Maybe after breakfast. Just be sure you have permission from an adult who is prepared to supervise. We wouldn't want Thor getting lost. In the meantime, he'll be safe in his pen." The one Seth had built. Everywhere she turned there were reminders of how impossible it was to push him from her thoughts.

Even without reminders she'd never forget him.

Thanks to Mercy and Sybil's understanding, Jayne wasn't forced to sit at Seth's side throughout breakfast.

"I'll be leaving today," Seth announced.

"You're welcome to stay," Eddie said. "I could use another man with the roundup approaching."

"I have to see to my pa."

Sybil sat at Jayne's side and reached out to squeeze her hand under cover of the table.

Jayne felt Linette's concerned look but studied her empty plate.

"Your hospitality has been most generous. Thank you," Seth continued, his words flat. Was he regretting his decision?

She stole a glance at him under protection of her eyelashes. He didn't look in her direction, but the set of his jaw allowed her no hope for a change of mind.

"I'll be on my way directly." He pushed to his feet. "It's been a pleasure. Again, thank you."

Jayne merely stared at a spot in the middle of the table as everyone offered goodbye wishes. When Eddie and Linette accompanied him to the door, she fled to her bedroom. She would not watch him ride away. She would not wave, nor call an agonized goodbye for fear it would turn into a plea to stay. Or at least a promise to return.

Instead, she sat on the edge of her bed, her hands pressed between her knees and whispered, "Goodbye, Seth. May God bless you." Her heart bled empty.

She heard chairs scuff across the floor in the kitchen, dishes rattle in the dishpan, cupboards open and close. Muted voices informed her the other women worked in the kitchen. The outer door slammed. Was it Eddie leaving? Or was it Grady?

She sighed. She couldn't hide here forever but she didn't move, either, not wanting to face the pitying looks from her friends. Nor have her situation discussed.

Her brocade bag, the one she carried her gun in, sat on a shelf in the wardrobe. She took it and left the room.

"I'm going to practice shooting," she announced. "Unless you need my help with anything." She addressed Linette.

"No, there are lots of people around to help with anything that needs doing."

"I'll be back later." She slipped out the back door before either Mercy or Sybil could voice an opinion. With heavy feet and a lifeless heart she made her way to the spot where the target waited.

She plopped her bag on the fallen log. It landed with a satisfying thud and she sat down beside it and stared at the ground in front of her feet.

She'd wanted to be independent. She'd achieved that. Strong. Self-sufficient. And alone. Even Smokey didn't follow her, preferring to stay and play with Thor.

Not that she was entirely alone. She had Mercy and Sybil, and Eddie and Linette and a dozen others around the ranch.

But with Seth gone, her heart echoed with emptiness.

A rustle in the underbrush jerked her attention to the side. Had Smokey decided to join her after all?

She squinted into the shadows but Smokey did not appear.

A dull sound came from behind her, making the hair on the back of her neck stand up. Someone was there. She edged her hand toward the bag and her gun.

"I'll take that out of harm's way."

At the gruff words, Jayne squealed and sprang to her feet. She stared at a man who was supposedly in jail. "You."

The beady blue eyes narrowed and Jayne realized too late that she shouldn't have let him know she recognized him.

"So you do remember me." He smirked.

"The Mountie said you were in jail."

He laughed, a mocking sound. "I was never in jail."

"But—" She wouldn't give him the satisfaction of asking who was in jail.

Seems he didn't need her to ask. "I fooled that policeman good, didn't I? All I had to do was find someone who looked a lot like me, persuade him he wanted my clothes. Sell him my ring and leave a few things in the pocket of my coat." He let loose another burst of ugly laughter.

She edged backward toward the trees as he talked, but he came forward, stepping over the log. "You aren't going anywhere, little lady."

She turned and ran, made two steps toward safety before his hard grasp on her arm jerked her around to face him.

"You know what I want."

She wasn't going to let him kill her and fought to escape his grip.

He grabbed both her arms and shook her hard. "My key. Where is my key?"

"I have no idea what you mean." He shook her so hard her teeth rattled.

"That's what Oliver said but I saw you with it before I had to run from the coppers. Didn't see it when I'd seen you later."

"You are mistaken." He'd followed her and spied on her? She felt dirty all over.

He grabbed at her throat.

She squeaked. Did he mean to choke her?

He yanked at the neck of her dress and pulled so hard she fell forward. Her dress gave way and she clutched at her throat to protect her modesty.

He pushed her head back to study her throat. "Where is it?"

"I don't know what you mean," she gasped.

His fingers bit into the flesh of her upper arm. "You can stop playing Miss Innocent," he snarled.

"But I honestly don't know." The anger in his eyes made her legs weak. She fought dizziness and tried to squirm free. As his fingers dug deeper she bit back a cry.

"I know you brought it with you. You wouldn't be fool enough to leave it behind."

She sucked in air and released it in a scream that she hoped carried to the ranch. *Please, God, let someone hear me.*

He slapped her face. "Stop that."

She took a deep breath.

Seeing she meant to scream again, he swung her about, pressing her back to his chest, and clamped his sticky palm over her mouth. His clothing smelled of old sweat. Her eyes watered and she clawed to escape his hold.

"You aren't going anywhere until you tell me where that key is."

She fought to free herself.

"Stop it or I'll have to get tough."

She would fight as long as she had strength. With a flash of insight, she realized fighting might be the wrong tactic and she made her body go limp.

"Now that's more like it." He bent to scoop her into his arms.

As soon as his hand released her, she flew from his arms. Her skirt caught her legs. She yanked it out of the way and continued her headlong flight.

The man uttered a curse.

His feet pounded after her.

Please, God. Help me.

He caught her, swept her off her feet. "You little witch. Get it through your silly head. You are not going anywhere until you tell me where that key is." He dragged her at his side like a sack of rotten potatoes.

She skidded to keep her feet under her.

He made it sound like he would release her if she could produce a key but she very much doubted he would.

They reached a dark, narrow break in the trees where a cold campfire suggested he had spent time here. A shadow moved. Had someone come to rescue her? But it was only his horse tethered out of sight.

He pushed her back against a tree, forced her to sit, and tied her hands and legs. His touch, far too intimate, made her skin crawl.

The look she gave him should have blistered his skin but he returned it with a leering grin.

"So what will it take to convince you to tell me where the key is?" He trailed his smelly finger along her cheek.

She shuddered. She only had to delay him. Eddie would discover her absence when she didn't show up for dinner.

Or would they think she wanted to be left alone?

Seth, why did you have to leave when I really and truly need you?

* * *

Seth had stayed up late last night making a belt for Buster. He'd given it to Eddie this morning. "A thank-you for Buster for taking care of my horse."

Eddie had examined it. "Nice tooling. You do this?"

"My pa taught me." Pa had given both his sons leatherworking tools on their twelfth birthday. Frank had never cared much for the work but Seth had become quite good at decorating leather pieces. Though Pa had never said so. Only those who bought the items had told him.

Seth had stayed long enough to eat a hearty breakfast, knowing it would be the last decent meal he got until he reached Corncrib. At the main road, he'd turned south, leaned over his horse and raced down the road.

He'd delayed his return far too long.

Pa would have every right to think he neglected him.

Only the truth was, he never had and never would. For a few days he'd taken care of a different responsibility. That was all. Pa had no reason to worry. Or condemn.

Why, even when Pa made unreasonable demands on Seth, he hadn't balked. Like the time he'd insisted they needed one more load of wood even though it was almost dark, cold and threatening to snow.

"It will snow before morning," Pa had warned. "Then it will be even harder to get the wood out. You want Ma and me to freeze to death this winter?"

Of course Seth didn't so he'd gone out in the deepening darkness, stumbling over roots he couldn't see. The horse tangled the rigging on a stump and it had taken Seth several hours to get everything sorted out and the wagon loaded. Snow began to fall long before he finished. By the time he got home he was soaked to the skin and so cold the marrow of his bones ached. But he still had to unload the wood, stack it in the shed and take care of the horse.

All Pa had said was, "You got it done? Good."

Not for the first time, he'd wondered if Pa wished Seth had died instead of Frank.

Seth would have gladly given his life for Frank's but he'd been unable to stop Frank from rushing onto the thin ice.

Pa had said so many hurtful things. Expected the impossible from Seth. Seth understood it was because Pa held him responsible for Frank's death.

So many instances came to mind as Seth rode away from Eden Valley Ranch and Jayne.

As he thought of never seeing Jayne again a groan ripped from the bottom of his insides, like a flash flood tearing up worries and concerns and memories by their roots, swirling them into a quagmire. He hunkered over the saddle horn as if he could block the pain.

Jayne had shared her worries and fears as if she thought he could help her keep them at bay. She had given him sweet kisses.

His fists tightened into knots at how empty his arms were. How barren his future. He longed to hold her next to his heart forever.

But he wasn't worthy.

He reined up and stared at the rocks next to the path.

Why did he think that? It wasn't as if he couldn't provide for a woman. He could work for Eddie. Or start his own ranch.

It wasn't as if he couldn't protect her. He'd shown that. Although, he hadn't really, had he? The Mountie had captured the man without incident. All Seth did was hang around for the sake of his conscience.

But he would have protected her if the need had arisen.

But somehow everything he'd done, or would have done, wasn't enough.

He continued to stare at the lifeless rock, hoping the answer would somehow appear.

For whom wasn't it enough?

Pa saw Frank and Sarah's accident as proof that Seth could never handle responsibility. He'd expected a lot from Seth and Seth always delivered. But he knew full well Pa was disappointed in him.

"You could never take care of a wife. It'd end up the same way it did with Frank."

Recalling Pa's words shook him to the core.

He'd heard the words enough times, though he couldn't say if it had been a hundred, a dozen…or only twice. But they were branded into his thoughts.

He believed them so firmly that he'd secretly vowed he would never take a wife.

But were the words true?

He shifted about, brought his gaze to the trees a few feet away. His throat tightened as he considered what being a husband involved.

There were certainly risks. Illness. Accidents. Wild animals. Childbirth.

Some he could guard against. Others, he would be helpless to do anything about.

Were his pa's words true?

Was his fear of commitment valid?

Was it possible to fulfill his duty to his pa and also be a husband?

And—the biggest question of all—did he dare risk having his heart ripped apart should any of those disasters befall?

What had Bertie said about God having His eye on the sparrows?

Any one of us is worth a whole lot more than a sparrow.

Worth more than a sparrow? Why he hardly gave them a thought.

Wasn't it Roper who looked at his children and said that God saw fit to bring them into their lives so he could surely trust God with their future, their health, their happiness?

Was it possible to trust a God he couldn't see? A God who didn't do things the way Seth thought they should be done?

Or was he simply finding a way to ease his way out of responsibilities that forced him to make a hard, unwelcome choice?

Was he looking for a way to backtrack? To settle into the groove he had dug himself into?

Pa or Jayne. Where did his heart belong?

He jumped off his horse and led him to the trees where he paced from the trail and back again, considering what he should do.

Go to Pa and care for him as was his duty.

Return to Jayne and follow the inclination of his heart.

Or do both…and perhaps fail both parties?

Finally, desperate for an answer, he fell to his knees by a tree. "God, if You care about a little worthless sparrow then I figure You care for me, a worthless man. Show me how to do what is right. Pa or Jayne. Or can I have them both?"

He surely didn't expect a bolt of lightning from the sky pointing the right direction any more than he expected an audible voice.

But he heard a bird nearby and located a nest of little ones. Only they weren't so little anymore. They were fully feathered and flew back and forth freely. Yet they continued to return to the nest where they'd been hatched.

Free to fly. Yet bound to their beginnings.

He had his answer. And he swung to the back of his horse and turned back toward the ranch.

He couldn't wait to tell Jayne his decision.

Chapter Seventeen

Jayne's arms hurt from being tied behind her. The ropes around her wrists bit into her flesh. Struggling in a vain attempt to free herself had rubbed her wrists raw. But her captor before her offered no relief. The dark pines pressed close on all sides, filling the narrow clearing with ominous shadows.

Fear clawed at her throat. Made it impossible to fill her lungs. *Be calm. Be brave.*

She swallowed hard. Maybe if she could divert him in some way...

"What's your name?" she asked.

"Why you want to know?" The man sat across the small clearing, a space of about eight feet, alternately scowling at her then chewing viciously on his fingernails.

"No matter. Just being polite." But she'd like to be able to tell his relatives—if he had any—when she shot him through the heart.

Her anger lasted but a second. He kept her brocade bag pressed to his side. She'd have to have wings to get it.

"Guess it don't matter if you know. I'm only keeping you 'till you come to your senses and tell me where the key is."

"Believe me, I'd tell you if I knew."

"Guess I don't believe you." He spit out a bit of fingernail. "Name's Harry Simms."

She didn't know whether to gag at the way he gnawed his fingers or laugh at such an innocuous name for a murderer. Instead, she fixed him with a look that stung her eyes. "Wish I could say it was a pleasure."

He gave a mirthless sound that she supposed was the closest he could come to a laugh. "I'll let you go anytime you agree to show me where the key is." He opened a can of beans. "You hungry?"

"No, thanks."

He scooped the beans out with his knife and ate them directly from the can.

She checked the position of the sun. Directly overhead. Wouldn't Eddie wonder why she hadn't returned for dinner? *Please show him where I am*, she prayed silently.

Harry cleaned out the can and tossed it into the woods. He lounged back, picking his teeth with a thin wooden toothpick. "I can wait all day. Can you?" He pulled his hat over his eyes. In a few minutes, he snored.

Jayne tugged at the ropes binding her. Harry might be a despicable man but he knew how to tie her so tight she couldn't get loose.

She considered her options. Enough time had passed she decided Eddie wasn't looking for her. At least he wasn't finding her.

What would happen if she told Harry she knew where the key was? She played through several scenarios. She could take him back to the ranch, and hope

Eddie or one of the other cowboys could stop him. Or lead him to the barn. Or take him... Where?

Every possibility ended with her having nothing to show him and by leading him to the ranch, possibly putting others in harm's way.

No. She must find a way to trick him out here where no one would get hurt but herself.

She prayed desperately for God to give her a really good idea. But nothing came to mind. She shuddered to think what would happen to her.

But no matter, she would not reveal her fear.

Nor would she let it control her.

God help me.

She could count on no other help but His.

Seth rode up to the ranch house. Had he arrived in time for dinner? Not that food interested him half as much as the certainty of seeing Jayne at the table.

He went to the back door to knock. Eddie opened it before his knuckles met the wood.

"Seth? Where did you come from?" Eddie glanced past him. "Is Jayne with you?"

"Me? Why would she be with me? I left earlier today. Alone. You know that." He pushed Eddie aside to glance into the kitchen. "Where's Jayne?" Everyone else sat around the table. Mercy's and Sybil's expressions were strained as if the skin on their faces had grown too tight. Linette pulled Grady to her lap and murmured comfort to the boy, although her eyes darkened and she looked worried.

Seth stepped into the room. "Where is she?"

They looked from one to the other.

Mercy answered. "She left right after you did. Said she was going shooting. But she hasn't come back."

Sybil rubbed a hand across her eyes. "We all assumed she just wanted to be left alone, but shouldn't she have come home for dinner?"

"Well, if that's all, I'll go get her." He dashed out the door and trotted up the hill. It would be easier to talk to her in the clearing where they had spent so many hours together. As he headed for the spot, he rehearsed what he would say. "I've come back for you." Hmm. That sounded a bit blunt. "I hope you care enough to—" Still not right. Surely the words would come when he saw her. Or maybe he'd say what he felt with a kiss.

"Jayne." She'd likely wonder why he'd come back and why he sounded so eager. "Jayne." He stepped into the clearing. The target was there, along with the log on which they'd sat to visit, and a few casings of spent shells. But not Jayne.

"Huh?" He turned full circle. Peered into the trees. "Jayne?" Had she heard him coming and been too angry to talk to him? "Jayne, come on. I came back to tell you that I care. I don't want to leave and never see you again." That should bring her out of hiding.

He held his breath and listened for the sound of her approach. The wind rustled leaves overhead. A pinecone rattled to the ground. A magpie squawked and scolded. Other birds chattered as they went about their business.

His breath whooshed out. "Jayne, are you hiding? Stop it. You're worrying me."

He waited but heard nothing except the sounds of nature. This was past being funny. She should make her presence known. He stepped into the trees and searched the nearby bushes. Where was she and why was she doing this?

No longer did he smile. No longer did he burst with

anticipation of telling her what he felt. Instead, he pressed his lips together tightly. When she finally decided to make herself known, he meant to tell her how foolish this game was.

He returned to the clearing and plunked down on the log. Maybe she'd slipped away while he beat the bushes and returned to the ranch.

With a deep sigh, he dropped his hands between his knees.

This was not at all how he'd pictured his return. He scuffed his heels back and forth. Maybe this was a sign from God that he should continue with his original plan and head for Corncrib.

Might as well go back to the ranch. Let her gloat that she'd fooled him.

A bit of pale wood caught his eye. He picked it from the ground.

A toothpick. A fancy, city-man toothpick. How could it be? Had the Englishman been here days before and dropped it? He ran his finger along its length. The tip was wet. It had been dropped recently. How was that possible? The Mountie had arrested the man.

Had he escaped?

Hot blood boiled from his heart. Had the murderer returned and found Jayne unguarded?

He slapped his forehead. Thrashing through the bushes looking for Jayne would certainly have warned the escapee of Seth's presence and could well have destroyed any trail.

He considered his options. Go back and inform Eddie or go after Jayne? The former would waste precious time but Eddie deserved to know.

He ran to the house as fast as his bowlegs allowed. Thankfully Eddie stood outside the door. Whether he meant to get back to work or waited for news of his sister made no difference to Seth. "I found this." He thrust the toothpick at Eddie. "It's like the one I found where the man had been watching Jayne the other day. He must have escaped. He must have taken her. I'm going to find her." The words came out in a rush.

Eddie slapped him on the back. "I'll get some cowboys together and we'll scour the country. We'll find her. We'll let you take that direction. We'll go there and there." He pointed then ducked into the house.

As Seth swung to the back of his horse he heard Eddie tell the women to pray. Then he turned his mind to what he would do and galloped back to the clearing. He tied the horse at the edge, pulled his pistol from his saddlebag and checked to make sure it was loaded before he tucked it into his waistband.

He searched every blade of grass, every leaf for a hint of the trail. "God, give me eyes to see, ears to hear and a way to protect her.

"Thank You," he murmured when he found the footprint of a man's boot in the soft ground. The imprint was different than the one he'd seen overlooking the ranch but it was possible the man had more than one set of footwear. He followed the direction it pointed, his eyes glued to the ground for another track. He reached a thin strip of grass without finding another track and straightened. His body ached and not from the position he'd held as he crept across the ground. Worry and failure clamored at his bones. There had to be a clue. Where would the man have taken her? He could not afford to waste time searching in the wrong direction. His ribs clamped down so hard it hurt to suck in air. The man had already committed a murder. Another would make little difference to him.

"Oh, God. Protect her." The whispered words ripped from his throat.

He forced himself to take in a slow breath and released it just as slowly. Where would the man go? Where would Seth go if he wanted to kidnap a young woman?

Mentally, he reviewed the surrounding area he had grown familiar with as he guarded Jayne. In a tiny clearing he remembered a circle of rocks that had indicated someone had once built a campfire there. The grass had been undisturbed when he'd found it so it hadn't been used recently. But perhaps someone else had discovered it and now used the spot.

He studied his surroundings to get his bearings. The place would be a ten-minute hike to his left, through some thick bushes. He would have to go slowly in order not to alert the Englishman. And he prayed this was the correct direction.

Parting the branches of the trees carefully, searching for a spongy area to place his foot, he started toward the spot.

He had stopped praying after Frank's death, but had started again since his arrival at the ranch. Now he prayed with urgency. He'd do his best to rescue Jayne and believe God would help.

If she was still alive.

He grabbed the nearest tree and leaned against the rough trunk as the words screamed through his head. Would he fail yet again to protect those he cared about?

Jayne, I love you. Please be safe.

Strength returned to his limbs. He stilled the urgency pressing at him to hurry, and made his careful, silent way toward the spot.

If she wasn't there...

He would not think of it.

But should it be true, he'd search to the ends of the earth until he found her.

He must be getting close and stopped to strain for any sound that would let him know if people were at the clearing. A rustle. A snuffling like a horse chewing grass. Satisfied that someone lay ahead he took a moment to plan his next move.

Harry jerked awake and glowered at Jayne. "I'm tired of this game." He lurched to his feet.

Jayne shrank back, her heart tightening. What would he do to her? She pushed her fear aside. Do something to distract him, she told herself. Think. What could she do? "What's so important about this key?" He had murdered for it. And likely would not hesitate to do so again.

Her mouth dried so much her tongue stuck to the roof of her mouth.

He gave a mirthless laugh. "Don't play games with me."

"It's no game. I don't know."

He sank back on his haunches and studied her.

She met his eyes and hoped she revealed none of her fear or loathing, only curious innocence.

"Huh. Guess Oliver was too smart to tell you."

"Tell me what?" She didn't have to pretend because she had no idea what he talked about.

He snorted. "Your friend was a cardsharp. A cheat. Did you know that?"

She shook her head. She knew Oliver had gambled. He'd made no secret of it. He often commented on how fortunate he'd been and said he'd won big. But would he cheat? At one time she would have instantly defended him but now she wondered. Had she really known anything about Oliver? He'd never talked about fears, hopes, or even his childhood, apart from the places he'd lived. Likewise, she had never confessed her doubts and fears to him.

Not like she had with Seth.

Oh, Seth. Why did you leave? We had something together.

Had the feeling only been on her side?

Harry shifted and spat and she spoke, desperate to keep him talking. So long as he talked, perhaps he wouldn't act. "I guess I didn't know him as well as I thought."

Harry grunted. "He fooled you, too, huh?"

She gave a half shrug. If she'd been fooled it was only because she was naïve. Or, as Seth said, foolish. She'd been so blind, so trusting, so needy that she hadn't even asked questions.

"So does this key have something to do with what Oliver might have done?"

Harry said a nasty word. Didn't bother to muffle it nor did he apologize. "That man of yours—"

She didn't object, even though Oliver was dead and could never be her man but also because she'd never felt like they'd had that sort of bond.

"He played a dirty hand of poker. Stole every penny I had. I ask you, how am I supposed to keep a household going without any money? Then he had the audacity to lock the money into a strongbox and taunt me with the key. The key he gave you. He said I'd never locate it either. But he didn't know how desperate I was. I should have known he wouldn't keep it on him. But I had to be certain. Surprised me to think he'd give it to you." The smile on his lips dripped evil. "Guess he didn't care much about your safety."

Jayne could not still the shudder that raced up her spine.

"Ha, ha. I see you think as little of him for doing that as I do." He sprang forward until he was practically nose to nose with Jayne.

Fear said to close her eyes. But she would never again give in to her fear because of this man and she opened her eyes wide and glared defiantly at him, ignoring the fetid smell of his breath.

"So, pretty lady, it's time to stop playing games. Where is the key?" He spat the words out, along with moisture that landed on her cheeks.

With no way to wipe off the drops, she ignored them and leaned forward as far as the ropes allowed. "I do not know." She delivered her words with as much force as he had.

His face reddened. "You are a fool."

She would not back down in face of his anger.

He clamped his fingers on her face, pressing her cheeks against her teeth until she tasted blood.

How could she give him something she didn't have? But the man was beyond reason. He believed she had a key to a strongbox and would not be convinced otherwise.

Reaching around her, deliberately pressing into her body, he cut through the ropes at her wrists, having no concern for the fact the blade nicked her skin.

The pain meant nothing to her. She'd face far worse before this ordeal ended but she would not give him the satisfaction of making her beg or cry. As she considered how she'd rip his eyeballs out if she got the chance, the pain disappeared, blocked by the desire to claw his face.

He sat back and looked at her. And laughed. "Don't think there is some way you can make me change my mind. Ha. I'm not giving up until I get that key." He grabbed her hands and dragged them to the front of her.

Pins and needles filled her arms. She wanted to rub them away but he held her in a cruel grip.

"I will find that key if I have to torture you to death."

"Shoot me and get it over with."

He laughed again, a wicked sound that would live forever in her brain. Though forever might be a matter of minutes. *God, I'm trusting You. Either rescue me or enable me to face this with dignity.*

"What good would that do me? Nope. I figure a few cuts with my knife and maybe a little sport with your body—" He eyed her breasts, leaving her no doubt what he meant. "I figure that will convince you to tell me where the key is."

Despite the shiver that passed through her, she clenched her teeth so hard she imagined the enamel cracked but she refused to reveal a shred of fear.

With a quick slash that trapped a scream in her throat, he cut the ropes holding her ankles and jerked her to her feet. "I've run out of patience."

Her legs numb from being bound, she struggled to stay upright as he dragged her across the clearing.

Oh, God. Her silent prayer wailed through her mind. Would He rescue her or take her to heaven? *Please make it swift and painless. Give me courage.*

But it wasn't courage she felt. It was cold, mind-sucking fear that drained her insides of strength. Her knees folded. But he held her by the elbows and continued their journey.

To what? She closed her eyes and did not let the possible answers come.

Chapter Eighteen

Seth edged closer, carefully silent.

He heard a man's guttural voice but had no way of knowing if it was the Englishman he suspected had taken Jayne. But who else would it be? When the voice came again, he detected an English accent.

No female voice came to him. Where was Jayne?

The man shuffled and grunted as if dragging something heavy across the grass. Something like a body.

Seth's limbs froze. He couldn't go on. Was it Jayne's body being dragged? Then fire burned through his veins. He would tear the man from limb to limb if he'd hurt Jayne.

His first instinct told him to beat through the bushes in a mad rush, but good sense told him surprise was his biggest weapon. So he checked each step before he lowered his foot.

A minute later he saw movement. A man's back. When the man shifted, Seth saw her. Jayne, her hair loose and tangled about her face. Was she alive? He couldn't tell from where he stood.

He edged closer, keeping a shield of trees before him. Jayne's eyes were wide, flashing anger, her jaw set.

His legs wobbled. She was alive. *Thank You, God.*

Her determination would serve her well.

The pair shifted. Jayne's pretty blue dress was torn, exposing her neck. Had he molested her? Harmed her? Bile rose in his throat and he choked back a growl. Any man who hurt Jayne would pay at Seth's hands. His fists curled. He would exact justice. Though hanging would be the man's due. His fists relaxed. He would let the law mete out justice.

How was he to get Jayne away? *God, help me.*

He edged to one side. If no one noticed him, he stood a chance of getting to the trees close to the man. From there he would burst forth and press his gun to the man's head. He palmed his pistol in preparation and began the slow circle to his left. He dared not rush. Any sound would alert the man and ruin the element of surprise. He sucked back a breath and held it as he slid through the trees.

The horse whinnied.

Seth jerked to a halt. If he didn't move the man might not notice him.

The scoundrel pulled Jayne to his chest. A metallic flash caught the sun's rays. Seth's heart slammed into his ribs as he saw the man held a knife to her throat.

"Who's there?" he called. Slowly he circled, his arm so tight about Jayne she clearly struggled to breathe.

Seth prayed the man would not see him.

"You. In the trees. Step out where I can see you."

So much for hoping for invisibility. He shoved his gun into his back waistband. If he got any sort of chance he would use it.

"Hands in the air."

The man had a voice of evil. But then Seth might have a prejudiced opinion.

He stepped into the clearing and smiled at Jayne. A tight smile he hoped offered encouragement.

Something flickered across her eyes. Her gaze darted to the side. He shifted slightly so he could look without being too obvious. Her brocade bag. No doubt she wanted the gun but he didn't need hers. He had one he meant to use.

"I wondered if you'd come looking for your lady friend."

"You wondered right. What do you want with her?"

"She knows and she's playing dumb."

Jayne managed to croak, "He thinks I have a key but I know nothing about one."

Seth glanced about. Pretended not to understand. "You think the key is here."

"I'm not stupid. She has it somewhere. I expect she brought it with her. Maybe brought the strongbox, too." He jerked her tighter against him and brought the knife closer to her throat. "Stop stalling and tell me where it is." He grunted as if an idea had embedded into his brain. "Better yet, show me." He shoved her forward, still gripping her arms.

Seth growled when she stumbled. "You're hurting her."

"Yeah. So what? It might convince her I'm serious."

"Harry, I believe you but I can't help you," Jayne managed to say. "You're mistaken about the key."

"I know what I saw."

"Harry, is it?" Seth asked. "Maybe you should listen to her."

"She's lying." He noticed that Seth has edged closer. "Stop right there. You must have a gun. Toss it aside."

Seth didn't move. Harry had no way of knowing he

had a gun at his back and Seth didn't intend for him to find out.

Harry pressed the knife tighter to Jayne's throat. A drop of crimson blood dripped from the blade.

A reeling sensation as big as the heavens swept over Seth. He had never before considered throwing caution to the wind. But he wanted nothing so much as to launch himself at Harry, wrench his knife from him, press it to his throat and apply enough pressure to bring out a few drops of the man's own blood.

Only the knowledge of how little it would take for that knife to end Jayne's life kept him from springing forward.

Seth kept his hands up. "You see any guns?"

"Don't toy with me. Turn around. Unless you'd like to see your lady friend bleed."

If the knife went any deeper, Jayne's life would be in danger. Seth turned slowly, knowing Harry couldn't miss his gun.

"So you think you can toy with me. Take it out slowly and toss it to the side. And no funny stuff."

What choice did he have? He couldn't hope to swing his gun into position without risking Jayne's life. So he gingerly pulled the gun from his waistband and tossed it to the side. But if he got the chance he would retrieve it and shoot the man.

Or if the man lowered the knife, he would snatch Jayne away. Let the man use the knife on Seth if he wanted but Seth would not stand by and watch Jayne hurt if he had it in his power to stop it.

"I might know what you're looking for. If you let her go, I'll take you there." If Harry would release Jayne...

"I don't think you're in a bargaining position.

Where's the key?" He spilled another drop of Jayne's blood.

"Look. Take my gun. You've got a knife. What chance do I have against you? But I won't take a step unless you let her go."

"You like to see her suffer, do you?"

"No. Stop." Harry would kill her if Seth kept it up. "I lied. I don't know anything about a key. I only hoped to trick you."

With a growl, the man shoved Jayne to one side, his hand holding her like a vise. "You think you can toy with me?" He lunged toward Seth.

Seth brought both hands down as hard as he could on Harry's arms. The man shrieked and loosened his grip on Jayne. Seth shoved her to the side. "Run. Get away."

Harry's knife slashed toward Seth's heart. He wrenched to one side. The knife caught him in the ribs. So this was what a knife wound felt like. Burning. Searing.

But the burning didn't slow him down. He had to protect Jayne. He threw reason and caution aside. His anger burned so fierce that if he'd been made of wood, he would have ignited and set both of them on fire. A satisfying picture.

"Seth, you're hurt."

Why was she still here? "Jayne, go get help." At least she'd be out of danger's way if she went after Eddie. Though he didn't expect help would arrive in time to do any good.

The knife came at him again. Seth grabbed Harry's wrist. Harry growled and tried to twist away. Seth would not release his arm. Out of the corner of his eye, he caught a flash of blue. Jayne! How could he protect her if she didn't use her common sense and leave?

* * *

Jayne's throat closed off as she watched Seth struggle to get the knife from Harry's hand. Seth expected her to leave. Run and get help.

But all thought of escape fled when she noticed blood trickled down Seth's side.

She had watched one man bleed to death. She would not let it happen again. She gritted her teeth. She would not run and leave Seth. There must be something she could do. Seth's gun. Where was it? There. Not two feet from where she stood.

Just as it had been when Harry had shot Oliver.

Only this time Jayne didn't intend to stand by and let it happen.

As the men struggled for the knife, their attention away from her, she rushed forward and scooped up the gun. She hadn't known Seth to carry a loaded pistol but prayed, *Lord, let it be loaded this time*. Without consciously considering Seth's step-by-step instructions, she took her stance and aimed. Her arm lowered. If she missed, she might hit Seth. Might kill him this time.

The pair shifted. Seth had Harry's knife-wielding hand by the wrist.

She aimed at Harry's head, refusing to think what might happen if she missed. She had to take her chances. She sucked in air, steadied her hand and squeezed the trigger.

The blast battered her eardrums. An acrid smell tainted the air.

Harry screamed. "You shot me."

Obviously not in the head or he wouldn't be yelling like that.

Harry held a bleeding hand. "Lady, you're crazy."

"Crazy enough not to stand by and let you hurt another person."

Seth pushed the man to the ground face down and planted his knee in the middle of his back. "Nice shot, Jayne," he said.

"I meant to hit him in the head," she admitted.

"You put him out of commission, that's the main thing. Grab a rope off his saddle."

She hurried to do his bidding.

He trussed the man up solidly then rushed to her side. He took the gun from her hand and stuck it in his waistband. He lifted up the front of her dress, pulled a handkerchief from his pocket and pressed it to her throat.

"Are you okay?" he asked, though his voice cracked.

"I'm fine." She touched her fingers to his ribs. "But you're hurt and I'm again responsible."

"No, he is." He nodded toward Harry Simms. "You saved us both."

"You'll never get away with this," Harry yelled.

They ignored his muttered complaints.

"I'm okay," Seth said.

Jayne's knees folded. Her vision blurred. Seth sank to the ground, taking her with him, and held her close. Shivers raced through her, rattling her teeth.

Seth rubbed her back. "You were very brave."

She clutched his shirtfront. They'd both end up stained with each other's blood. She should likely care and do something about it, but instead she merely held on to him.

He pressed his cheek to her hair.

"Where did you come from?" she asked. "I thought you left."

"I did. But I came back."

She didn't want to leave the shelter of his arms but

she must see his face when she asked her next question. "Why did you come back?"

"Because of you."

That didn't provide any information.

Harry thrashed about. "You can't do this to me."

Now was not the time and place to ask questions. She pushed to her feet. "We need to get you to the ranch and tend that wound."

"My horse isn't far away."

"I'll get it." He must feel worse than he cared to admit because he sat there as she headed for the place he indicated.

But she had gone only a few yards when Eddie, Slim and Roper rode into view.

"I heard a gunshot," Eddie said when he saw her.

She nodded, her voice suddenly gone.

Eddie dropped from his horse and raced to her side. "You're hurt." Blood from Seth's wound blotched her dress. Perhaps a drop or two of her own had spattered on her bodice.

"I'm okay. Seth has a knife wound." She led them back to the clearing.

Seth struggled to his feet. "Good to see you."

Eddie jerked Harry to his feet. Slim brought his horse forward and they swung him into the saddle. No one paid attention to Harry's continued protests except Eddie.

"You kidnapped my sister. That's a capital offense."

Harry glowered. "She's got something of mine."

"I don't want to hear it."

Roper led Seth's horse forward and Seth swung into the saddle. Jayne noticed his lips were white and suspected he was in a lot of pain.

His gaze met hers and he smiled in a slow, intimate

way that touched her heart. Whatever his reason for returning, they could wait until the business with Harry Simms was over and done with to discuss it.

Eddie pulled her up behind him and they rode for home.

As soon as the women saw them, they rushed forward. Linette immediately guided Seth upstairs. She would tend his wound and make sure he would live. But Jayne's heart followed him up the steps. She couldn't wait to have him to herself so he could explain why he'd returned.

Mercy and Sybil took Jayne under their wings and helped her change into a clean dress. They demanded all the details of what happened.

Sybil tenderly washed Jayne's neck. "It's only a nick."

"You really shot him?" Mercy asked again.

"I had no choice. He meant to kill Seth."

"You're a very brave woman," Sybil said.

"And a good shot." Mercy's voice was filled with awe.

Her strength returned. She could finally look at the situation fully. "I'm not a good shot. I meant to shoot him in the head but somehow managed to hit his hand."

Mercy and Sybil stared at her. Mercy started to laugh. Then Sybil joined her.

Jayne stared at them both. "I might have hit Seth."

"You already did once and he survived," Mercy managed to gasp out.

"But at least you did what you could." Sybil choked out the words in between laughter.

Poor Seth. She truly might have injured him again.

What must he think? He'd taught her all he knew and she still couldn't hit what she aimed at.

A tickle began beneath her ribs and raced upward to escape as a burst of laughter.

The three of them fell on her bed and laughed out their tension and fear and relief.

After a moment, Jayne sobered. "I hope the knife wound isn't too serious. Let's see if Linette is done yet." If she was and Seth felt up to being on his feet, Jayne meant to have a talk with him.

The three returned to the kitchen where Eddie waited for her. "Sit down. Tell me what happened."

Mercy and Sybil sat beside her. Before she began, Linette returned. "I want to hear, too."

"So do I." A deep, familiar voice drew her attention to Seth.

"Are you okay?"

"I've been hurt worse. I was shot once, you know." His grin said he meant it to be teasing.

"I'm sorry. Somehow I feel I am to blame for this time, too."

Mercy moved over and made room for him at Jayne's side.

"You likely saved our lives."

She nodded. He'd said it before. All she had to do was believe it.

She turned to her brother and began her account of the day's events. "Harry Simms is his name. He was never arrested." She told how Harry had set up some poor man to appear to be him.

She told every detail. "He wants a key that I don't have." She ended by relating how she'd missed her target.

"I meant to shoot him in the head."

Her friends muffled a laugh but Eddie smiled at her. "My little sister can take care of herself."

"She sure can," Seth answered.

Their praise gave her food for thought. She had taken action rather than cowered in fear. She'd missed her intended target but nevertheless had disarmed the man.

Yes, she could take care of herself.

But she'd learned a second, equally valuable lesson.

Taking care of herself could be a lonely business unless she had a partner.

Why had Seth come back?

Chapter Nineteen

Jayne hoped she and Seth would get a chance to talk but Linette had supper ready and after the meal, everyone continued to hang about.

Mercy and Sybil didn't leave her side, as if afraid she would disappear again.

"You aren't leaving again in the morning?" Jayne managed to ask Seth as they all clustered about the table, reading the newspapers brought back from town. It grew increasingly obvious that no one intended to leave Seth and Jayne alone. Whether intentional or not, she couldn't say.

He shook his head. His eyes promised they would talk. And with that she had to be content.

Around the table Sybil covered a yawn and Linette's head bobbed.

"We've kept you up long enough." Sybil patted Linette's arm.

Jayne's sister-in-law had weary lines about her eyes, from hard work and her pregnancy. Jayne sprang to her feet. How selfish to be thinking only of getting a chance to talk to Seth. "Yes, it's time for bed."

Mercy rose and the three friends headed down the hall to their bedrooms.

Jayne paused just before she ducked out of sight and called "Good night." She meant it for all of them but her gaze went only to Seth who stood in the hallway that went in the other direction.

His smile blessed her as he lifted a hand in a tiny wave.

Until tomorrow, she promised herself as she went to her room. He had come back. Surely that meant good news for her.

She didn't have the strength to think of other reasons he might have returned.

The girls had made her put on the dress she'd worn when Seth had taken them to the waterfall up the mountain. When she'd taken it off she hadn't planned to wear it ever again. It reminded her of his announcement that he meant to leave. He'd given her no reason to hope he'd come back or that he cared for her in the slightest.

Now she willingly hoped and believed he'd changed his mind.

She lifted the skirt to her nose and breathed deeply of the memories. The cool dampness of the spray of water, the sweet pine scent. She touched her fingertips to her lips, recalling the warmth of his kiss. How she'd thought it so full of promise.

Perhaps there would yet be a promise. She jammed her hand into the pocket. Her fingers encountered something hard. She dug deep and pulled out a little stone.

Her heart swelled with hope as she cupped it in her palm. Smooth and heart shaped, it had lain hidden in her pocket, forgotten until now.

A tremble filled her heart. The promise of that day had disappeared as Seth rode away. But now he had returned.

Hope danced across her nerves.

Clutching the rock, she went to her trunk and dug through the contents until she found her little treasure box. In it were items of sentimental value. She set it on her bed. A smile caught her lips as she opened it and lifted out a tiny gold locket. Mother and Father had given it to her when she was six years old. Perhaps one day she could pass it on to a daughter. Her throat tightened, as she pictured a tiny girl with hazel eyes like Seth's and a smile that turned her heart to liquid honey.

She set aside the locket and picked up a valentine card her sisters, Bess and Anne, had made for her. For days they had labored over their secret. Bess was only about twelve years old and Anne nine at the time. The card they'd crafted was a little uneven in places but every time Jayne looked at it she remembered the way they had smiled as they presented it to her.

Next were four picture cards from the trip when Father had taken them to Paris. She sat back on her heels. Life had seemed so simple then. She would never have believed so much tragedy would hit her in a few short years.

She put the cards on the bed beside the other things and put her heart-shaped rock on the bottom of the box. Right beside the locket Oliver had given her. She touched the heart and key. Stirred them across the bottom.

The key didn't match the heart for proportions. It was too large and heavy. Oliver had said she needed a big key because he had a big heart. At the time she'd put it down to Oliver's likeness for doing things in a large way.

Where's the key? Harry had been sure she had it. Insisted he'd seen it. Was this what he meant? Could this be the key he sought?

A key to what? She studied it for a long time, searching her mind for a clue. What had Oliver said when he gave it to her? Nothing that seemed to indicate anything unusual. But several times he'd caught the charms as they hung from her neck and then said something cryptic. *You have the key to my heart and so much more.*

Another conversation surfaced in her mind.

"Of course." Now it all made sense.

She returned to the kitchen. It was dark. But she saw light in the hall. She found Eddie in the library, entering figures into a ledger.

He set aside the pen as she entered. "How are you doing?"

She shrugged. "Fine. I found this. Oliver gave it to me on a chain with a locket."

Eddie examined it carefully. "It seems rather large to hang on a chain about your neck."

She nodded. "I thought so, too, but it seemed sweet of Oliver to give it to me." And then Oliver had died and she couldn't bear anything that made her remember the details of his death so she'd put it in her treasure box and forgotten it as she tried to forget about Oliver's murder.

"Oliver used to joke about a box he'd asked to store in a garden shed on our property. Said he didn't think his parents would value it as they should and might even destroy it. He said someone had given it to him. He valued it for some reason, though he never said why." She'd never thought to ask him. Or if she had, she'd quickly dismissed her curiosity. Oliver did not like her to ask too many questions. "I asked the gardener if he minded and of course he didn't. I think this is what Harry was after."

"I think you're right. I'll send the key to Father to check out."

"If the box is full of money as Harry said, who does it belong to?"

"I really don't know. I guess Father will have to get his lawyer to sort things out. I don't think you need to worry about it, though." He leaned back and studied her. "I guess that solves the mystery surrounding Harry."

"Now I can rest in peace. Not that I think he'll ever be a threat to me again."

"What about Seth?"

She blinked. "Seth was never a threat to me."

"Not physically. But I think emotionally he can hurt you very badly. Did he say why he came back?"

"We haven't had a chance to discuss it." She tipped her chin in a gesture of determination. "We will in the morning."

He laughed at her little show of firmness. "Let me know how it goes."

She rose, bent to kiss him on the forehead and pat his shoulder. "I'll tell you what you need to know."

He grinned. "Getting real independent, are you?"

She smiled down at him. "Not so independent I don't need friends and family." And a husband.

He opened his mouth, likely to add the same words she'd added silently.

She patted his shoulder again, not giving him a chance. "Good night, big brother."

"Good night, little sister. Though not so little as you used to be."

Nor so weak or fearful, she added silently.

Seth's injured side did not pose a hindrance to his sleep. But his thoughts did. He still didn't know what he meant to say to Jayne.

Not that her friends and family had allowed him a

chance to talk to her. Maybe they purposely prevented it. After all, he had left her. And they'd all seen her hurt.

But he would speak to her alone and he'd do his best to find the words to explain why he'd returned.

He rose early the next morning and made his way to the kitchen. Jayne was there preparing a bottle for Thor as he'd hoped.

"I'll help you feed him." Did she understand he wouldn't accept any excuses to avoid him?

She nodded. "Come along, then."

They traipsed down the hill toward the barn. Out of habit, he reached out to pull her to his side but the danger of a murderer watching her was over. And he didn't want to cloud his mind with the joy of her pressed close. He dropped his arm and allowed a few inches between them.

Thor greeted them and bunted against Jayne in his eagerness for the bottle.

He didn't say what his heart felt as the fawn sucked. It was too easy to be distracted by Thor's playfulness.

"I found the key," she said. She must have noticed his confusion. "The one Harry wanted."

"I thought you didn't know anything about it." His blood thundered against the top of his head. Had she put them both in mortal danger for a lie?

"It was a key Oliver had given me with a heart-shaped locket. I'd forgotten all about it. I found it last night when I was poking through my stuff." She ducked her head as if to check on the fawn but maybe also to hide her face from him. Did she regret his return? Maybe she'd been relieved to have him leave.

No. He would not entertain doubt. He would explain his reason for coming back and let her respond.

The fawn finished and turned to play with Smokey.

Jayne faced him, her eyes dark, allowing him to read nothing. "Seth, why did you come back?"

"I came to ask you to go with me."

Her mouth dropped open. She closed it and swallowed hard. "Why?"

"Because I have to take care of my pa."

"You don't need me for that."

He wasn't explaining himself well. "On my ride south I started to recall things my pa said to me. Hard things."

She nodded.

"He blamed me for Frank's death. He had taught us to watch out for each other and I failed."

"You didn't fail." She brushed her hand along his arm. "You tried to stop them. The choice was theirs."

"I know that but I still feel Pa's accusation." He found strength in the look she gave him. "He said I would likely fail to take care of my parents, too."

She squeezed his arm.

"There's more." His throat tightened so his voice cracked. "Pa told me I could never take care of a wife. I guess I believed him."

She waited, a curtain closing her thoughts to him.

"Until yesterday."

Her eyes looked hopeful and guarded at the same time.

He hated that he was responsible for the latter emotion. "Yesterday I stopped and thought of all that Pa said. I realized that just 'cause he said it didn't make it true."

She nodded. "That's so."

"But even if it isn't true, marriage is a risk. So many bad things can happen."

"And so many good things."

"Yes. I made a decision to trust God with the future and enjoy the present."

"I'm glad." Her voice was quiet, overly controlled.

"I want you to come with me. Meet Pa. I will have to stay and care for him. It's my duty and I would never neglect him."

"I wouldn't expect you to."

"Will you come?"

She lowered her head so he couldn't see her eyes or read her expression.

"I can't bear to leave you behind."

"It wouldn't be proper for me to go with you. An unmarried woman." She shook her head.

"But what if we're married?"

Her head came up. Her eyes widened. "Married? What are you talking about?"

He furrowed his brow. "Isn't it obvious? I love you and want you to come with me."

"Whoa, there, cowboy. Back up a minute. What did you say?"

He slapped his forehead. He'd forgotten the most important thing he meant to say. He tipped Jayne's chin up and studied her eyes, her beautiful skin, her firm little chin.

He jerked his thoughts back to the words he wanted to get just right. "Jayne Gardiner, I love you with my whole heart. I want to spend the rest of my life with you, sharing the good times and the bad. Growing old and gray. I want to hold you next to my heart." He patted his shoulder. "Right here where you belong. Jayne, will you marry me and make me the happiest man in the world?"

Her eyes filled with such warmth and joy he could

hardly meet her gaze. "Yes." She laughed. "Yes, yes, yes, yes, yes."

He caught her to him and kissed her. When her arms pressed into his back he sighed. He'd come home where he belonged.

He ended the kiss and smiled into her welcoming gaze. "Does that mean you love me?"

"Seth Collins, I love you so much I wonder my heart doesn't explode."

"Is that good?" he teased.

"Oh, it's very good." She tilted her head to the side. "How long have you known you loved me?"

"I don't know. I guess I knew it when you stood in my arms, insisting you would learn to shoot even though you were scared to death of guns."

"It took you long enough to say it."

He nodded. "I had learned to shut my heart to love and focus only on responsibilities."

"I'm sorry your father said such unkind things. I expect he spoke out of his own grief and pain." She pressed her palm to his cheek and he turned to kiss it.

He nodded. "I guess so. But if I ever say anything that hurtful please remind me of the power words have."

"You mean like this? Seth, I loved you when you pulled that wad of money from your boot so intent on caring for your pa you would have bled to death trying to get to him. I loved you when you made sure I knew how to shoot. I especially loved you when you held my hand steady when I couldn't keep my eyes open. I knew then that you were the kind of man who would walk at my side, helping me and supporting me." Her voice fell to a whisper. "I thank God He brought us together."

"About God. I have stopped shutting Him out, too. I prayed when you disappeared. I believe God led me to you and helped us escape." He laughed. "Though you shooting Harry's hand certainly made it possible."

She shuddered. "I dare not think how close I came to shooting you."

He shook his head. "I was never in danger. You're a better shot than you know. Jayne, what about coming with me to see Pa?"

She pressed her head to his shoulder. "That's something we need to discuss. It takes time to plan a wedding and make arrangements."

"Time is something I don't have. Pa has been alone for days. I don't know if he's being taken care of or not. I have to do my duty." Not that it was duty alone that drove him. He had always planned to take care of Pa. That hadn't changed.

She clutched his shirtfront. "I know. I can't bear to let you go. But waiting for me will only delay you longer."

He did something he hadn't done in a very long time. "Jayne, let's pray about it and trust God to provide a way." He took her hands, pressed them to his chest and bowed his head until it touched hers. "Our Father in heaven. First of all, I want to thank You for Jayne. For bringing us together and for making her strong and brave. I don't want to leave her but my pa needs me. Could You bless our love by providing a way for us to stay together? Amen." It was the longest prayer he'd ever prayed and the most sincere and urgent.

"God will provide," she whispered. "Now I promised Eddie I'd tell him anything he needed to know. I want him to know about us."

Eddie, Linette and the others were gathered round the table for breakfast when they returned.

"Finally," Mercy said. "Eddie was about to send out a search party."

"No need," Seth said. They stood side by side, facing Eddie. "Jayne has agreed to marry me."

Eddie stood and grabbed Seth's hand. "Congratulations. You've made a good choice." He hugged Jayne.

The others clustered around them, offering congratulations.

"You're getting married?" Grady asked.

Jayne hugged the little boy. "Yes."

"Are you going to live here?"

She lifted her face to Seth. Her coffee-brown eyes promised so much he wanted to shout with joy. "I don't know where we'll live. We haven't figured that out yet."

Where were they going to live? What about Pa?

The questions hammered the inside of his head. If only he could stay here and forget his responsibilities. But he couldn't.

Was their love strong enough to survive the uncertainty of their future?

Chapter Twenty

❧

"Have you made any wedding plans?" Linette asked.

"No," Jayne said. It had been only a few minutes since they'd confessed their love. She wanted to twirl down the hall, laugh with joy and stand out in the sunshine to shout to the heavens. She gave Seth a slow, deliberate look. He met her gaze, his forest-green eyes full of longing.

Mercy nudged her. "Ahem."

Jayne blinked, smiled distractedly and tried to remember what the conversation involved.

But she couldn't focus on anything apart from the questions burning her mind. When would they marry? Where would they live? So many things to work out. And so little time.

As soon as breakfast was over and she'd helped with the dishes, she hurried outside to find Seth.

He came around the house. "I've been waiting for you."

Her heart swelled with sweetness to know he wanted to spend the rest of his life with her.

He held his hand out to her and they walked to the

clearing where they'd spent so much time, and sat on the log.

"I will always think of this as our special place," she said.

He pulled her close. "But this is your special place." He pressed her head to the hollow of his shoulder.

"My place. I like that."

For several minutes they didn't move. She would gladly have spent the day there.

"We need to make plans." His words disturbed her peace.

"I suppose we do." She sat up and turned so she could watch his face as they talked.

"I love this country."

Her heart leaped within her. Was he going to stay here after all? Dreams filled her head. A little home for the two of them. Visits with Linette and her friends. Keeping house.

He sighed. "If I had time I would look about for a piece of land to start my own place."

She began to decorate a house—a big table in the kitchen so she could do lots of baking and canning like Linette did and entertain visitors. Maybe she'd make a quilt for their bedroom. Light flooded a secret place behind her heart. A place that until now had been unknown.

"But I doubt Pa will want to move."

Her dreams disappeared in the blink of an eye. "What will you do in Corncrib?"

"I'll work for ranchers. Do odd jobs. Whatever I can find that will allow me to be home every day to care for Pa."

She touched his freshly shaven cheek. "I'll help you."

He nodded, his eyes flooding with so many things—

determination, love, surprise, as if he didn't believe that love possible. "I don't want to leave you."

"You go. Look after your pa. I'll wait until you sort things out." A lump in her throat cut off her flow of words.

He pulled her close, cupped his hand to her head. "It kills me to think of leaving you but I must."

Perhaps it was only because her ear was pressed to his chest that his words seemed more like a growl.

They clung to each other, till finally a sigh rippled from him. "I'll stay the day."

Did the thought of only one day hurt him as much as it did her? She hoped so, yet she didn't want to add to his distress.

"A day will be wonderful." She would do her utmost to make it a day of sweet memories that would make him never forget how much he loved her and she loved him. Her decision made, she kissed him soundly. "Let's go on a picnic."

"I'll enjoy whatever we do. So long as we are together." He pulled her to him and kissed her. She sighed and leaned into his embrace. Maybe they could stay here and forget everything and everyone but this moment and each other.

But she wanted to know everything about him. She loved listening to the beat of his heart but wanted to listen to the words of his heart, as well.

So they returned to the house where Linette helped Jayne prepare a lunch to take with them. Jayne explained Seth would be leaving tomorrow and she wanted to be alone with him.

"I'm sorry you only have today," Linette said. "Enjoy it to the fullest."

They set out with no destination in mind, talking as

they walked. They reached an open area that let them see the rolling hills that flowed away from the mountains.

"This looks like a good place." Seth spread the blanket Jayne had brought and they sat side by side looking out at the vista before them.

For a moment, they didn't say anything.

"What kind of house will we have?"

Seth leaned back on his elbows and tickled her neck with a blade of grass. "Pa's house is small. Two bedrooms upstairs but he sleeps in a bedroom on the main floor. We'll have our privacy."

"I wasn't worried about that. I'm simply trying to imagine your home."

He sat up. "If I could start my own ranch, I'd build a solid house, frame or log. I'd start small and add on rooms as our family grew."

She turned on her side to face him. "Family?"

He touched her cheek. "Don't you want children?"

She brought his fingers to her lips and kissed them. "I want a little boy with dark brown hair and hazel eyes and the sweetest face in the world."

"Jayne." His voice thickened and he drew her in for a kiss. Then he smiled at her. "I want a little girl with coffee-brown hair and brown eyes that would make it hard for me to be stern."

"Only two?" she asked.

"More would be nice."

She sighed and lay back to look at the fluffy clouds overhead. "Tell me about your childhood."

"Before Frank's death?"

Sensing that his childhood ended after the accident, she murmured agreement.

He told of a stern father and a gentle mother who

taught the boys responsibility and hard work but who also engaged in outings to church gatherings, town fairs and who played board games with their sons and read to them.

"But there was no more of that after Frank died."

She opened her arms and pulled him close, holding him like he'd not been held since that awful day. If only she could kiss away all the pain of his past. She vowed she would try her best to do so.

Her eyes filled with tears, and she blinked them away. She would bravely face his departure and leave him only the memory of this day and her smile.

Her tears would be shed in the privacy of her own room.

His heart so heavy it pressed against the soles of his boots, Seth saddled his horse the next morning. Every heartbeat squeezed out shards of glass, tearing his veins to shreds.

He must go but it would be the hardest thing he'd ever done.

Jayne waited for him outside the barn. He led the horse out and stopped. What did he say to describe his reluctance to leave her? He simply pulled her into his arms and hoped she understood.

She clung to him so hard the knife wound in his side hurt but he welcomed the pain. It would serve as a diversion in the days to follow.

"I can't promise when I'll get back." They had decided he would make arrangements for someone to care for Pa so he could come back. They would marry then return to Corncrib. He glanced past the ranch buildings. How he'd like to start fresh with land of his own. Perhaps God would allow it in the future.

For now he was grateful for the blessing he had and he pulled Jayne closer.

"I'll be here waiting and watching." The words grated from her throat, and he knew she found this parting as difficult as he did.

He would be brave for her sake.

He tipped her head up and gave her a kiss so full of hunger and missing and loving that she gasped then returned the kiss with equal emotion.

He tore himself away. "I must go." He'd already said goodbye to the others. A groan threatened to escape as he turned toward his horse and swung into the saddle.

His smile barely moved his lips but it was the best he could produce and he took Jayne's outstretched hand and held it a moment. Regret dulled her eyes. His likely revealed the same emotion. "Until later."

She nodded.

Looking to neither the right nor the left he bent low and raced from the yard.

"Whoa!"

He jerked up at the word, fought to control his mount and stared at a covered wagon he'd almost run into. He squinted at the older couple driving the rig. It couldn't be....

"Hello, son."

"Pa!" Not another word came to his befuddled brain.

"You look surprised."

"I guess I am!"

"But Crawford wrote you. Told you I was marrying and headed out here to visit you."

"Married?" He looked at the woman at Pa's side.

"Meet my wife, Edna."

He doffed his hat.

"Howdy," she said, grinning at his confusion. "Looks like you didn't get the letter."

"I did but most of the words were smudged. I only knew Crawford had left. I figured you were home waiting for me to finally show up."

"Nope. I been busy with my own affairs." He patted Edna's arm.

Eddie signaled from the house to bring them in.

"Come and meet the Eden Valley Ranch crew."

Jayne had climbed the hill and stood at Eddie's side, her hand shading her eyes as she watched him.

Pa was here. He was well enough to drive the wagon, though his face drooped on one side. Seth didn't know what it meant but one thing was certain: He didn't have to go to Corncrib. His heart bounced from rib to rib in joy.

"Take the wagon to the door," he called to his pa then turned his horse, raced to Jayne's side where he jumped to the ground and swept her into his arms. He swung her about in a big circle.

"Seth, are you crazy?"

"Crazy about you." He kissed her nose.

When the wagon reached the house, Pa and Edna stepped down. Seth kept Jayne at his side as he went to Pa's side. "Jayne, this is my pa and his new wife."

She looked up at him in wonder and surprise. "You mean—"

He pulled her close to his heart. "I don't have to go to Corncrib."

Her eyes said she understood what this meant as clearly as he. He led her to Pa and Edna. "I'd like you to meet my intended, Jayne Gardiner."

Pa gave Jayne a quick study then shook her hand.

Edna gave Pa a scolding look. "Pshaw, what's wrong with you, Murdo? She's family." She hugged Jayne.

Seth swallowed a lump then turned to the others.

He waited until introductions were made and Linette invited the guests inside before he took Jayne's arm and drew her down to the river. Pa surely had a story to tell but it could wait.

Once they were in the shelter of trees he turned her into his arms. "When can we get married?"

She kissed him. "I love you, too."

They returned in time to partake of dinner. Afterward, Pa said he wanted to talk to Seth. "Bring Jayne along, too."

"Feel free to use the front room," Linette said.

They retired there.

Pa leaned forward. His right arm still didn't move a hundred percent correctly.

"I can't believe how improved you are." Seth shook his head. "I expected to find you an invalid."

"Crawford did a world of good. But it was Edna moving in next door that did the most for me." He took her hand as he talked. "She lost her husband and son in a horrible accident. Her husband had been cleaning a gun and accidently shot their boy. When he saw what he'd done he turned the gun on himself. He left Edna to deal with it on her own."

"It was difficult," Edna said. "But I've discovered what doesn't kill you makes you strong."

Seth grinned at Jayne. "I think we're also learning that. And that God is always there to help us."

Pa continued. "As Edna told me what she'd dealt with and I saw how she shone like gold despite her trials—"

Edna made a dismissive noise but gave Pa a grateful smile.

Pa nodded. "I realized I had allowed bitterness and blame to become my way of life." He reached for Seth's hand and held it in his own.

What was this all about? Did Pa mean to clear his conscience by laying the blame firmly at Seth's feet? His heart ticked in steady, warning beats.

"Seth, I said cruel and untrue things to you. I don't know if you recall them or if you believed them. I regret them. It wasn't your fault Frank died. And despite the things I said, and the times I failed to show appreciation, you have been a fine, upstanding person. I'm proud to call you son. Can you forgive me for the wrong things I've said and done?"

Seth's lungs emptied in a rush. "Pa, I forgive you." The power of Pa's words had started to fade when he met Jayne. They had grown fainter as he grew to love her and lost most of their power when he stopped on the trail and decided to throw off their chains.

Pa's apology forever erased them from his heart.

When Pa and Edna left them a few minutes later, Seth turned to Jayne. "We can start with a brand-new, clean slate. How does that feel?"

"It's wonderful." She kissed him then they moved to the window to look out on the ranch.

He looked past the buildings to the promise of a bright future in God's generous plan.

Epilogue

Three weeks later

Jayne looked at her reflection in the mirror.

"You look lovely," Sybil said. "The new dress was a good idea if I do say so myself."

Linette and Sybil had offered to make her a wedding dress to remember. She'd refused. "I'm to be a rancher's wife. I prefer something plain so I can use it again."

"A nice dress can never go amiss," Sybil had said. "Allow us to do this."

"I'm glad you persuaded me." Jayne loved the dress. Made of ecru satin with seven rows of green piping at the wrists and a row of green-covered buttons down the front, it was dressy enough to be special and yet she would be comfortable wearing it to church and other special events in the future. The waist dipped in the front. The neckline ended in a small stand-up collar. "It's lovely." She faced her friends. "So are you."

Mercy wore a dark blue dress that brought out her beauty. Sybil shone in a golden dress.

Eddie appeared at the door, handsome in his dark jacket and white shirt. "Are you ready?"

She nodded. Mercy and Sybil left the house ahead of her and Jayne took Eddie's arm for the walk to the clearing where she and Seth had decided to get married—the same clearing where they had spent many happy hours. "Still no word about the box Harry Simms was after?"

Eddie smiled down at her. "It's too early to get a reply from across the ocean but Father will take care of it. You needn't give it another thought."

"I won't." Her life was too full of joy and love to be concerned with the past.

They paused to let Mercy and Sybil walk down the grassy aisle ahead of them.

Then they stepped into sight. The assembled people turned. She felt their smiles. Their love.

She spared a glance about. She and her friends had spent hours preparing the clearing for this day. They'd gathered wild flowers and placed them in containers around the circle, and Sybil had hung pink, red and white ribbons from the trees. Jayne smiled. It was perfect.

This day was perfect, blessed with sunshine and a breeze that rustled the leaves overhead enough to prevent the air from becoming too warm.

She scanned the crowd. Everyone from the ranch was there, and Seth's pa and Edna, who had decided to live in Edendale.

Buster looked like a new person. He'd taken his first month's pay, gotten a haircut, a new shirt and pair of trousers. He wore the belt Seth had made him.

Her heart swelled with pride at Seth's skill and generosity.

Eddie had arranged a preacher from Fort Macleod to perform the ceremony. He stood patiently at the front.

She had resisted looking at Seth until now because she knew once she saw him, nothing else would register.

His smile blazed at her.

His hair had been trimmed. He wore a white shirt and a dark gray vest that emphasized his coloring.

She drew in a breath and held it.

"I can't believe I'm marrying such a handsome man," she whispered to Eddie.

"He's marrying a beautiful woman."

"Thank you." Her eyes on Seth, she walked at Eddie's side until he released her to Seth.

"To have and to hold from this day forth."

The words rang in her mind as they went through the rest of the ceremony then returned to the ranch to a beautiful meal the women had prepared. They ate outside.

Then at some invisible signal, likely from Linette, the people filed by Seth and Jayne to congratulate them and say goodbye as they made their way to their own homes.

Seth smiled down at Jayne. "Dear wife, it seems we can finally go home."

"Husband, that sounds real good."

They went to the small cabin across from the cookhouse where Linette and Eddie had spent their first winter.

Seth swept her into his arms and carried her over the threshold. He kissed her soundly before depositing her on her feet.

"Our first home together," she said, her voice filled with joy.

"Next spring I will find land and build a house on our own ranch."

She wrapped her arms around his neck. "I don't care

where we live so long as we're together. You are mine to have and to hold for the rest of my life."

He kissed her. It was the beginning of their lives together.

God had blessed her beyond measure.

* * * * *

IF YOU ENJOYED THIS BOOK
WE THINK YOU WILL ALSO LOVE

LOVE INSPIRED

INSPIRATIONAL ROMANCE

Uplifting stories of faith, forgiveness and hope.

Fall in love with stories where faith helps
guide you through life's challenges, and discover
the promise of a new beginning.

6 NEW BOOKS AVAILABLE EVERY MONTH!

LOVE INSPIRED

INSPIRATIONAL ROMANCE

UPLIFTING STORIES OF FAITH, FORGIVENESS AND HOPE.

Join our social communities to connect with other readers who share your love!

Sign up for the Love Inspired newsletter at **LoveInspired.com** to be the first to find out about upcoming titles, special promotions and exclusive content.

CONNECT WITH US AT:

Facebook.com/LoveInspiredBooks

Twitter.com/LoveInspiredBks

Facebook.com/groups/HarlequinConnection